THE IRON CROWN

L.L. MACRAE

Don't dream your adventures

— live them

L.L. Macrae

24.7.22

Cover by: Psycat Studios
Maps by: Domino44maps

Printed and bound in Great Britain by Clays Ltd, Elcograf S.p.A.

www.llmacrae.com

For Pipkin.

My king, my rock, my soulmate.

ALSO BY L.L. MACRAE

DRAGON SPIRITS

The Iron Crown

The Shadow Gate

ACKNOWLEDGMENTS

I cannot thank Olivia enough. If it weren't for her, this would remain a collection of notes and disparate ideas floating across various documents, never to be woven together into the book you're reading now. Also everything would be much more rubbish. And probably make no sense. From providing encouragement, brainstorming ideas, or yelling at me to get the next chapter written, she's been instrumental at every stage of writing.

Thank you also to Eike W., my chief curse writer, who helped define the backbone of this trilogy. Without Eike, the main driving force of the plot would be far weaker. Her ideas, enthusiasm, and positivity helped keep me motivated —especially at the earliest parts of the process where everything seemed insurmountable.

And my eternal gratitude goes out to Ellie, Josephine, Laura, and Maxine, my unflappable beta readers, who gave me critique and confidence in equal measure. From general feedback to specific plot points, adding detail and providing clarity, they helped make this book the best it could be. So many details were caught or expanded on because of them, bringing *The Iron Crown* to a truly vibrant shine!

To anyone who purchases my book, I am eternally grateful. It would mean the world and more if you would be kind enough to review *The Iron Crown*.

POLAR SEA

FOXMOUTH

SHRINE OF TORIAKEN

NETHAL

WESTBROOK

EASTBROOK

LASEEN OCEAN

HORUSH

HILLSBRIN

SHRINE OF MIROTH

NORTHBOURNE

THE SALT SEA

TONMOUTH

MARLRUSH FORTRESS

SOUTHBOURNE

PORT FRICKLEY

THE SPINDLE WOODS

SPINDLEFORD

SHRINE OF ALNOTHEN

SHRINE OF YAKRIS

FELLWOOD

SHRINE OF GHYRAM

CLIFFTON

ORDONA

VAELAR

MEADOWHILL

HERSTLOCH

SHRINE OF NEROS

SEGANDIS

HOGSBROOKE

BALEOWTOWN

SALTASH FOREST

ULBRIDGE

ISLE OF SALT

DOMINO44 MAPS

ETROVIA

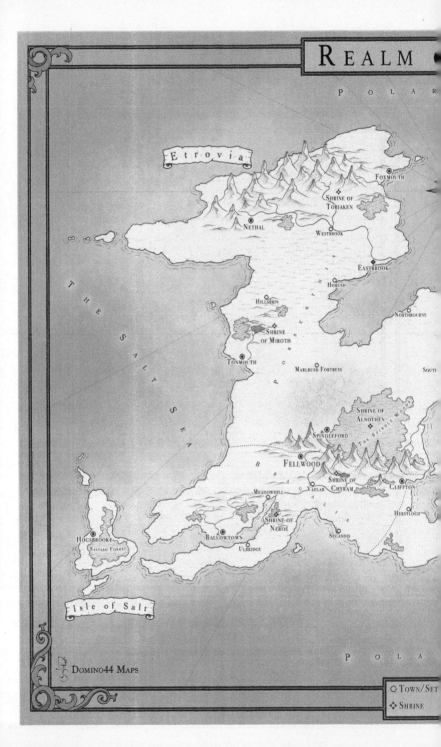

PART I

What belonged to thyne,
Now stolen as mine.
Memories, once crystal clear,
Are lost, leaving only fear.

1
THE AWAKENING
FENN

Foul.

Brackish and thick, the putrid sludge pulled Fenn deeper in, filling his nose with its awful stench. He flailed, weak, the strength sucked from his arms. Every movement made it worse and his head pounded in time with his pulse. His chest tightened in panic—both at his critical situation and the suddenness with which he found himself in it. Fenn had no recollection of falling into a bog, or even where he'd been before.

Where *was* he?

Gulping down lungfuls of air, he cast his gaze about, looking for anything he could use to get himself out of the swampy mud. Enormous trees surrounded the fetid pool on all sides, their vast canopy throwing the small clearing into shades of mottled green. Weak sunlight filtered through the broad leaves, bathing him in dappled shadow. A few vines trailed down the ancient trunks, thorns protruding from their green flesh. Some reached the edge of the pool, their ends disappearing into the brown-black mud—the closest thing he could reach.

He spun in place, squelching as he sunk further in. The mud was up to his waist, and he could hardly feel his legs.

Shit.

What was this place?

How did he get here?

He hadn't been in a forest, had he? He couldn't remember, couldn't *think*.

Questions for later—if he didn't get himself out right now, there wouldn't *be* a later.

Reaching forward, Fenn stretched his arms out, fingertips just grazing the nearest of the vines where they settled on the pool's edge. Sweat rolled down his arms and dampened his clammy hands. He managed to grab one vine between his first two fingers, but it slipped out of his grasp.

Fenn groaned with the effort. Bubbles on the surface of the viscous liquid burst and cold mud slapped against his bare arms, coating them in thick, brown ooze. The foul stench made him gag, and he bit down on his instinct to cover his face with his arm—that was only going to make the smell worse. He screwed up his nose, as if that would somehow lessen the intensity of the odour.

He sank deeper, the cold now creeping up his lower back.

'Help!' His voice cracked, as if it hadn't been used for some time. Clearing his throat, Fenn called out again, 'Can anyone hear me? Can someone help?' He didn't like how thin and reedy his voice sounded, small against the dark, foreboding forest. A few birds took flight, their fluttering sending feathers down between the green, leaving an eerie stillness to the humid glade.

With difficulty, he swallowed and reached for the vine again, this time catching his thumb along one of the long thorns and tearing his flesh open. Withdrawing it with a yelp of pain, he shoved his thumb into his mouth, then immediately spat out bloodied mud and retched. Idiot!

Using his shoulder to wipe away the sweat dripping

down his temple, he tried to throw himself towards the edge. Cold, wet sludge kept him from taking more than a step and pulled him down more. He squeezed his eyes shut, desperate to hide from the headache that throbbed incessantly at his forehead, and hoped to wake from whatever nightmare his mind had decided to inflict upon him. 'Hello? Please!' Fenn called again, volume rising with panic.

There *had* to be someone nearby. Forests were usually full of people gathering wood, setting traps, picking herbs and flowers.

No-one replied.

Nothing moved, save the few leaves that dropped to the ground in the birds' wake.

Stomach sinking, he realised there was no-one there. No-one coming to help. He had to get out of this himself, otherwise he'd die. Drowning in muddy sludge had never before crossed his mind as a way his life could end, and he had no intention of letting the possibility become a reality.

There was nothing for it. Grimacing in anticipation of the coming pain, Fenn threw himself forward with all the strength he could muster and grabbed the closest vine with both hands. His muscles spasmed as he overexerted himself, and he ignored the twinge. Thorns dug into his palms, then his thumbs, as he tightened his grip. He winced as they pierced his skin—better a short, sharp pain now than a slow death later.

Slowly, due to the thick sludge and his own dwindling stamina, Fenn pulled himself along the vine, inching towards the edge of the pool. Every movement pushed the thorns in further, deepening the cuts across his skin. Moving through the mud sapped his strength, but he soldiered through it. One thorn snapped off under his finger, flicking mud at him as it fell. Fenn turned his chin at the last second, the gloop spattering along his right cheek, narrowly avoiding his eye.

5

One arm over the other, he pulled himself towards safety. He was halfway there, now. Slow and steady.

Another two thorns snapped away, and a deep growl reverberated across the surface of the mud.

'You're pulling my thorns out!'

Fenn stilled at the sudden, ferocious voice. Fat chunks of mud dropped from his arm and slapped back into the pool, but he ignored the stench rising from it. His heart thundered in his chest, eyes wide as he gazed around for whoever had shouted at him.

When the voice didn't speak again, and quite certain he was becoming delirious in the fumes emitted from the muddy swamp, Fenn continued to heave himself along the vine, redoubling his attempts to free himself. A fourth thorn snapped away with a crack.

Just as the edge was within grasping distance, another of the trailing vines rose from the ground and thwacked him across the chest.

Fenn coughed violently, stunned.

Had...had the vine *deliberately* attacked him? It couldn't have.

'Get. Off!' The vine in his hands shuddered, recoiling from him as if alive, dragging its thorns along his bare arms and leaving a trail of raw scratches.

'I'm trying!' Fenn couldn't believe he was talking to a vine. Arguing with one.

He must be more delirious than he'd realised.

Fenn tightened his hold on the tip of the vine and hurled himself through the last few feet of mud. He pulled harder to speed his approach, and the vine snapped just before he reached safety. Flailing forward, fingers scrabbling against the wet grass that lined the edge of the pool, Fenn heaved himself out of the mud as it tried to suck him back in.

He managed to stay on his hands and knees for a few seconds before collapsing onto the dew-covered grass, panting heavily. Glancing back down at himself, he realised he'd lost a shoe somewhere in the fetid pool. There was no going back for it now. His lower half was completely caked in the stinking, oozing mud, and all his clothes were ruined, anyway. It hardly mattered that he was missing a shoe, too.

Besides, that was the least of his worries.

The vine had spoken to him, hadn't it? Or had that been part of a headache-induced hallucination? The pain hadn't left him. And the vine wasn't speaking now. There were distant sounds in the trees: birds and squirrels chittering, the drip of water somewhere, the rustle of leaves in the breeze.

Nothing here was familiar. And nothing made any sense. He had no idea where he was, how he'd got there, or—more worryingly, now he had time to consider it—no recollection of *who* he was. Where had he been? Who...who was he?

Fenn.

His name floated up from the darkness of his mind. But other than that? There was...nothing. The more he tried to think, the less he knew. Memories slipped through his grasp like water through his fingers. His mind was a tangle of confusion, as though a dense fog had taken up residence and settled down over everything that made sense.

Several lines of crimson criss-crossed his flushed arms and hands, the stinging intensifying now he was still, especially where the stinking mud touched it. He raised his left arm to his face, wondering if there was poison in the thorns. Perhaps that was causing the hallucinations? The memory issues?

Something moved just outside his peripheral vision. A shadow, shifting along the leaf litter covering the forest floor. Fenn turned, breath held in case it was one of the numerous predators that made the trees their home. After saving himself from drowning, it would be just his luck to be devoured by a bear.

A hiss rippled through the undergrowth.

Fenn froze.

Perhaps it wasn't a bear. They didn't hiss.

'Who...who's there?' He staggered to his feet, wet mud dripping from his body, trying to get a better look between the trees. His one bare foot squelched with each step, and he suppressed a shudder. He hadn't fully recovered from the talking vine—if it really *had* been talking—and wasn't sure he could face a new threat quite so soon.

A sudden cold wind snaked through the trees, turning the damp air into freezing mist. The grass wilted away, shrinking down to the ground. Even the trees seemed to sag. Fenn shivered at the drop in temperature and the growing tension that came with it. The hiss sounded again—no more than a few feet away.

The hairs on the back of his neck stood up as the mist crept across the mud pool, frosting the top layer. Fenn saw his breath in the air on his next exhale, and gritted his teeth, expecting to be snatched away and eaten by some frost monster.

'My, my, my...where have you come from?'

It wasn't the vine talking. Not this time. The disembodied voice came from the mist itself—across the pool within the shadows, just hidden out of view. Not trusting himself to speak, Fenn kept his mouth shut and eyes wide open, ready to react.

The hiss shifted into a low growl, and the mist coalesced on top of the frozen mud pool. It churned like water over a fall, until solid shapes formed. A sinuous, reptilian body. Scales. Claws. Wings. A tail. Two golden eyes with vertical slit pupils that stared directly at him.

Fenn's breath caught. Even if he'd wanted to talk, he couldn't. His voice had left him.

The dragon's nostrils flared, sending up a plume of smoke that joined the mist wreathing the trees. Its skin was mottled green, like the forest around it, with darker stippling along its back and legs. Its wings were thin and membranous, the pattern on its skin identical to the tree's leaves. Four large horns protruded from the back of its head, and long, green vines dangled between them. Although easily as large as the bear Fenn feared it had been, it wasn't as bulky, and it shimmered in the pale sunlight—becoming translucent every few seconds.

Waiting for a response, the dragon flexed its wings.

Memory loss was one thing. A talking plant was another. Now a dragon had appeared out of the mist, Fenn was sure he wasn't entirely in his right mind. He blinked rapidly, hoping to clear the visual and auditory hallucinations he was *most definitely* experiencing. But the dragon remained. If anything, it looked mildly irritated at being ignored. Another plume of smoke rose from its nostrils and one long, sharp fang protruded from its upper jaw.

'What...are you?' It was a stupid question, but the only one Fenn could come up with. He took a few steps away from the now icy mud pool and the dragon standing atop it.

Lowering its head to the torn vine, the dragon breathed gently over it, and a cloud of thick, green smoke drifted out from its jaws. At the smoke's touch, the vine's tendrils lifted, wrapped around one another, and knitted themselves back together, as if Fenn had never ripped it. Even the lost thorns regrew, pushing through the vine's flesh like new teeth.

The dragon let out another growl, its muscles bunched up as it studied Fenn through bright, golden eyes. In a flash, the dragon charged at him. Fenn leapt back, tripping over a tree root and slamming the back of his head against the trunk. The dragon roared as it leapt into the sky with a beat of its wings, before it shifted into a thousand green scales that burst into fragments of light.

Fenn gasped in shock and watched as overhead, every individual scale shifted from light into countless silver butterflies. Air forced from his lungs, Fenn could do nothing but groan and gaze up in wonder as the thousand butterflies reformed overhead, turning back into the translucent green dragon that soared underneath the canopy, mist wreathing its limbs.

A shaft of sunlight broke through the leaves and cast rainbows of light on the forest floor where it touched the dragon. It arced in the sky, powering on wings of pressed silver, before it dived towards the ground—directly at him.

Fenn covered his head, bracing for impact, for the death he'd escaped prior to finally catch him.

Nothing happened.

Hardly able to believe he'd cheated death again, he cautiously opened one eye to see four enormous talons less than an inch from his face. He quickly pushed himself up to sit.

'You're supposed to answer when you are asked a question.' Disdain was evident in the dragon's tone.

Fenn blinked stupidly for longer than he wanted to. Was it a dream? Had to be. It was a damned vivid one if so. He'd have to swear off wine forever more. 'Um. Sorry?'

The dragon snorted, clearly unimpressed.

The headache that had been throbbing at his temples increased. He had a sudden urge to vomit, but he held himself together before he could begin retching. Any earlier dread he'd felt had washed away by the sheer absurdity of it all.

'I ask again. Where have you come from?'

In truth, Fenn wanted to know that himself. If *he* didn't know, how was he expected to tell anyone else? Instead, he opted to ask the dragon a question to stall for time, hoping hitting his head against the tree trunk might force some of his memories back into existence. 'Where did *you* come from?'

'You cannot tell? Foolish creature. I am the spirit of this forest.'

Its voice was soft and languid. *'You are in* my *domain. Causing damage. I heard the vines cry out.'*

Now Fenn *knew* he was dreaming. 'How can you be...a forest? A spirit? You're as real as I am.' As if to prove his point, he reached out and touched the creature's smooth scales, accidentally wiping mud across its warm snout.

The dragon snarled, and realising his transgression, Fenn immediately withdrew his hand.

'You dare *touch the Spirit of Salt Ash? I have cursed people for far less.'* Flames danced in its open jaws.

Despite the clear warning, Fenn sensed a little amusement from the dragon. 'I've never seen a spirit before. Never *been* here before. How was I supposed to know?'

Another rumble from the dragon. More amusement. It didn't seem to care about the smear of mud across its muzzle. *'How can you be unaware of Tassar's Guardians? Are you sick? Tainted in some way?'*

Fenn avoided the dragon's questions as he tried to think of a way out of his situation. The filthy mud stuck his clothes to his skin and he shuddered at the sensation. 'Are you going to kill me?'

The dragon considered for several long seconds. *'No.'*

He gulped down a lungful of air as if it would give him strength and confidence. 'Then can you help me? I don't know where I am. *Who* I am! Or where I'm from.'

The dragon's pupils dilated. *'You are in my domain, lost one. I told you. Salt Ash.'*

'What's that?'

Tilting its head to one side, the dragon let out a plume of smoke from its nostrils. *'You really do not know? How fascinating...'*

The dragon's reluctance to give him a straight answer was infuriating, and already Fenn could feel the strength leaving his knees. 'Please! If you won't kill me, help me!'

Something low rumbled in the dragon's vast chest that

was akin to laughter. *'I will watch you for a while. You are... interesting. If you harm my domain again, I shall kill you, and you shall be a feast for my forest.'*

Fenn didn't question it. An argument was a poor choice when the predator had already agreed he wasn't going to eat him. He licked his lips and let out a slow breath to steady his nerves.

The dragon leaned forward and brushed Fenn's forehead with its muzzle, then with a sudden burst of speed, passed *through* him and the tree, and fire sparked across Fenn's chest for a heartbeat. The dragon again shifted into a myriad of light and silver butterflies, and disappeared into the depths of the trees.

It was as if the entire forest burst into life in his head. Every bird, every insect, every animal that made this place its home was alive in his mind. All the flowers, grass, trees, plants. An explosion of light and sound and motion. He heard each and every one, their voices high and laughing, or low and rumbling. A perfect balance of chaos, surrounded by the dragon's fire.

Fenn's headache intensified. He sank to one knee and clutched his head with both hands. He could do nothing but focus on his breathing as the fire in his body dimmed. With every exhale, the intensity of the forest dwindled, slowly softening, lessening, until he was left in the humid glade with only his own, shallow breathing for company.

His arms tingled all over from his wounds, sweat dripped down his nose, and every muscle trembled. He wasn't sure he could even wipe his face without passing out.

Somewhere behind him, a twig snapped.

Fenn gasped in surprise and fear.

Footsteps. And a voice. Two voices. Both female.

'...This stinking swamp.'

'It wasn't there yesterday! You know what Hassen is like. Just having fun when he gets bored.'

'Gods, I miss the mountains. No swamps. No spirits. Just clear air, excellent views, and water that doesn't randomly change based on a spirit's sense of *fun*.'

Responding laughter. 'You told me if you saw another mountain again it'd be too soon.'

'A *lot* changes in seven years, Jisyel. I'm just tired of traipsing through a forest where trees constantly shift and repulsive bogs appear every handful of days.'

More laughter, from the one referred to as Jisyel. Her voice was flighty, constantly on the edge of giggles, as if everything amused her.

Fenn squatted down beside the tree, leaning on it for support, and waited for them to appear.

'I know, I know. "You can take the Bragalian out of the mountain, but not the mountain out of the Bragalian." Calidra, you *can* go back anytime you want. Nothing's keeping you here!'

Calidra snorted. 'You're doing a good job of that.'

The voices grew louder. They couldn't have been more than a handful of paces away.

Fenn gulped, wondering whether it would be better to try and get away, hide, or remain where he was. And hope they didn't hurt him—or worse—the moment they spotted him.

But he'd survived an encounter with a dragon spirit. Surely he could survive these two? And if the dragon wasn't prepared to help, perhaps *they* would be. It wasn't as if he had many other options. He turned to face them when his legs cramped up and he stumbled to the ground with a yelp of agony.

Perfect. Absolutely perfect.

Almost at the same time, the two women appeared on the far side of the glade. The taller one stopped by the edge of the mud, one hand on her hip, frowning. Sunlight lit up her pale skin and bright auburn hair, making her seem as

13

translucent as the dragon. 'Strange. It's iced over. Hassen must've been here recently.'

'A shame he didn't bother to restore the bog to the pond it should've been.' The second woman, Calidra, pinched the bridge of her nose. She was shorter than Jisyel, her skin nut brown, with quick eyes that spotted Fenn a heartbeat later. She drew a long hunting dagger from her belt and held it up, the blade glinting silver. 'You. Boy. I see you. Step out of the shadows before my blade finds you.' Even from across the glade, her gaze was intense.

Fenn gulped, trembling all over. Jisyel appeared unarmed, but that didn't mean she couldn't hurt him, too. He tried to straighten up and winced, doubling over again.

'I am running out of patience. Do you have a strong desire to die today?'

'Okay, okay. Wait a second, please! I'm hurt!' Glad he'd found his voice before Calidra had decided to act, Fenn raised both hands and stumbled out of the tree's shadow, his legs screaming in pain. He knew he must have been quite a sight, his entire lower-half was black with rapidly-drying mud, blood flowed down his arms, and the rest of him was as dishevelled as a street urchin.

'What are you doing down there?' Calidra pressed, her knife held high, with no signs of being lowered. She'd cut straight to the point, not even bothering to ask about his bizarre appearance.

'I...don't know,' Fenn answered. It sounded ridiculous, even to him, but there was no other answer. 'Honestly, I'm not in this state by choice!' He offered a grin.

Jisyel laughed and shook her head, but Calidra was unmoved. If anything, her scowl deepened.

Licking his lips, he dropped the humour. Clearly it wouldn't help. 'I think I hit my head. Woke up in the middle of that.' He gestured to the mud pool. 'Before it was iced, I mean. Can you tell me where I am? There was a dragon, called himself a forest spirit and—'

'Hassen cursed you?' Calidra interrupted, raising an eyebrow and lowering her blade slightly, her demeanour softening.

'Cursed me?' Fenn repeated.

'He's been known to' Jisyel gave a cautious smile and pressed on Calidra's arm, forcing the other woman to lower her dagger. 'What about before that? Where are you from?'

Fenn shrugged. 'I really don't know. It…my head hurts so much.' He clutched it with one hand, swaying on his feet. 'Please, I…I need help.'

Calidra pulled away from Jisyel and raised her blade again. 'Could be a trick.'

'I'm not lying!'

'Relax, Cal. I don't think it's hogshit. He seems desperate,' Jisyel said. 'Why not bring him to gran? Not like he can hurt us in the state he's in.'

Calidra huffed at Jisyel's words and brusquely sheathed her dagger, evidently deciding he posed no threat. 'Can't take him back. Bell will throw a fit, and he'll stink up the whole place.'

'Nonsense. A bath and some new clothes and he'll be fine. Can't just leave him out here, can we?' Jisyel gestured towards Fenn with an open palm. 'Look, he doesn't even have both his shoes!'

'Of *course* we can leave him. Who knows what some raving lunatic will do? Especially if Hassen's cursed him. You don't have to help *everyone* who wanders through the forest! Best march him to port and send him to the mainland. The Inquisitors will pick him up soon enough. *They* can deal with him.'

'With what papers? Look at him, Calidra. Poor thing's been dragged through that mud. Hassen's obviously had some fun with him. He wouldn't last two minutes in Bragalia by himself, and you know it.'

Calidra rolled her eyes as if this was an argument she'd had many times before. 'Well, just leave him here, then. Perhaps a bear or a pack of forest wolves'll have him and—'

'Please!' Fenn hobbled around the bog towards them, leaving muddy prints across the vibrant green grass. His vision flickered in terror at the thought of being thrown to the wolves. 'I'm no good for eating! Just give me a chance? A bit of help? I'll do what you need. Clean. Cook.' He thought desperately for some way he could make himself useful. 'Whatever you need! I just need to get my head sorted and—' Fenn swayed again, the stabbing headache almost crushing his ability to speak. Desperate, he tried to argue his case. 'A few days, I just…I…'

With a groan of agony, he collapsed.

SOFT COTTON SHEETS. A pillow stuffed with goose down. The richly floral scent of lavender soap.

Fenn forced his eyes open and found himself lying in bed in a small room. His skin tingled, and he looked down to see a thick, green paste smeared over the cuts on his arms. Touching it with his fingertips, he brought them close to his face and, after a cautious sniff, frowned. It smelled awful—worse even than the swamp sludge. It had to be medicine of some sort. Medicine always smelled awful. The paste had numbed his wounds, however, and even his headache had lessened to a more manageable level.

Most of the mud had been washed from his arms, but he could still feel it caked around his waist and legs. He shuddered at the feeling and sat up gingerly. Glancing around, he tried to recognise something, anything. Three more beds were nestled against the far wall of the comfortable room, which had been furnished with a bookshelf, wardrobe, a low table with a large bowl of steaming water and a nub of soap, and a wooden chair at the end of each bed. There was a painting on the wall depicting a farmstead and pigs bristling with hair wandering around in front of a gate. The door to the room was made of heavy wood, but was closed.

Nothing stood out. He drew a blank. Clearly several people could sleep in the room, but he couldn't tell more than that.

Had he been here before and forgotten, like everything else? Or was this place somewhere new?

An open window beside his bed let in the deep, orange light of sunset, and he wondered how long he'd been asleep. Dust motes fluttered in the shaft of light, oddly calming as he watched them.

Muffled voices drifted up from somewhere below him—so he was upstairs. He held himself still, trying to listen. He couldn't be sure, but it sounded like Calidra and Jisyel, along with other voices. The floorboards were too thick for him to make much sense of what was being said, but he could tell the voices were raised with some emotion he couldn't place.

He lifted the sheets off himself, desperate to get to the bowl of water and clean off the sticky mud, when footsteps thundered towards the closed door.

Sinking back into the pillow and closing his eyes, he held his breath as the door burst open.

'Calidra, please! Wait!'

Aware that two people had entered the room, but afraid to open his eyes and show he was awake, Fenn concentrated on his breathing and keeping as quiet as possible.

Someone threw open the wardrobe in the room's corner and began rifling through the clothes, contents spilling out and rolling onto the wooden floorboards.

'Tell me what the message said! No-one ever bothers to

17

send us stuff out here, don't hog it all to yourself!' Jisyel's voice pleaded.

More shuffling of clothes. Drawers were opened, then aggressively slammed shut. Feet stomped around the room, and Fenn felt the radiating anger even through his closed eyelids.

'Please? Cal?' Jisyel's tone was no longer light. Utterly serious.

Calidra took a deep breath. 'Jisyel...' She sounded distant, as if she stood far away and not on the other side of the room. 'It came from Fellwood. It...it stated that a terrible sickness had taken the life of the Laird, and I am requested at his funeral, one week hence.'

Unable to resist any longer, Fenn turned his head minutely and opened one eye.

Jisyel rested a hand on Calidra's cheek, the rest of her cheeriness diminishing. 'Calidra...'

The other woman trembled and looked away, her hands balling into fists as she whispered, 'It's father. He's...finally gone.'

18

2

THE BEGINNING

CALIDRA

'Oh. He's awake!' Jisyel gasped.

The young man glanced up from his bed, looking far less disoriented than Calidra had expected given his earlier bewilderment. She narrowed her eyes, waiting for any sign of deception. Had he been listening to her conversation with Jisyel?

'Um. Guessing you two brought me inside? Thanks.'

'You feeling any better?' Jisyel asked, ever eager.

'Ready to tell us who you are?' Calidra added before Jisyel could get too carried away with the pleasantries of hospitality. She wasn't entirely certain she trusted his amnesiac story, it was too convenient. Thieves and opportunists used any excuse to manipulate you, and she didn't put it past this lad, no matter how pathetic he appeared. Whatever he was hiding, she'd find it.

He pushed himself up onto his elbows. 'Hey, I'm not that much younger than you!'

Calidra folded her arms over her chest, her earlier sadness and rage about the message she'd received evaporating. Her familial obligations could wait. This boy was a potential threat right in front of them. And she'd caught him, now. 'So how old are you, then? Telling the truth would be a good start to gaining our trust.'

She saw him think, screwing up his face like a toddler. Eventually, he shrugged. 'I...I'm not sure. And I'm not lying, either, before you accuse me of that again!' He sank down a little in the sheets. 'Were those vines really talking to me? Or did I hit my head before I almost drowned in that bog?'

Calidra scowled, her eyebrows furrowing. How could he not have been in a living forest before? Something was off about him.

Jisyel put a hand on Calidra's shoulder. 'Hey. Hassen is capable of all sorts of things. The lad is clearly hurt. Maybe you could *try* to be nice?' She crossed the room and perched on the edge of the bed. 'I'm Jisyel, lovely to meet you! This is an inn in Hogsbrook, on the Isle of Salt. That's Calidra,' she jerked a thumb over her shoulder, 'and my gran, Bellandri, owns this inn. She's downstairs. And yes, the plants here can talk. Lots of forests are the same. It's pretty common when it has a spirit.'

He took it all in, and nodded. 'I'm Fenn.'

Jisyel smiled, politely waiting.

'I...can't tell you much more than that. My mind's blank. I don't even know how I got here.'

Calidra fought to hold her snort in. 'That's rather convenient, don't you think?'

'I guess it looks bad, but *I'm* the one shaken up by it. Imagine if *you* woke up in the middle of a mud bog with no idea who you were or how you'd got there!'

He made an interesting point, but she wasn't convinced.

Jisyel leaned forward. 'In all honesty, that bog wasn't there yesterday. Hassen—the spirit of the forest here—has a habit of playing games and messing us around. He even—'

'That's enough, Jisyel. Don't need to tell him your whole life story,' Calidra interrupted, speaking between gritted teeth.

Jisyel coughed and tucked a few loose strands of hair behind her ears. 'Yes, well. Strange things occur on this island. You turning up in the middle of it with no memory isn't even the strangest thing to happen this month!'

'Stupid cursed rock.' Calidra looked out the window at the sunset and the dark forest beyond.

Jisyel grinned broadly. 'It's not cursed, that's just what the mainlanders say about the island. And anyway, she *claims* to hate it, but she's stuck around for seven years!'

Calidra stiffened, the only way she could hold back the tide of emotions that threatened to flood her at the mention of seven years. She didn't like showing emotions at the best of times, and she had no intention of letting the stranger see her weakness. 'Well, that's about to change, isn't it? So, Fenn, where are you from? Your accent isn't Porsenthian. Nor any of the Bragalian dialects. Not Olmese, either.'

Fenn visibly gulped.

Jisyel continued the line of enquiry, 'Castrin? Ulnoth? Any of those names helping you remember? Spirits bless me, don't say you're Egyean!'

'I don't know!' Fenn threw up his hands, exasperated. 'I can't explain how, or why. I *know* night follows day, rain follows grey clouds, fire burns. But when it comes to *me*? Who I am? My home? My family? There's...nothing. A fog, maybe. I know my name is Fenn. Bar that? Nothing...But, maybe if I rest for a few days, some of the confusion might lift?' He gripped the bed sheets tightly, though Calidra couldn't tell if it was in frustration or fear.

Either way, his emotions were so raw, Calidra softened her voice. 'And if it doesn't lift?'

Fenn didn't reply, just kept his gaze on the floorboards.

Jisyel cleared her throat, clearly uncomfortable. 'Anything, no matter how bad, recovers after some time, doesn't it? Broken bones. Even the pain of grieving a loved one eventually passes.' She gave Calidra a pointed look. 'You'll just have to be patient, that's all.'

Calidra let out a long sigh. There were too many emotions today, in this room. And it stank of glinoc paste and putrid, drying mud. She needed some fresh air.

'Fenn, are you hungry?' Jisyel asked him.

'Starving.'

'All right. Clean yourself up in here. There's plenty of spare clothes in the wardrobe,' she gestured to the mess of clothing Calidra had made moments before Fenn awoke, 'help yourself to whatever you want. We'll be downstairs when you're ready, and get you a plate of something.'

He nodded, shoulders dropping in relief. 'Thank you. I really appreciate it.'

Calidra didn't wait for more conversation. Picking up the few items of clothing she'd specifically wanted, she left the room, some of her anger dissipating. If she kept herself busy, she didn't need to think about Bragalia, about going back.

The strange boy was a welcome distraction from what she knew would be Jisyel's well-meaning but ineffective advice on facing her family again. She dumped her effects outside the door and marched towards the stairs, her anger now a gentle simmer.

Thankfully, the messenger had left by the time she reached the ground floor. Few people stayed on the Isle of Salt longer than was necessary—Jisyel had that right, most people from the mainland believed the island to be cursed, and Hassen's ever-changing moods fuelled that theory. But, even Hassen's mischievous ways didn't dissuade mainlanders coming to see the vast forest of Salt Ash, the steep cliffs, or enjoying the delicacies of the remote Porsenthian island. Boats came and went to the mainland once a week, twice during high trade, and no doubt the messenger wanted to get back on the boat to Bragalia the moment it finished unhauling and re-loading its cargo.

Bellandri already had a steaming mug of coffee waiting for Calidra at her regular table in the inn's large dining room, the smell of it easing her fears and aches more than anything else could. She'd added cinnamon too, and Calidra loved the old woman for the way she cared for her in the little details.

The Hog's Tusk was Bellandri's pride and joy, an inn that she had run alone for the past forty-three years, and raised Jisyel in after her mother's sudden passing. She had a habit of helping those washed up on the island, getting them back on their feet again and setting them to rights.

It had been the same with Calidra.

Most went back home, however. Yet, after seven years, Calidra was still here.

As much as she grumbled and complained about the Isle of Salt, the terrible weather, the lack of decent food—or coffee—and Hassen most of all, for her, it was better than going back to the mainland. And it wasn't for lack of trying—it had become an annual argument she'd had with Jisyel. Calidra had tried to explain that going back home wasn't that simple. Forgetting the fact she hated water—it was one of the few things in the world that scared her besides her mother's wrath—her family was so disjointed and broken that she didn't even *want* to go back. She'd lost her sister some years prior, and now her father, too. There was simply too much pain baked into where she'd come from.

She took a long sip of her coffee, savouring the taste of home, as the crumpled paper in her pocket weighed heavy on her chest. Her father. She'd not seen him in twelve years. Not seen her mother in eight.

And everything was about to be undone. The new life she'd tried to forge on the cold rock in the middle of the Salt Sea was about to be torn away from her. Jisyel was getting her wish, and she was going to regret ever suggesting coming to Bragalia with her.

Calidra took her hunting dagger from her pocket and

23

balanced it on the table. The ogee pattern on the hilt was typically Bragalian—a memento of her sister. She stared at it, watching light glint off the blade's edge.

There were no patrons in *The Hog's Tusk*. It was the wrong time of year for fishing, not that the place improved much in summer, but the driving rains and stiff sea wind tended to keep all but the hardiest of travellers away. The wood and stone walls creaked in the low wind that howled on the peak where the inn had been built some four hundred years prior, a comforting sound.

Calidra cupped her mug with both hands lest she grabbed the letter and threw it in the fireplace. That would be bad. She'd learned a long time ago to keep a careful hold of her more impulsive reactions. But it didn't make it any easier.

'Bad news?' Bellandri asked, exiting the back room of the inn, bringing the smell of the kitchens with her. She had a rag over one shoulder and wiped her hands on an apron already smudged with soot and flour. Her weatherbeaten skin was deeply tanned and lined with creases, probably made worse by her almost perpetual grin. Having spent most of her life in a physically demanding job, Bellandri's gait was sure across the slightly swaying inn floor as she meandered through the empty tables to Calidra.

'You could say that.' Calidra glanced up as Jisyel came down the stairs, refolding the clothes she'd dumped outside the bedroom door. 'Or it's good news. Depends on your perspective.'

'Oh?' Bellandri raised an eyebrow, a wisp of grey hair floating above her forehead like antennae. Despite there being two generations between Bellandri and Jisyel, they shared such a likeness they could be mother and daughter. Calidra supposed they were, all but biologically. 'How's the young man doing?'

Jisyel slumped into a chair beside Calidra and brought out a small bag of nuts she'd had in her pocket. She popped a handful out of their shells, palmed them into her mouth, and crunched down. 'Other than not having a clue who or where he is, I'd say he's doing pretty well. Gonna have to rinse out the tub once he's done, I reckon. Mud's gonna get *everywhere*.'

'I don't understand why Hassen made the bog in the first place,' Calidra said, eying the nut shells and dust covering the table with distaste. She loved Jisyel, but by the spirits, the woman was the messiest person she'd ever met.

'Boredom, I say. Think about it. An immortal spirit stuck on this island. You'd change things around just because you could, too.' Jisyel grinned, her hair sticking out at odd angles in the same way as her grandmother's.

'Corrupted, more like.' Calidra shook her head.

'I wouldn't go that far. Hassen isn't corrupted. Spirits take me, you'd *know* if you met a corrupted one. They only get like that when they're dying, anyway.' Bellandri made the torteth sign across her forehead, an old gesture to ward off the attention of spirits that might do you harm, which Calidra found utterly ridiculous superstition. 'He's just…a bit of a trickster. Mischievous, like most children are. Some years we've been struggling so badly that we wouldn't have survived at all if it weren't for him.'

'Glad I wasn't here for those,' Calidra said with a barely suppressed shudder. She didn't want to think about how the island could be worse than it already was.

'Gran's just joking. *Apparently* everything was more awful back then, but I don't remember it like that at all.' Jisyel emptied the rest of the bag's contents onto her upturned hand, then shoved the nuts into her mouth—shells and all. 'Anyway. Be nice to have a new friend, eh?'

Calidra looked away, vaguely repulsed. She could imagine the tough, bitter shells, their fine hairs like a broom head, and the thought of it almost made her gag. She'd tried to tell Jisyel it wasn't good for her to eat those blasted shells, but the woman had laughed it off and eaten them anyway, gleeful at Calidra's obvious discomfort.

'Well, perhaps if *you'd* showed a bit more respect to the forest spirit, *you* wouldn't have ended up with *that.*' Bellandri gestured vaguely in Jisyel's direction.

Jisyel grinned, as if she hadn't the faintest idea what her grandmother meant.

Calidra fought to keep her eyes from rolling. Jisyel's *affliction* for reckless naivety had always been with her. Hassen had simply made things worse. 'Fenn is *not* our friend. And what're we going to do with him? Leave him here? Not like we have enough guests at the moment to warrant another pair of hands. How do we know he isn't here to steal something?'

Bellandri lifted her mug and let out a short bark of laughter. 'Oh no, the good coffee beans. Whatever will I do if those disappear overnight?'

'*I'd* be upset.'

Jisyel playfully nudged Calidra's arm. 'Yes, but *you* aren't going to be here long enough to be upset, are you? I'll be with you, you know. You don't have to go back to Bragalia alone. I always said I would go. Now it's finally time.'

Calidra bit her lower lip. Damn Jisyel for bringing her attention back to Bragalia.

'Are you going to tell me what the letter says? That messenger was in a terrible rush.' Bellandri sat back, giving her some space.

After a moment of internal debate, Calidra fished the paper out and smoothed it on the table. Bellandri couldn't read, so there was no point in passing it to the older woman. She cleared her throat and spoke slowly. It was no easier than reading it the first time. If anything, it was harder, because she knew what was coming and could do nothing about it.

It was the first letter she'd received from home in six

years. The only correspondence before that had been from her mother confirming no more funds would be sent. Clearly, she'd embarrassed the family by ending up on the supposedly cursed Isle of Salt.

Though it had been expected, it had still hurt.

When Calidra was finished, Bellandri nodded knowingly. 'Ah. I see what you mean about it being good and bad news. You know the boat leaves in the morning? If you don't go, it'll be another—'

'I know,' Calidra snapped, regretting her disrespect but unable to stop herself. If she didn't make the boat, she'd have to wait a week for the next one. She'd miss the funeral.

Probably her mother deliberately sending the messenger late, forcing her to come home before she could think or talk herself out of it.

She wasn't sure she wanted to go. If she even *could* go.

It had been so long, and that particular wound hadn't healed. If anything, it had festered over the years. She didn't know what she'd do if she returned home to find everything had gone to rot. Calidra bit her lip again, thinking.

'It'll be fine. I've been badgering you about it for years, so it's about time you check in on things. And anyway, didn't you mention wanting to take Fenn to the mainland?' Jisyel suggested, leaning on one arm on the table. 'No point him staying here, all confused.'

'True. He'd probably get under my feet, sweet as he is,' Bellandri agreed.

Calidra's face heated up. She knew what they were getting at. Take Fenn to the mainland, and while they were in Bragalia, she might as well go home to Fellwood. She hated that they were right and let out another long sigh.

'I've a friend in Ballowtown. Ashothka,' Bellandri said. 'You can stay with him for a night or two when you arrive, while you sort out things for Fenn. He'll give you some coin and make reservations for you at inns along the way. He owes me a few favours.'

'Ashothka? That's an Olmese name,' Calidra said. The same as her mother.

Bellandri nodded. 'Believe it or not, I had a life before retiring here on my little salted island. Anyway, Ashothka helped me smuggle a few things from time to time. So don't be too shocked if you aren't staying somewhere as lovely as *The Hog's Tusk* when you get there.'

'Ballowtown's awful, anyway,' Calidra said, remembering the crowds from the last time she'd passed through.

'Where's awful?'

They all glanced up at the staircase, where Fenn had crept part-way down without any of them noticing. His hair was damp and his arms were red from the paste, but he looked much better now he was clean.

'My granddaughter and Calidra are taking a trip to the mainland. You'll be going with them,' Bellandri said brightly. She stood up and crossed to the bottom of the stairs, where she helped Fenn down the last few steps, which were partly missing. She brushed him down none-too-gently with her hands until she was satisfied with his appearance. 'Well you don't scrub up half bad, do you? I'm Bellandri, welcome to my inn. Go on, go on, sit down. I'll get you something to eat.' She pushed him towards the table.

'Don't fuss over him so much, Bell,' Calidra said.

'Nonsense. I did the same to you, Calidra. Leave him be.' The old woman bustled away into the back room, the door sending more smells of food as it swung open.

Calidra regarded Fenn, then begrudgingly pulled out a chair for him. Now he wasn't covered in mud, he looked less pathetic. Still scrawny and lost-looking, but sturdier than she had initially given him credit for. 'I don't suppose you remember anything about Ballowtown?'

He shook his head and sheepishly crossed the room to

their table, looking vaguely put out after Bellandri's man-handling.

'One of the biggest towns in Bragalia. Port town. And the closest place on the mainland that we can reach from here.' She didn't know why she was explaining it to him, but Jisyel and Bellandri's confidence in his innocence made her give him the benefit of the doubt. She didn't relish the idea of having to explain things to him every five minutes, and couldn't wait to palm him off to the Inquisitors once they reached Bragalia. She had enough of her own problems to deal with without adding Fenn to the mix.

'Oh, hogshit!' Jisyel sat up straight. 'They won't let him into town without paperwork. They'll just leave him on the boat to come back here!'

Jisyel had a point. Calidra's gaze narrowed on Fenn, now sporting new, mud-free clothes. 'Where are your old clothes? You had no papers on you?'

Fenn shrugged, the faintly bemused look still plastered on his face, which irritated Calidra more than she cared to admit.

Calidra thought. 'Well, I guess it's not unheard of that you came here from Porsenthia. Or somewhere else.'

'What's wrong?' Fenn asked.

'Bragalia is divided into different cantons. You need the right papers to pass between them, which are usually issued by the Laird of that canton. If you don't have the right papers, you aren't going anywhere. And Bragalia is the nearest land to the Isle of Salt. Wherever you came from, it was most likely you travelled through Bragalia. Which you couldn't have done without the right paperwork...So I suppose you came from somewhere else?'

Fenn shrugged again. 'I'm sorry, Calidra. Believe me, no-one is more frustrated than I am.' He rested his elbows on the table and leaned on them.

Calidra frowned, trying to work out *where* he'd come from, if not Bragalia.

'But what does all that stuff about cantons have to do with Ballowtown?' Fenn asked, his attention split between Calidra and Jisyel.

'It's part of Bragalia. No papers, no travel. You won't get onto the mainland, they'll just send you back on the boat here. Except, it only travels once per week, so you'd be stuck there for a week, unable to go anywhere.'

'Well, we'll just have to get Fenn some forged papers then, won't we?' Bellandri came back from the kitchen, a platter held easily in the crook of one arm, a large coffee pot in her other, and three mugs looped on the end of her fingers.

'Forgeries?' Calidra's eyebrows shot up.

'Oh, come now. Even the daughter of a Laird knows these things happen from time to time, *Miss Vantonen*.' Bellandri gently set the array on the table and shoved the platter towards Fenn. 'Come on, eat up. Need to plump you up a bit. Salt Sea can be a cruel thing to cross this time of year.' She patted his back in encouragement.

It was a platter of cooked sausage—cured and smoked from the colour and smell—cabbage salad, some fresh bread swathed in melted butter, and Bragalian pickles.

Fenn stared at the platter, his hands firmly by his sides. 'Shouldn't I...do something for this?'

'You are a guest, Fenn. Your job is to sit there and be fed. Eat,' Bellandri demanded, as she poured coffee for them.

Fenn did as he was told, and there was enough on the platter for them all to share.

Calidra gratefully took another coffee, the hot steam calming her. It helped her realise the decision had already been made, she just needed to accept it. 'Okay, okay. Fine. I have to go back to Fellwood, I see that. Better to go now than wait another seven years, I suppose. Fenn, you can travel with us. But you'll be the Inquisitors' problem once we're on the mainland. I'm not babysitting anyone. It's hard enough making sure Jisyel doesn't get into trouble!'

'Yes, she is a bit of a scatterbrain isn't she? I don't know what she'd do without you,' Bellandri said fondly, patting her granddaughter's hand. 'Calidra, that's a very sensible decision. I'm proud of you.' She raised her mug high. 'I just hope it's not Torsten there.'

Calidra did roll her eyes, then. 'There's no chance the Master Inquisitor will be that far south. I've not heard of him being out of Porsenthia in years.'

'Well, just keep an eye on Fenn. Maybe his memory will be back by then and you won't need the Inquisitors at all,' Bellandri spoke cooly, watching Fenn as he ate. She poured him another mug of coffee once he'd finished. 'Poor lad. It's not much but I'll make sure you don't go without tonight!'

'Time to pack?' Jisyel stood up, the movement making Fenn pause.

'I suppose.' Calidra hated how sudden everything was. She resigned herself to the decision and got to her feet. 'We'll need to leave at dawn to get to the boat in time. Best get your head down early.'

Fenn nodded. If he had any doubts, he hid them well. 'I'll be ready. I hope getting to the mainland will help, all this chaos and confusion is sickening.'

'I'm sure it will, dear.' Bellandri reached over and squeezed his wrist, as if he was another of her grandchildren. 'At least you'll be in tip top shape for travel after my excellent hospitality.'

CALIDRA DIDN'T SLEEP that night.

Too many thoughts and emotions cascaded through her mind, not permitting her a moment's peace. A wave of nausea spiked at the thought of crossing the cold expanse of water, but she pushed it away. Coffee would solve that. Or at least make it more tolerable.

Fenn was the least of her concerns, though he was a complete mystery. Perhaps Hassen *had* cursed him. She was already up, washed, and dressed before the first of the sun's rays lit the horizon. She was downstairs, polishing off a breakfast of eggs, tomatoes, mushrooms, and potato, and had downed her second coffee, when Fenn and Jisyel joined her.

Jisyel yawned widely, rubbing her eyes clear of sleep. She'd never been a morning person, but even Calidra could see how excited she was for the trip with the smile that refused to leave her lips.

Bellandri had stocked their bags with plenty of supplies for the journey. It would be four or five days' travel to Fellwood from Ballowtown, but they had enough food to last them three weeks. 'Are we expecting some catastrophe to befall us?'

'Of course not, but there's no need to take lean rations. Anxiety is worse on an empty stomach.' Bellandri pulled Calidra into a rough embrace, squeezing her so hard that she thought she was going to bring up her breakfast again.

She hugged Jisyel and Fenn, too, showing him as much warmth as she was used to giving family, then walked the three of them to the edge of the inn's grounds. She carefully handed Fenn a sealed envelope, decorated in gold filigree, and told him to keep it safe. She kissed Jisyel twice on each cheek and smoothed her unruly hair until Jisyel pulled away with a giggle. Then, Bellandri turned to Calidra. 'Whatever happens, whatever decisions you make, you know you'll always have a home at *The Hog's Tusk*, Calidra. Always.'

Calidra's breath hitched at the sudden surge of emotion that powered through her. She bit down on her lip to keep it from wobbling. Bellandri had been more a mother to her than anyone in her own family ever had been. 'Thank you.' Her words came out more breathless than she'd expected.

'Keep a close eye on my granddaughter, please. And Fenn, poor lad. Don't let anything happen to them, will you?'

'I won't.' Calidra turned to catch up with Jisyel and Fenn, but Bellandri kept hold of her hand.

'Calidra. Promise me. You're as much my granddaughter as Jisyel is. You're family.'

A lump formed in the back of her throat. 'I promise.'

Bellandri smiled, her face cracking into all her wrinkles and crow's feet. 'There's a good lass. I'll see you again, soon?'

Not trusting her voice, Calidra nodded and hurried to catch up to the others.

Jisyel had already led Fenn down the path towards the trees. They needed to keep a brisk pace to make the boat before it left, and they were racing the rising sun.

Thankfully, they didn't encounter Hassen, Spirit of Salt Ash, on their way through the forest, for which Calidra was immensely grateful. She didn't have patience for the trickster spirit at the best of times, and certainly not while they were on a tight deadline.

It was a relief when the cold, green Salt Sea came into view, the waters choppy as they were prone to be. Despite her unease at being on open water, she picked up her speed. A thick layer of dark cloud had rolled in, and the three of them sprinted the last few legs of the journey to the dock to beat the inevitable deluge.

The first few raindrops spattered down as they boarded the waiting schooner. When not transporting people to and from Bragalia and the Isle of Salt, it tended to fish in the southern part of the Salt Sea, along the island's north and eastern coastlines. With a crew of six, it was far from the gallant sailing vessels common in southern Bragalia, but having spent the best part of a decade on the island, Calidra recognised them all, and even knew a few by name.

Most were ready to be off before the weather turned, and none paid Fenn the least bit of attention, which was a relief.

She wasn't sure she could stomach more questions while so queasy.

With a deep breath, Calidra stepped off the land and onto the boat, clutching onto Jisyel's arm as much for comfort as to steady herself.

'Perhaps this is a good omen?' Jisyel said, setting down her bag and finding a place to sit for the journey. 'You going back, I mean. After all these years. It's exciting!'

'Perhaps. Just not going back under the best circumstances, am I?' Calidra didn't believe it was a good omen. She shuddered at the boat's unsteadiness underfoot, and gritted her teeth against the growing nausea, already at the base of her throat. She told herself it was just the wind in *The Hog's Tusk*, and that she was perfectly safe.

The crew got on with the bustle of getting the schooner away on their journey, unfurling sails and pulling on ropes. She spotted the messenger from yesterday curled up in a bundle of thick furs and boiled leather. Evidently he'd paid the captain to spend the night on the boat, preferring that to sleeping upon the Isle of Salt. She smirked. Calidra had quickly learned there was very little to that "cursed" rumour, and even Bellandri laughed at the soft-bellied mainlanders who were too scared to stay more than a couple of nights on the island.

Her gaze found Fenn and lingered on him. The young man stood on the starboard side, peering over the edge like a child seeing the sea for the first time, his eyes wide in wonder. 'What do you think of him?'

'Hmm? Who?' Jisyel replied with another yawn. Even the brisk walk had failed to wake her more.

'The lad. Fenn.' Calidra gestured with her chin.

'Oh. I don't know. He seems okay. You don't trust him?'

'Jisyel, it took me three years before I trusted *you*.'

She snorted at that. 'I don't think he's dangerous. He didn't steal anything, I checked his room this morning.'

'Jisyel, you're so tired in the mornings that you wouldn't notice if your own arm was missing.'

The boat lurched forward, water slapping at the hull, and Calidra couldn't suppress a gasp of fear. One hand instantly went to the knife at her belt, then stopped. Her blade couldn't do anything against the sea. It was part of the reason she felt so uneasy on water.

'It's okay.' Jisyel took her free hand and gave it a squeeze. 'We'll be in Ballowtown by lunchtime, if Neros is kind.'

Calidra nodded, eyes scanning the waters ahead for any sign of the Spirit of the Lasseen Ocean, which bordered the Salt Sea to the south. A far larger body of water, the Lasseen Ocean had given rise to a powerful dragon spirit, Neros, who was famed to make travel across her waters treacherous whenever she was in a foul mood.

Their course would take them swiftly inland, hopefully before they attracted the attention of any spirits, yet Calidra couldn't help but worry at the thought of it.

She kept staring at Fenn, his hair quickly windswept, white flakes of salt streaking it within minutes of leaving the island, awe clear on his face. She wondered if he'd ever seen a boat before—or if it was something he'd forgotten. The idea of losing her memories, her sense of *self*, terrified her. It was the thing that kept you sharp, aware of dangers, and able to react swiftly.

Something gnawed at her about him, and it was more than her general dislike for strangers and overly cautious nature. But Bellandri and Jisyel were happy enough, and if he had been cursed by Hassen, it explained his confusion.

She wondered if they might unearth more answers if they stayed with him, instead of handing him over to the Inquisitors at the first opportunity. The doubt sat at the back of her mind like a toad on a sunny stone. It had no intention of moving.

Handing him over would just be another example of running away from her responsibilities.

Calidra turned her mind to Bragalia. Her father had died. Her family had completely ripped itself apart. She half-expected to find a warzone in Fellwood, and wondered how much had changed in all the time she'd been away. Would anything even be as she remembered it?

Wrapping her arm around Jisyel—although more to support herself than anything else—she sighed as the boat rocked below them. 'Spirits bless me, what's waiting back home?'

3

THE CROSSING

FENN

Fenn had quickly realised there was nothing to be gained by arguing with Calidra.

Jisyel was far less sour and had been considerably more patient with him, but he remained at their mercy. If they decided to throw him overboard—not that he *really* thought they would—he'd be able to do very little about it.

He'd not yet regained the full strength in his arms, and was shaky on his legs. The fog within his mind hadn't lifted either, even after a decent night's sleep, and he didn't know what any of it meant.

They'd said the Isle of Salt was cursed. Had *it* caused the issue? Was Hassen, the spirit of the forest there, responsible? Or was it mere coincidence? Squeezing his eyes shut, he tried to think. Tried to recall something, *anything*.

It caused a flare of pain behind his eyes, and he clutched onto the handrail of the boat to keep his balance. Swaying at the lull of the sea underneath, he was amazed at such power held within the water. He was tiny before it; weak and insignificant. He wondered if he was heading towards his home, whether he would even remember it if he saw it. Was anyone looking for him right now, wondering what mess

37

he'd got himself into this time? Why he'd disappeared so suddenly?

Bragalia.

It *sounded* important, the way Calidra, Jisyel, and Bellandri had spoken of the place. Clearly it was important to Calidra, who despite her obvious discomfort on the boat still walked with confidence and certainty—unlike himself and Jisyel.

He was frustrated at not knowing things, for being caught up in the tide of events like a piece of driftwood. His grip tightened on the rail, knuckles whitening.

Once they were on the mainland, he was sure to find someone who knew more. Someone who *wanted* to help him. Chancing a look back at Calidra and Jisyel, a pang of resentment grew. They didn't care about him. And why would they? He was a stranger to them. They had their own problems to deal with without worrying about a lost, confused amnesiac who was getting in their way.

At least they'd shown him some kindness.

He doubted it would last once they made reached the mainland.

Pulling out the envelope Bellandri had given him, Fenn carefully turned it away from the strong winds and opened it. For a moment, he was afraid he'd lost his ability to read, but then the words came swimming back into focus—even if he didn't understand half of them.

The bearer of this pass may be permitted to travel between the Isle of Salt and two Bragalian cantons, including the gates at Ballowtown and Fellwood, as decreed and signed by Vantonen, Laird of Fellwood, Bragalia.

FENN SWALLOWED. Calidra's father was a Laird. Bellandri had said as much when she'd fed them. Vantonen must be the family name.

And he'd died.

It was one thing to forge papers, it was another to use the signature of a dead man for gain. He suddenly felt sick, but it was too late to do anything about it now. Without the paper, he'd be stranded on the cursed island with Bellandri's overbearing fuss on one side, and Hassen tormenting him on the other.

Slipping the paper back in his pocket, he sighed, turning his gaze back to the unending green-grey streak of cold seawater. Leaning over the rail, he peered into the murk, stunned to see a shoal of fish swimming alongside the boat.

He *knew* he recognised the species, but the name of the fish never materialised in his thoughts. They were large and slender, with powerful tails for swimming in the rough waters. He counted over thirty of them, and far more swam deeper, their shapes hardly more than shadows in the waters' depths. One splashed upwards, breaking the surface of the cold, foamy sea for a split second, then dived back to join the others in its shoal.

Fenn lifted a hand to touch the spray on his cheek, shivering at the water's temperature, and wondered if he'd ever seen this sea before.

He was less panicked than yesterday, more frustrated than anything else. He'd expected the events of the previous day to fade into nothing, lost like things from before, but he could recall everything from the moment he'd been stuck in the bog.

Had that been an awakening of sorts?

Everything was too confusing, made too little sense.

The boat lurched, cresting a rising swell, and Fenn staggered, grasping the handrail again and peering overboard. A large, dark shadow appeared on the horizon, heading towards the mainland faster than their boat. Vaguely humanoid, with long arms that appeared to drag along the waves behind it, the sight of it made his mouth run dry.

Fenn tried to keep his footing without losing sight of the shadow. 'Calidra? Jisyel?' he called over his shoulder, not willing to pull his gaze from the horizon. 'What's that?'

Calidra was beside him moments after he'd called. She staggered under the moving boat and clutched the rail with one hand, her dagger already drawn and ready. 'What is it?'

'There. Looks like...a creature of some sort?' He pointed with one hand, though unsteady.

She followed his gesture and narrowed her eyes. 'I don't see anything.'

Fenn blinked. The horizon was clear. 'It...I saw...'

She glanced up and down the horizon line.

'It was right there!'

'Don't make things up, Fenn. It's not helping your case.' She turned away.

'But I didn't!' He watched her return to her seat by Jisyel, sheathing her dagger and shaking her head. Fenn turned back to the horizon, which was clear save the rolling, grey clouds that threatened more rain. He had definitely seen something. Hadn't he?

'Best sit down and get some rest, Fenn. It'll be a few hours before we get to Ballowtown,' Jisyel called.

Despite his growing unease, Fenn left the side of the boat and made his way over to the two women, sitting down heavily and folding his arms against the chill sea air. His headache was a constant companion now, occasionally causing his vision to flicker.

Perhaps he *had* been seeing things.

By the time the mainland came into view, the sun was already low and the temperature had plummeted. Although even at its zenith, the warmth had done nothing against the freezing wind over the Salt Sea, which bit deep, chilling his bones. Fenn was glad he'd chosen a thick, fur-lined doublet and a long overtunic from the wardrobe at *The Hog's Tusk*. He'd been cold on the island, and on learning he'd be crossing water, he thought more layers would be better.

Not to mention he had no idea what awaited him in Bragalia.

He fought to keep from shivering as the schooner took them up a narrow bay towards their destination, and land encased them on either side.

'See anything you recognise, yet?' Jisyel asked, ever positive. She strolled along the deck, and flakes of the thin, sugary pastry she held fluttered away in the wind. She quickly took another bite lest more of it was lost to sea.

'Still nothing.' Fenn could always lie. *Try* to appease them. But then he was sure they'd question him further, and his lie would quickly unravel. It wasn't something he wanted to chance, especially not with Calidra so quick to grab her hunting dagger.

'Jisyel, you don't need to eat again so soon. Especially not after being on the moving boat. You'll be sick,' Calidra admonished.

Jisyel shoved the rest of the pastry into her mouth with a bright grin and ignored her. 'We'll be docking soon. That's Ballowtown there, Fenn. See those buildings where the land slopes up?'

He stood up to get a better view of the large town nestled against the water's edge like a cat waiting to pounce on an unsuspecting fish. He wondered if the town would dig its claws into him, too.

'It gets all sorts of people. Bragalians, mostly, but usually merchants and traders, people passing through. Much busier

41

than on the island. You're not afraid of crowds, are you? Don't worry if you are, we'll keep you in one piece until we can figure out what's going on.'

Fenn idly scratched his eyebrow, watching as the town grew closer. Although grateful for Jisyel's kind words, he knew the sooner they docked, the sooner he'd be palmed off to the Inquisitors, whoever they were. They didn't sound particularly friendly, and his stomach was already in knots at how quickly everything was happening to him.

There was a bustle of activity across the schooner as the crew slowly brought the ship into port, confidently avoiding other vessels already docked, heading out to sea, or further inland. The bottom half of every vessel was darkened by time in the water, with barnacles and sea molluscs clinging to the lower parts of their hulls.

Fenn suddenly wondered if he would have been better off staying on the Isle of Salt and taking his chances with Hassen. He glanced at the horizon again, in case the shadow had reappeared, but it was as empty as when Calidra had taken a look. Typical.

'Hope my gran sent out a fast pigeon, otherwise we'll be waiting forever for Ashothka.' Jisyel rested one hand on her hip, the other shielding her eyes from the low, evening sunlight. Crowds were gathered along the docks, seagulls screeched overhead despite the dying light, and salt wind filled the air. The place was a bundle of energy, noise, and movement. Officers in whale skin coats and thick rubber boots paced the edge of the docks, reams of paperwork under their arms as they barked orders at the gathered people, pointing them in different directions, directing carriages of cargo, and yelling at the boat crews.

On the far side of the docks, Fenn saw three young men, not much older than himself, with their hands chained. They were being led away by another officer with a longsword, and his stomach dropped at the sight.

'Probably stowaways.' Calidra was beside him again, watching the dock with a calm confidence. 'That'd be you if it weren't for that paperwork. Keep hold of it, you understand?'

Fenn gripped the envelope tightly in his pocket and took a deep breath to steady his nerves. There was no need to be pessimistic. So far, luck *had* been with him. He just had to hope it lasted a bit longer—until his memories returned and he could get back to whatever home he'd left behind. His family—if he had any—must be worried sick.

As if sensing his sudden panic, Calidra turned to him. 'Don't worry. I'm the daughter of a Laird, remember. No-one is going to question me.' Her voice was smooth and confident, and it eased his nerves somewhat.

'All right, all right, get in line. Papers at the ready,' an officer barked up at them as the captain brought the schooner in, the dock suddenly very close. He was tall and burly, with a thick beard of black and grey, his eyes hidden by a helm of iron worn low upon his head. A dragon insignia had been burnished into it, the same insignia as on his and the other officers' cloaks.

With a gentle bump, the schooner nudged the dock, and the crew scrambled to pull out the gangplank for their passengers.

Taking a step back, the waiting officer stared down at his papers and pulled out a quill.

The messenger, who had ignored them throughout their trip, marched off the boat first, and raised his chin to address the officer. 'Mias Uselin. I'm a messenger bound by Fellwood, I left on yesterday's boat. You should have my name listed. Quickly now, I've urgent work to attend to.'

'Uselin...Uselin...' The officer ran his index finger along presumably a line of names, muttering under his breath as he did so.

Fenn peered cautiously around Calidra's shoulder, who

stood next in line. Jisyel remained behind him, and offered an encouraging smile. 'It's just a formality, don't worry.'

He didn't like being told not to worry so often. If anything, it had the opposite effect, and his heart was already thumping loudly.

While the officer dealt with the paperwork, Fenn turned his attention to the rest of Ballowtown, which rose up beyond the docks like mushrooms atop a large boulder. There were many buildings, most three or four storeys high, each with the same red tiled rooftops. Several spires reached higher, here and there, which Fenn assumed were churches or watchtowers—a few even had large, iron bells in them. Several buildings had already been lit, their windows providing a cool, yellow light as dusk fell across town.

'Next,' barked the officer, waving away Mias and looking up to see Calidra.

'Calidra Vantonen, of Fellwood, daughter of the Laird. With me is my partner, Jisyel and my servant, Fenn, of Salt Ash.'

Fenn held in his gasp at that, but the officer didn't notice. He thumbed through the papers, turning over a few leaves, then frowning. 'Your Ladyship, you are listed, as is Jisyel, as residents of the island. But...the servant, Fenn, he...I can't seem to find a record—'

'Are you questioning me?' Calidra raised one eyebrow.

'Ah. No! Of course not, it's just...I...I can't seem to...If I could just see his papers, please....'

'So you *are* questioning me.' Her voice had taken on an edge, and the man gulped. Despite standing a clear head and a half over Calidra, he shrank away and adjusted his helm.

'Certainly not, Your Ladyship. I just...I wouldn't mind... him travelling with you is normally fine, it's just...'

'Just *what?*'

'Well, the Master Inquisitor is on his way. On business of the Iron Crown. Been a lot more persons unaccounted for,

44

recently. In Bragalia, I mean. I can't risk any slip ups, I'm sure you understand. Why, even your father has a reputation for—'

'That's quite enough. Fenn. Show him your papers,' Calidra snapped.

Shuffling forward, Fenn pulled out the envelope and handed it to the officer, wondering if he'd seen through their ruse and he'd have to make a run for it. He glanced around, looking for any potential openings. But the place was busy, full of officers, sailors, and townspeople. And it wasn't as if he had the first idea of where he'd go even if he managed to get through all of them.

He didn't want to end up in chains, especially not for a crime he'd not committed.

With several muttered apologies, the officer quickly skimmed his paper and then, satisfied, stamped it with the same dragon insignia that adorned his uniform. 'Thank you, Your Ladyship. Welcome back to Bragalia. I wish you safe—'

'Fine. Let's go.' Calidra cut him off again and ushered Jisyel and Fenn forward. She strode past the rest of the berthed ships and out of the busy docks without a look back.

'Calidra, what—' Fenn ventured, but was silenced with a glare colder than he'd seen from her before. He kept his hands in his pockets, struggling to keep up with the pace Calidra set as she led them down a wide, cobblestone path, past taverns and shops, and into the heart of Ballowtown, which had started to come alive with evening activity.

Lamps were being lit, with several burning in an ethereal purple that cast peculiar shadows on the walls between buildings. Fenn was quite sure he heard the fire whispering, but the words were just too low for him to catch any detail.

When they were some minutes walk from the sea, Jisyel spoke, her voice shaking. 'The Master Inquisitor, did I hear that right?'

'Apparently so. What he's doing all the way down here, I

have no idea.' Calidra replied, no longer angry. She sounded afraid.

'On the dock, the officer said, "persons unaccounted for." What does that mean? People without papers?' Fenn asked, thinking back to the line of people he'd seen in chains.

'Pretty much,' Jisyel said. 'Bragalia and Porsenthia share a border. It can be easy for stowaways to cross countries.'

'I wonder if they're like me.' Fenn hadn't meant to say it aloud, but the words left his mouth before he could stop himself.

'Like you? You mean…suffering from memory loss?' Jisyel asked.

'What if it's happened to others, too? Happening to them right now?' Fenn wasn't sure if he *wanted* to to be true, couldn't tell if it would be a good or a bad thing.

'Let's just find Ashothka and get settled. If I don't sit down somewhere solid soon, I'll vomit.' Calidra brushed her forehead with the back of one hand. 'Damned crossing never gets any easier.'

CALIDRA AND JISYEL were familiar with Ballowtown, so it didn't take the two women long to reach a particular tavern in the heart of the place, *Seafarer's Haven*. It was a large, vibrant building, heard for some distance before they saw it. Bellandri had instructed them to wait for Ashothka there, if he wasn't already at the docks. That way, they could get a hot meal and stay in shelter if the weather was poor. Judging by the dark clouds overhead, they didn't have long before the weather turned.

Fenn had been dizzy with the sights and sounds of Ballowtown, it was so overwhelming. Each street was paved with flat stone slabs, or large round cobblestones. Stone buildings with red tiled roofs appeared to be the trademark of the town, and after more than a handful of turns down side streets and across squares, he was confused. Everywhere looked the same, and there were numerous alleyways between the tall buildings, many of which were lit by those strange, purple lanterns.

He was able to keep a sense of where the sea was, for the most part—if anything he could always use his sense of smell to find his way back there—but as the shadows lengthened and his legs ached for rest, he was looking forward to sitting down to some food.

As they crossed one of Ballowtown's many squares, something drew his attention to the far side. It was the shadow-like creature that he'd seen before, looming out from one of the alleys, half-lost in darkness. Its edges blurred, as if it wasn't quite there. The air surrounding it rippled, and he rubbed his eyes to clear his vision, to no avail. Something about it felt wrong. Very wrong. But he couldn't put his finger on why.

Fenn stumbled on a cobblestone, and Jisyel caught him by the arm.

'You okay?'

'Y—yeah,' he muttered, clutching his shin where he'd caught it. He could have sworn a pair of amber eyes glowed from the alleyway, but when he looked back, it was gone.

Delirious. He was completely delirious.

Calidra found them a table in the corner of the busy tavern, at least twice the size of *The Hog's Tusk*, and bursting with patrons—most of whom smelled of the sea, which he supposed was what gave the place its name. Several people hunched over large mugs of hot, steaming drinks at the bar, while others ate furiously, devouring platters of seafood as if they had the gullets of gulls.

Unnerved by sighting something unknown, Fenn kept quiet, lest anyone else tried to question who he was and what right he had to be there. He was glad the large table of officers opposite them were more interested in their ale than in the flood of people coming and going.

He hoped they were off duty.

A large fire roared fiercely in the hearth, and Fenn slipped out of his overtunic, unable to rid himself of the doubt nagging at the back of his mind. What *was* that creature? Another spirit? It didn't look like Hassen. He thought about it while they got comfortable at the table, checking out the other patrons for signs of Ashothka.

When Calidra rejoined them a few minutes later, bringing three mugs of coffee, Jisyel whispered, 'Cal, should we really be here? There are officers over there. What if they check Fenn?'

'Nonsense.' Calidra didn't bother to look at them. 'The portmaster checked his papers, no-one will question him now he's already in town.'

'But Torsten...'

'I'm sure Torsten will be very busy with whatever business has brought him here. He won't care for one young lad already in town, blending in with everyone else. Drink. It'll be fine.'

'You're probably right...' Jisyel didn't sound convinced. She leaned on her elbow and tried not to look at the officers, their laughter rising every few minutes as they drank more. 'I don't like it. They make me uncomfortable.'

'You're the one who wanted me to come back to Bragalia. I've made the crossing. Don't change your mind about it now!'

Jisyel sighed.

Fenn glanced around, wondering about the other patrons here. Close to them, a trio of women laughed, sharing a large, tin pitcher of something foul-smelling; a brooding man with dark hair and gold rings in his ears, more interested in the pie on his plate than anyone else, ignored them; two men argued over whether Bragalian or Olmese steel was better; a tall man thumbed through a stack of papers, his plate of food untouched, and kept throwing anxious glances towards the officers.

Could anyone here be someone he knew? Had known?

On the table to their right, two men played a board game with several pieces, each carved from different coloured wood. Black. Grey. Brown. Cream. Blue. Red. They were moved in seemingly random ways, some several squares at a time. One of the players moved two red pieces, carved to look like broken trees, and his opponent let out a disappointed groan.

'Rehkaro.'

Fenn glanced up to find Jisyel watching him. 'That's the game?'

'It's an old Bragalian game for keeping young children and old men quiet.' Jisyel rubbed her upper arms. 'I just hope Ashothka gets here soon. This place is too busy for my head.'

'You'll feel better once you have some food. Shouldn't be too long before they bring it out. I got you hot onion soup,' Calidra said, and Jisyel immediately brightened.

Fenn could see the edge of the street through one of the tavern's small windows, and he watched as night enveloped Ballowtown. He kept staring in case the shadow creature wandered past again, but the coast remained clear. Their food came; empty plates went. Still no sign of Ashothka. His stomach sank, and he wondered whether it was too late to run for it, after all.

Without Ashothka, he didn't know what they'd do next. Bellandri's contact was supposed to give them a place to stay, and help them on their way. If Ashothka wasn't coming, he might as well go it alone. That way, he wouldn't be ignored and dismissed by Calidra, who clearly had her own reasons for coming to Bragalia.

Calidra drummed her fingers on the table, the only sign she was growing more worried as time ticked by.

At least they hadn't rid themselves of him at the first opportunity—they seemed to want him to be okay and on his way before they let him go—but Calidra and Jisyel's visible nerves weren't just to do with him. Ashothka was a contact of Bellandri, someone she trusted.

Had he ignored Bellandri's message? Hadn't he received it?

It was getting late, and there was no reason for the lack of response. Rain spattered on the thick, glass windows, the clouds finally releasing their bounty, and a peal of thunder rolled overhead.

'If I knew his address, we could just go there,' Jisyel gave words to the thoughts clearly on everyone's minds. 'We'll just have to keep waiting. Stay here tonight, if he doesn't show. We have enough coin for a room between us, don't we?'

Calidra's fingers continued to drum.

'Should we ask after Ashothka? If he lives in town, maybe someone here knows him?' Fenn suggested, trying to be helpful.

Calidra dismissed him with a wave of her hand. 'Don't be ridiculous, Fenn. Everyone in their right mind is suspicious. No-one is going to help a group of strangers. Not unless there's something in it for them. People aren't like that.'

'That's a bit harsh?'

'Being harsh is expected. You should get used to it.'

Several patrons had left, but the tavern remained relatively full. Could Ashothka be one of these people and they hadn't realised? He opened his mouth to suggest that very thing, when the tavern doors burst open, bringing in a wash of rainwater. That in itself wasn't unusual, people had been coming and going all evening, but the three people who stood in the doorway drew the eye of everyone present.

A man stood ahead of the other two, his black cloak lined with silver fur, the same dragon insignia on it—as well as his helm, shield, and the scabbard that held a longsword at his

50

hip. Gold edged his half-armour, too, the only distinction in his uniform from the two with him.

One of his companions, a narrow-shouldered man with sandy-coloured hair, walked through the crowd to the bar, ignoring the stares of those around him. The other, a slender woman with dark, braided hair reaching her waist, took one step to the right, standing at attention beside the door.

'Torsten. Queen Surayo's Master Inquisitor,' Jisyel whispered, her face suddenly close to Fenn's ear.

He didn't need her to tell him that. By the hush that took over the tavern, it was clear these officers were of a different caste to those already inebriated.

Torsten joined the officers at their table, one member standing and giving up their seat, then conversation within the large room resumed, albeit quieter and less rowdy than before.

'Should we...go?' Fenn whispered, making to grab his overtunic again.

Jisyel rested a hand on his arm, giving Calidra an accusatory look in the same motion. She whispered, 'That other Inquisitor is by the door. They'll be noting who leaves now that Torsten's here. Can't go now, it'll look suspicious. Maybe they're just here for a drink, not on business. It's late.'

Fenn lowered his head, leaning over his folded arms, staring at the officers' table and trying to work out what was being discussed. It was hard to make out anything above the murmur of the tavern, clinking crockery, and the occasional loud belch.

A few words floated above the general cacophony and he focussed on the snatches of conversation that reached him.

'...sign of it...'

Narrowing his eyes, Fenn scooted over on his bench, trying to get closer. Were they talking about the same creature he'd seen?

'...lost...Too easy to hide...deadwater town.'

'...what kind of creature...'

'Could be dangerous if we don't...'

'Fenn, what are you—'

He tumbled off the edge of the bench, hardly aware of Calidra's hissed warning. He smacked his nose painfully on the wooden floor, inhaling dried ale and dust. His headache, which had subsided after a full belly and a mug of coffee, flared back with a violent fury that left him seeing stars.

'Hmm. Trying to listen in on official Inquisitor business, boy?'

Fenn held his nose tenderly, afraid he'd broken it, and a trickle of blood leaked from one nostril. He was infuriated with being shoved around by someone else, yet again. 'You're having a conversation in a public house. Of *course* people are going to listen in.'

He was aware of Jisyel's sudden gasp, before a hand grabbed him by the scruff and roughly yanked him to his feet —where he stared directly up at Torsten.

'Do you have any idea who I am?' Torsten's voice was flat, without the anger Fenn had expected, but his blue eyes burned with barely concealed outrage. He was clean shaven, with sallow skin and thin lips.

Fenn gasped with sickening realisation that he'd pushed it too far. Torsten clearly was not in a mood for jokes, nor was he about to cede any ground. Fenn recalled the few snippets of conversation he'd overheard, combined it with the shadow he'd seen earlier, and took a wild guess. 'The creature you're hunting? I've seen it.' He'd blurted out the words before realising what he'd said.

It took Torsten by surprise, too, the man's cold eyes narrowing down at him. 'What did you see, boy?'

Fenn wanted to turn around and look at Calidra and Jisyel, maybe take some comfort from them, but he didn't dare look away from the Inquisitor. Most of the talk in the tavern had ground to a halt, all eyes and ears on the pair. He wasn't sure about his guess, but it was too late to backtrack now. Fenn continued, 'I...I saw...it was a shadow. A huge creature, in Ballowtown. First saw it on the Salt Sea, and then again earlier—'

'You talking about Neros?' Torsten sneered, his shoulders dropping slightly.

Fenn's mind went blank. 'I—No, wait...Who's Neros?'

Torsten visibly relaxed, one hand resting on the pommel of his sword. He let out a short bark of laughter. 'Who's Neros he says? That's a question we've heard a few times over the past few days, haven't we, Nadja?'

The woman at the door nodded once. 'Twelve times, sir.'

'Mmhmm. Twelve times,' Torsten repeated, leisurely turning back to Fenn.

Fenn had no idea what "twelve times" meant, or why Torsten had changed his stance from aggressive to relaxed, almost lackadaisical. He swallowed. 'A shadow it was, sir,' he thought he should add the honorific, now he was on the back foot.

'You saw a spirit. Nothing more.'

'No! I've *seen* a spirit, and this wasn't that!'

'You were mistaken. It was a spirit.'

Fenn continued to argue the point, angered at being ignored and dismissed. He racked his brain, trying to remember more details about the shadow creature to prove his truthfulness. 'It was huge. It had amber eyes and long arms...and it felt...wrong. Like it shouldn't be here.'

Torsten's jovial grin disappeared immediately, replaced by a tight-lipped grimace. 'And you, boy? Should *you* be here?'

Fenn stammered, unsure what to say, what was expected of him. His papers were in the pocket of his overtunic, thrown across the back of the chair Jisyel sat in. 'I have papers. Stamped by the portmaster.'

Torsten raised an eyebrow but said nothing. Fenn took

that as permission to retrieve it, so he whipped around and darted over to the other side of his table. Jisyel and Calidra stared at him, Jisyel with wide eyes, Calidra with narrowed ones. Both were tense, braced as if for combat.

Withdrawing the envelope, Fenn held it up to the Master Inquisitor, who took it without breaking eye contact. When Fenn defiantly stared back, Torsten scowled and briefly glanced at the paper. 'Interesting. But a forgery. Laird Vantonen is several days dead, and could not have signed this paper. You dare travel through the Queen's lands unwatched?'

'S—Surayo?' Sheer panic froze Fenn in place. He couldn't think, let alone speak coherently.

'I think you're a clever one, boy. But you can't fool me.' Torsten drew his sword, cruelty glinting in his eyes as he grinned at Fenn. 'You shall join the other twelve lost souls we've picked up, though I must say, you are the only one to have made it this far. Most have no idea who the queen even is.' He curled his lip as if in disgust. 'Nadja. Irons.'

Fenn gasped. So there *were* others like him.

'Fenn!' Jisyel cried from their table.

Before Torsten's companion could move, one of the patrons by the bar stood up, the wooden stool scraping against the floor as he did so, attracting everyone's attention. 'Don't bother, Nadja. Torsten, you should take a night off for once. It'll do you some good.'

Outraged, Torsten whirled around to face the man, his sword levelled at him. In the low light of the tavern, Fenn noticed a patch of rust dotted along the blade's dull side. He might not have known much about his situation, but he was fairly certain swords had to be rust-free to be any good. Frowning, he looked at the man who'd spoken out against the Master Inquisitor, daring to hope at a possible escape.

At the possibility that someone *wanted* to help him.

The man had several golden hoops in his ears, a short, a

deep scar across his left eyebrow and another across his cheek, and dark hair that grew thick down his neck. Even in the heat of the inn, he wore a heavy bearskin cloak that made him seem half-wild. He drank directly from a large bottle of red wine, which he placed on the bar before looking straight at the Inquisitor. 'Put that away, Torsten. I ain't here to cause trouble.'

Torsten sucked in a breath and pursed his lips. 'I had not expected to see you, General.'

'Nor I you, but that's how the world works. Full of surprises sometimes. And it's *former* General, you know that.' He gestured with his chin in Fenn's general direction. 'Lad's with me. I've been summoned to Fellwood. Some training contract for the Laird's youngest. Fenn's my apprentice. Want to check *my* papers?'

Torsten sheathed his sword so aggressively, he knocked his own drink off the table where it landed with a heavy clunk and rolled across the floor. Indignant with rage, but apparently unable to do anything about it, Torsten straightened his uniform. 'Not necessary, Varlot. We'll get back to work.'

4

THE SHADOW

TORSTEN

Of all the countries of Tassar, Bragalia was the worst.

It was a cesspit of differing bloodlines, pseudo-royalty, and a streak of stubbornness that would put a mule to shame. It didn't help that the food was terrible and the wine was worse.

The Porsenthian Emperors had greatly diminished Bragalia over the centuries, as they'd expanded their country further and further south. They'd won land against Bragalians of old after a number of violent skirmishes, all aided by the strength of Toriaken. Now, all that was left of the country were five weak cantons of even weaker Lairds—one of whom had recently died—who'd agreed to swear fealty to Porsenthia to save what was left of their lands.

Even their military was poorly trained—a mish-mash of warriors sent by the various Lairds as part of their truce, whose drills, conduct, and competence varied widely. Being here, in this country, made him feel sick. It was a far cry from the orderly Porsenthia, where Queen Surayo reigned supreme and standards were higher.

Bragalia was bearable at night, but even the heavy rain

that had accompanied his arrival in Ballowtown brought with it an uncomfortable heat. It had been a necessary trip, though, by direct order of the queen.

He glared at the lad, Fenn, as he chatted happily to Varlot. He wondered whether the boy had any idea how close he'd come to being locked up and brought back with the other prisoners. The fact he'd suggested they were hunting something had thrown Torsten off. Not even the other Inquisitors were aware of his true task. As far as anyone was concerned, there'd been an infection or illness running through Bragalia; people were turning up with no knowledge of who they were, where they were, or where they'd come from. In fact, they didn't know anything at all. Lost, bedraggled amnesiacs without links to other people or places, and the Inquisitors had been sent to round them up for more *thorough* questioning. That was a job that awaited him back in the Porsenthian capital, and he was rather looking forward to it.

There'd been no explanation for their appearances, nor why there were so many of them. And more were turning up all the time, much to his irritation.

This sort of rounding up wasn't the kind of thing he usually got involved in, but Queen Surayo had insisted he accompany the other Inquisitors—it was a solid enough reason for him to be there, if uncommon, while he investigated his true task: determining whether Porsenthia was in peril.

Queen Surayo was a mage, and the workings of her magic were largely a mystery to him. She'd been convinced *something* approached the borders of her empire, but hadn't been certain what, or even whether it was a threat. Torsten, of course, had been sent to investigate under the ruse of the other Inquisitors' work.

Torsten picked up the mug he'd knocked to the floor and sat back at the officers' table.

Fenn needed to be watched, as far as he was concerned.

The lad had a forged paper, and anyone who had a forgery was up to no good. If he, too, was part of the lost souls appearing, he had more wits about him than most. That, in itself, usually meant trouble. And Torsten always had a good nose for finding trouble.

He threw a glance over his shoulder, narrowing his eyes at Varlot, who'd joined Fenn's table. The women there were worth noting, too. The Porsenthian was nothing special, if somewhat aggravating with her loud voice and propensity to giggle. And judging by her high cheekbones, the Bragalian woman had some Olmese in her, too. His lip curled at the thought of those sandy griffin-lovers, and an old scar under his ribs flared at the memory.

'Sarron.' He turned to the Inquisitor who'd come inside with him, who was currently inspecting the bottom of his third mug of ale, evidently as uncomfortable at the table with the Bragalian officers as Torsten was, and coping with it in the only way he knew how—unhealthily. 'I want you to watch Varlot. Might be he *is* headed to Fellwood, but if he has an interest in Fenn, I want to know why. Keep out of sight.'

'Yes, sir.' Sarron was young and inexperienced, but Nadja had vouched for him, and she was one of the few people in the world whose opinion he actually valued. So far, the young Inquisitor had done little wrong, but he'd also done little to impress. Perhaps this would be a task where he would show his usefulness. At least he obeyed without question, even if he had quite the taste for alcohol. Such things could be overlooked as long as he completed his job with the efficiency the Inquisitors were known for. This would be a fine estimator of that.

Order given, Torsten returned his attention to the map spread out across the table. Of the eleven officers present, all but one were Bragalian, as was to be expected, and they meekly obeyed his orders and answered questions fully. The first two lost souls had turned up to the west of the Spindle Woods about a week prior, with several more picked up along the Bragalian border. Today, the port masters had rounded up another three, bringing their total captives to twelve.

Although Fenn was out of his clutches, he was certain the boy was part of the same problem. Whatever that problem was. It seemed to be a Bragalian issue, one he didn't care for. Or, perhaps, Fenn had been coincidentally and conveniently unlucky with his timings. Torsten wondered if too long spent in his role had made him paranoid, seeing problems and conspiracies when there were none.

As he scoured the map, he thought of the queen's words. Where she'd felt her magic stir, where she thought the threats might be coming from. There'd been rumours across this spirits-forsaken stinking pit of a country of a wild beast attacking. According to the reports, this *beast* had eluded sight and sound, leaving only death behind in a few remote areas. Torsten had assumed it was the mad ravings of someone cursed by a spirit, or who had perhaps sighted a corrupted spirit, and in their ignorance had neither the education nor common sense to realise what it was.

Either way, he was certain this was a waste of his time. But he couldn't disobey.

The queen knew something and wasn't telling him.

He wondered if Fenn really *had* seen something, or if he'd allowed his imagination to run away with him as he'd hoped to bargain for his freedom. Torsten scoffed. If there was any truth to the rumours, the creature wouldn't be in the middle of one of Bragalia's biggest towns.

Giving up on ale, Torsten poured himself a glass of wine from the bottle on the table. He wrinkled his nose at the sweetness of it, and continued to read the reports of Ballowtown's officers, glancing at the map every so often to get his bearings when a town or village was mentioned.

Varlot's presence distracted him more than he would have liked. Their last meeting had been several years prior, on the battlefield under a sky of iron. Blood had slicked—

No.

He could dwell on the past another time. There were other matters which demanded his attention. He cleared his throat and addressed the officers. 'We'll see if the ships bring in any more people over the next few days. Then, we'll head north with the stowaways you've picked up.'

'What about that lad? Fenn?' one officer asked. He acted the most senior at the table, the first to throw his opinion into conversation, and drank more heavily even than Sarron.

Torsten hadn't bothered to learn his name. 'He's in Varlot's charge. I've no interest in dealing with the general. Neither should you.'

'No. Of course not.' He sat back in his chair, deflating.

'Not upset are you?'

'He'll be loose in Bragalia. *You* thought his papers were forged. Doesn't that warrant some questioning? Even if you don't take him back?'

Torsten shrugged. 'As I said, it's Varlot's business now. We'll have more than enough of these lost souls to conduct a thorough investigation. Should more turn up after we leave, have them locked away and notify the Inquisitors immediately. I'll ensure to keep a post at Spindleford to receive birds. They'll be well positioned for speedier travel. Tonmouth, too, if we need eyes on the Salt Sea. If we can figure out where they're coming from, we can put a stop to it. Might be some new smuggling racket from Olmir taking advantage of the empty seas. We'll get to the bottom of it soon enough.'

Thankfully, the officer agreed without argument, and Torsten decided it was time to retire for the evening. He'd had enough of Bragalian ale and wine for one night, and he needed to make his own report—easier done in seclusion than with so many eyes and ears close by. His iron dagger, issued by the queen, hung on his belt, patiently waiting. He ignored it. She knew where he was. She could wait on him for once.

A bell rang out over the pouring rain, high and clear.

Torsten turned his ear to the door, one hand already on his sword. To his left, Sarron got to his feet. Despite the amount of ale he'd consumed, he was steady. 'The watchtower?'

Two more bells, one much further away from the tavern, the other somewhere to the east of town.

'Towers,' Torsten corrected.

'An attack?'

Not replying to the Inquisitor, Torsten faced the table and drew his sword. 'On your feet, officers!'

Annoyed by their slow response, Torsten was already out the door, Sarron and Nadja on his heels, before most had roused themselves from their chairs. It wasn't strictly speaking his job to help, but he wasn't going to sit around and do nothing while trouble befell the town. He stood several paces outside the tavern door, multiple bells ringing and rain pelting the ground, as he assessed the situation. 'Nadja, east. Sarron, west. I'll go north. We sweep the streets and meet by the sea.'

'Sir!' Both Inquisitors drew their weapons and raced off into the dark streets.

'Always drama where you're concerned,' Varlot's voice was tinged with amusement.

More people had crowded at the door, several spilling onto the street despite the rain and the obvious warnings sounding across Ballowtown.

He didn't have time for this. 'Why don't you make yourself useful, General, and keep these stupid sea dogs inside and *out* of my way.'

61

Torsten put on his helm and headed straight across the square, slipping between two buildings as he raced due north, following the sound of the nearest bell. What could possibly be cause for the alarm? Had another Laird decided to take Ballowtown by force? Bragalia was always criss-crossed with border fights and combative skirmishes. Getting caught in another would be more than a minor inconvenience. He needed to assert his authority and put a stop to it before it had a chance to get started.

He heard footsteps behind him—several people had chosen to follow—but he paid them no attention. He had authority on matters of Porsenthian state and law, not whether some foolhardy Bragalian wanted to throw their life away in a silly warriors' confrontation.

Rain bounced off his helm, the noise echoing loudly, but he kept his breathing even despite the distraction, focussing on where he was going, and keeping his eyes peeled for any signs of violence. Most of the streets were empty—people always wanted to keep out of the rain—for which he was thankful. Fewer people to make a nuisance of themselves.

Unlike most, Torsten welcomed the rain. His sword glinted in the low moonlight, eager to taste blood. It *had* been a while since he'd last fought, and he relished the idea. Perhaps being sent to Bragalia had its advantages.

Skidding to a halt as the road ended, splitting off to his left and right as the expanse of the Salt Bay opened up ahead of him, Torsten took a moment to catch his breath. He could just about make out the wide bridge leading to southern Bragalia. It was cloaked in shadow, closed at sundown, and built over one of the narrower parts of the strip of water.

He was near one of the watchtowers, whose bell continued to ring, and several uniformed guards hurried out onto the street to greet him.

Torsten didn't hesitate in demanding an explanation. 'What's going on? Another canton attacking the town?'

One officer shook her head. 'No, Inquisitor. Some young lad came staggering along the waterway, his arm shredded. Screaming bloody murder.'

'Where?'

'I sent Foxel to take him to the—'

'Not the lad, where was he *attacked*?' Torsten glared at her.

She pointed towards the dark cobblestone path that ran along the body of water. 'Not sure exactly, but he came from over there. Babbling about a monster.'

'Rubbish. Probably one of the large mountain cats, or a bear.'

'With respect, Inquisitor, we're nowhere near the mountains,' she replied, not shying away from his dismissal.

'There are hills to the north of Ballowtown, are there not?'

She pulled a face. 'He was scared out of his mind.'

'Then it's a good thing he's away from the situation, isn't it? Get back to your towers. Keep civilians inside and off the streets.'

'Shouldn't we help?' Another officer stepped forward, a longsword clutched in both hands. 'It was one of our own what was hurt.'

Torsten frowned at his poor grammar and shook his head. This could have been part of what Surayo's magic had warned, and he decided to pull rank. 'It's part of official Inquisitor business. Get back to your posts.'

They obeyed, reluctantly, the female officer scowling at him all the while, but he waved them away. It *could* have been a beast of the wilds, starving or sick, and had made a desperate attempt to hunt within the town. A lone boy would have made an easy target.

'It felt wrong...Like it shouldn't be here.'

He gritted his teeth at the memory of Fenn's words and hurried onwards, squinting in the rain now blowing directly into his face, driven by the winds across the water. A long minute passed as he jogged, the cold water to his right, buildings on the edge of Ballowtown to his left. It wouldn't be long before he'd catch up with Nadja making her sweep towards him.

Another minute. Nothing, save the occasional slap of water as something underneath broke the surface—most probably a fish.

He came to a halt. How far could a young boy have staggered while losing blood? Suddenly feeling foolish, he sheathed his sword and shook his head. Stupid Bragalians getting themselves worked up over nothing. It was wet out with the heavy rain. Probably the boy had slipped and hit his head, and was now babbling nonsensities.

Torsten was annoyed with himself for jumping up so quickly, like an apprentice eager to impress.

There wasn't anything worth his time in this damned—

Something shifted in the air, the rain rippling unnaturally. There was the metallic tang of magic on the back of his throat—but it wasn't Toriaken, not any spirit he knew. It was something *far* deadlier.

Surayo's decision to send him into Bragalia suddenly became clear. 'Miroth, I might need you,' he muttered under his breath, squeezing the hilt of his sword and drawing it again.

An enormous shadow darted towards his face.

Torsten reacted instinctively, moving backwards as swiftly as the shadow attacked, then he stepped to the side and brought his sword up in a sharp arc—more to get the thing away from him than in any sort of trained manoeuvre.

It withdrew with a low growl, and Torsten squared himself to face it. Hunkered down against the wet path, the shadow creature was easily the width of a carriage, and twice as tall, with long arms that dragged along the ground. He'd never seen a bear—any creature—of a size to match it. Was it...? It couldn't be...

64

'Foul spirit, why do you attack me so?'

Two small lights appeared near the creature's swirling black and purple centre, amber pinpricks that seemed to be eyes. *You are faster than the others.*

Its voice echoed in his head.

Torsten held his sword high, both hands grasping the hilt, ready to put more strength into his next blow. He had to be certain of what it was. 'I have done nothing to you. Are you the spirit of some misbegotten river? Cursed to roam without a domain?'

'I...'

Whatever the creature wanted to say, it was lost as it surged forward again, letting out a shriek so low that Torsten thought his eardrums would burst. He slipped into his training—Inquisitors were expected to have the same competency as any individual in the Porsenthian army— and rushed to meet the creature with his own sword, *Tinebás*.

Flesh and metal met in a shower of sparks, and Torsten fully expected to drive his blade deep into the creature's gut, but it hit a hard, solid mass somewhere in its centre. The creature didn't bellow in pain, simply moved forward, forcing Torsten back.

It was stronger than he was.

Yanking *Tinebás* from the creature, Torsten whirled to the side, letting his enemy's momentum carry it past, while he swiftly arced his sword downwards for another strike on its legs. The edge caught onto something, cutting into flesh and spilling dark ichor onto the waterlogged road.

It smelled of rotten flesh, fermented fruit, and death.

Gagging, Torsten leaped backwards as the creature struck at him again, clawed appendages bursting from its body in unexpected places. He slashed at them, knocking them away or slicing a few before they reached him. More ichor fell, more stench filled the street.

He'd never fought a spirit before. Most people didn't live if they challenged one.

The ichor. The shape. The *smell* of the thing...

'Spirits take me, what *is* that?'

Torsten turned to see Fenn, Varlot, and the women from the table. He spat a curse. 'Get out of here you fools!'

'Why? Looks like you could do with some help!' Varlot said with a smirk, his axe in hand.

Torsten was about to curse, then the creature was upon him again. He could spare them no more attention as he deflected another blow, stepping to the side, his sword raised high. The way it shrieked, he wouldn't be surprised if it brought the entire town to them.

He needed to get this mess under control, before anyone else saw the thing and jumped to their own conclusions.

Attacking with violent fury, Torsten met its every strike with one of his own, countering whenever he spotted an opening.

The creature circled him, darting in low and leaping high, swiping with ever larger claws that left enormous gouges on the road. Mis-timing one jump, it fell against the wall of the nearest building—a florist, Torsten realised—and crashed through the walls, sending buds and vases smashing in all directions. One ceramic pot flew through the air, and though Torsten avoided it, the pot shattered on the ground beside him, one shard nicking him just below the knee.

Gasping in pain, though adrenaline kept the worst of it at bay, he darted away from the debris.

It had been too long since he'd tasted battle, and although he'd always dismissed such tasks as grunt work, dusting off the cobwebs gave him a grim pleasure, even through the pain. He savoured the adrenaline, let it fuel his strength and desire to be victorious.

Pulling itself from the collapsed wall and shaking off

several ruined bouquets, the creature let out a low, keening whine, eyes searching for its target.

Though Torsten was right in front of it, the thing decided to launch itself at Fenn and the others. The Bragalian pushed Fenn out of the way, stepping protectively in front of the Porsenthian woman. She held up a dagger to the creature in defiance. Varlot, too, stood ready to fight beside her, his axe raised.

'Calidra!' Fenn yelped, crouching down as the incoming creature bore down on them.

The Bragalian, Calidra, slashed haphazardly at the creature with her long dagger—more for hunting than combat—driving it away from the other woman. Despite her poor choice of weapon, she moved confidently, every step planted as she pushed the creature back, unfazed by the slippery ground. Clearly, she was a trained fighter.

Roaring at the new combatant, the shadow attacked Calidra, though she deftly avoided its strikes, always keeping it away from her companions. Varlot, too, stepped into the fray, shouting his own war-cry as he swung his axe as easily as Calidra thrust her dagger.

Torsten's eyes widened in sudden realisation. The Laird of Fellwood had several children, and he knew the eldest was named Calidra. It would explain why Fenn's papers had been supposedly signed by Vantonen. This woman, Calidra, *had* to be the heir to Fellwood.

He was never usually wrong, and the thought he'd made a mistake gnawed at him more painfully than the wound on his knee. Already, blood trickled down his shin. Another mistake to cover up.

Torsten's lip curled as the two battled fiercely. What had become of the spirit to make it act so? It was either corrupted beyond all hope or...or it was Myrish.

That wasn't possible. *Couldn't* be possible.

This needed to stop. Now.

'You. Spirit!' Torsten raised his sword to the creature. Hacking at it like it was some common beast was not going to be effective.

'Torsten, you need help!' Calidra called.

He snorted. 'I do not need help from the likes of *you*, Bragalian.'

Before either of them could say anything more, the creature shot forward, sending forth multiple appendages, its claws digging into the ground, the fallen building, debris, anything it could reach. Torsten charged forward, slicing away as many of them as he could reach with devastating accuracy. Varlot appeared on the monster's other side, his axe expertly slamming into its blind side and causing it to let out another shriek as it whirled around to face him. In the next moment, Calidra buried her dagger deep into the creature's exposed flank.

The shadow creature span in a circle, sending out great swipes of its claws to push its aggressors away, and let out another low bellow.

Where was Nadja? If it was Myrish, if there was even a chance it *could* be, he needed the creature to die before anyone else saw it. And he wasn't sure he could manage that without another Inquisitor fighting with him.

Between the three of them, they subdued the creature—its attacks came less frequently, with less speed, and it didn't take long before it tried to flee.

Torsten stepped in front of it, panting heavily, and blocked its path. With a violent slash, he brought *Tinebás* down and sank it deep into the creature's mass. Ichor burst from the wound in a shower that coated him with the dark ooze. Wrenching his sword to the side, he tore a gaping hole in the middle of the beast, and it shrieked again, rolling onto the ground as if in submission.

Torsten took a steadying breath, doing his best to keep his hands from shaking.

'You...filthy...' The creature's words came out as a wheeze, and it shuddered with the effort of speaking.

'Get back from it! It's not safe!' Fenn called from several paces away. Although his eyes were wide with fear, he had an arm in front of the Porsenthian woman, blocking the creature's way with his own body.

Varlot spun his axe casually, as if they were in the training ring, not a life-or-death battle against an unknown spirit. 'Nothing to worry about, lad. It'll—'

The writhing mass of shadows leapt to its feet with a suddenness that he hadn't seen before. With another furious bellow, it barrelled towards Torsten, its movements wild and erratic. It pounced, crashed into him, and clawed frantically.

Torsten lost his grip on his sword and punched the creature, aiming for what he thought were its eyes. In retaliation, it bit down on his arm. Whatever teeth it had dented his vambrace, but the metal was slick, and it couldn't grip. Torsten grabbed hold of whatever he could reach—flesh, teeth, eyes—squeezing tightly. Its teeth pierced his thick leather gloves and Torsten pulled *hard*—until the creature released him with a furious snarl.

He was back on his feet in an instant, sword scooped up in the same movement. It was time for this thing to die. Before he could drive his sword into it, one claw slammed into Torsten's head, bouncing off his iron helm.

It whirled around again, then charged at Calidra, knocking her violently to the ground. Her back cracked on the stones and she cried out. Caught between the creature and the churning waters of the bay, she raised her hand, dagger still grasped in her trembling fingers.

It wouldn't save her.

The others ran towards her, desperation lending them speed, but the gap was too great.

Metal ringing in his ears, Torsten thrust his sword forward, the tip aimed at the creature, already five or six feet away. 'Miroth. I call upon your strength.' Though the words were whispered under his breath, half-gasped more than commanded, the effect was immediate. *Tinebás* lit up like a torch, flames licking the metal with a blinding flash.

The creature hesitated, as if sensing the spirit's power.

It was all Torsten needed.

Fire plumed from the tip of his sword, shooting forward with such speed that it lit up the shadow creature instantly. The noise emitted from the creature was like nothing Torsten had ever heard before—a wailing howl that cut through to his bones—and he watched with grim satisfaction as it burned. It stumbled over, writhing, its body jerking as the fire sank deep into its flesh.

The other woman hauled Calidra to her feet, who had regained sense enough to push the others away, even as they struggled in the chaos. 'Back! Get back!' Calidra pushed them, almost violently.

With a final cry of anguish, the creature careened into the group, rolled over the edge of the road, and splashed into the churning waters of the Salt Bay. The wave it produced engulfed the docks in silt-rich, freezing water, and crashed into the bridge leading to the south of the bay. Stone and wood crumbled in the explosion, water was thrown up several feet high, then rained down in a splatter of drizzle.

If the sound of battle hadn't attracted attention, *that* explosion would.

Torsten frowned, mildly annoyed he'd not managed to get a solid answer from the thing, then looked down at his hand to inspect the damage the creature had left on his armour. His fist was still closed where he'd grabbed at the thing's face, and when he opened it, he saw one of the creature's fangs, coated in the same ichor that covered the road.

He smiled. Whatever secrets the queen had hidden from him, he'd have his answer soon enough.

'Master Inquisitor!' Nadja called from further along the road.

He looked up and saw her sprinting towards him, her sword drawn, though the threat had passed.

'I've never known your timing to be so ridiculously poor,' he said. The fire had burnt off the gore coating his sword, and he sheathed it as the Inquisitor reached him.

'I was held up. Trying to disperse the crowds itching to see what all the chaos was.'

Torsten nodded. It wasn't a good excuse, but he was in a better mood now the thing had been dealt with, and he had some evidence that he could investigate.

'Jisyel!' Calidra screamed, drawing his attention.

The Bragalian and Varlot stood on the edge of the road, peering into the dark water. 'Jisyel!' Calidra called again, her voice pitched in obvious distress. Varlot stood beside her, axe forgotten on the ground as he paced alongside the bay, calling for Fenn and Jisyel.

Torsten turned away from them and back to Nadja. 'You kept the locals clear, I hope?'

'Yes, sir. Most wanted to help. Word has spread that a young boy was attacked.'

'Hmm. Has he said by what?'

'No sir. He's not of sound mind, from what they were saying. May not survive due to the amount of blood he's lost.'

Torsten's mind whirled. 'Good. Let's keep it that way. An unfortunate accident by one of those large cats that prowl the hills near here.' In his periphery, Calidra waved at him, evidently trying to get his attention. Varlot had taken off his boots and was already waist-deep in the water, one arm clutching the edge in case he was swept away by the swift current.

He frowned.

'Sir?' Nadja brought his attention back. She pointed at the black ichor that had settled in thick puddles on the road.

'It was rabid.' Torsten dismissed her querying look with a wave. 'You and Sarron will get this mess cleaned up.'

Nadja stiffened but did not object.

Calidra stormed over to him. 'Inquisitor! Why aren't you *doing* something?'

He scowled. 'What's the matter, woman?'

'Jisyel's gone! She and Fenn were knocked into the water when that...that...*thing* fell in!'

Varlot pulled himself out of the bay with effort. He took several heaving breaths and leaned on his thighs, shaking his head as a puddle formed under him.

Torsten couldn't make out any details, couldn't even see the water moving, it was too dark. 'Go in and get her then, if you're that worried. It's not my problem.'

'Not your problem?' Calidra brandished her knife. '*You're* the Master Inquisitor!'

'Yes. And my problems have nothing to do with a lost soul and some random woman.' He gestured towards Varlot. 'Fenn is in his charge, if I recall rightly. Have *him* help you. And get yourself seen by a medic, you're delirious. Wounds from a rabid animal ought to be addressed quickly. Besides, this area is now off limits by my orders.'

She glared at him, a defiant, furious gaze that matched his own stubbornness.

He ignored it. 'Get moving, Bragalian, before I arrest you for trespassing.'

5

THE GENERAL

CALIDRA

J isyel was gone. She'd disappeared into the dark
waters of the Salt Bay along with the shadow-like
creature they'd fought—and Fenn, too. She stared
out at it, desperate to jump in, but unable to get past
her fear of water. It crippled her.

'Keep my granddaughter safe.' That's what Bellandri had
told her only *hours* before.

Jisyel was certainly *not* safe.

Calidra's rising panic and dawning realisation of the
gravity of the situation pushed out all logical thought. Her
breathing hitched as the seconds ticked past.

Varlot had tried to follow them into the water and
quickly crawled back out—the current here was too swift.
Too dangerous.

Torsten, bastard that he was, couldn't care less. Had just
told them to get out of his way and leave the area. The other
Inquisitor with him, Nadja, she thought her name was, had
offered a thin smile of condolence before carrying out
Torsten's orders and starting to clean up the scene of the
battle. As if nothing had happened.

As if Jisyel wasn't gone.

Only a *day* after they'd left the Isle of Salt.

Calidra began to protest. 'But—'

'Orders are orders. As the daughter of a Laird, *you* should know that.' Nadja brushed past her to reach a particularly thick puddle of dark ooze the creature had bled. She glanced back up at her, and with more kindness, said, 'The other Inquisitors and I will be here the rest of the night, I expect. We'll keep an eye out for your friends.'

It was a dismissal. Kind and polite as it could be, but a dismissal all the same. Ignoring it would bring Torsten's attention back to her, and after all the stories of the Master Inquisitor's cruel nature, she knew irritating him wasn't something she should do.

But Calidra wasn't sure she could even bring herself to leave, her gaze drawn back to the water, hoping to see a hand or body break the surface, swimming back towards them.

Varlot paced nearby, but whatever sway he had over Torsten, he didn't call upon it here. He approached her and gave a comforting smile. He'd tried to help. Braved the water when she couldn't. And it was impossible to go after them. 'Calidra, I'll help you get back to the tavern. Looks like you took quite a beating from that thing.'

She hadn't even realised her injuries in the panic of losing Jisyel, and now he'd mentioned it, her bruised arms and legs thrummed with pain.

Calidra knew Jisyel was a strong swimmer, but if she'd taken a hit to the head, or if the current was too swift, or if she tried to help Fenn—sweet, silly thing that she was, it was likely she *would*—she might end up drowning in her attempts. It would be just like her to die a heroic death. It had been chaos, with the monster crashing into them. Jisyel had grabbed hold of Fenn, tried to keep him safe, and the pair had been flung into the water as if they weighed nothing.

Damned stupid Fenn. He'd brought the Inquisitors' attention to them, and now...and now...

'Jisyel!' Calidra called out again, her voice echoing into nothingness over the dark water, swallowed by the rain that continued to fall. 'Please!'

'Come on.' Varlot held out his arm, but she refused it, pacing along the line of the water and looking out, decidedly ignoring Nadja's stares. 'Jisyel!' Her only answer were more splashes as chunks of the bridge fell into the water, great boulders of stone sending up a shower of spray as they plunged into the bay.

What if...what if one landed right on Jisyel? Crushed her skull and shattered her bones.

Calidra tried not to think of that, but her mind reeled, whirling with worst-case scenario after worst-case scenario. She hardly realised when Varlot's strong arms helped her back to her feet. When had she sunk to her knees? Why did she ache so much?

'We'll take it gently back.' Varlot's voice was low and soothing.

Although Calidra knew the man by reputation, she didn't know him personally, and it was all suddenly too much for her. 'No! Jisyel! I have to get to her!'

But when she gazed out at the vast expanse of black water, her legs turned to mush, and they buckled. There was no way she could convince herself to get in there. Not even for Jisyel. She was too afraid.

Too *weak*.

Fighting the lump at the back of her throat and the stinging behind her eyes that were always a precursor to tears, she flailed her arms, weakly waving them. 'Jisyel...'

'Really, now. I don't want to have to arrest you for your conduct. That wouldn't look good for your family, would it?' Nadja walked over to them, one hand on the hilt of her sword. All kindness had left her eyes.

Varlot gently, but firmly, steered her away from the water's edge, lifting her back onto her feet and continuing to support her. 'Thank you, Inquisitor. I'll look after her from here. Let me know if you spot our…companions?'

Nadja nodded once.

Calidra looked back at Torsten, who was deep in conversation with another Inquisitor with sandy-coloured hair. She'd not even realised he had turned up. Her throat dried and her vision swirled. 'I think…I think I'm going to be sick.'

CALIDRA WAS BARELY aware of their walk back to *The Seafarer's Haven*. Bellandri's friend, Ashothka, had never turned up. Which meant she had nowhere to stay, either. How had she lost everything so quickly?

She threw up twice on their way back into the heart of Ballowtown, and Varlot helped her up into a quiet room on the third floor, leaving a bucket beside the bed as he went back outside, closing the door behind him.

She clutched the bedsheets as grief and despair warred within her. Varlot was out there, in the rain and darkness, looking for Jisyel. Fenn. She wanted to be out there as well, she *should* have been out there with him, searching.

But it was dark.

Dangerous.

And she was in no fit state to be looking for anyone. She clung to the hope he would return with good news as exhaustion gave way to a nightmare-fuelled sleep.

Calidra woke up several more times through the night, vomiting until nothing but bile burned her throat. Alternating between vomiting and crying, she trembled under the bedsheets, her mind a whirlwind of emotion and confusion. Time seemed to spin, and everything that had once made sense unravelled.

Bellandri's words echoed. *'Keep my granddaughter safe.'*

Less than a day off the island and everything had gone

mad. This was why returning to Bragalia had always been such a terrible idea. Nothing good could come of it.

Exhausted, she rolled over on the hard bed, kicking the sheets off herself. She automatically reached for Jisyel, for comfort, but her hand fell through empty air. She sobbed, then. It had been a long time since she'd really let her emotions get the better of her. Feeling horrific, and desperate for a hug that she couldn't have, she dozed off again.

Sometime after the sun had risen, a knock at the door brought Calidra to full alertness instantly. She glanced around the room, taking a moment to recognise where she was and reorientate herself, and brace for the pain as she remembered Jisyel wasn't there.

Though she winced at the difficulty of getting to her feet, she crossed the room quickly, pushing her hair out of her eyes. With a deep breath, trying to inspire some non-existent confidence from whatever strength she had in reserve, she opened the door. 'Varlot?'

Sunlight streamed in from the bright corridor behind him, and she stood back to let him in, heedless of the smell of vomit that no doubt permeated.

Varlot's cloak was soaked, as were his boots, and he brought in mud. 'I thought you might need something to drink.' He handed Calidra a small, tin jug, liquid sloshing inside.

'Did you find Jisyel?'

He didn't reply, walking past her with heavy steps. Even in his tiredness, sopping wet and post-battle with a terrifying shadow-creature, the man radiated strength. It was no wonder he'd been so highly ranked within the Porsenthian army.

She lifted the jug's lid and gave it a cautious sniff—lemon and a mixture of herbs she faintly recognised. She sipped, grateful it was only lukewarm, then wandered over to the bed and sat down, wearier than ever. There were so many things happening. She should apologise for the mess. Be thankful for the tea. Ask about the money she owed him for the room he'd so generously furnished her with. Make sure *he* was okay after spending a night outside searching in the cold rain.

But she could only focus on one thing. 'Varlot? Tell me you found her?'

'Damn Inquisitors are crawling all over the place. Won't let anyone near the site.' Varlot shrugged out of his cloak, then laid it neatly over the back of one chair.

Without his cloak, she saw scars littered his muscular arms. Some looked quite fresh. She wondered if he fought for fun or glory, or if trouble had a habit of finding him.

'No sign of Fenn and Jisyel. Or whatever that creature was. They're definitely not in Ballowtown. Might have washed up on the other side of the bay...'

Calidra's heart soared as she latched onto the possibility of hope. 'She's a strong swimmer, Jisyel.'

Varlot nodded and exhaled sharply. He walked over to the window, drew the curtain, and lifted the pane open, letting cool air stream into the stuffy room.

She watched him carefully as he gazed out the open window. He'd told them he'd helped Fenn because of an old rivalry with Torsten. That he enjoyed making life difficult for the Master Inquisitor whenever the opportunity arose. Was it worth having someone around who liked to poke sleeping dragons? Attracting Torsten's attention was never a good thing. And yet, Varlot seemed genuinely to want to help Fenn.

More than that, she *needed* him. Without Varlot, she was effectively on her own. Having him as an ally would keep her safe, there was no doubt about that.

Varlot said, 'Bridge is out, too. Saw a few officers try and cross, but more of the stone crumbled and a handful of them ended up in the water. That'll take a while to repair, need to ship the stone in from the mountains.'

Her earlier joy shattered. 'So...I can't cross?'

'You'd have to go all the way up to Meadowhill, cross the river, then come back south.'

Calidra *knew* that. She was Bragalian, she knew her own country and its geography. But she didn't know if another bridge had been built further inland in the years she'd been away. Still, she appreciated Varlot's thorough explanation. At least he cared.

It was probably more than she deserved.

She thought about what to do next. Meadowhill was just over halfway between Ballowtown and Fellwood. Jisyel knew that, too. If...if Jisyel had made it to the other side, perhaps she'd continue north, and they'd meet up at Meadowhill. She licked her lips, considering. Of course, Varlot could be mistaken, and Jisyel and Fenn had drowned together, never to be seen again.

The thought threatened to turn her stomach, so she took another sip of her herbal tea, hoping it would settle her body, if not her emotions. She looked at Varlot, a former General within the Porsenthian army, and wondered what he was doing in Bragalia. Even when she thought back to the conversation they'd had at the table, before everything had gone mad, she'd been suspicious of him. Then again, she was suspicious of everyone.

A training contract in Fellwood wasn't uncommon; her parents often hired specialists or tutors to work in their household. She'd had several throughout her own childhood, including a weapons master.

But he was *particularly* interested in Fenn. Something about it felt off, and she didn't know if she was simply on edge because of what had happened. Was he telling the truth? She needed to figure it out. Needed to see if she could trust him. 'Did you lie to Torsten?'

79

Varlot's gaze, which had been firmly locked on outside the window, whipped around to her. His eyebrows knitted together. 'Lie?'

'About Fellwood. My father...'

'Passed away, I know. And I'm sorry for your loss.' Varlot returned his attention to the window, staring out at the street below, his emotions guarded. 'He'd been sick a while. It was to be expected.'

Again, Calidra knew, but she let it slide, holding back her natural reaction to correct him. If Jisyel were here, she'd tell Calidra she ought to be grateful. That he'd done so much to help her. But she couldn't quite bring herself to vocalise that.

'I suppose he didn't want to leave his youngest kid without any sort of fighting experience. That's why he contracted me. Unusual, but money is money. I do it every now and then. Torsten knows that.'

'Only the best for father.' Calidra rolled her eyes and took a larger gulp of her drink. It was somehow too bitter and too sweet, and she'd give anything for a steaming mug of cinnamon coffee instead, but it had quenched her stomach's desire to vomit. For now, she'd give Varlot the benefit of the doubt—as long as he was helping her, Jisyel, and Fenn. He was handy with his axe, and clearly resourceful. Useful to have around.

She didn't *want* to think about home, about what was left of her family, but she couldn't help it. Her brother, Paicha, had only been a toddler when she'd last seen him. She doubted she'd even recognise him, or he her. Calidra abruptly changed the subject before another pain grew too strongly in her chest. 'Was this your room?'

'Yes.'

'Why did you give it to me?'

Varlot shrugged. 'You needed it. What's wrong? Not good enough for the Laird's daughter?'

'Nothing's wrong.' She wasn't a fan of his humour.

Calidra chewed her lip. She had a funeral to get to and Varlot had a training contract. But she didn't want to leave, couldn't even *consider* leaving, in case Jisyel and Fenn had washed up further along the coast. What if they were making their way back to Ballowtown right now? Jisyel would be irate if she finally made it back to the inn only to find Calidra gone.

She sighed. With the Inquisitors forbidding anyone from going near the bay, it would be pointless trying to look again. Varlot had spent all night looking. And Jisyel *could* swim. There was a good chance they'd made it to the other side of the bay.

She hoped Fenn could swim, too, unless that was another thing he'd conveniently forgotten.

Perhaps she should wait *one* day. Just in case. A single day wouldn't put her too far behind schedule, she'd just have to travel faster for the rest of the way to Fellwood to make it home in time for her father's funeral. The message that she'd received on the Isle of Salt had said she had a week before the funeral. She'd have a handful of days to make it.

As soon as she thought about waiting another day, it seemed the best thing to do, and some of the tension eased from her shoulders. 'Varlot. I'd like to stay one more night, if that's okay. In case Jisyel comes back.'

'Fenn too?'

'Of course Fenn, too.'

He scratched the side of his chin.

'There'll be payment, of course. I...travel light, but as we're both heading to Fellwood, you'll get your coin there.' It was a white lie. She *did* travel light, but that was because her funds had been cut off, not out of choice. She had no idea if her mother would allow Varlot to take more coin as payment for looking after her, but that was an argument—no, conversation—for later.

His jaw tightened. 'Fine. I'll get another room, assuming they still have openings.'

At his abrupt change, Calidra wondered if she'd offended him somehow. Despite living on the Isle of Salt for several years, she wasn't completely familiar with Porsenthian culture and expectations. They were isolated on the island, at any rate. Anything Jisyel and Bellandri did couldn't necessarily be parallelled on the mainland.

She didn't have time to tiptoe around customs and familiarities, though. Not while Jisyel—and Fenn, she reminded herself—were lost, possibly injured. 'I'm going back to the water, see if I can—'

'No. Torsten is arresting anyone who ventures too close. Best to keep away, Calidra.'

'But—'

'I know Torsten more than anyone. Better to keep off his bad side. Better to keep out of his notice completely, if I'm honest.'

Calidra didn't like it. She hated being told what to do, especially where Jisyel was concerned. But getting herself arrested wasn't going to help anyone's situation. She massaged her temples, angry at herself for letting things get out of hand so quickly. She sat, quiet, sipping from her drink every so often, while her mind reeled from the night's events.

'I want to know what that thing was.'

Varlot's voice brought her from her thoughts. 'I beg your pardon?' In the panic of losing Jisyel, she'd almost forgotten the cause of the chaos.

'The thing Torsten and I fought. Never seen a spirit like that before, and I've fought pretty much everything on this continent.'

Calidra thought back to the battle, mildly annoyed he'd excluded her from the list of combatants—she'd done her part, too, even if she only had a hunting dagger. But the details of what they fought hadn't meant anything to her, so she hadn't paid much attention. 'Corrupted spirit, I guess.'

'Was it?'

'Why else would it attack? Or look like that? I've never seen one before, have you?'

Varlot shook his head and ran a hand through his dark hair. It was greying at the temples, but he was handsome in a rugged sort of way. Past his prime, perhaps, and arrogant from his time in the army, but not unlikeable. Had a wife and son too, if she remembered rightly.

Calidra tried to channel Jisyel's positive thinking and decided to show him some courtesy after all he'd done for her. For them. 'Thank you, Varlot. For...everything. We were fortunate to have crossed paths. Fenn's lucky, too. Torsten would've whisked him away, otherwise.'

He inclined his head in acknowledgement, then continued to look out of the window. 'He's a good lad, Fenn. Reminds me of my boy. Anyway, this place is gonna be crawling with Inquisitors.' Resentment laced his voice, turning his words sharp and bitter. 'Best get out of here soon.'

Calidra frowned. She wanted to wait until the next morning—to give herself time to rest as much as wait for Jisyel and Fenn. There was no chance she'd leave earlier. 'Tomorrow, we'll leave.'

He didn't seem to hear her. 'The people. "Lost souls," Torsten keeps calling 'em. You remember? That's why there are so many Inquisitors right now.'

'Yes. Well, I'm sure stowaways turn up from time to time? I imagine northern Bragalia is in a bit of a state after my father's passing. It isn't often that a Laird dies.'

'Not like this. Torsten wouldn't get involved unless it was something important.' Varlot didn't say any more on the matter and they fell into silence.

Calidra didn't know. She had too much on her mind with

her own family matters and Jisyel falling into the water to really care about why Torsten was down here. It may be that the lost souls and Fenn were connected, but she simply didn't have the brainpower to think about that right now.

Her immediate situation and survival was the only thing she could consider. Varlot was a curiosity, too. Calidra had always wondered why a man of Varlot's standing—and ability —had left the Porsenthian army. He didn't seem any worse for it, and she wondered if it had anything to do with Torsten or the rivalry he claimed to have with the Master Inquisitor. If the truce between Porsenthia and Bragalia wasn't in effect, she'd be Varlot's enemy. Her throat tightened at the thought. Perhaps she was fortunate he'd taken an interest in Fenn.

It didn't matter that Bragalia had been an ally to Porsenthia for close to six decades. For many people, centuries of hatred and violence weren't so easily erased. The memories of that time were fresh for many.

She should have paid more attention. Perhaps then she could have done something to stop what had happened. She'd been too preoccupied with her irritation at having to babysit Fenn, too focussed on herself and Jisyel, keeping an eye out for Ashothka, figuring out what she'd say to her mother when they finally reached Fellwood. As far as she was concerned, Fenn becoming someone else's problem was relieving her of that burden.

Calidra was determined to put things to rights.

VARLOT HADN'T BEEN happy about waiting another day before leaving, but Calidra had promised him extra coin, and that appeared persuasive enough to get the man to stay with fewer complaints. He had gone into town shortly after the first morning, on his own business that he'd not shared with her. She didn't care. She had too much on her mind to worry about what her new companion was up to, and her bruises needed time to heal.

It gave her the space to think, plan, and get herself recovered and ready to travel.

Luckily, she had the majority of their supplies, and though she'd have preferred a hot meal cooked by the tavern, Calidra stuck with the food Bellandri had packed to keep her spending as low as possible. She tried to make sense of things; Ashothka hadn't met them. Had something happened to him? It meant her way forward was less sure. A shadow creature of some sort had attacked the town—perhaps a corrupted spirit. Jisyel and Fenn had fallen in the water, possibly drowned or washed away. Lost souls like Fenn were cropping up everywhere, and Queen Surayo had sent her Inquisitors—including one of the Master Inquisitors—as far south as Bragalia to get control of the situation. Not to mention her father had died and she needed to return home in the next few days to not only see the funeral, but face her mother again.

Could she even go back to the Isle of Salt if the worst had happened to Jisyel? The island had been her home, Bellandri her new family.

She didn't think she could ever face Bellandri again.

Deep down, she knew that Jisyel and Fenn weren't coming back to town, but something prevented her from leaving straightaway. It might've been guilt more than any real expectation they'd stroll back into the inn, but waiting gave her some element of control, even if it was futile. Her constant worry gave way to exhaustion, which made her her second sleep marginally better than her first.

She was disturbed awake in the middle of the night when Varlot returned from his business in town—which became apparent as he fell into a deep sleep on the floor under the

85

window, stinking of wine, a deep cut across the knuckles on his right hand.

Calidra said nothing the next morning. Everyone had their issues, and she needed his help more than she needed to criticise his life choices. Honestly, as long as he helped her, she didn't really care. But to appease his desire to steer clear of the Inquisitors, they left at first light.

Varlot strongly believed Jisyel and Fenn were on the south side of the bay, already making their way onwards, and sitting around waiting frustrated him.

Despite there being no sign of Jisyel or Fenn, and more Inquisitors arriving, Calidra left Ballowtown with a heavy heart.

It would be simple enough to get to Meadowhill—they just needed to follow the river up through the hills. The town sat comfortably on the far side of a small forest, about a day's walk away, if they didn't take too many breaks and kept a brisk pace. Calidra was unsure what Varlot's mood would be the morning after his drinking session, but aside from being bleary-eyed, was as spritely as before.

'Thank you again for your patronage! It's always an honour to have you here, General! Even if you're passing through at the last minute, we're happy to help you!'

Varlot nodded and gave the innkeeper a smile.

The man beamed at the attention. 'You take care of yourselves, you hear? Wild cats and bears are everywhere these days.' The innkeeper waved them away, parroting Inquisitor Torsten's warning. 'Get yourself a decent weapon at the smith's, won't you? You can't be too careful!'

Calidra didn't bother to respond—she didn't know what had attacked Ballowtown, but she'd put money on it *not* being a bear or cat. Even if they were to encounter one such animal, her dagger and Varlot's axe would be more than enough to keep them away.

She and Varlot made their way to the north-eastern edge

of town, avoiding any streets that even gave them a glimpse of the bay, before following the water upriver.

Calidra forced herself not to look back.

'Jisyel and Fenn will be waiting in Meadowhill,' Varlot said with certainty. 'You'll see I'm right when we get there.'

She wasn't convinced and gave him a tight smile in response. She had no choice but to keep going.

Most of the morning passed in silence, which suited Calidra just fine. She'd have preferred a distraction to missing Jisyel so keenly, but by following the river and thinking about getting to Meadowhill as quickly as possible, she had something to focus her attention on.

The path north was wide and well-maintained, and much of it was paved with the flat, grey stones she remembered from her childhood home. Her leather boots felt heavy on the stones, and she longed to swap to more comfortable Bragalian sandals, but she didn't have any. As the sun rose, they passed several people—merchants, bards, and other travellers like themselves. Thankfully, Varlot seemed as averse to attention as she did, and they skirted around most people without much more than the expected, 'good mornings,' and, 'safe travels.'

Curious as she was about Varlot's reasons for being here, she didn't ask. It wasn't her business, and she didn't want to upset him and lose his aid. His reputation in the Porsenthian army was well-known, and she'd need him if they encountered any more trouble. The man was supposedly impossible to kill.

And as much as she claimed otherwise, she wasn't entirely sure she could cope being back in Bragalia alone.

Shortly before midday, they took a break in the shade of a willow tree where the path widened beside the river. Ahead, the trees thickened into a forest that loomed at the base of the hills surrounding Meadowhill. Far below them and to the south, the bay glistened in the sunlight. She hoped that on the other side, Jisyel and Fenn were safe and well. She'd never forgive herself otherwise.

The spot they'd picked to rest in was clearly popular among travellers, because a handful of carriages, wooden stalls, and tents had been set up—a makeshift marketplace that was able to move at a moment's notice—and the place was bustling with a small crowd. Almost everyone present was Bragalian, with a handful of Olmese dotted in between, standing out in their fine, coloured silks.

Several had taken an interest in them, with one man challenging Varlot to a friendly spar so he could show off in front of his children. Varlot had politely declined, even turning red when the man's wife had given him a kiss on the cheek for humouring her husband.

The pair of them found a shady spot to sit down away from the bustle. Calidra was impressed with how he handled the attention. She'd probably have chased them away with her dagger by now, but Varlot took it all in his stride. Even though several people were throwing glances in their direction, none of it was menacing. In fact, two young women—who had to be young enough to be Varlot's daughters—kept giggling and looking over at him, as if he was their first crush.

She rolled her eyes and kept her attention on the other people—listening for signs of Jisyel, Fenn, or any Inquisitors. News travelled quickly in a place like this.

Conversations drifted over to them, mostly about the attack in Ballowtown and the Inquisitors taking away the "lost souls" who had appeared throughout the country over the past few days. Yet, for all the amnesiacs, no-one was talking about relatives or friends who'd disappeared.

She found that peculiar.

Calidra shared a look with Varlot, who shrugged and turned away. 'It's not for us to deal with. We need to get to Fellwood, that's all we have to worry about.'

Although she agreed, the sight of seeing her home country in such turmoil ate at her. She was the daughter of a Laird. These people were her responsibility, in a way. It didn't matter that she didn't wield the power of her parents. Their discomfort and fear bothered her.

Having been gone so long, there was no chance of being recognised, especially in this canton, and she wondered what things were like at home. She watched an Olmese family, three young children laughing and chasing one another in and out of the river's shallows while a young woman with a long skirt that draped on the ground leaned over a piece of coloured fabric, and was mending it with a needle and thread. Beside them, a group of five adults sat around a makeshift table playing dice and eating sticks of meat.

Varlot leaned forward, watching the dice with interest.

Emotions warred within her at the sight. Her mother was Olmese, but Calidra had never spent much time in the desert country bar a handful of childhood visits.

Seeing the happy family only brought her situation into stark realisation. Everything she'd run from.

Her mother's sentiment about preferring some Porsenthian woman over her own people floated to the top of her mind, and she angrily shoved it away, locking it up along with other memories of her family.

One of the Bragalians selling fish from a stall threw up his arms in despair, and the sudden movement caught Calidra's attention.

'No money, no fish!' bellowed the stallholder, trying to snatch back the wrapped parcel he'd given a woman with dirty blonde hair.

'But I have...I thought I had...'

'You have empty pockets!'

More people were turning to watch, pausing in their conversations.

'Give it back, you thief!' He rushed around the side of his

stall, upending a bucket of fish in his haste to grab the woman by her arm. 'Stop where you are!'

The woman sank to the ground, one hand held defensively across her face, the other clutching the parcel as if her life depended on it. 'Please! I'm starving! I haven't eaten in three days!' She trembled in his grasp.

'Then go to Ballowtown or Ulbridge and find an officer, or beg the Laird for help! Don't steal from *me*!' He wrenched the parcel from her as a crowd gathered around them. Some called out to the pair, defending the fisherman's rights. Others pleaded mercy, stating how thin and frail the woman was, and didn't everyone deserve food if it saved their life?

Calidra balled her hands. The woman had the same panicked expression as Fenn.

'Stop that!' one man yelled, barging forward to restrain the stallholder. 'There's no need to be so aggressive!'

'*I'll* pay for her!' Another man stepped forward, fist clenched around a handful of coins.

'She should be taught a lesson!' The stallholder yanked the woman to her feet. 'You're one of those wandering idiots, aren't you? Lost all thought and memory? I heard Torsten himself was in Ballowtown. Perhaps I'll take you there and get a nice fat reward for helping the Iron Crown's Inquisitors!'

At mention of the Porsenthian queen, an explosion of activity filled the clearing. Calidra immediately got to her feet, her dagger drawn without thinking.

Varlot put a hand on her shoulder. 'Careful. Not our fight.'

Calidra hesitated, caught between wanting to help one of her own people, and not getting involved. Eventually, reluctantly, she sat down again, but kept her dagger drawn, carefully watching.

In a matter of moments, it was over. Three people had restrained the amnesiac woman, and the fisherman had returned to his stall, angrily picking up the scattered fish and broken crates. Although the crowd began to disperse, several people loitered, speaking in low voices that Calidra couldn't catch.

'If the Inquisitors are paying people for these lost souls...' Varlot trailed off, his gaze steely.

'Fenn...'

'You would've let Torsten take the lad.' He had a silver coin in his hand, rolling it back and forth across his knuckles absently as he watched what was left of the commotion. One knuckle had a deep cut that was scabbing over.

Calidra turned away from Varlot. She *had* wanted to dump Fenn off with the Inquisitors, but things had quickly gone south, and now she wasn't so sure. Fenn hadn't been her problem, and she hadn't wanted him to be. But he was clearly part of a bigger puzzle.

She wondered if Varlot knew that, and whether his claim that he'd helped Fenn simply because he reminded him of his son—and he enjoyed riling Torsten—was a poor cover up. Calidra couldn't help but notice how driven he was by money. And, if she was being honest with herself, she wasn't sure someone like Varlot *would* help a stranger simply on the basis of looking like a relative. His rivalry with Torsten bothered her, and she wondered whether the hatchet they needed to bury was far bigger than he'd let on.

As the woman was led away by the trio towards Ballow-town and the tension amongst the gathered group eased, Calidra finally sheathed her dagger and frowned. She didn't know who to trust.

And she didn't know what any of it meant.

91

6

THE PRIESTESS

FENN

N ever in his life did Fenn want to set foot in water
again.

No fishing. No more boats. And absolutely no
swimming.

Admittedly, the excursion hadn't been by choice, but a dip
in freezing cold water with a terrifying shadow-creature had
been traumatic enough that he started to tremble every time
he looked out at the bay.

Jisyel was far better off than himself, aside from a nasty
gash across her cheek, which she didn't seem aware of. He'd
coughed up water while she'd managed to get a fire going.
She'd wanted to get back to Calidra as soon as possible, but
had said that wasn't going to happen if they died of the cold.
Although he'd sat beside the crackling flames all night—
mostly in wonder at her resourcefulness even in a crisis—
he'd felt frozen to his bones. He'd assumed Calidra would be
better at that sort of thing. Swimming. Survival. Practical
things.

He looked at Jisyel with more respect, even as his teeth
chattered.

They'd dragged themselves out of the water and onto

land, stumbling along blindly in the dark until Jisyel had told them they could stop and rest. It wasn't much shelter from the rain that continued to pour—overhanging boulders and large trees kept the worst of it off, but it was still very cold, and very wet.

Shivering, disorientated, and having swallowed too much water, Fenn had collapsed, not even caring if the shadow creature found and consumed him. Jisyel had insisted they change out of their sodden clothes and hung them over some tree branches to dry beside the fire. Fenn had barely enough energy for that, but thankfully any embarrassment he might have felt by stripping down in front of her was overtaken by their situation and the fact it was pitch dark.

'She better not do anything stupid,' Jisyel muttered, more to herself than Fenn.

'What?' He mumbled through chattering teeth.

'Woman is terrified of water, you know? Almost threw up on the boat over here. She can swim but...when she panics, she's worse than me!' Jisyel's constant stream of talk seemed more to self-soothe than to actually engage in conversation with him. 'She better be okay. She better be thinking properly. Like she always tells *me*!'

Fenn remembered Calidra's obvious discomfort on the boat—it had bordered on fear. It made sense she'd be equally uncomfortable in the bay, and if she'd been thrown in along with them or deliberately jumped in, it wasn't going to end well. He'd thought of Calidra as logical, focussed. Surely she wouldn't have put herself in danger?

'Aren't you cold?' Fenn stared up in astonishment at the woman, who paced impatiently along the edge of their shelter, staring out into the rain and the bay beyond, evidently worried Calidra *had* jumped in. She didn't seem to notice the cold water that she'd been drenched in, absently picking her sodden clothes off, her attention never wavering from the bay. She didn't even shiver.

'Oh. I don't much feel the cold,' Jisyel muttered by way of explanation when she caught him staring. 'Have to remember to do things, sometimes. Or Calidra reminds me. It's fine.' She gave him a smile, though it didn't reach her eyes. Despite her words, goosebumps had risen along her arms, and her fingers had started to turn blue.

'Just stay near the fire. Your fingers!'

She glanced at her hands and backed up to the fire, facing the water all the while.

He wondered at her disconnect, but there were bigger things on his mind—like whether the creature would wash up with them and start attacking again. Everything had happened so quickly, been so hectic, that he hadn't been able to keep track of what had happened. He hadn't even realised *Jisyel* had been with him until he'd pulled himself onto land.

In two days, he'd nearly died twice. Both by drowning.

He wrapped his arms tightly around himself and tried not to fall asleep. He needed to stay awake in case Calidra and Varlot made it across—if they'd jumped in, of course. It would certainly even their odds if the shadow creature appeared again and they had to fight. He didn't have a weapon, and neither did Jisyel. Their chances wouldn't be great if the worst should happen, and even if…

Fenn blinked awake as the warmth of the morning sun lit up his surroundings, taking the edge off the chill. He hadn't realised he'd fallen asleep, but he'd dozed off while huddled around his own knees, and all his joints were stiff and sore. Thankfully the rain had blown away in the night, leaving numerous puddles sparkling in the sun. Jisyel stood a short way off, staring over the water, her back to him.

'Any sign of them?' Fenn ventured. His throat was raw from all the water he'd swallowed and coughed back up.

Jisyel shook her head. She'd been worried the night before, uncertain and talking herself through her emotions. But now he was confident she was scared, really scared, for the first time since they'd met. She only wore her under-clothing and her auburn hair was a mess of tangled knots. It didn't look like Jisyel had slept at all. 'She can swim. She *can*.'

'Maybe she washed up further down the bay? It's been hours since we were thrown in.'

'Maybe...' Jisyel sighed. 'Maybe...'

Fenn poked at their extinguished fire with a stick, ashes blowing in the wind, and stifled a yawn, glad there had been no sign of the shadow creature. Torsten's flaming sword had certainly done some damage, and Varlot and Calidra had fought well.

Their clothes had dried somewhat, and although there were a few damp patches here and there, it was a far cry from the cold, wet mess they'd been the night before. Quickly dressing, he fumbled with the laces across his trousers and looked around. Now the sun had come up, he could see a narrow dirt path that ran behind the boulders they'd sheltered beside. 'I'll...take a wander down the path. See if I can spot her? Try not to worry, Jisyel.'

Jisyel nodded, barely moving, and Fenn headed away from their makeshift camp, eager to get the blood flowing in his stiff limbs and some warmth into his body.

It was early; the sun a sliver of yellow peeking above the horizon, and after the previous night's dramatic events, Fenn hoped he *wouldn't* see anyone save Calidra or Varlot. He wasn't sure he had the energy to engage in conversation with a stranger if they tried to talk to him.

As he walked along the dirt path, boots squelching in the muddy puddles where he couldn't avoid them, he wondered whether he was originally from this place. Calidra had been unsure about his accent, but then again, she'd been unsure about everything about him.

This was the second morning since he'd "awoken," on the Isle of Salt and he'd yet to remember anything from *before*. Fenn wondered if it was the same for the others who'd lost their memories. Had it been some traumatic event they'd all been caught in? Losing their memories at the exact same moment? Or had they been picked, one at a time, all memory loss staggered across a group of unlucky people?

Birdsong filled the air as small creatures awoke with the rising sun. If he closed his eyes, he could forget everything that had happened the previous night. That it was a calm, quiet morning like any other, with nothing wrong—no friends hurt or missing.

He carefully peered past every tree and rock, checking everywhere he could see as methodically as possible—grateful none of the plants or foliage shouted at him like they'd done on the Isle of Salt.

But there was no sign of Calidra or Varlot.

It wasn't necessarily a bad thing. They could still be safe in Ballowtown.

Things had been looking up for him, with Varlot appearing only briefly before everything had gone mad. He'd saved him from Torsten—whatever the Inquisitor had been about to do—and he'd lost Varlot immediately after.

Calidra hadn't seemed happy about Varlot stepping in to help, especially not against Torsten. Then again, she seemed grumpy about everything unless it was Jisyel. But Calidra's unhappiness had gone out the window the moment the watchtower bells rang. She was the daughter of a Laird, responsible, in some way, for the people of her country. Although they weren't in her home canton, and she had no reason to get involved, she'd wanted to see with her own eyes what the cause of the distress was.

Varlot had been intrigued, too, and had followed Calidra's lead into the rainy streets. Jisyel had tried to argue against it —she'd been uncomfortable since arriving at the tavern and seeing the officers seated—but Calidra clearly was the more stubborn of the two.

And once again, Fenn had been swept up in events outside of his control.

Would staying on the island with Hassen really have been so bad? At least the dragon hadn't tried to kill him. His chest burned suddenly, as if flame thrashed inside, and he coughed up more water.

Wiping his mouth, he stared out at the bay. He didn't know whether Calidra and Varlot had been flung into it, but was certain he'd have come across them by now if they had. The water was swiftly flowing and choppy in the wind. It wasn't too hard to imagine they'd been swept away, carried down by the fast-flowing current, like the creature seemingly had been.

No. He couldn't think like that. Wouldn't.

Jisyel was already on the brink of panic, and he didn't want to make things worse. They'd be okay if they stuck together—he just needed to show Jisyel how he could help. Staying level-headed was the only way they were getting out of this mess.

Fenn continued to patrol the bank until the sun had risen enough that he began to sweat. It wouldn't be long before the people who lived on this side of the bay would be up and about, and not wishing to get into another confrontation for which he was ill-prepared, Fenn hurried back to the low outcropping of rock where they'd camped. He shook his head. 'No sign of them.'

Jisyel had dressed while he'd been away, and braided her hair to keep it out of her face. The gash on her cheek had stopped bleeding, but it didn't look like it would stay that way for long.

'How do we get back to Ballowtown?' Fenn asked, trying to be practical. 'Calidra and Varlot aren't here, I'm sure of it. So we'll have to go back to them.'

'But the bridge across the bay was damaged.'

'Isn't there another way across?'

'Not unless we walk all the way inland and around. It'd take days. And we'd be halfway to Fellwood by then, anyway.'

Fenn frowned, trying to think. They needed to be practical. 'If they didn't fall in…If they're okay…'

'What would Calidra do…? She…she *would* go on, wouldn't she? Come on, Jisyel, think, *think*…' She chewed her thumbnail.

'Maybe Calidra's waiting in Ballowtown?'

'Maybe…But she has a funeral to get back to. She's on a timer for that. She might…she might have to keep going.'

'She wouldn't wait for you to get back to Ballowtown?' Fenn found Jisyel's words a bit of a shock. He'd assumed the only thing Calidra cared about was waving her knife at strangers and making sure Jisyel was okay.

Jisyel shook her head. 'It's…a long story. This is her last chance to have a relationship with her family there. Her mother, really. She's put off going home for years. This funeral has finally given her the push to get back.' Jisyel sounded confident, if worried.

'Oh.' Fenn wasn't sure what to say. It was strange, Calidra looking to rekindle her own family. He was doing something similar. Except, Calidra *knew* where hers was. 'You're *sure* she'd keep going?'

'I'm sure. When I…when *we* don't turn up in Ballowtown this morning, she'll have no need to keep waiting.'

Fenn thought it harsh, but from what he'd seen of Calidra, she was ever logical and practical. His stomach growled. 'Well, if there's no way across, we have to keep going to Fellwood, too?' It was the only thing they *could* do. 'And we can't wait here when Calidra has all our supplies. Maybe we'll catch up with her on the way, if we're quick?' Despite the morning light chasing away the chill of the night, Fenn knew they would need food and water soon. He reached into his pocket, pulling out the papers Bellandri had given him. Although wet, the paper was thick and undamaged, and the writing remained legible.

Jisyel shook her head. 'That doesn't mean anything. South of the bay, we're in a different canton.'

Fenn raised his shoulders. He was starting to get used to not understanding what people said, but it didn't get any less frustrating.

'You aren't allowed to be here, Fenn. It's ruled by a different Laird now we're this side of the bay. And anyway, Torsten doubted its authenticity. Another Inquisitor could, too. Seems there's loads of them here right now.'

'Because of the other lost souls.' He'd been thinking about it for a while.

'I don't know why they're here.' She rubbed her eyes, then sighed, as if suddenly overwhelmed.

Fenn dared to hope she wouldn't hand him over. After meeting Torsten and the other Inquisitors, he'd rather take his chances alone in the wild. There'd been something dark in the man's eyes, a spark of cruelty that made his blood run cold.

To be locked up by him was something Fenn *never* wanted to happen.

He decided to take a risk. Thinking quickly, he said, 'Jisyel. Let me help you get back to Calidra. Just…don't hand me over to the Inquisitors.' It was clear that Jisyel needed encouragement, if not outright help, and with her in turmoil after everything that happened, he had to try. 'I can help point out if you're in danger of losing a finger or something, seeing as you seem to struggle to feel those things.'

Jisyel's face dropped, her usually easy smile disappearing.

'You didn't feel the cold of the water. Didn't even know about that cut on your face 'til I pointed it out.' Fenn gestured to her cheek. 'Even your fingers were turning blue and you had no idea. And you said Calidra had to remind you of things. Something wrong with *your* memory, too?'

99

Jisyel's gaze lowered, as if she was suddenly self-conscious. 'Hassen.'

It took Fenn a second to recall the name. 'The…Spirit of Salt Ash?'

She nodded, glancing away, almost shy. 'Three years ago…I was young and stupid. More reckless back then, if you can believe it. I managed to get on his bad side and he cursed me. Now, I can't…feel anything.' She raised a hand to her cheek, rested it on the cut and stared at the dried blood on her palm with faint surprise. 'Pain. Pleasure. Cold. Heat. Even food.'

A pang of sympathy rippled through Fenn's chest. 'You know what it's like to lose something, then. Some part of you that you're sure should be there?'

'Yes.' That one word from Jisyel endeared her to Fenn more than any action could.

'I want to find my memory, if it's possible. I don't know why this has happened to me, to all those other people, and I don't know how to fix it. But I'm going to try. I have to! If you hand me over to the Inquisitors, what's to stop Torsten driving that sword through me for looking at him the wrong way? He seemed keen enough.'

Jisyel shook her head. 'Torsten is a whole other class. Most Inquisitors are a shade more reasonable.'

Fenn shuddered. 'Even so, I don't want to be locked up. I *want* to know who I am. The answers are going to be out there, not in an Inquisitor's cell.'

Jisyel held her shoulder and looked away. 'It was unkind of Calidra to suggest dumping you on the Inquisitors—'

'It's fine.' He took a breath, steadying his frustration at his situation. Calidra had wanted him gone, but Jisyel had been more reluctant. With Calidra out of the picture for now, he had to take his chance with Jisyel. Convince her to *not* get rid of him, that helping each other was the best option for them both. 'But *I'll* help you, Jisyel, and you can help me? Perhaps, together, we'll be able to figure out a cure for whatever our curses are?'

Jisyel sighed. 'No offence, Fenn. You seem like a good lad, but we don't know you and—'

'I don't know you either!' Fenn interrupted, his frustration growing. 'But we've been thrown into this situation, so why not make the most of it?'

'Calidra would laugh at you and leave you here.'

Fenn shrugged. 'Maybe she would...But she's suspicious of everything and everyone, isn't she? And she's *not* here. Maybe by the time we catch up with them, things'll be clearer for me? I'll remember who I am, where I live, and be able to make my own way?'

'And if you don't?'

He didn't want to think about that. 'You never found a cure for your curse on the island. Maybe you will, here. What's to say I won't, too? Clearly there's a lot of us looking for answers at the moment.'

Jisyel dragged her hands down her face, then returned her attention to the water. Her smile faltered for a moment, then it returned, bigger than before. 'You're right. I can't do anything by sitting here and staring. Calidra will keep moving. We'll do the same.' Making her way back to their makeshift camp, she pulled down the last few bits of clothing from the branch they were drying on—her jacket, boots, and a sodden bag. She rifled through it then pouted, suddenly looking childish. 'Pastries are ruined.'

Fenn shook his head, realising what her curse meant. 'But...but you can't even taste them?'

'I *remember* what they taste like! Sometimes there's a hint of sugar on my tongue!'

Fenn grinned.

After throwing out whatever was of no use, Jisyel shouldered her bag and nodded to him. 'We'll follow the bay inland, further east. Without Ashothka, we're pretty poor, so there's no chance of getting supplies in Ulbridge. The sooner we get moving, the better off we'll be. Like you said, maybe we'll catch up with Calidra!' She'd cast away all sadness and was eager to get going.

Fenn buttoned up his doublet and nodded, following Jisyel as she led them away. Even with the immediate risk of being thrown to the Inquisitors removed, he knew they'd found themselves in a difficult situation. With no food, water, or coin, they were exposed and vulnerable.

Chimney smoke rose somewhere to the north and Fenn pointed. 'Might be some people over there who can help us?' He remembered Torsten's cold stare and shivered. 'Just hope there aren't any Inquisitors.'

Jisyel didn't object, and the pair of them headed away from the water and deeper into unknown territory. It took them only a handful of minutes to reach the source of the chimney smoke. A collection of steep-roofed buildings were gathered around a small farm. Each building was made of stone, rather than brick in Ballowton, but none had the strange purple lanterns or heavily paved streets.

There was only one road through the hamlet, with half a dozen buildings on either side, and fields sprawling out beyond. Of the few people who were up and around, most wore sleeveless tunics and heavy boots. All of them were carrying farming tools or animal feed.

One young boy of seven or eight carried a basket of eggs under one arm, and he was the first to notice Fenn and Jisyel. After taking one look at them, he raced off into the largest building, eggs forgotten on the side of the path.

Less than a minute later, a burly man exited what must have been his home, the boy following at his heels like an obedient dog. With short-cropped hair, neatly trimmed beard, and a confident stride, he appeared to be a leader of sorts. He adjusted his hat as he strode towards them.

'Can you help us please?' Jisyel hurried over to him,

before he'd even had a chance to speak. 'There was an attack in Ballowtown last night. We were caught in it and need food, help, whatever you can—'

'Ursah! It's not the Myr. Stop trying to get out of your chores!' The man smacked the boy over the head with his hat none-too-gently.

The boy—Ursah—let out a squeak and ran back to his forgotten eggs, then raced down the street and through an open gate into the nearest field.

Fenn scratched his nose. 'The Myr?'

'There are Myr here?' Jisyel flinched as if she'd been struck.

Replacing his hat on his head, the man shrugged. 'Sometimes. Well. Before that *queen* made everything worse.'

Jisyel looked around warily. 'You really had the Myr here? But...but it's so *normal*.'

The man folded his arms. 'The Myr *are* normal. Just a natural part of life. We learned to live with them out here.' He appraised her and narrowed his eyes. 'Not that I expect a Porsenthian to understand that.'

'*How?*' Jisyel was incredulous. 'They...they *kill* people! Destroy food!'

He curled his lip. 'You sound like those damned Inquisitors. Sure. They came every so often and we lost some of our weaker folk. But that's the nature of them. Death. We all gotta face it sometime. Now we have to give more money to that Iron Queen and get hounded by her Inquisitors if we don't pay up enough! Like we should be *grateful*!'

Fenn nudged Jisyel's shoulder. 'We came here for help, not to irritate him!'

'Fenn! He's talking about the *Myr* like they aren't a threat!'

He didn't understand what that meant, but the man was getting more irate.

'I don't have anything spare to help beggars. Go to the shrine. Beg for food there.'

Fenn could understand he and Jisyel probably looked in quite a sorry state—bedraggled as they were—but the man's assumption stung.

Exasperated, Jisyel threw up her hands. 'But—'

The man grabbed a scythe that had been resting against the wall and brandished it. 'Go beg somewhere else, or I'll assume you're here to steal.'

Unnerved by his hostility, Fenn pulled on Jisyel's sleeve, forcing her away.

'Please!' Jisyel tried again, before Fenn yanked her away and they hurried off.

Though the man hadn't been as cruel as Torsten, Fenn could see the same anger simmering under the surface. This time, there was no Varlot to help.

They didn't stop running until they reached the waters of the bay again, though they were further up than where they'd crawled out the previous night. Fenn sat on the damp grass and tilted his head back as he caught his breath, wondering what the Myr were and why Jisyel was so afraid of them.

Equally, he worried about Inquisitors and the locals here who were unhappy to see what they believed to be a pair of beggars. He needed to get away. 'What about my papers? How soon can we get out of this canton if I shouldn't be here?'

'Well, that guy might have been rude, but he wasn't wrong. There's a shrine not too far from here, a pretty big one. Might be we can get one of the priests there to vouch for you and give us something to eat, too.'

'A priest?'

'Of course. Each shrine worships a particular spirit—they call themselves Tassar's Guardians—so a word from one of their priests covers more than just a single canton. It should keep you safe from the Inquisitors. And they should have food and supplies, too. They're always helping those in need,

104

ever since the wars. I'm an idiot for not thinking of the shrine first.'

Fenn vaguely recalled Hassen saying something about being one of Tassar's Guardians, but he didn't ask more questions about that or the Myr—he'd risk confusing himself and getting overwhelmed again. The fog of his mind had yet to lift, but his headache, though much eased, was a constant companion. It wouldn't be long before the Bragalian sun bore down on them and worsened it. He wondered if it would finally disappear when his memories returned, as if his brain was constantly trying to remember and the effort caused him pain.

They kept to the edge of the water, keeping within sight of it at all times lest they stumbled upon more unfriendly locals. Jisyel said she'd been on this side of the bay only twice before, and there were a number of smaller villages and settlements that they were probably better off avoiding.

With a sigh, he fell into step behind Jisyel, hoping that when his memories finally returned, it would bring under-standing.

'THIS IS *SUCH* HOGSHIT!' Jisyel huffed in frustration.

They'd been walking all morning and most of the after-noon, and the path they'd been following had disappeared several times under large puddles of mud and wet grass—leftovers from the previous night's rainstorm. While they'd been careful to go around as much as possible, both were caked up to their waists in filth. It brought back rather unpleasant memories of the Isle of Salt.

Fenn's body ached as he tried to keep up with Jisyel, who'd hardly slowed her pace all day until they'd hit the mud. He tried not to laugh at her evident frustration at the lack of solid ground and offered her his hand for the third time in as many minutes.

With mud sucking at their every step, it was slow going. The shrine they were heading for dominated the horizon— sea-green stone spires curving on either side of the enormous, reflective building like a pair of giant wings. Two slender pillars flanked the shrine, and the building's cone-shaped roof pierced the sky like an arrow.

He'd been in awe when he'd first spotted it, but soon after, Jisyel had been bogged down by the sludgy path, and her complaints hadn't let up since the first deep mud puddle.

'We're nearly there, Jisyel. Just a bit further!' Fenn tried to comfort her, but she ignored him, too annoyed by the mud.

'I can't even *feel* it,' she said, despairing, 'every step is such an effort. It's so bloody annoying!' She hauled herself out of one spot, and took an enormous step forward, only to immediately sink into another puddle, right up to her knee.

Fenn grinned and offered his hand to help her forward again. At least she didn't have to worry about aching legs like he did. But that might be rubbing salt in the wound, so he kept that thought to himself.

She took his hand and pulled herself out of the mud— leaving her boot stuck in place. 'Doesn't help that we're going to Neros's Shrine. Fanatical worshippers.'

'Is that a problem?' Fenn looked up at the shrine, suddenly more foreboding than wondrous.

Jisyel swore again and yanked her boot free with a loud squelch, mud splattering up her tunic. 'Well, beggars can't be choosers, I suppose.'

Fenn helped her across the rest of the sludgy mud to the stone path that marked the end of walking on grass and dirt. Thankfully, the road to the shrine had been paved, and it was a relief to finally have something solid underfoot.

He wiped his muddy hands on his doublet. 'Right! Now we're out of that!' he gestured vaguely at the way they'd come, 'is there anything I should know? Do? Before we get to the shrine?' The last thing he wanted was another incident like with Torsten.

Jisyel thought, her frustration easing now she was out of the mud. 'Hmm. I don't think so.'

'Sure? I don't even know who Neros *is*.'

'Ah.' She stopped in her tracks and turned to him with a frown, as if suddenly remembering he knew nothing. 'Neros is the Spirit of the Lasseen Ocean.'

Fenn briefly recalled a conversation about that spirit on the boat to Bragalia. 'Of the sea?'

She nodded. 'Like Hassen is the Spirit of Salt Ash, the forest on the Isle of Salt? That's his domain. He *is* the forest. If it were to be cut down or burned, Hassen would disappear. Likewise, Neros is the Spirit of the Lasseen Ocean. She *is* the water, and the water is her. As it's a bigger domain, she is *much* more powerful. Any forest that's big enough will usually become a spirit. That's why there are so many forest spirits, you know?'

He didn't know, but he gestured for her to continue, glad for the explanation. It was more than he'd received from Calidra—getting *anything* from that woman was more likely to earn him a scowl or a knife waved in his face than the requested answers.

'Same with lakes. Mountains. Any area that has enough life energy. Which includes people living nearby.'

Fenn struggled to imagine what a mountain spirit might look like, how big one might be, but he didn't interrupt.

'But, Neros is…different from other spirits. She doesn't offer her followers boons, but neither does she harm people. Directly, anyway.'

'I didn't know spirits did that.'

'Oh yes.' Jisyel continued down the path towards the shrine.

Lines of soil had been dug up on either side, flowers

planted and opening their vibrant petals to the sunshine. Most were blue or green, with a few white ones dotted in here and there to break up the colour. Fenn didn't recognise any of them. He wanted to spend a minute or two to look at them, partly to see if any jogged his memory and partly just to enjoy their fragrant scent—a nice change after the silty waters of the bay and the muddy path they'd just fought their way along.

Jisyel said, 'It's why most people worship a particular spirit. They hope to get their blessing, or something that'll help their lives. But Neros doesn't do any of that. She ignores her worshippers. And even though her shrine is one of the most glorious in all of Tassar, Neros doesn't even acknowledge it.'

'So why do people worship her? If they don't get anything out of it?'

'That's why they're considered fanatics.' Jisyel shrugged. 'Joining one of the orders is too much work as far as I'm concerned. I just want *one* spirit to get rid of Hassen's curse, I don't care which.'

Fenn mulled it over. The neat lines of flowerbeds expanded out into dozens of rows, with a number of trees providing shady corners here and there. To one side, a large field grew potatoes; another grew beans; a third, carrots. Nestled between them were other vegetables and plants that he didn't recognise. Water fountains appeared among the foliage, too, each one bigger than the one before, and the larger ones were adorned with statues carved from marble— depicting flowing water, fish, and even the dragon spirit herself. The closer they got to the shrine, the more elaborate the decorations. His stomach rumbled at the sight of the vegetables, and he considered sneaking into the field to pick a few, when he spotted several people crouched over the plants wearing wide-brimmed straw hats, tending to the gardens.

A few glanced up as they passed, but most were too interested in their work to pay them any mind. He stopped where he was and looked back across the fields and plants. It was nice to not be stared at for once, as if he was a sudden and unwanted growth that had sprouted on someone's arm. 'No-one's interested in us?'

'Come on, quickly. You must be starving.'

Fenn's stomach growled as if in response, and he quickened his pace. If he'd even considered stealing vegetables, he *really* needed a meal. 'You don't get hungry?'

'Oh I do. I just don't feel it. Better to eat little and often, in case no-one's around to remind me I'll collapse because I last ate breakfast three days before.'

Fenn chuckled at that.

More wildflowers dotted the lush grass surrounding the shrine, which seemed to rise from the ground like an ocean wave. At first, Fenn had thought it was made of glass, but up close, he could see it was some sort of stone, polished to glint in the sun. Water cascaded down the side of the shrine, plunging into a narrow moat that encircled the building. Dark green and red sea grasses floated on the water, swaying gently in the current caused by the waterfall.

At the centre of the building, an enormous stone door lay wide open, a dragon carved onto it in gold, wings extended in all their splendour, mouth open to spew flames. The door had to be fifteen feet tall, and wide enough for two carriages to drive through.

A large crowd congregated in the courtyard. Some people saw to the myriad of plants and water features dotted around the shrine's entranceway, while others stirred enormous cookpots, serving steaming stew in small, wooden bowls to a queue of waiting people. Aside from the hungry people, everyone else wore long, flowing robes in shades of silver, cream, or blue.

Poorer folk wore plain robes of roughspun cotton,

though a few had been dyed brown or grey. Many were thin and underfed, and several sported injuries that the priests—Fenn assumed the robed people were priests—were helping with.

He wondered if any of them had fled here from the hamlets and villages surrounding Ballowtown, scared off by recent attacks.

'Can we have something to eat, too?' Jisyel had already crossed the wide courtyard and was speaking with the nearest robed man as he served food from a cookpot.

He was tall with ginger hair, his skin pale in comparison to most of the Bragalians gathered. He had an intricate tattoo in blue-green ink on the back of his left hand. Lines swirled around one another, similar to waves of water. 'Talk to one of the priests inside, first. These people have been waiting here all night.' He gestured to the line with a long, metal ladle, brown gravy and chunks of carrot dripping from it.

Fenn tried to keep himself from drooling at the sight.

Jisyel waved him over enthusiastically. 'Inside, Fenn! Come on.'

Taking another moment to look around and gather his courage, he hurried past the people queueing for food and caught up to Jisyel who waited for him at the open doorway. She stamped her feet by the door, and chunks of dried mud fell off her boots on the grey stone.

Fenn copied the motion, following her inside, eyes round in awe. The grey stone floor quickly gave way to a mosaic of blue and green tiles, all in irregular shapes and varnished so smooth he slipped over. Jisyel caught him before he cracked a limb on the floor, the two of them balancing each other.

Incense burned somewhere deep within the shrine, and the scent of salt, honey, and something pungent like moss hit his nose. His eyes watered at the strength of it, and he struggled not to cough in case it would be disrespectful. Inside was vast, the ceiling so tall it was bathed in shadow far above him. Deep alcoves had been carved into the walls at regular intervals, the sound of running water somehow louder, and Fenn wondered if there were more waterfalls inside, even though he couldn't see them. It certainly *felt* like a shrine to the sea.

The few people who were inside drifted about in soft slippers and long robes like ghosts. They spoke in hushed voices which were swallowed by the expanse.

Jisyel approached the nearest priest, whose cream robes were edged in gold. His tattoo was more elaborate than the man who'd been serving food—it disappeared up his sleeve. She clutched his arm, stopping him mid-step. 'Please, we need—'

The priest peered down his nose at her for a long moment before pulling his sleeve away with a dismissive snort. 'Leave this sacred place, cursed one. Neros does not welcome you.'

Unperturbed, Jisyel scurried across the delicate floor, her steps echoing loudly, to grab the attention of the next—a priestess, her dark hair threaded with silver. Wearing silver robes that shimmered in the low light, she gave Jisyel a few seconds longer than the other priest, before gesturing to the door and speaking in a dialect Fenn couldn't understand.

Jisyel tried with three others, the pair of them walking deeper into the shrine, where the incense grew stronger. His heart sank with every rejection, yet Jisyel grew more animated, ever more determined to get them something to eat. 'Doesn't anyone here care if we starve? If we're cursed, surely we're *more* deserving of help?'

Her shouts caught the notice of more priests and priestesses, who shuffled towards them, arms wide as they herded the duo back to the door. 'There is no food for those without peace. You are both tainted and cannot enjoy Neros's bounty. Cleanse yourselves, then you may return to this sacred place.'

The dismissal hurt, but Fenn mirrored Jisyel's determination and tried his luck, too. 'A small bowl each, then we'll be on our way? Please?'

But they ignored him, ushering the pair towards the door.

If they weren't willing to share food, why would they be willing to vouch for him and sign new papers to let him travel? Fenn's stomach knotted at the thought of ending up with the Inquisitors despite everything, and fury burned hot in his chest. He'd fight his way out, if he had to. If they tried to chain him up or throw him in prison.

Back in the sunlit courtyard, Fenn took a deep breath. The heavy smells within the shrine had worsened his headache, and he turned to Jisyel. 'Is there another shrine somewhere near? We aren't getting anywhere with this one. I thought you said they helped people in need?'

Jisyel ran a hand through her hair and shook her head. 'I can't believe it! I *knew* they were a bit weird here. Didn't realise they were so nasty, too.' She stuck out her tongue at the shrine and snorted at the priests and priestesses gathered in the courtyard. 'Stupid shrine. Stupid spirits. Stupid, stupid, stupid!'

'I'm glad I wasn't the only one who didn't know they wouldn't help.' Fenn doubted it would comfort Jisyel, but it was nice that he wasn't on the back foot alone. 'Although after that experience, I wish I'd stayed without a memory of this place.'

'Without a memory?'

They whirled round at the sound of a woman's voice and came face to face with another priestess. Her robes had been cream, once, but they had patches of grey and white where sections had been bleached in the sun, and there were several holes dotted her long sleeves as if a moth had had its way with it. Through the holes, her intricate, green-silver tattoo was visible as it ran up her arm. Her short, curled blonde hair and pale blue eyes were in contrast to her light brown skin, and she seemed to glow in the sunlight, picturesque. Despite a thin, white scar across her right eye, she was the picture of serenity. 'Another amnesiac, are you? There've been so many lately. You did well to avoid the Inquisitors. I heard Torsten himself has travelled to Bragalia.'

'Your friends said I was tainted.' Fenn folded his arms. Suddenly Calidra's mindset of treating everyone with suspicion didn't seem like such a bad idea. 'And I met Torsten in Ballowtown, as a matter of fact.'

The priestess raised an eyebrow. 'A stroke of luck that you weren't taken.'

'Our luck's run out.' Jisyel stepped forward. 'The city was attacked and we were thrown into the bay. We were separated from our friend—Calidra Vantonen, daughter of the Laird of Fellwood. We don't have any food, coin, or supplies. Please, can you spare a bowl of stew? We'll be out of here straight after, promise! Surely you can't turn us away if we need help?'

'If you wouldn't mind vouching for me, that would help us get out of here sooner,' Fenn added, latching onto Jisyel's words.

The priestess chuckled, the sound somehow too low, as if it didn't suit her petite frame. 'How can I vouch for you if I don't know you?'

'S—sorry! My name is Fenn.' He straightened up and brushed away dirt and mud from his doublet, aware he looked rather dishevelled. Cautious or not, he *had* to impress her. They'd run out of people who'd even *look* at him without turning up their noses. Although calm and serene, the priestess seemed different from the others at the shrine— even ignoring her scar. She'd certainly not been brought up in the order to have acquired something like *that*. Fenn tried not to stare at it.

'I'm Jisyel Herbst. My grandmother, Bellandri, owns a tavern in Hogsbrook.'

'Ah, so you're from the island.' It was a statement, not a

question.

Jisyel nodded, one eye twitching.

'Well. That explains *your* curse, Jisyel. It must be tricky with Hassen. Such a young spirit. So mischievous, and with the arrogance of youth, too.' She narrowed her eyes at Fenn. 'But it does not explain *you*, amnesiac.'

'He's been cursed, too. Hassen sometimes goes on sprees. He turned a perfectly good pond into a muddy bog just the other day!' Jisyel cut in, almost shoving Fenn to one side to keep the priestess's attention on her. 'Might we know your name, Priestess of Neros? To formally ask your aid?'

Fenn would have protested at being pushed out the way again—he was beyond sick and tired of that—but he held his tongue. He didn't want to blow it again, like he'd done with Torsten.

The priestess stared at him for several long moments. He found his gaze drawn to the scar on her face again, and he quickly looked away, cheeks reddening.

'Selys Ioran, of Segandis,' she said after a moment. 'My heart bleeds for the lost souls of Bragalia. There are so many. I've seen them from a distance, taken away by Inquisitors. But I've not seen one up close until you, Fenn.'

'Segandis? Lots of pirates down there.' Jisyel took a step backwards. 'How'd you end up here?'

'So, you'll help me?' Where Selys came from meant nothing, and Fenn hoped she could help him. He offered the priestess the biggest grin he could, as if that alone would persuade her.

'Having seen you now, I think there *is* a cure for your curse, though you may not like it.'

The world seemed to spin, and Fenn staggered under the sudden surge of pain through his head and hope in his chest. All of a sudden he found it difficult to breathe.

Selys didn't notice. 'Jisyel, you've clearly been affected by Hassen. But *you*, Fenn? On you, I sense the touch of the Myr.'

7

THE MESSAGE
TORSTEN

Drab scrubland rolled past the open window. Clumps of dust were thrown up by the horses' hooves and the large, rattling carriage wheels. Above the soft yellows and browns, the cloudless blue sky was harsh. It mirrored Torsten's frustration at being in this place.

They'd left Ballowtown early, before dawn, at his behest. Nadja and Sarron had done a decent job of the cleanup, and he'd been sure to pass on official word that it had been a rabid animal which had attacked. He expected the Bragalians to accept that, especially as it came from the Master Inquisitor. Regardless of how they felt about him, his words carried weight.

But the particulars weren't important.

As long as the people remained oblivious to the Myrish spirit—he couldn't think what else it could be—nothing else mattered. With the Iron Crown in power, they were safe from the Myr. Porsenthia and Bragalia had put their faith in that fact, and nothing was permitted to shake it.

Even the other Inquisitors knew nothing about his task of

7

115

looking into Queen Surayo's concerns, and his hardest job right now was keeping it that way. Nadja, in particular, appeared to consider questioning his orders more than ever, especially after she'd come across the scene of the battle. She wasn't an idiot, and knew it wasn't a wild bear. He'd need to nip that in the bud.

If only he'd *known* he was dealing with something Myrish, he'd have kept his Inquisitors away to begin with. Fewer eyes to see and fewer mouths to gossip. Why hadn't the queen been honest with him if she'd truly been concerned that the Myr were returning?

Perhaps she'd not believed it possible.

She'd been too afraid to give it words.

At least *he* now knew it was something Myrish—but what, exactly, he couldn't say. He'd fought his share of them while they'd been at war, but their spirits were so numerous, so vast and ever-changing, constructs of pure magic, that he'd never learned the differences between them.

They all died the same way.

Toriaken and the Porsenthian military had made sure of that.

Even *he'd* assumed Surayo was mistaken, and worried over nothing. He hadn't truly expected to see the presence of any danger, let alone the Myr. Perhaps her magic was not as flawless as she'd led everyone to believe. Her threads of farsight weaved across her empire like a spider's web, waiting for the tell-tale touch of their enemies.

Torsten had no real understanding of how it worked, but the mage queen hadn't done wrong up until now.

Before he could do anything else to contribute to his queen's Myrish cover up, he needed to travel north. He'd not expected to be thrown into battle, nor call upon Miroth's strength to survive it, and that power had to be restored. *That* was more important than anything else, and he weathered Nadja's confused scowls and questioning glances as they left Ballowtown behind far sooner than they'd expected.

After a few hours on the road, Nadja broke the silence of the carriage, 'We've left days earlier than we were scheduled.' It wasn't a question, no doubt her words were strategically chosen to avoid his rebuke.

Torsten replied, 'We've rounded up the lost souls from Ballowtown. No need to stay in Bragalia longer than necessary.'

'Of course, sir.' Nadja gave him a sharp nod, then returned her gaze to the window, unwilling to speak further.

Over the bumpy terrain, their journey was far from smooth, but they'd covered a decent amount of ground already that morning. They'd left the hills surrounding Ballowtown far behind, and the high Bragalian Mountains loomed to the east. Once past their shadows, they'd be back on Porsenthian soil, and he would be able to breathe a sigh of relief.

Another bump over the dusty land sent a shiver of pain down Torsten's back and he winced. These cross-country trips were getting to be more of a hindrance every time. As a crown dependency, they were as safe in Bragalia as they would be in Porsenthia, but the land was scattered and chaotic, ruled by Lairds—little more than warlords with more gold, sense, or man power than their rivals—which always made discussions tense. Violence was a constant threat to Inquisitors, and with all the lost souls suddenly appearing, Torsten had his work cut out to maintain order among the people, whether Porsenthian or Bragalian.

Torsten had left Sarron in Ballowtown, having tasked the young Inquisitor with trailing Varlot. Torsten had given him strict instructions to report only to himself, even if it meant waiting until they returned to Eastbrook before getting an update. He'd sent Sarron on the mission partly to test the

Inquisitor's skills, but also because he wanted Varlot watched. Having the former General back in the open had thrown his normally infallible demeanour, and he wanted to know what the man was up to.

Harder to kill than a cockroach, Varlot had survived more than his fair share of battles against opponents—both Myrish and otherwise. But he'd quit the army unceremoniously after being found attacking other soldiers after one too many drinks. It had been allowed to slide up until one new recruit had ended up paralyzed from the neck down. Even Varlot's proficiency on the battlefield hadn't saved him from a dismissal.

The recruit had been the queen's cousin.

And yet, Torsten was only a Master Inquisitor because of Varlot.

Had Varlot not been dismissed, Torsten would never have been chosen for the promotion.

Although Varlot was prone to violence, especially after a drink, he hadn't been responsible for the soldier's paralysis.

Torsten had. One of his questionings gone wrong in his overzealousness.

He folded his arms and pushed away those memories of his past, and warmth flooded his chest to help ease the darkness away. Reminiscing was never a good thing. What mattered was what lay ahead of him.

Torsten and the other Inquisitors were fortunate that Queen Surayo was linked with Toriaken, the Spirit of Iron. It meant most communication with her was not done via written reports sent by pigeons, ravens, or horses, as was the norm in other countries. Instead, *they* had a direct link to their queen which negated the need for such slow, primitive communication.

Tinebás hung at his hip, the tiny spot of rust glinting dully in the light that streamed through the carriage window. On his other hip was sheathed a slender dagger, identical to all those given to Inquisitors or high-ranking palace or government officials. Forged of iron, it was heavy, crude, and more ornamental than a functioning weapon.

But it was their link to the queen through her spirit, when called upon.

Her way of keeping tabs on them, on obtaining information as quickly as it was learned, without straining her magic or being too invasive—making it a useful tool for quick messages and sharing information. It had been part of why the Porsenthian Empire had been so formidable over the centuries, and Surayo, the current Supreme Ruler and Queen-Empress, had followed in her parent's footsteps to keep her people in line and safe from the Myr.

Torsten held in a snort.

She would be expecting a report by now. The previous night, in fact, and she never appreciated lateness. He folded his arms and shifted on the slightly padded seat, ignoring the incessant weight on his hip. She could wait for now.

Leaning his head back to rest on the wooden board, he closed his eyes, exhaling slowly. If he wasn't careful, the carriage movement would lull him into sleep. It would not do to lose focus while in Bragalia.

The creature had been destroyed, of that he was sure. There weren't many things that could survive the direct flames of a spirit, even a young one like Miroth. But he wondered if there were others, slinking into Porsenthia and hiding in the shadows. The thought of it made his skin crawl. Those creatures back again, scuttling in the darkness, bringing death and misery everywhere they went. No. It had to be just one Myrish creature.

The idea that there could be more of these things…

He shuddered, ignoring it for now. Miroth's need was more pressing. Once he'd visited the shine, things would—

'Torsten, sir?'

Nadja's query brought Torsten's attention back to the

carriage. He glanced out the window first—in case some threat was hurtling towards them—before looking at his comrade.

'Shouldn't we have spoken with Queen Surayo?'

Torsten narrowed his eyes slightly, but Nadja held his gaze. She was experienced and efficient enough to be considered for promotion to Master Inquisitor, and she knew her worth. 'Our orders—'

'Come from me, do they not?'

Nadja nodded.

'We *are* following my latest orders. Nothing else is your concern.' Torsten's voice was clipped, hardly concealing his frustration.

'The sooner we're back in Porsenthia the better,' Nadja said, unfazed by Torsten's annoyance, 'I don't like the reported sightings of the Myr.'

'Nonsense,' Torsten said. 'The Myr wouldn't dare set foot on our land. Not while Toriaken breathes.'

'Perhaps. But the reports are what they are.'

'You believe some foolish peasants' account of what they saw over Queen Surayo's magic? Over Toriaken?' Torsten lifted his chin. 'She would sense the moment any Myrish magic set foot on the continent.'

Nadja shifted, clearly uncomfortable. 'Most reports are not without merit.'

'The same thing as in Ballowtown, I'm sure. Possibly a plague or some disease that's taken hold of a few wild creatures. Or a corrupted spirit causing issues. With the Laird of Fellwood dead, the Bragalians are on edge, looking for any reason to turn to violence. What if they burned down a forest or poisoned a lake? Spirits tend to take offense to that sort of thing.' It wasn't completely unheard of. Spirits grew mischievous or bored with people, and often impacted Tassar in strange or frightening ways when their domains were harmed. Even Miroth behaved unpredictably at times, and Torsten was bonded with him. 'Our job is to investigate those lost souls and bring them in for questioning. If the Myr *were* here, you'd know.'

'I should hope so.'

'Even if it were true, we have the queen's magic, the Porsenthian forces, and Toriaken himself. Nadja, curiosity is useful, but do not let it become a burden. We are safe.'

THEY STOPPED and set up camp after six hours on the dusty road, their small caravan of three horse-drawn wagons parking in a loose circle, the Salt Sea far in the distance to the west. Queen Surayo had sent five Apprentice Inquisitors alongside himself and his two comrades to investigate the amnesiacs, most of whom busied themselves with tending the horses, getting a fire going, and cooking food. Three of them sorted out the lost souls they'd collected, ensuring they had fresh water and something to eat.

Torsten didn't bother himself with the prisoners. They were traitors, each and every one. Part of some conspiracy against the Iron Crown, he was certain of it.

Either that, or they were pretending to know nothing so they could take advantage of the Inquisitors' generosity. If the rules were completely up to him, he'd have them chained and flogged until they began speaking sense. Surayo had too much of a soft touch, regardless of what the general populace thought.

'Have a message sent to Tonmouth so they are aware of our arrival,' Torsten addressed Nadja. 'I want them to be ready to receive us. No delays.'

'Yes sir.'

Torsten cast his gaze skywards, squinting at the bright sun. He couldn't put her off any longer.

The other Inquisitors set up camp with practiced efficiency while Nadja made her way to their supply of red pigeons, parchment already in hand. Everyone had their role, and they worked together like cogs in clockwork. As they didn't need direct supervision or additional orders, Torsten made his way across the clearing, heading up a gentle slope. Here, grass grew in thick tufts, dryer than in Porsenthia, but a far cry from the brown scrubland further south. That, alone, made him more comfortable. He was on the edge of home.

Once he was a suitable distance from camp, Torsten knelt down beside a hedgerow, careful to avoid thorns and jutting branches, and pulled the ornate iron dagger from his belt. A ruby had been pressed into the hilt, and he rubbed his thumb against it briefly. Even in his gloved hand, the dagger was warm—though he was never sure if it was Toriaken or Surayo. In one, smooth movement, he plunged it tip-first into the soil, tapping into the spirit's magic.

Toriaken was powerful, could split his consciousness across anything made of iron, but he still had to be called upon. If he spent all his awareness across every instance of iron in Tassar, he'd never be able to fight. This was a direct link to the spirit—to Queen Surayo herself—in a way that did not drain the dragon's power too much.

Torsten only just had time to scramble backwards before the blade lit up, light bursting forth in a barrage of flaming sparks. It fizzed like molten steel plunged in cold water.

Despite the shower of fire, none of the dry grass caught— it was an illusion, nothing more.

'You're late.'

The woman's voice that emanated from the fire was laced with barely suppressed anger, lowering her regal tone into a warning snarl.

Carefully pushing his face into a mask of impassivity—it was never a good idea to show weakness or vulnerability in front of a spirit—Torsten took a breath and waited for the illusion to complete. It didn't take long. Over his many years of service to the Iron Crown, he'd seen Toriaken form from the iron dagger hundreds, perhaps thousands of times. Even so, his heart often skipped a beat at the sight of the enormous spirit forming on the grass beside the blade—looking at him with the queen's eyes, and speaking with the queen's tongue.

Toriaken, the Spirit of Iron, was one of the most powerful dragons in all of Tassar. At more than two hundred feet in length and with a wingspan twice as long, Toriaken dwarfed practically every other dragon in existence. Yet the one before him now was a shadow of that greatness; hardly a quarter of the size, but no less imposing.

Unlike most spirits, who were bound to their domains—a forest, a mountain, an ocean—Toriaken's domain covered almost every inch of the world. Everywhere iron could be found, deep within the ground, gave the spirit power. His soul had been bound in a sword by one of Queen Surayo's ancestors, and the spirit had served her bloodline ever since. While his true form and power remained by the queen's side at all times, he had enough influence over the iron given to the Inquisitors that he could see and hear through it when required to do so.

It was this ability that enabled Queen Surayo's eyes and ears to cover all of her lands through her Inquisitors, or anyone else that carried one of the many iron daggers she used for long-distance communication.

Though only an illusion, an echo of Toriaken's real power, the cinereous dragon which stood in front of the iron dagger towered above Torsten, scales glinting dully. Steam poured from his nostrils with every breath, misting around his bulky body and blown by a wind that Torsten could not feel. Six thick horns protruded from the back of his head; two more from his lower jaw; and a twin line of sharp ridges jutted out along his spine, running all the way down to the enormous, spiked club at the end of his long tail. Toriaken peered down at the Inquisitor, waiting.

If Torsten were to be brave—or stupid—enough to approach, he would walk straight through the apparition. But the dragon was so vast that even a mirage was an impressive sight. It demanded reverence.

'There was an incident in Ballowtown,' Torsten said by way of explanation. He was certain not to apologise for his lateness, which he knew was rude, and not something he'd permit from anyone else, but he enjoyed keeping the queen hanging on his words. She was more powerful than he by far, so he took whatever opportunities for control he could get. And considering she'd sent him away to investigate something she'd not even shared the details of—any Myrish creature could easily kill an individual—he was less keen than usual to be forthright with her for the slight. He straightened up and put his arms behind his back. 'No Inquisitor deaths, though a couple of the townsfolk were injured. We left early this morning and it's possible they will live.'

'And...? What incident?'

Torsten knew she was asking whether her fears *had* been correct. He wondered whether she'd suspected it was the Myr all along, and decided not to tell him. He'd been sent to investigate in the dark, like a lamb to slaughter. If he hadn't been so good at his job, he would've probably died.

He held the queen in the palm of his hand. To tell the truth, that the Myr were back, would reveal a chink in her supposedly infallible iron armour. To lie would reassure her, and turn her attention away from himself while he conducted his own investigations on the scope of the problem. If a few more Bragalians died while he did so, it was a small price to pay.

He decided to stroke her ego while skirting the details. 'In truth, I'm not sure, your Majesty. The creature was not one I am familiar with. Some old spirit, perhaps? But the citizens and officers of Ballowtown agree it was some rabid animal. A bear or wild cat is the story being circulated. They do not look to you with any suspicion.'

'As well they should not!' Toriaken replied with Surayo's voice, the reply a little too sharp, giving away her fear.

Torsten held back a smile.

'You destroyed it?'

'I did.' Torsten kept his arms stiff. He had a sudden urge to grab hold of the tooth in his pocket he'd claimed from the creature, and inspect it. 'As we speak, we're on the edge of southern Porsenthia. It shouldn't be more than a few days until we return to the capital. There was, however, some truth to the reports of an influx of people without papers. Seems there are over a dozen of these lost souls wandering around.'

'In Bragalia?'

'Yes, though I wonder whether there will be others in Porsenthia soon, if not already..'

'Hmm.'

Torsten said nothing more while the queen thought. As long as she was slightly off-kilter, she was less formidable, and that gave him the breathing room he wanted. Once he'd worked out the significance of the threat, he could adjust his actions accordingly.

After a moment, the dragon lashed his tail. 'I must act as if our enemies are moving against me. If the Myr have recovered...that is my greatest concern. I had thought the last major strike in Malbosh would have put a stop to them for good. The armistice should still be in effect and there are none of their artefacts left to give them strength. I wonder...'

There it was. Admission. 'There is nothing to wonder, my queen. Things are as they should be.' His forehead glistened with a fine sheen of sweat. Perhaps if he had been in the presence of Surayo herself, she'd be able to see through his dismissal. But she was hundreds of leagues away, speaking with her magic through the spirit of a dragon, and that meant he could get away with more. She had less chance of picking up minute details that might give away his white lies.

'Are they?' Toriaken fixed his attention on him, his deep blue eyes vast and empty as midnight.

He rolled his shoulders. 'Should anything change, I shall of course inform you. Otherwise, we will return to Eastbrook with the lost souls we've collected. I would be more interested in the Bragalians and the Olmese flouting your rules than about what's left of the Myr.'

'Perhaps. I wonder if these...lost souls...have anything to do with the disturbance I felt.'

'You are certain about your magic?'

'It was very slight...'

'Would you like me to bring in another mage to the palace? Perhaps a Bragalian—'

'No.'

Torsten frowned, but smoothed his face back into a neutral expression a moment later. He hoped the dragon hadn't noticed. Deciding to ease her worries, he said, 'Beggars and peasants turn up everywhere, especially in Bragalia. Cursed knaves. Wretched, the lot of them. Summer will be bountiful, it always brings out the scavengers. And the Fellwood Laird's death will have brought more chaos, no doubt.'

'I'm sure there will be answers soon enough.'

Torsten dropped his gaze for a moment.

'Something bothers you, Master Inquisitor?' Toriaken let out a snarl. 'What else have you seen?'

He swallowed, thinking quickly. 'The former General was in Ballowtown.'

'Varlot?'

'Yes. I sent Sarron to tail him.'

'What does he think he's doing?' A wave of heat washed

over him as the queen's fury echoed through the dragon's fire.

'Precisely why I sent an Inquisitor after him.' Torsten took a step back as if mildly inconvenienced by the surge in temperature. He shook his head. 'Then…if there is nothing else, my queen?'

'Very well. I will see you when you reach Eastbrook, Torsten. Ensure your return is timely. Report immediately if there are any changes. Toriaken will fly south and patrol the border in case anything tries to enter Porsenthia.'

Torsten sank to one knee again, bowing his head low. He'd never been comfortable exposing his neck to Toriaken, even if he was an illusion. The whumpf of fire told him the spirit had dissipated and when Torsten stood up again, he allowed his frown to linger. 'Suspicious woman.'

He supposed she needed to have a healthy dose of caution. Anyone did if they wanted to retain a position of power. He wondered whether there was a real Myrish threat within their borders. None of their spirits had been seen anywhere on the Etrovian continent for five years. Perhaps it had just been one, desperate creature, forced into Bragalia by circumstance.

Whatever the reason for it being here, he'd disposed of it.

However, there was no way of knowing if there were any more. Were they truly on the cusp of a new invasion?

Surayo's magic was rarely wrong, whatever he thought of the queen herself, and it bothered him that he didn't have all the answers. Until he knew more, had a handle on the situation, there was no need to inform her, or the other Inquisitors.

He took a few steps forward then knelt down, collecting the iron dagger. It seemed to weigh more than before. Slipping it back into his belt, Torsten looked to the west, where the Salt Sea was a thin line of grey-green on the edge of the horizon.

If there were Myrish spirits here, the armistice would be broken.

And they'd be on the brink of another war.

He needed to get to Miroth's Shrine, first. Then he could return to the palace.

8

THE FORSAKEN

CALIDRA

On the second morning in Meadowhill, Calidra couldn't take waiting any longer. 'Jisyel should have been here by now!'

Varlot glanced up from the table, his attention pulled from the coins he was counting out. They had a reasonable amount, but they'd need to be frugal if it was to last. He said nothing and went back to counting, but Calidra could sense his growing impatience, and the frustration that spilled from it. Although he'd been nothing but cordial to her, she knew she was pushing her luck by forcing them to wait.

They'd shared a ramshackle room above a butcher's shop on the edge of town—again under Varlot's coin—but it had been cheap, with a good view of the river and the main road into town. If Jisyel and Fenn were coming, they'd spot them first from their vantage point, and had taken turns to keep watch while the other rested.

Calidra knew she was prone to bouts of anxiety—often unwarranted—and Jisyel was the one who kept her grounded, but this time it felt like the *right* emotion to have. Jisyel and Fenn could be long-drowned by now, their bloated corpses already washed out to sea. Or devoured by some predatory fish.

The idea of it made her want to vomit again.

Almost as bad was her dependence on Varlot. Without him, she had less coin, no comfort, and no way to cope. If he grew bored of her, or decided his own contract to her family was of greater importance, and left, there would be nothing she could do about it. It was a delicate balance—abide by his travelling wishes as much as possible while looking for Jisyel.

She, too, was on a deadline. The funeral was in two days, and she'd wasted so much time sitting around, waiting, hoping, doing nothing. Like an idiot. If she didn't make it in time, she'd never have a chance at rebuilding the relationship with her family. Would never be able to bring Jisyel into it, either. She could cope without her mother's acceptance. But it didn't stop her being desperate for it all the same.

Going back home to Fellwood was something she'd put off for eight years. The message had been sent with the expectation of her attendance at the funeral—and she *did* want to go—she just didn't want to deal with her mother while there. All her memories of her mother revolved around being punished whenever she did something wrong—which had been constantly throughout her childhood. Or she'd be punished if she did something in a way her mother disapproved of. And it went deeper than that, not that Calidra wanted to dwell on her mother's penchant for guilt-tripping, manipulation, and anger issues. But it had moulded her into the person she was today.

It was no wonder she'd spent so long running from it, running from *her*. Calidra had buried her head and pretended those problems didn't exist for close to a decade, that she didn't know how to face them again.

Wasn't sure she *could*.

If she turned up too late, tail between her legs, she might

as well have not bothered ever leaving the island. She could already imagine her mother's sour expression, the bite in her voice, at her lateness. Her disrespect. Just another failure. Another *disappointment*.

Calidra took a steadying breath, wondering if she should ever have left the island with Jisyel.

'The funeral is overmorrow, isn't it? We can't really wait any longer if you want to make it in time.' Varlot's tone was gentle, but firm. And, of course, he was absolutely right. Even if Jisyel and Fenn were to stroll into Meadowhill in the next minute, they'd be hard-pushed to reach Fellwood in time.

'What if Fenn and Jisyel passed through? They could be in Fellwood already, waiting for you? Or part-way, in Vaelar? Depends where the water spat them out.'

Calidra whirled around at Varlot's suggestion. She'd been so preoccupied with worst case scenarios and guilting herself for leaving Jisyel behind that she'd not even considered that possibility. 'In Fellwood so soon?'

Varlot shrugged, putting the coins in a drawstring bag. 'You waited a day in Ballowtown. Another here. They could easily have been in and out of Meadowhill before we even arrived.'

Her heart soared for a brief moment, then critical suspicion—ever-present—reared its head. Varlot wanted to get to Fellwood as quickly as he could. He had a contract for one, and would be paid for babysitting her, for another. It was possible he just wanted to keep them moving in as polite a way as possible for his own gains.

The smile fell off her lips, replaced by a frown. And yet, he *could* be correct. 'Jisyel...'

'You have an entire canton to be thinking of, Calidra. With the Laird dead, shouldn't you be getting to Fellwood sooner rather than later? Not worrying about one woman? She's from the Isle of Salt, right? So she's Porsenthian? Don't you think it's a bit silly for the daughter of a Bragalian Laird to bother herself with that?'

Heat flushed up her neck. Coincidence or not, what Varlot said was dangerously close to her mother's last words to her. It drove out logic and filled her head with the frustrating emotion that often blocked everything else out: anger.

'I'm allowed to worry about whoever I want!' Her words were out before she could stop them, she hadn't even been aware she'd thought them. 'Bragalia doesn't exactly need me, anyway. There are half a dozen Lairds and queen's Inquisitors doing a good enough job of that. And mother has always ruled the canton while father defended the borders.'

She scowled at Varlot, a former General in the Porsenthian army, a highly decorated military war-hero, who had survived numerous battles and claimed to be impossible to kill. He was so sure of himself, so confident. The complete opposite of her.

It was no wonder he wasn't bothered by any of her concerns.

She hadn't known what to do, only that she *couldn't* leave Jisyel. Now they were at Meadowhill, she had three choices. Hurry on to Fellwood, probably cross-country because of the amount of time she'd wasted already; continue following the river to the next town, Vaelar, and hope to catch up with Jisyel and Fenn there; or give up on the funeral entirely and head south, down towards Ulbridge, and hope to find Jisyel somewhere along the bay.

Was it worth invoking her mother's fury to confirm Jisyel was alive?

Absolutely.

But Varlot had to continue. *He* was under no obligation to traipse around Bragalia with her while she looked for her lost love. It would mean she'd be alone without shelter for however long it took to find Jisyel and Fenn.

If she found her.

Varlot secured the bag and put it in his inside pocket, then stood up. Despite Calidra's height, he loomed a foot over her. 'Look, Calidra. I know a thing or two about not facing your problems, believe me. But you got responsibilities in Fellwood, and so do I. Fenn and Jisyel will be there. Pack up your stuff, let's get going No more moping around.'

She glowered at him. Being told what to do had never gone down well, but she held back her anger. It bubbled near the surface. She *needed* him. Outside her own family's canton, no-one was likely to offer help. In fact, most Lairds were a hairs' breadth from open war with each other. It wasn't as if she could just ask a stranger for coin.

But, like at the bay, she didn't trust herself to do what she wanted alone. The last time she'd done that, she'd washed up on the Isle of Salt after a year of wandering aimlessly through Bragalia, unsure if she was running away from or towards danger. It had only been thanks to Bellandri's kindness that she'd survived at all. And Jisyel, of course, had helped her stay.

Calidra looked out the window, her gaze drawn by movement. Two people had walked through the town's gate, but they were a pair of Bragalian men. Beyond the gate were wheat fields, where farmers were already harvesting crops. Buzzards circled overhead, occasionally swooping down to grab field mice or rodents.

She massaged her temple. She didn't like any of it.

She really *was* alone again.

Already her heart thundered in her chest and anxiety twisted cold in her gut. She wiped her suddenly sweating hands on her tunic. Whatever decision she made, she wouldn't like. 'Fine. We'll cut straight north and catch up on lost time.' And she hoped Varlot was right—that Jisyel and Fenn would already be there, waiting for her.

If not. If Jisyel wasn't in Fellwood…She'd *force* her mother to put together a search party. Armed, armoured scouts on horseback to cover the ground quickly. Fanning out and searching every road methodically.

Her mother wanted to rebuild their relationship, fine. She'd do something to help Jisyel.

Damn it, she wished she'd thought of that sooner. She *was* the daughter of a Laird. She *had* some power. She might as well embrace it to help Jisyel and Fenn. If she hadn't spent so much time *wallowing* and being weak...

They packed up quickly and Calidra ensured her trusty dagger was in its sheath at her belt. A memento from her sister, from her home. Her family's crest was etched into the handle—three white feathers tipped in gold on an ogee-patterned background—she was never without it. Calidra triple-checked it was securely attached before following Varlot out of the cramped room and down the rickety wooden stairs to the wide alley below.

Meadowhill was smaller than Ballowtown or Fellwood—more of a large village than anything else—but it was already bustling with people despite the early hour. Built on the side of a river and straddling two cantons, it was a wonder the place hadn't grown bigger over time. It was a stark reminder that she'd be in her home canton once they left via Meadowhill's eastern gate.

She scanned the crowd, ever-cautious, before leaving the alleyway. Most villagers were Bragalian, and probably lived there. She spotted one sandy-haired Porsenthian in uniform, and realised he was an Inquisitor. Although she'd done nothing wrong, and had every right to be where she was, the sight of him was an uncomfortable reminder of what had happened in Ballowtown.

'Best keep away from them.' Varlot grabbed her arm and pulled her into the market crowd, away from the Inquisitor, who hadn't noticed them.

'Worried?' Calidra asked, drawing up her hood.

'Keeping us safe. *Move*,' Varlot replied. They picked their way through the crowd quickly and turned down another main street, leaving the bustle—and the Inquisitor—behind.

Now they were heading towards Meadowhill's eastern gate, the mountains beyond loomed even bigger, almost threatening. It wouldn't be long before she'd be able to see the shining gold of Chyram's Shrine glinting in the sun. The thought of it made her want to retch, and she forced her attention back to the street she walked down. Varlot, already several paces ahead of her, marched confidently through the thinner crowds, every step filled with purpose. People parted for him as if he were a riverboat, and she followed hurriedly in his wake, trying to convince herself she was doing the right thing.

A child wailed somewhere ahead, the shrill cry high and piercing, and Calidra peeked around the edge of her hood, curious.

Outside a small, dilapidated cottage, a woman sat on a large, wooden chair, nursing an infant. Her thick, dark hair was draped over one shoulder, and although she couldn't have been older than thirty-five, she had the worry lines of a seventy-year-old creased around her eyes and mouth. A young girl who looked around seven years old cried inces-santly, tears streaming down her dusty cheeks as she clutched the woman's skirts. Her face was smeared with dirt, and her clothes weren't much more than tattered rags. She had the same nut brown skin as Calidra, who wondered if the girl was from Fellwood.

It was that similarity that slowed Calidra's step. She paused beside the low fence marking the cottage's boundary. Flowers grew by the fence posts, adding a splash of colour to the ramshackle building. 'What's wrong?'

The woman glanced up sharply, then softened when she saw Calidra's concerned look. 'She's dying, sigya.' Her accent was thick, in a regional dialect Calidra only had a passing familiarity with. She'd also used the formal honorific to address Calidra. Literally translated, it meant blessed one— something that her sister had often been called, but never her.

Calidra nodded in acknowledgement, a lump forming in her throat. 'Dying? How? She doesn't look hurt.'

At the sudden attention on her, the girl blinked furiously and turned away from Calidra's curious stare, burying her face in the faded yellow cotton of the woman's skirt, her cries continuing.

'You okay?' Varlot returned to her side, one hand resting on the hilt of his axe. 'Thought we were getting out of here?'

'Porsenthians. Everywhere these days. Didn't you take enough from us already? Now you darken our mornings!' the woman snapped, her calm composure gone in a heartbeat.

Varlot faced her, unflinching. 'I do as my queen commands. As should you. Or have you forgotten the reach of The Iron Crown?'

Calidra rested a hand on his forearm before he could draw his axe. 'Sorry, mahdol,' she apologised, using the old term for mother in Low Bragalian. She hoped it would placate her. 'We were just passing through.' Against her better instincts, she added, 'Is there anything we can do for the elthian?' Another Low Bragalian term. It felt strange on her tongue, after so many years without speaking a word in the language.

Still scowling at Varlot, the woman cupped the girl's back and pressed her close, the thick cotton muffling her tears. 'No, sigya. She is beyond all help. I travelled to Vaelar, tried to beg the aid of one of Chyram's priests. If I had more gold, I could take her to a better doctor. One in Fellwood, or Cliffton. But they refused. They *refused* me, sigya! An old mahdol like me! Who has nothing!' Letting go of the child, she gestured to her cottage—the roof tiles were in poor condition and several were missing, and even the stone walls of the building crumbled in places.

Calidra dropped her gaze, memories of people begging at her childhood home flashing before her, desperate for her sister's aid. She blinked the memory away. That had been a *long* time ago.

The mahdol continued, oblivious, 'It's nearly a month since she turned up in Meadowhill. Washed down the river like a caught fish. She and a younger boy, who was already drowned when we found them. Each day she worsens. Pain in her head. No idea where she came from.'

Calidra and Varlot shared a worried glance.

'And everyday she screams. It won't be long now, I think. It is like a heatless fever has taken her. The Inquisitors passed through a few days back. I hid her. Muffled her screams with a washcloth until they'd gone. But she's soon for the spirit world, I think. Better she passes here, among her own people, than bound by that Iron Crown.' She spat the words out, and the child whimpered beside her. She wiped away the girl's tears with one thumb, her other hand adjusting the infant swaddled in the clothes across her breast. 'A sigya like you must have more important matters than a lost elthian or a poor mahdol. And your Porsenthian companion is keen to get away.' She eyed Varlot with obvious distaste.

Despite being soothed, the young girl sobbed again, her voice cracking from weeks of crying, and Calidra's heart broke. She stared at the back of the child's head, wondering how much hurt and fear she must've experienced. If the mahdol was correct, it would be over soon. Not that it made it any easier. If she could have wished away the girl's suffering, she would have. 'Keep her hidden. There's an Inquisitor in town today.' Calidra turned away, unable to endure the child's crying. Her own eyes burned with the threat of tears, and she strode towards the edge of town, Varlot following behind her.

Neither said a word.

❄

MUCH OF WESTERN Bragalia was flat, with only the hills
further south and the mountains further north breaking up
the landscape. While it made the trek over the fields easier,
the sun beat down mercilessly overhead, and it didn't take
long before both Calidra and Varlot were struggling. Their
pace slowed, and sweat dripped down Calidra's shoulders.

Her head was full of worry for Jisyel and Fenn, and the
distraction slowed her down even more. She'd decided to
hurry to Fellwood, omitting another stop in Vaelar, on the
assumption that Jisyel and Fenn were already at her home,
waiting for her. Even if they weren't, she'd be in a better
position to at least *do* something about it.

She grunted as her calf twinged in pain at the steep
incline.

'Not having a tough time are you?'

Calidra grimaced. 'Like you aren't, too?'

'This? This is nothing!' Varlot laughed and hefted his axe
higher across his back as if it weighed the same as her own
dagger. 'When you've spent three days fighting the Myr in
high summer, *then* you get to complain.'

'Three days?'

'Without cover, mind you.'

There were only a handful of conflicts against the Myr in
recent memory, and only one sprang to mind at his description of a battle in the open in the middle of summer. It had
scarred Tassar like nothing before, leaving the land itself
dead and withered. '*You* were at the Battle of Marlrush?' She
nearly stumbled on a thorny plant jutting out from the dry
grass and managed to catch herself before she fell.

Varlot snorted. 'You *do* realise I was one of the Generals
in the Porsenthian army, right?'

'Of course. But I thought…'

'You thought what?'

Calidra wasn't sure. The Battle of Marlrush had been one of the last, largest confrontations on this continent between The Iron Crown and the Myr, almost a decade prior. And it wasn't as if she'd kept tabs on Porsenthian personnel while she'd been away from home. That was her father's job, not hers. 'I'm not sure. I thought that battle was after your time.'

'Hmph. It was my last major conflict. I left shortly after.'

Calidra didn't want to linger on her lack of knowledge, so she shifted the conversation as the sloping ground eased. 'What was it like? That…confrontation. Queen Surayo was there, wasn't she? With Toriaken?' She remembered all the household staff had been talking about it. A great victory against the Myr, if harshly won.

For a long time, Varlot didn't say anything, and Calidra wondered if she'd insulted him somehow. Dark mountains lined the horizon, mist wreathing their peaks.

'I remember…The skies were black with arrows. Death rained down on everything. Our army. The Myr.'

A cold shiver ran up Calidra's spine at his words, and she remembered the chaotic fighting in Ballowtown from the other night. She'd never seen a creature like it, spirit or animal. And no matter his position, Torsten was an arse whose words she had no reason to believe. 'Did they all die? The Myr?'

'Most. The rest fled not long after Toriaken joined the fray. Nothing can stand up to a spirit that powerful. Not even the Myr.' He shook his head and heaved a long sigh. 'That lad, Fenn. Reminds me so much of my son.'

It was the second time he'd mentioned it since Fenn and Jisyel had fallen into the bay. She didn't know how he could make the connection—he'd only met him for a few minutes. 'Does he really?'

'He's got that same fire in his eyes. Got courage. Not

many will stand up to Torsten, even grown men! Good lad, he is. Will be good to see him again, soon. Put a blade in his hand and make sure he can defend himself properly next time.'

Calidra chewed her bottom lip. Both Jisyel and Bellandri had been happy to give Fenn a chance. So had Varlot. But she'd always been suspicious of people and hadn't been completely sure of Fenn, either. Now that she'd learned there were others like him...

Her mind wandered back to the dying child in Meadowhill.

No memory. Constant head pain.

Were they related? The same as the lost souls the Inquisitors had been after in Ballowtown? The same as Fenn? Was he destined to worsen over the coming days, until he died screaming? 'That poor child.'

Varlot snorted and continued on up the grassy slope.

Calidra couldn't abide his rudeness. 'What's that for? She's so young! It's hardly fair.'

'Oh yes. Very sad. I don't know why that stupid woman kept hold of her.'

'Wait a minute. *You* were the one who didn't want Torsten to take Fenn. Why is it okay for that little elthian to be chained up by the Inquisitors?' Calidra hurried to catch up to him, her calves burning at the sudden exertion.

'I didn't say that.'

'What *did* you mean, then?'

Varlot and Calidra crested the hill and peered down at the rolling plains before them. To their right, a long, narrow river flowed down from the mountains, cutting the plains in two with a line of azure. To their left, the grass continued all the way to the horizon, turning brown as it did, until it ended at the Salt Sea. Directly ahead, at the foot of one mountain, Fellwood awaited them. And beyond the mountains lay Porsenthia, and all the power of The Iron Crown and her Inquisitors.

A cool breeze ran across the grasses, making them sway.

'Better off killing her.'

Varlot spoke so harshly that it took Calidra a few seconds to realise he was talking about the girl. It took all her effort not to let her mouth hang open. 'How can you say such a thing?'

'She's suffering. Lost her brother already, by the sound of it. Why keep her alive? Just another mouth to feed.'

Calidra couldn't believe it. 'And what if Fenn ends up that way? Would you kill him, too? Or what if it had been *your* child?'

Varlot paused and faced her. 'It's not the same thing.'

'Why not? What happened to your son? You've said Fenn reminds you of him. So tell me.'

'You've never killed anyone, have you?'

She didn't like him skirting around her question. 'What difference does that make? It's not right to—'

'I have. Countless people. I'm pretty well acquainted with it, as a matter of fact.'

Calidra narrowed her eyes, one hand already on her dagger. She didn't know what she meant to do with it, but she refused to let some Porsenthian speak to her in that tone without consequence.

Varlot scoffed. 'Like that butter knife would do me any harm. What I'm *trying* to tell you is sometimes…sometimes it's better they don't suffer. Four of my closest friends. Brothers, really. One had an arrow through his lung. Couldn't breathe. Every movement filled his chest with more blood. Lying there on the battlefield, surrounded by the corpses of our friends, the Myr skulking between bodies, looking for more of the living to slaughter.'

'That's…that's awful…'

'Another had his skull caved in by Myrish magic. Top of

141

his head was a bloody pulp and he was missing half his jaw and one eye. Still talking. Told me he could *see* the bloody spirit world. Could see his Ma standing beside us, calling for him.'

'I don't—'

'Third had a blade of ice slash through him. Myrish magic, tougher than steel, it is. Even iron. Carved him open throat to thigh. You've never seen so much blood come out of a man, let me tell you.'

'Please. No more—'

'You say I should've kept *them* alive? In agony? Delirious? Until help got there? *If* help got there? On the hope that they *might* survive? Suffering all that time, some begging for release?'

Calidra didn't say anything. She found she couldn't look away from his hard stare.

He continued, wearing a smirk of grim victory. 'Of course not. I gave them mercy. Same as what I'd have given that girl if the woman hadn't been there. Would *you* have done that? Given her peace from her suffering?'

Calidra dropped her hand from her dagger, her fingers trembling.

'I didn't think so.'

She tried to think of something to say. But no matter how hard she tried, nothing would be appropriate after Varlot's admissions. How could *anything* she say match up to what he'd been through? He'd lived through war. Battles. Death. Probably had to face choices no-one should ever have to.

Suddenly feeling small and insignificant, as if her own troubles weren't worth considering, Calidra opened her mouth to mutter an apology when a shadow fell across them, freezing her in her tracks. They'd left Meadowhill under a cloudless sky, and that hadn't changed through the morning. She looked up, startled.

The creature was upon them before Calidra even understood what was happening. A surge of darkness swallowed her, and her shriek of surprise was instantly snuffed out. Something slammed into the side of her head, knocking her so hard to the ground her vision danced.

Before she had any time to register pain, there was a weight on her neck—pressing her cheek into the ground. She couldn't breathe. Panic flared, and she scrambled for her dagger—the only thing she had to hand.

Hot, acrid breath filled her nostrils and she gagged. Combined with the weight on her neck, the dusty grass being shoved in her face, and the disgusting smell, Calidra was choking.

The creature's snarls were thunder in her chest, driving away everything else.

Her fingers wrapped around the hilt of her dagger and she yanked it out of its sheath. Without the time or energy to take in a breath or gather her strength, she shoved it as hard as she could into the thing above her—its massive weight pinning her body to the ground. Whatever it was hardly flinched at the dagger, and Calidra twisted the blade, forcing it into the creature as deeply as she could.

Something sharp cut into the meat of her shoulder as she fought back, but she ignored the hot, wetness dripping down her arm. She still couldn't see who—or what—she fought, couldn't do anything but think of surviving.

Then, suddenly, the pressure was gone.

Bright light flooded her vision as the darkness left her and she found herself staring up into the blue sky. Coughing, she got to her feet, one arm on her shoulder, as she looked around for her attacker.

Varlot was locked in combat with the creature; his axe had already taken a chunk out of its flesh.

Her stomach dropped. It was another of the shadow-like creatures, though not as large as the one from Ballowtown. It had six limbs, each ending in a single, hooked claw, and a wide, flat head, its mouth a gaping hole.

Compared to Varlot, the muscular man in the bearskin cloak, the creature appeared weak, frail almost. He passed the axe from one hand to the other, stepping around the creature and pushing it away from Calidra. Varlot darted forward, his axe a flurry of furious blows. Every strike found its mark, and a particularly heavy thrust spilled dark ichor from the creature's flank.

It let out a shriek that cut through the air, then charged at Varlot, slashing its front appendages like a pair of deadly scythes. Varlot parried one, scooting under the creature's guard and smashing the flat of hix axe into the creature's other legs.

With another ear-splitting cry, it tumbled to the ground.

Varlot swung again, the force of his blow so great that he severed one of the creature's legs. More ichor spilled, steam rising from it.

Another sharp cry pulled Calidra's attention from the battle.

Something low rumbled through the air, and only when it passed under the sun did she recognise the shape. 'A griffin!'

Varlot had his axe clutched in both hands a second later, the blade held up defensively, and he backed up to Calidra. 'Attack from above, too?'

As he spoke, the griffin descended towards them, enormous feathered wings sending gusts of wind with every powerful beat. Its legs were outstretched, talons open as if to pluck them where they stood.

Calidra and Valot leapt backwards as the griffin's talons slashed into the creature's hide, gouging deeper than the axe had.

It let out another cry of pain so loud it shook Calidra's bones. She covered her ears, wincing at the noise.

Unperturbed, the griffin hovered in place, its front claws raking down the creature's body with such aggression that it was invulnerable. More black ichor coated the ground, and still the griffin attacked, darting forward with its curved beak to pierce one of the creature's legs.

With one, final, scream of fury, the creature withdrew into itself, spun in a circle, then raced away—darting for the horizon.

Calidra leaned heavily against Varlot, panting for breath.

'I thought there weren't any griffins in Bragalia!'

'There aren't any *wild* ones,' she clarified. Seeing the creature brought a flood of emotions. Her mother kept a pair of griffins, originally brought with her from Olmir, who roamed their villa and grounds as if they owned the place. They were a smaller, more delicate subspecies bred for companionship—the beast that flew above them was far larger; a war breed that had greater strength and intelligence.

The griffin turned its orange eye on them and flew low, swooping in close.

Varlot raised his weapon and pushed Clidra away with his free hand.

'Lower your axe, Varlot.'

'Are you mad, woman? Look at the size of the talons on that thing!'

'Easy! Easy!' A voice called, somewhat muffled above the creature's movements.

Calidra leapt to the side, giving the griffin more room to land. It was tall, easily eleven feet high at the shoulder, and yet it landed with a surprising amount of grace—the ground hardly trembled under it. Black feathers shimmered almost purple under the bright sunlight, shifting cleanly into smooth, dark fur and two massive hind paws. The talons that protruded from its forelegs were each longer than Calidra's dagger, and its massive, curved beak looked like it would have no trouble tearing her apart.

'Careful down there!'

She peered around the griffin's menacing beak, trying not to look at its deep orange eyes, to the rider atop its back.

'Watch it! That thing nearly crushed us when it landed!' Varlot pointed his axe squarely at the griffin, who ignored it.

'Lath, would you mind?'

The griffin let out a sharp cry, part-snarl, part-shriek, and slowly knelt its forelimbs—enabling the rider to more easily slide out of his harness and down the massive creature's side to the ground.

He was young, younger than Calidra would have expected for a griffin rider, with smooth, tawny skin, high cheekbones, and green silk robes that instantly made him recognisable as Olmese. His bare arms were muscular—as would be expected in his role—but the rest of him was lean and athletic under the light scale armour across his chest and torso. Compared to Varlot's decades of experience, he seemed only just out of training. But he wore two golden torcs around his left wrist and Calidra realised he was no ordinary messenger. It should have been obvious from the size of the griffin he rode, but the torcs signified his status as a warrior—those were only given for duelling victories or bravery in battle.

'Didn't you hear me? I said you nearly crushed us!' Varlot raised his voice.

'Forgive me if you were afraid. Hailathlyl hasn't had any accidents in years.'

'Afraid?' Varlot repeated, voice rising.

'Varlot, calm down. We aren't in any danger now.' Calidra checked the wound on her shoulder. It was shallow, her thick cloak taking most of the damage. As long as she kept it clean, she'd be fine.

Griffins were enormous predators, rarely seen outside of Olmir, and almost never in Porsenthia. She imagined it was Varlot's first time seeing one up close, and privately smiled at his disquiet. She nodded to the rider, a broad smile across

146

her lips. 'Welcome to Bragalia, friend. Your timing was excellent.' It had been too long since she'd last been in Olmir, let alone seen any griffins, and she was awe-struck by the creature.

'Thank you for your welcome. I'd hoped not to encounter one of those creatures.' The rider crossed one arm over his chest and inclined his head. 'I had not expected to see anyone in the open. Bragalia won't remain safe for long.'

'We saw another of those…creatures in Ballowtown. But that one was smaller. Are there more of them?' Calidra asked, quickly deciding that if she had any more bad luck, then she really *had* been a fool to leave the Isle of Salt. For all its discomfort, it was at least out of the way of the dangerous problems that were apparently constant occurrences on the mainland.

Varlot, too, had become attentive, and even sheathed his axe to better pay attention.

'Unfortunately. Their numbers are growing, but their movement is slow. We have time.' He stroked the griffin's side affectionately, earning a low purr from the creature—Hailathlyl, she remembered. The rider continued, 'We travel to Fellwood. My brothers and sisters have flown to the other cantons. Several more are on their way to Eastbrook.'

'To speak with the queen?' Varlot surmised.

He nodded, grave, and his easy smile faded. 'Yes. Though it pains us to speak with the Iron Queen, we must. The Myr have returned.'

I t was the first time Fenn had seen death up close. Certainly the first time he remembered it. Who knew what he'd seen or done in his past, before he'd awoken on the Isle of Salt in the middle of a muddy bog. Nothing from before then had come back to him, and the harder he tried to remember, the more his head throbbed. As much as not knowing ate at him, and worrying about what important knowledge was lost, he tried not to think about it.

Right now, it was easy *not* to think.

Selys had provided him with more explanation of the state of the Bragalian people in the past few minutes than anyone else had thus far. Before she could explain more, she and a handful of other priests and priestesses underwent one of their daily rituals—performing rites on the dead.

He rested his chin in his hands, thinking about everything she'd told him. None of it was familiar, but he understood the hurt and pain so many people here felt.

Even though Bragalia hadn't been at war with Porsenthia for decades, nor the Myr for only a handful of years, death was still rife in the poorer communities given the Lairds' constant confrontations with each other. Starvation and disease usually went hand in hand within the more isolated hamlets and villages, with one's chances of survival linked to the Laird in control of the canton. More generous Lairds provided for their people. Those who were more interested in hoarding land and resources to themselves often let their people starve while they warred for glory, greatness, and greed.

It gave some explanation for the hostility he'd experienced earlier.

According to Selys, it was worse further south and east, where cantons were more prone to conflict. But Ulbridge's canton, where the Shrine of Neros had been built, was relatively peaceful. It meant that a steady stream of injured, dying, or dead, made their way here for funeral rites and cremation, entombment, or burial at sea. As Neros was the Spirit of the Lasseen Ocean, many were dealt with by the third option—especially those who had no relatives.

Fenn wondered if he'd have the same fate if he died without ever regaining his memories.

'The casualties of war never end,' Jisyel whispered. They watched the rites from a short distance away, under the shade of an apple tree whose fruit had yet to ripen. Pink blossoms drifted down every so often, caught in the strong breeze, adding an ethereal tone to proceedings. How could something so beautiful frame something so horrific?

'It seems a harsh place. More than the Isle of Salt,' Fenn replied.

Jisyel drew her knees up to her chest and hugged them. 'In some ways, yes. Lots of places still haven't fully recovered from...the Myr.'

They sat on a low stone wall that ringed the shrine, watching quietly and keeping themselves out of the way. Thanks to Selys, they'd been able to have something to eat, and she'd even brought them a bucket of warm water each to get cleaned up.

Cleaning the silt out of his hair and clothes had done more to cheer up Fenn than a belly full of hot stew, and he could actually relax if it weren't for the tension that had grown between himself and Jisyel since Selys had made her observation.

He'd been touched by the Myr.

Even without any knowledge of who or what they were, he'd shuddered at the priestess's words.

Jisyel had done her best to explain what was happening at the shrine—no doubt to keep herself from thinking about what Selys had said. She spoke about the different cantons of Bragalia and where Calidra was from, expanding on Selys's earlier words. She'd skirted around the topic of the Myr as much as she could, clearly uncomfortable discussing it.

He remembered the man had said they were death. And judging by Jisyel's reaction, they invoked fear more than anything else.

But Fenn had to know more.

If the Myr were responsible for what had happened to him, he *needed* to know why and demand they undid whatever they'd done to him.

He watched the procession of robed priests and priestesses walking past weeping, kneeling relatives. They watched their loved ones bound in thin linen, their faces showed varying degrees of grief—from sadness to stoicism, anger to fear. Fenn wondered if he had any relatives who were going through the same gamut of emotions, or whether they were all dead, and *he* should be the one upset.

One priestess, her hair already thin and grey, bent crookedly to place a small fruit cake at the throat of the body she'd been wrapping. She then placed a small wooden spoon in her right hand, and a folded apron in her left, before gently binding them all with the off-white linen that every member of the dead had been wrapped in.

Behind the priestess, other members of Neros's order

were doing the same—placing small trinkets in each hand, or at the throat of the deceased. He couldn't figure out any pattern to it. Some were given food, others items of clothing, jewellery, or tools.

'Why's she doing that?' Fenn gestured to the priestess.

Jisyel turned away, her shoulders stiff. 'Better to ask them.'

He shifted where he sat, hurt by her dismissiveness. It was worse coming from Jisyel, who was usually so light-hearted and prone to laughter, and never took anything too seriously. 'I'm still the same person, you know? I don't know what happened to me.'

She sighed, hunkering into herself.

'Jisyel?'

'I know, Fenn. I just...the Myr...it...' Again, she huddled into her knees, facing away from him. Her easy smile and happy-go-lucky attitude had been forgotten, and Fenn suddenly felt very unwelcome.

Before he could say anything more, Selys returned to them, her sleeves rolled up to her elbows, a streak of dark blood across one arm. 'That's all I can do. Now, they will burn, or be washed away by Neros.'

They looked back to where the bound bodies were carefully being carried on thin planks of wood through the spattering of trees dotted around the shrine's western side, to the water that flowed swiftly beyond.

'Here.' Selys pulled out three small cups from within her robes, and a half-full bottle of a liquid so dark red it seemed black. 'A toast to their passing.'

Fenn wasn't sure about it, but when he saw Selys only gave them a few drops each, he sipped it to be polite. He wasn't sure if it was wine—it didn't taste like anything he remembered, which admittedly wasn't much. Sweet and salty at the same time, it tasted of fruit gone bad in the sun. It coated the back of his throat and he suddenly wished he had water to get rid of the taste.

He forced his attention back to Selys, who despite confidently stating he'd been Myr-touched, wasn't as repulsed by him as Jisyel was. 'I saw the priests and priestesses putting items with bodies before wrapping them. Why?'

'Because you leave the world as you enter it—naked, squealing, with no notion of who you are or what your purpose is. We decorate the bodies so when the soul reaches the spirit world, they will know who they were.' Selys faced the water, watching the burials, unflinching. 'A mother. A warrior. A baker. They can remember their essence and be at peace.'

'How do you know who they were?'

'Those who bring them tell us.'

'What if they don't know?'

Selys turned to him and gave Fenn a small, knowing smile. 'We choose for them. You do not want to be lost in the spirit world.'

Fenn gestured to the landscape around him. 'I'm already lost in this one. Wouldn't make much difference for me.' He pushed himself off the wall. He wasn't above begging, but it was obvious he needed the priestess to have any chance of crossing through Bragalia. 'Selys. Please. Tell me how this... this...curse can be lifted. Is there something you can do?'

'It's beyond me, I'm afraid. The Myr are too powerful.'

Fell dropped his shoulders, letting his frustration show. He'd tried to keep his emotions under wraps after blurting out his annoyance at Master Inquisitor Torsten and almost getting himself arrested, but his patience was wearing thin. 'Is there *anyone* who can help? I thought things would go back to normal after a few days, but nothing's changed. I remember waking up on the Isle of Salt and *nothing* before that. Every time I try and think, my headache worsens.' He clutched his head as a particularly sharp spike of pain blazed across his temple. 'If there's a way to stop this, I *want* to know.'

'You may not like the answer,' Selys replied.

'It can't be worse than this. What if I have friends? Family? What if I was doing important work somewhere?'

Jisyel sat up straight. 'I know I'm going to sound like Calidra, but...Fenn, what if you're an enemy?'

'To who? Have I hurt you?'

'You've been touched by the *Myr*! *Tainted.*'

Annoyance flared across his chest, bright and hot. How could she say that after they'd helped each other so much? 'And how is that my fault, Jisyel? You were happy enough to help me before. Why does the cause of my memory loss make any difference?'

'Because the Myr have been trying to wipe us out for *centuries*!' Jisyel shouted. 'Say what you want about the queen, but she's the *only* thing keeping the continent safe! And now you're here, and all those lost souls, what if you're all part of some Myrish sneak attack?'

Fenn raised his hands, afraid someone near the shrine might have overheard. 'Jisyel, sshh!'

'No! I will *not* sshh!'

'I don't know anything about the Myr! About *myself*! How could I possibly be part of an attack?'

'Stay calm, please.' Selys raised a hand to both of them. 'All the amnesiacs that I've seen, even at a distance, were weak, disorientated. Several have even died. I would not think that was the most effective fighting force, would you? Don't let your bias cloud what's right in front of you, Jisyel. Anyway, you said Fenn had helped you. Surely if he worked for the Myr, he'd have left you for dead?'

Jisyel hugged herself. 'I...I just don't know what's going on. Cal's not here and...' She seemed on the verge of tears. Now her walls had broken down, Fenn could see how vulnerable and scared she was.

'It's worse for me, Jisyel,' he said gently, trying to let his anger dissipate, 'you're scared. I know. So am I.'

Jisyel gently touched his shoulder. She took several long breaths and shook her head. 'I'm sorry, Fenn. I didn't mean... I just...the Myr are *terrifying*. You should hear the stories! And Calidra is always telling me that I'm too reckless, always getting into trouble and doing something stupid. So, I thought I'd gone and done it again, and...and that wasn't fair on you.'

He squeezed her hand. He'd not expected an apology, and was glad he'd not lost his only friend already. 'Selys, please, if you can give me any information at all, I'd appreciate the help.'

The priestess pulled her robes back down her arms as she thought. Behind the trio, the final rites had been completed, with mourners lingering on the bank as they stared out across the water. Most of the priests and priestesses had made their way back to the shrine, with several heading inside. It made the courtyard appear suddenly empty.

Selys tilted her head, and in a low, almost conspiratorial voice, whispered, 'You'd need something of Myrish origin to help you.'

Fenn grimaced. 'There's no other way? No other spirit that could help?'

'Possibly. But you'd need a very powerful spirit. And the only one I can think of that holds a candle to Myrish magic is Toriaken.' Selys suppressed a laugh. 'Best of luck with *that*.'

'The queen's dragon?' Fenn groaned. 'Can't you do something?'

'Me? If only. I'm no High Priestess, and Neros doesn't bless any of her followers, unfortunately.' Selys genuinely looked remorseful.

'What's a High Priestess?'

'Someone who has devoted their life to their spirit, like

154

me, but has *also* received a boon. Their spirit has chosen to bless them, and thus shares their power with that individual.'

'Like...Jisyel's curse?' Fenn tried to fit the pieces together in a way that made sense.

'Well, Jisyel is the opposite, I'd say. Spirits can bless or curse anyone they choose. Understanding them and working towards acquiring a blessing is why many people join an order and get this.' Selys raised her left hand, her tattoo in full view.

'How do you get a blessing?' Fenn wondered if he could get one, it would be an easy way to cure his curse.

Selys laughed. 'Unfortunately all spirits are rather fickle. And as I said, Toriaken is the only one I know of who could possibly destroy that Myrish magic.'

He could hardly believe it. Going anywhere near the queen, even to ask for help, would surely result in his immediate arrest by her Inquisitors. He supposed he could chance it, and hope he was able to request an audience with Queen Surayo before anything awful happened to him. Torsten's smug smile appeared in his mind's eye, and he shook his head with a shiver. Fat chance of that happening. 'I don't suppose there's anything Myrish conveniently located in that shrine that could help?'

Jisyel let out a startled yelp that she quickly bit back down, covering her mouth with both hands.

Selys shook her head. 'Anyone harbouring something Myrish would be executed for high treason, Fenn. You won't find any of their artefacts near here.'

'High treason?' The more Selys spoke, the worse things seemed to get.

Selys glanced at Jisyel and smiled. 'Well, Queen Surayo saved us all from the Myr, ending the war five years ago. Even *talking* about the Myr now is the worst kind of insult to her.'

He pulled at his hair. 'So my options are talk to a queen

whose Inquisitors want me arrested, or find something impossible? Is that right?'

Selys laughed, her eyes twinkling. 'I didn't say that. I just said anyone who *had* such a thing would be executed for high treason.'

Fenn had been about to argue when her words sunk in. Ignoring Jisyel's fierce stare, he crossed the short distance to Selys and reached for the priestess's hand. 'You…you know someone?'

With a smile, she pulled her hands away from him and smoothed down her robe. 'I know *of* some*thing*.'

'Where?' Already, his breathing quickened. Was this finally his path to ridding himself of the curse? He knew next to nothing about Selys aside from the fact she didn't behave like the other priestesses of Neros, but right now, he was pinning his hopes on her being correct.

'A Myrish…construct. It's a creature, of sorts, created through their magic. Said to live in the Nethal Mountains in northern Porsenthia, at the site of an ancient battle.'

Jisyel stood up, joining them. 'Priestess Selys, with respect, you're talking about a sailor's myth.'

'Am I?'

'What myth?' Fenn looked between the two women. 'Can you *please* remember that I don't know *anything* about what's going on?'

Jisyel stared at him intensely, as if she'd never seen him before.

He hated being under scrutiny. 'Do the Myr normally do this to people? Take their memories? I'm guessing not by the way everyone's reacted to me and the others.'

'They usually massacre us.' Selys's voice was flat. 'They've not set foot on the continent for five years. Queen Surayo finally brought the armistice, and we've enjoyed peace ever since. Porsenthia even more so than Bragalia. She may rule with an Iron Dragon, but there's no more risk of Myrish death spirits snatching us from our beds. So you turning up, Myr-touched, without memory...all those other lost souls could be the same.'

'Something's happening, that's for certain. Would explain why Torsten himself was in Ballowtown.' Jisyel chewed her thumb.

'It *is* unusual for the Master Inquisitor to leave Porsenthia.' Selys nodded.

'More than that, there was an attack in Ballowtown—'

'A creature of shadow,' Fenn interrupted, pleased he finally had some knowledge to contribute. 'Something about it that made my skin crawl. It was something dark. Evil. I don't know, perhaps *that* was a Myr?'

'No. The Myr don't look like that,' Jisyel said, 'but maybe it was one of their spirits? Or a construct of theirs? They have so many.'

Fenn swallowed. Suddenly all the strange pieces of the puzzle appeared to fit together. He wasn't sure how, but everything felt connected. His memory loss, and those of the other unfortunate people. The attack on Ballowtown. The Inquisitors—and Torsten—investigating. Now, Selys had confirmed the origin of his amnesia, perhaps it was related to the creature attack as well.

And at the centre of it all: the Myr.

'Why haven't they been here in five years?' Fenn asked. 'How did the queen defeat them?' He was no fighter, but if he could somehow replicate what she had done, it might drive away the Myrish magic in his own body and mind.

Selys sat down on the wall. 'Like I said, Queen Surayo arranged an armistice. She ended the war. Prior to that, the Myr would attack us. Sometimes every day. Sometimes we'd go a whole year without encountering them. They'd kill people first with their death spirits, then swoop in to take the life from the land. The army would drive them off eventually, though there are a few places in Porsenthia that bear the scars of the larger conflicts.' She sighed. 'During those, Tori-aken led us to victory. He's one of the most powerful dragon spirits. Although I'm sure Neros is equally capable.'

Selys touched her dangling earrings, beads of jade. 'The Myr were persistent, until five years ago, when the queen attacked them in their homeland. A few weeks after her return, she declared peace. We've not been attacked by the Myr since. We assumed it was the end to centuries of fight-ing. We were finally at peace.'

Another wave of pain surged through his head and he let out a small gasp. Was it getting worse? Maybe he was imag-ining it. 'Somehow I think peace is over.'

From the sounds of things, an answer could lie in the Myr's homelands, wherever that was. Otherwise, Selys had given him an option—even though Jisyel didn't seem to believe it was real.

'Fenn, we better keep moving. The funeral isn't far off, and we need to get to Fellwood. Calidra's probably on her way there now.' Jisyel rubbed her shoulders as if cold.

'What about this Myrish creature in Porsenthia, Selys? You said it was near Nethal? Some ancient battle site? Can it really help me?' Fenn watched Selys carefully, looking for any signs of deception.

'I can't say for certain. But your curse *is* of Myrish origin. Unless you can have Toriaken himself help you, I'd say it was your best bet.' Selys raised one hand to touch the soft blos-soms on the tree that grew over the wall, the dappled shade dancing across her face.

Fenn made his decision. 'Then that's where I have to go.'

'Will you? And what if you discover something about yourself, who you were, that you'd prefer not to know?' Selys raised an amused eyebrow.

Honestly, Fenn didn't care. 'Anything is better than this! If that's my best bet, that's what I'm doing. I don't have a choice. And Jisyel, you can tell Calidra she doesn't need to babysit me anymore. Neither do you. I'll go there alone, and won't be in your way.'

'Fenn!' Jisyel grabbed his arm before he could head off. 'Wait, don't walk away! You could be picked up by the Inquisitors! And if they find out what you are? Where you're going? Fenn, you'll be imprisoned and probably hanged!'

'What choice do I have, Jisyel?' It wasn't an easy decision, but it was the only one he had.

'At least come with me as far as Fellwood? It's on the Porsenthian border, anyway. Varlot will be on his way too, I'm sure. He said he had a training contract. And he helped you once before; maybe he can help you again? Maybe...we all could? If this really is a bigger problem, if the Myr really *are* back, then we need to warn them before it's too late.'

Cold fear snaked its way through Fenn's gut at her words.

She was right. It wasn't just about him—one unlucky man who'd been caught up in some misfortune. It was all connected. And it was about *more* than him. Dozens more people. If he'd been lucky enough to not immediately be arrested, then he had to do something with his freedom. More than finding out answers for himself—if people were in danger of the Myr attacking, if another massacre loomed on the horizon...if more of those creatures could appear, he *had* to do what he could to help.

'People will panic if they realise Queen Surayo can't protect them anymore. If the Myr walk in our country openly, attacking who they want!' Jisyel's nervous gaze flicked to the water, as if something might burst forth and attack.

'Fenn? I'll vouch for you,' Selys said at length.

Fenn straightened up. 'You will?'

The priestess nodded. 'Something is happening. Not just in Bragalia, but across the world. Something that could shake everything to its foundations. If the Myrish curse is part of it, and if the answers you seek are connected, I wish to know. The dragon spirits are the Guardians of Tassar. Neros must know. The other spirits must know.'

Fenn was shocked at Selys's openness.

'Life is fragile, Fenn. It must be protected. Perhaps Neros put you on the path to come here, so I might learn more.'

He understood that. And the Myr were death. They were against everything Selys and her spirit stood for.

The priestess continued, 'It means I'll have to accompany you. Our word is solid, but doesn't carry the weight of a Laird's authority. I can't just write a paper and send you on your way. But I can vouch for you and state that we are on a pilgrimage. In the name of Neros.'

'You'd *lie*?' Jisyel was aghast.

Selys smiled, her eyes twinkling again. 'I would. It would be in service to Tassar. I can accept that term.'

'Even if it means...dealing with the Myr? Or whatever their creature is? In Porsenthia?' Fenn ventured, wanting to make absolutely sure the priestess knew what she was signing herself up for. 'Won't that bring us closer to Queen Surayo and her Inquisitors?'

'Yes. I am not as black and white as Surayo's law. I can see this might be a way forward for Bragalia, Porsenthia. For Tassar itself. This could be something of value.'

'Are you even allowed to leave the shrine?' Jisyel asked.

Selys laughed, her voice high and musical. Genuine. 'I'm a Priestess of Neros, as wild and free as the sea itself. Our order is not as strict as others, and my deity does not punish me when I serve others instead of her.'

'How soon can we leave?' Fenn asked, eager to be off. 'Calidra could be halfway to Fellwood by now!'

Jisyel said, 'If that's true, we might meet up with her in Vaelar. We'll follow the river east, see if she's in town. If not, and we've missed her, we'll go straight to Fellwood. Two days, that's all it'll take us, if we leave right now.'

Excitement grew. *Finally*, he had an answer.

Or the path to a potential answer.

He knew why he didn't have a memory—it had been taken by the Myr. While there was no explanation as to why, nor his constant headache, or why so many others had fallen victim to this curse—it was more of an answer than he'd had since waking up on the island.

If anything, his headache had been slowly worsening, and despite being painful, it was a worry. Selys had said other lost souls had died. The thought he was on a time limit made him more determined; drove him to search harder for a cure. For answers.

If he didn't solve this soon, he might well die.

And then Tassar would have no idea what was about to happen—whether the Myr were truly back or not.

Instead of aimlessly wandering Bragalia, following Jisyel and Calidra in the hope of discovering a clue, he had something to hold onto. Something tangible. Varlot, and now Selys, had helped him out of a difficult situation, and he owed them both. He was grateful not everyone was as suspicious and harsh as Calidra had been. She'd been wrong about that.

'I'll need to get supplies and inform the order that I'm leaving the shrine for a while. Truth be told, I think they'll be happy to get rid of me for a bit.' Selys began to walk up the paved path to the vast building.

'Happy? Why?' Fenn frowned.

'I think that's a tale for later. We're short on time, aren't we?' She laughed again, then headed back, almost running the short distance to the shrine's open door.

'Are all priestesses like that?' Fenn asked.

'The others in the shrine weren't, were they? And to be honest, I've not really met any. No-one cares for Hassen enough to build a shrine on the Isle of Salt. He's not worshipped like many of the bigger spirits are.'

'Should we be suspicious? What's she done that the other priests don't like her?'

'I think we should be *grateful* we're getting help. It would have been difficult to make it all the way to Fellwood, otherwise. Although if Calidra's not there...' Jisyel trailed off, her voice dropping.

'She'll be fine. I'm sure she didn't fall into the water. And she has Varlot, too. They're probably already waiting in Fellwood, wondering what's taking us so long!'

Jisyel brightened at that.

Now that he had a clear idea of what to do next, humour came easily, replacing the constant frustration and building anger. He could forgive Jisyel's earlier suspicions, and wanted to know more about the Myr—as much as he could learn.

And Jisyel was right, they had help now. More than that, Selys wanted to get him all the way to his end goal, instead of him being a nuisance that was in her way. He knew he might not like what waited for him at the end, Selys had been sure to warn him, but he *would* be ready to face it by the time he got there.

Far beyond the boundary of the shrine, a vast mountain range rose up from the grassland. Dark, monstrous rocks that served as a landmark and a milestone. Fellwood sat at the base of the mountain, and Porsenthia lay beyond that.

Once in Porsenthia, he would be closer to his answers— whatever they might be. If the Myrish construct could undo what had been done, he'd be free. And then, without the burden of amnesia, he'd know who he was, what had been done to him, and *why*.

Perhaps he was Porsenthian after all, and Calidra had been wrong about him. Perhaps his family were worried sick, and his friends would laugh about his misadventure once he got back to them.

Fenn was already grinning to himself, earning a curious

stare from Jisyel, when Selys exited the shrine. It took him a few seconds to realise it *was* the priestess—she was nigh unrecognisable.

Her cotton robes and flat shoes had been swapped for boiled leather armour, a long, sleeveless over-cloak trimmed with dark feathers, and a pair of worn leather boots. While the attire was a change, the biggest shock was the enormous glaive she carried across her shoulder. It protruded three feet above her head, the bladed tip sharp and vicious. Silk ribbons of different colours adorned the shaft, along with a dangling, jade bead that had a dragon's head carved into its broad, oval face. She'd also slung a large sack over her other shoulder, though it didn't look full, and was in the process of adjusting the space to add a bottle of wine. Without her soft priestess robes, the scar on her face somehow seemed more livid.

'Right. Shall we get going while we have the light?' Her tone had changed completely, as if her sister spoke and not the priestess they'd been talking to only minutes before.

He remembered Jisyel mentioning pirates were common in the place she was from, and it now made sense. 'Selys...?' Fenn gaped.

'Ah!' Selys reached into her cloak and held out a slim sheet of paper, the ink still wet. 'Here. This should keep the Inquisitors off our backs. Ready?'

Fenn's grin matched hers, and Selys stretched her hands above her head, the joints popping loudly. She let out a sigh of relief and shook out her fingers.

He didn't know much about priests and priestesses, nor the spirits they served. But he decided there and then that Selys was a *most* unholy priestess.

10

THE PAST

TORSTEN

I t was dusk when the caravans reached Tonmouth. Streaks of orange and plum coloured the sky as the last of the light faded. Already, the moon had risen, its jagged northern edge like a gaping mouth ready to swallow the stars.

They'd travelled up the western coast of Porsenthia, as far from the deadlands as was possible, and they'd made good time. Now, Torsten could restore his power.

A small band of soldiers met them at the town gates, and helped with their horses and carrying their supplies. Pleased their message had been received in a timely fashion, he left Nadja in charge of unloading and liaising with the officials of Tonmouth, quickly crossing through the places he'd played as a child until he reached the quieter streets.

Oil lamps had already been lit, bathing the familiar streets in a warm, orange glow. Fountains and aqueducts had been built throughout Tonmouth, and he was never far from the sound of running water. Many people lingered in their doorways or at windows to watch the arrival with interest, but Torsten paid them no mind, intent on his own goal.

Once on the outskirts, he followed the freshwater that fed

the town upriver, to the hills north-east of Tonmouth. The route was well-practiced, and he cut across the darkening landscape as easily as a cat in pitch-dark. Ahead, highlighted by the last of the sun's light, a shrine rose from the hillside. Tall and narrow, it was not as glorious as the shrine of Tori-aken or Neros, but it served its purpose. Simply looking upon it gave him more energy, and he quickened his pace, until he sprinted through the undergrowth.

His thighs burned by the time he reached the shrine's bare, stony courtyard. At this altitude, he had a good view of the lake whence Miroth's power came, and he paused to both catch his breath and take a good look at the water. It had dried up far more than when he'd last seen it.

That was a problem.

The courtyard was empty of plants or decoration, and the flagstones were in dire need of maintenance. Several holes had appeared since his last visit—eroded by rain, snow, and wind—and determined weeds pushed through. It didn't look like it had been swept in some time. Dried rushes and leaves covered the usually pristine courtyard, with thick clumps of cobwebs gathered along the walls of the shrine itself. The priests here clearly needed more donations to keep the place looking presentable.

Torsten didn't bother to hide his scowl at the old priest who hobbled out to greet him. The old man struggled with the heavy stone door, hoiking up his robes before he tripped over them. 'Master Inquisitor! We had not expected your visit for—'

'Plans change. Clear the shrine at once. I wish to speak with Miroth.'

The priest hesitated for the briefest moment, then bowed low and backed away, out of Torsten's path. 'Yes. Of course. There aren't many here at this late hour. Lord Miroth has been—'

'Good. I do not wish to be disturbed.' Torsten didn't give

165

the man a chance to get his words out, nor did he reasonably expect anyone else to be in the shrine despite his order to clear it. Miroth was a weak spirit of a dying lake, barely alive himself. No-one would *choose* to worship him, not when he didn't have the strength to offer any boons.

Not anymore.

Torsten unsheathed the iron dagger at his belt and handed it to the priest. 'I will retrieve this once I am done. Ensure it is returned in *exactly* the same condition as I have given it.' Miroth would know he carried the dagger, but there was no need to bring the offensive item into his shrine and disrespect the spirit further.

With another bow, the priest said, 'Of course, Inquisitor.'

The building's interior was vaulted, as most shrines were, and the darkness of the ceiling pressed down on him like a physical weight. He'd always found it oppressive, yet it was also a strangely familiar comfort.

He delved deeper into the shrine's interior, through a low door at the back of the entrance chamber and down narrow corridors that twisted and turned. Taking one torch from its bracket on the wall, Torsten used its light to find his way to a chamber in the deepest part of the shrine, hardly thinking about the route, he'd taken it so many times. The light was comfort rather than a necessity.

Lingering outside the closed door, Torsten took a deep breath, steadying himself. *This* was why he'd left Ballowtown in such a rush, why he'd ignored his queen, and forced their pace.

When he decided he was as ready as he would ever be, he pushed open the final interior door—made of wood, a dragon flying out of the lake carved into it—and walked into the chamber. The door protested slightly, catching on the uneven flagstone floor and sending dust rolling into the circular room. No windows adorned the walls, and there were no other doors leading out. Directly ahead, a handful of steps led up to a stone altar in the room's centre, illuminated by a thin shaft of moonlight where parts of the roof had broken away, bathing the floor in white and silver.

Half a rusty sword had been buried deep in the altar, its hilt broken.

One hand brushed *Tinebás* at his hip, the movement not of his own control.

He shivered and made his way towards the altar, as if drawn like a moth to flame. Several chunks of stone crumbled away from the steps as he walked up them, and he adjusted his footing. With each step, the metallic taste of the spirit's magic grew stronger in the air, and the same awe that had overcome him as a boy manifested again.

That sensation never really went away.

'*We are brothers, you and I,*' The voice spoke in his ear.

Abruptly, magic surged.

Torsten's vision flared brightly, and images filled the empty chamber with a powerful illusion drawn from his memories as a boy. In a heartbeat, he was not standing in a shrine to his spirit—he was a child again, reliving a powerful memory, and the scene played out in vivid detail. Every sight and sound was the same, every sensation and scent, from the wind ruffling his hair to the smell of wildflowers.

His village, Tonmouth, had grown quickly over recent months; dozens more families joined the village built by the side of the lake—an influx of life energy had flooded the area, and unbeknownst to anyone, Miroth, Spirit of Tonmouth Lake, had formed.

Torsten had first encountered Miroth when he was eleven or twelve years old. Already a loner, playing on the edge of the other children of his village, he'd taken to wandering close to the lake and exploring by himself. He'd never been as big or strong as the other children his own age, and even a few who were younger than him were robust enough to physically push him around. With his father working away for months at a time at the palace, and his mother busy with young twin babies, Torsten was left to his own devices, and was usually drawn to the lake, away from the other children who tormented him.

It was a hot day in mid-summer, and the sun beat down on him relentlessly.

'We are brothers. You and I.'

The hissed voice had startled Torsten so much that he'd stumbled over his own feet and fallen backwards onto the rocky ground, slicing his palm open where he'd braced against the fall. Wincing at the streak of crimson bright against his pale skin, Torsten had clutched the wound while frantically looking around for whoever had spoken to him, sweat already sticking his hair to his forehead.

'If this is another silly joke, it's not funny!' Torsten called out, expecting it to be yet another trick the village boys were playing on him. But when no-one appeared howling with laughter at scaring him, Torsten frowned. He'd *definitely* heard a voice, like a hiss, whispering right in his ear.

Gingerly getting to his feet, his bloodied hand held tight, Torsten gazed around, unsure. He'd had a recent growth spurt and was uncomfortable in his developing body, with his gangly legs and lack of muscle. Rocks and pebbles rolled around underfoot, and he was careful where he stepped lest he added a sprained ankle to his list of injuries.

'Is someone there?' Against the backdrop of the rich, blue lake, his voice both echoed and was swallowed up. Birds squawked in fright and flew away, leaving him utterly alone. Unease slowly crept along his back, turning his already unsteady legs weak. He was filled with a sudden and desperate need to expel his bladder.

Torsten's nerve broke.

He turned to run away, to get back to the village before something terrible happened, when something sharp caught his jacket.

'Don't leave. Your brother here.'

The voice alone almost made him fall over again, and he staggered, trying to pull free of whatever held him. In his desperation to get away, he sank to his knees, rocks digging into his shins. 'Let go of me!'

Abruptly, whatever had snagged on his jacket released him, and he fell forwards, face in the dirt. Coughing, Torsten pushed himself onto his hands and knees and looked back over his shoulder. He gasped at the sight, it was so unexpected and awe-inspiring. A dragon, no bigger than a house-cat, curled up beside a boulder, tail wrapped around its body several times.

Torsten had often encountered snakes on the far side of the lake, hiding underneath rocks and waiting to strike at unwary animals. Although it was very clearly a dragon—blue light emanated from every one of its scales and it watched Torsten with eyes of liquid silver—it reminded him of the venomous snakes he'd always been sure to avoid.

'Y—you called me...brother?' Torsten squeaked, frustrated at his weak voice. This was a *spirit*. Something that people *worshipped*. But he didn't know any that were as small as this one. 'Are you sick, too? You're so small.'

The dragon bristled, its under-developed wings flapping uselessly. *'You and I. Need help.'*

'I don't need help.' It was an instinctive response, one he muttered multiple times a day. A defensive mechanism.

'You bleed.'

Torsten lifted his palm. The cut was deep, and red coated most of his fingers. Only after seeing it did he feel the pain, and he winced again. His knees, too, had been skinned, and the cool breeze on his legs made the scrape sting.

'I don't need help,' he repeated, even as tears pricked his eyes. If any of the other village children were there, they'd start pointing and laughing at him for crying. But up here, on the rocks surrounding the lake, far from the village, there was no-one to see him. No-one to laugh and jeer at his tears.

He chewed his lip, biting down almost until he pierced skin.

'I can stop that. Bleeding. If you help me.'

'You're a spirit, aren't you? Why do *you* need help?' He sank down to the ground, half-crouched, half-squatted, chin resting on his knees, and stared at the blood that dripped down his shin. His skin was dirty, the grime accumulated over the past few days. Torsten picked at it, keeping his bottom lip from quivering, fighting desperately to stop the tears before they fell.

He was afraid. Of the children. Of the pain in his body. Of the spirit, even if it was small and sickly like he was.

'I am. Of the lake. I know this. But...I am new. To this world. I do not understand. You creatures. The way you behave is. Strange. To me.'

Torsten glanced at the dragon curled up around itself, glowing gently in the sunshine. Sharp, hungry-looking fangs poked out from its lips. He didn't know what the spirit's problems meant, or why he should be concerned with them. 'So what?'

Another hiss. *'You are one. Of them. Yet you are apart. We are brothers, you and I. We can. Help each other.'*

He didn't understand why the creature spoke so haltingly, but he supposed the dragon was right. He *was* apart from the other children of his village. He'd always been excluded from their games, or been picked on. And for no good reason, either. 'Can you stop that happening?'

Torsten didn't explain what he meant, but the dragon nodded, as if it understood exactly his problems. *'My power. Will be yours. If you help me. And I will learn. What you know.*

About this world. We will be bonded. As brothers should be.'

Torsten's attention drifted from his scabbing knee to his shoes, which were leather and peeling away. He rubbed at a clump of dried mud above his toe. He didn't know what to say, so he kept his mouth shut, still fighting tears.

'We will be friends.'

That made him pause. Friends? He'd never had a friend before. Not a real one.

'Would you like that?'

He pressed his chin deeper in between his knees, crouching lower to the ground, refusing to speak in case his voice cracked again. There was a particularly stubborn lump of dirt on the end of his shoe. Some of it got under his nail, and he frowned, bottom lip poking out.

'I would like. To be your friend. Brother.'

Torsten wavered, listening but holding back his reaction. Then, dirt removed, he nodded. The gesture was so small he didn't think the dragon would be able to see.

But it reacted immediately—lunging forward with all the speed of a striking snake. It passed *through* Torsten, muffling his sudden scream with its wings. Every one of its claws, small but tremendously sharp, punctured the boy's flesh.

Then everything was fire.

WHEN TORSTEN HAD AWOKEN, the broken moon had already chased the sun away, and night blanketed the lakeside. His breath misted in the air in front of his face, and a thin layer of frost dusted the tops of the rocks, but Torsten hardly noticed the cold.

There was no sign of the dragon, but his chest burned with a warmth that had never been there before. And, along with the fire, was the knowledge of the spirit's name: Miroth.

Eventually, he followed the river down from the lake back

into town, where he found several villagers searching for him, flaming torches held high. Even the boys who bullied him mercilessly were out looking, annoyance on their faces while worry lines etched the adults'.

'Look! There he is!' One boy pointed, waving his torch to alert the others.

The cry went up quickly, shouts staggered through the streets and even the trees surrounding the growing village. 'Torsten's here!'

'The lad's safe!'

'Everyone get back, he's okay!'

His mother, so rarely able to offer him any time given the new babies, ran to him and clutched him close to her apron. She held him tighter than he'd ever remembered, and told him how glad she was that he'd returned home safe, that she loved him and never wanted to see any harm befall him.

In the days that followed, with Miroth whispering in his ear, Torsten was able to put a stop to the bullying—suddenly able to physically overpower the other boys. He pushed back when they started on him, giving them a real fight instead of cowering as they were used to. When he threw the first boy to the ground, the others attacked him as a group.

He was able to beat each of them—even breaking the leg of one boy three years his senior.

No-one knew it had been Miroth.

But Torsten's reputation began to grow that day.

And over the following months, Tonmouth realised a new spirit had formed out of their lake. Miroth never spoke of his bond to Torsten, nor Torsten of his, but in becoming a some-what unwitting priest—the first to receive the spirit's boon—he'd given the newly fledged spirit access to a fountain of information that made him formidable.

Miroth grew in size, accelerated by the shrine built in his honour, until he was as powerful as any other lake or forest spirit.

The constant illnesses that had plagued Torsten as a boy disappeared; he was able to breathe clearly, able to run for longer, and never again caught a fever. Muscle grew as his body filled out, and with it, a harsh severity. He no longer permitted anyone to push him around, and rarely gave newcomers the chance.

Torsten shuddered. His breaths were ragged and his chest was tight. He'd been standing by the altar for some time, lost in the memories of the past. It was a memory Miroth loved reliving—when he had become *something*. When they had become bonded brothers.

Today, some thirty years after Miroth's emergence, the lake had spoiled—water from the Salt Sea entering the lake and poisoning it of life—crippling Miroth and reducing his power.

Torsten could understand why the spirit preferred to take on the appearance of his younger, more powerful self, instead of what he had become. Could understand why the dragon forced him to relive the memory every time he visited.

As powerful as spirits were, and even though he drew strength from his bond with Torsten, they were ultimately bound to their domains. Whenever it was damaged—or destroyed—they vanished.

Miroth only just clutched onto the essence of life, and Torsten knew the spirit would be angered at having had its power drained when he'd called upon it in Ballowtown.

But that was done, now. In the past. The only thing to do was move forward.

Images flickered and died as Miroth reached the end of the memory, light fading, replaced by the pale moonlight from above. Torsten sucked in a deep breath as the spirit ceded control, now satisfied after reliving the memory.

'Miroth. It has been too long.' Torsten sank to one knee in reverence of his spirit. Respect always had to be given.

'Brother. I felt your need of me. You took. Much.'

'For which I am grateful. As ever.' Torsten stood. His left hand throbbed, a memory of the old wound twinging as it was prone to do in Miroth's presence.

'You still carry. The iron dagger,' Miroth stated. The spirit was vaguely corporeal, barely more than thick fog lingering around the rusted sword plunged in the altar.

'The Iron Queen is powerful. Toriaken is invulnerable.'

'Water. Rusts. Iron.' The snarl from Miroth set the hairs on the back of Torsten's neck standing up. 'You came. To mock me? After I aided you? I am already weak.' Twin pinpricks of silver flashed with the spirit's anger, and a cloud of smoke floated into the chamber. The hint of the dragon's tail lashed back and forth, passing through the altar several times.

'It was necessary, my lord. And Iron is a tool. I must use all tools available to me.' Torsten kept his voice low. He placed his hands behind his back and paced, slowly circling the altar. Moving helped him feel safer. Miroth was unlikely to hurt him—in truth, Torsten didn't think the spirit was *capable* of it—but he felt the dragon's anger, disappointment, and hurt as keenly as he felt the stones underfoot. They shared emotions, sometimes thoughts. 'I have come to restore you of the power I took. And I need knowledge.'

Miroth's own movement quietened, and the spirit watched Torsten with every fibre of his focus and attention. 'Restore?'

'Yes, my lord. I always keep you at the forefront of my mind.'

Torsten nearly staggered with the wave of adoration that flooded him.

Miroth sent wave after wave of joyous rapture. 'Yes, yes. Brother, you are always kind. Always considerate. Come closer, please.'

Hurrying to obey, Torsten crouched low beside the altar,

as if he were that eleven-year-old boy again, conspiring with a newly fledged spirit—the first to ever lay eyes on it.

Pressure filled the chamber as Miroth's excitement grew. The dragon, more mist than scales, swirled around the altar, and wind rushed through Torsten's hair. A few loose pebbles rolled around in the strong breeze, rattling against the chamber walls.

When it died down, Torsten grinned. 'My lord. Can you take power from this? It…I think it is another spirit. One far inferior to you.' Holding out his left hand, he slowly opened his fist to reveal the tooth of the Myrish creature flat on his palm.

'*Inferior creature!*' Miroth repeated, a distinct note of amusement in his voice. As the spirit came closer, more of its body became physical. A long, narrow snout, a short, slender neck, webbing between the small spines across its jaw and back. Scales of dusty blue and silver lined the dragon's body, and Miroth kept its small wings tucked tight against its sides.

Nostrils twitching, Miroth lowered its head to Torsten's palm, holding still for several seconds. Then, the dragon recoiled. '*The Myr.*'

'Yes. I killed one of their spirits. There is power in their bodies. Magic.'

'*Power.*' Miroth lunged forward, snapping at Torsten's hand.

Resisting the urge to flinch at the dragon's fangs scraping against his skin, Torsten stood once Miroth had devoured the tooth, and waited with bated breath.

Dust blew up around the floor as Miroth spun around the small chamber, then a flash of orange glinted in the moonlight as he brought forth flames. The dragon let out a roar, the sound somewhat strangled—Miroth had never been particularly vocal—and a crack of magic flooded the chamber for an instant.

Torsten was quite sure everyone in Tonmouth had felt it.

Then, as quickly as it had started, it was over. Miroth stilled, opening his wings to fill the chamber as the mist dissipated, and the dragon spirit truly appeared, glorious and powerful.

Torsten sank to his knees again, this time of his own volition, sharing in Miroth's jubilation of having his strength restored. It wasn't enough, of course. Miroth's domain remained poisoned and dying, draining away a little more each day, but he was no longer an echo of himself. At least, until Torsten needed to call upon his power in battle again.

'My lord...' Torsten's voice was breathy. 'You are magnificent.'

'*I am always magnificent, brother.*' Miroth's soft, halting voice had faded, replaced by a stronger one that snarled with confidence.

Torsten smiled and the earlier tightness of his chest lifted. 'That you are, my lord. What can you tell me about the Myr?'

Pillars of steam streaked from Miroth's nostrils and the delicate webbing between his horns quivered. Miroth sat down, the chamber trembling at the movement, and contemplated. '*I see now. The Myr are again on the rise.*'

'What? How could you possibly know that?' He didn't mean the words to come out so accusatory, but he couldn't fathom Miroth's certainty. All he'd devoured was the tooth of another spirit, and Miroth remained cooped up in its own shrine. He couldn't remember the last time the dragon had ventured outside.

Confusion cascaded through his mind until Miroth abruptly cut them off with another snort of fire. '*What I ate, brother? What you killed? It was something the Myr only sent out at the height of their power. Something not seen in Porsenthia in over five years.*'

Torsten was certain his heart stopped beating. Goosebumps had risen on his arms, and every old injury and wound he'd collected over his forty-three years ached with dread. Whatever Miroth knew, whatever the dragon spirit was about to say, Torsten *knew* it couldn't be possible.

'*One of their most loathsome creations. A Myrish death spirit.*'

11

THE MATRIARCH
CALIDRA

Extending his hand in the traditional Porsenthian greeting, the griffin rider nodded at Varlot. 'Pleased to meet you. I am Amsel Bala Uben.'

Calidra couldn't stop her eyebrows from raising. Bala was her mother's original surname, before she'd married her father and taken Vantonen. She knew her mother had siblings, though she hadn't met them all. And while Bala wasn't a hugely uncommon Olmese surname, she couldn't get past the idea that Amsel could be related to her—a cousin, perhaps?

And more than that, Uben was often added to the names of those of very high standing, even royalty. Was Amsel a *prince*?

Though clearly ruffled by the appearance of the griffin, Varlot took Amsel's hand in his own—almost crushing the other man's fingers judging by the sound of popping joints—and shook it once. 'Varlot Keir. Olmese, huh?'

Amsel brightened. '*The* Varlot Keir? Of Porsenthia? I am honoured to be in the presence of such a famed warrior.' He grabbed Varlot's hand with his other, as if to show his reverence. 'Yes! I live in Ordana, the capital. You should—'

'Never wanted to go to the desert, to be honest. Too hot.' He gestured to his broad body and heavy bearskin cloak, his wide smile doing enough to explain his words. Just like everyone else who had been excited to meet him, Varlot was clearly unfazed at being recognised by Amsel.

Although she, too, was drawn to his charismatic nature, she couldn't hide a noise of frustration at Varlot's rudeness at who she thought might be royalty.

If Amsel noticed, he didn't say anything about it. 'Ordana is only on the edge of the dunes. And if you think Olmir is just a desert, you're an uneducated fool. We have desert, yes, and oases, forests, even snow to the north.' Amsel's easy smile hadn't left his face, and he watched Varlot with clear amusement. 'It's the perfect training ground for any warrior, and of course, the only place in all of Tassar where we have such magnificent creatures as Hailathlyl.' To prove his point, he scratched the enormous griffin under her chin, where her feathers were soft and smooth.

She purred appreciatively.

'Consider me told,' Varlot muttered, but much of his earlier frustration appeared to have left him. 'Can't blame me for being worried. Not every day a thing like *that* comes crashing down on you!'

Calidra let out a held breath. She hadn't been entirely sure whether Varlot would have attacked Amsel or his griffin, which would have ended very badly for them both. 'Neither of us expected a griffin or rider here,' she said, trying to clear the air. 'Or whatever that creature was, to be honest. I am Calidra Vantonen. You said you were travelling to my home, Fellwood?'

Amsel took a step back, then scrutinised her. 'Cal...Calidra?'

She nodded, suddenly unsure.

Hailathlyl snapped her beak and nudged Amsel none-too-lightly. 'Her blood is the same. She is one of Furyn Bala's daughters.'

'It talked!' Varlot gasped, his hands held up in a peaceable gesture. Credit to him, he didn't back away, but he was clearly alarmed at the talking griffin.

The griffin turned her head and stared at him, before snorting and nuzzling Amsel.

'Yes, this is Hailathlyl. She is my companion,' Amsel said.

'Hai...hai...haith?' Varlot tried to sound out the name.

'Hai-lath-lyl,' Amsel said, speaking each syllable slowly. 'She is one of the finest, isn't she?'

'I don't mind a good horse, Amsel. A griffin might be a bit much!' Varlot laughed, easing into conversation with the other warrior, any discomfort quickly fading.

Calidra, unsurprised at the griffin's speech, trembled at the mention of her mother's name. She'd always thought it had been spelled with one superfluous letter, and those unpleasant childhood memories were never far from the surface.

She balled her fists. 'I am. My father, Laird Vantonen, passed away. I'm on my way to the funeral.' She kept her voice flat, without emotion. Precise and to the point. Calidra knew she wasn't talking to her mother—not yet, anyway— but her defences were back up, and speaking in a monotone voice, without showing any emotion, any weakness, was one of the first and easiest ways she could protect herself.

Amsel tilted his head, mirroring Hailathlyl's bird-like movement, then shrugged, getting back into business. 'We don't have much time, Calidra, Varlot. If you're travelling to Fellwood, we should go together. We can go faster on Hailathlyl, and it isn't safe to be on foot in Bragalia.'

'I can keep us out of trouble if it finds us again,' Varlot argued. He eyed the griffin with increasing uncertainty.

Amsel shook his head and gestured to Hailathlyl, who gently laid down on the browning grass, lowering her head as she did so. He stroked the feathers above her eyes with the back of his hand, earning him a loud purr, before walking to the harnessed saddle at her back. 'She is strong enough to carry us all. Even *you*, Varlot,' he added with a wry grin, 'come. We will be in Fellwood in a couple of hours.'

Varlot shook his head, but he clearly wasn't willing to be shown up in front of Amsel, and didn't retreat despite his obvious hesitancy. He fumbled with the fastenings on his cloak, paying more attention to them than Amsel or the war griffin.

Hours *were* better than days, especially as Calidra was already late and apparently the Myr had entered her home country. But hours would put her squarely in front of her mother far sooner than she had prepared herself for. That alone kept her rooted to the spot.

All of a sudden the sun seemed to beat down on her too much, and she became aware of her skin prickling under it. Her breathing grew shallow.

'Calidra?' Varlot broke her from her thoughts and fear.

'Hmm?'

'You okay?' He put a hand on her shoulder, steadying her.

Although she'd never enjoyed accepting help, which proved she was weak enough to require it in the first place, she leaned against his hand. Varlot was strong, much stronger than she was. She imagined he could probably carry her in one arm and not even break a sweat.

So when her knees trembled, her legs threatening to buckle under her, she knew Varlot would keep her standing.

'Want a hand up?' Varlot suggested.

Even though she wasn't sure she could entirely trust him, didn't know his true interest in Fenn—or in helping her, for that matter, other than for coin—he was all she had at that moment. She nodded. The trembling had reached her arms, now, a surge of emotion and panic roiling inside her, fuelling her paralysis.

She couldn't stumble now. Not in front of Varlot. She couldn't stand the idea of being weak in front of him.

'We'll have a better view of everything from up there.' Varlot supported Calidra as they walked over to the waiting griffin. 'Amsel spotted us easily enough. Maybe we'll get a glimpse of Fenn and Jisyel, too?'

Her eyes widened at the suggestion. 'Oh. Yes. Yes!'

Amsel, already sitting in position and waiting patiently, offered Calidra a hand. She took it, climbing up the harness, stepping neatly over the griffin's back and into the saddle. Surrounded by a raised wooden rail that provided a small amount of safety, Calidra gingerly sat down, not wanting to cause the griffin any discomfort or irritation. The saddle itself was made of soft leather, thickly cushioned, and dressed in ornately stitched designs, traditionally in Olmese reds and greens.

Another flavour of home, of her mother.

But she couldn't deny it was *almost* comfortable. Hailathlyl was easily large enough to carry five or six people, and though Calidra had ridden a griffin once as a child— and fallen off, though not from a great height—she was not nearly as afraid as she thought she would be.

Her feet found a broad wooden ledge in place of stirrups, her legs bent more than would be comfortable on a horse, but the griffin was an altogether different creature. Hailathlyl let out another squawk, her feathers ruffling in the stiff breeze that fluttered across the open land.

She fumbled with the straps, clipping herself in, as Varlot joined them in the seat behind her. 'Good thing we travel light,' Varlot mused, tightening his cloak all the way up to his throat.

Amsel laughed. 'Hailathlyl is for war. She can carry six Olmese, fully armed and armoured, *and* their supplies.' He patted her neck affectionately.

'Someone approaches. Porsenthian.' Another beak snap

182

and the griffin's enormous head turned sharply to face Meadowhill.

From her vantage point, Calidra could see some distance, all the way to Meadowhill itself. Her gaze drifted the river as it flowed downhill, and spotted a single person wandering up the path alongside the water. 'Jisyel?'

Another squawk from Hailathlyl, this one sounded impatient. 'Male Porsenthian. Inquisitor.'

'Is it Torsten?' Varlot asked, now strapped in himself. 'We should go.'

'Unfortunately Hailathlyl hasn't met many Inquisitors to tell them apart. But I agree. We should be in the air now and on the way. Just in case there's trouble.'

'Didn't you say you were talking to Inquisitors? About the Myr?' Calidra asked, holding onto the harness straps to avoid clutching at the griffin's feathers.

'My brothers and sisters are. I won't interfere. My own orders take me to Fellwood.'

Calidra squinted, trying to see for herself. But no matter how hard she stared, her eyes would never be as sharp as a griffin's. 'We're looking for someone also on their way to Fellwood. Friends of ours. Jisyel and Fenn. They're...' she hesitated, 'Porsenthians. Can Hailathlyl see them?'

'If they are under us when we are on the way, Hailathlyl will see them, yes.' Amsel nodded, certain. He watched the Inquisitor a moment longer, then let out a sigh of irritation. 'Hold on. Hailathlyl, fly.'

Amsel's instruction was clear, and the griffin reacted as if struck by lightning. Calidra felt Hailathlyl's muscles bunch underneath her, the only physical warning something was about to happen, then they were shooting high into the air. Tears streamed down her cheeks as they cut through the wind like a knife. Dimly aware of the enormous wings beating to either side of her, Calidra was glad of the rail surrounding the harness. She gripped onto it so tightly her fingers went numb, and though she was desperate to wipe her eyes of tears, she dared not unclench her muscles, quite certain she'd left her stomach somewhere on the grasses below.

How long they climbed, she couldn't tell. It was one, long, exhilarating blur. But when she felt able to breathe again, the wind no longer screamed around her. They'd levelled out, the griffin's broad wings soaring on a thermal of warm air that gently kissed her face.

Rushing wind buffeted her, and she could barely hear anything over it, but the flight was altogether less aggressive than take off had been.

Carefully, slowly, she released the handrail one finger at a time. Her skin was dry and stiff, and she massaged her hands, trying to get the feeling back. Behind her, Varlot said something, but his voice was lost to the wind. Even turning to face him was uncomfortable, she'd strapped herself in so tightly, so she just shook her head. Conversation would have to wait.

Once their flight was gentler, she peered over the edge to get her bearings—and nearly brought up her breakfast.

Water, she *knew* she didn't like. But up until now, she'd never had any problems with heights. Although she couldn't guess at their altitude, the drop below made her grasp onto the rail with renewed terror.

Meadowhill sat in the distance astride the river, and the Inquisitor below was a dark smudge on the green and brown landscape. How they were supposed to see *anyone* from such a height was beyond Calidra, but she supposed Hailathlyl had done most of the seeing. She'd have to rely on the griffin's incredible eyesight if they had any chance of coming across Jisyel and Fenn on their way to Fellwood.

If Amsel was correct, and they'd be there in a few hours, it didn't give them much time to look.

But it did give her an idea.

If the worst happened; if they arrived in Fellwood and

there was no sign of Jisyel or Fenn, she would get a search party together. She'd ask Amsel to lead from the sky. On the back of Hailathlyl, they could cover more ground more quickly than any scouting party, even on horseback. And they were much more used to scouting from so high.

Her mother would probably be against the idea, but Calidra disregarded the concern. Griffins obeyed their Olmese riders. It wasn't something that her mother could forbid. Calidra would have to simply ask Amsel nicely. If he was a cousin of hers, perhaps the familial obligation would get him to agree.

It was a poor way of behaving—forcing someone to go out of their way to help you—but if Fellwood was empty, Calidra wasn't sure how she was going to cope.

And at least she would be doing *something*.

HAILATHLYL DESCENDED after several hours on the wing, the mountains growing closer ahead of them. Calidra had quickly recovered after the beginning of their flight, had almost enjoyed it for the last hour or so, once the fear had dissipated.

But as they came down, realisation dawned.

It was time to face her mother.

And she was facing her *without* Jisyel.

In truth, Calidra had only felt able to face her mother with Jisyel by her side. Now she had to endure it alone, like she was a helpless girl again; a child, unable to stand up for herself.

Hailathlyl slowed as she brought them down upon Fellwood, and the surging wind lessened somewhat, enabling her to hear Amsel's careful instructions to the griffin.

Fellwood hadn't changed much in eight years, although it was difficult to tell from above. Groves of peach trees surrounded the palatial villa at the town's highest plateau—her childhood home. A white marble wall surrounded the grounds, keeping the distinction between the Laird's residence and the rest of Fellwood clear. Calidra vividly remembered the day that a group of desperate beggars had scaled the wall, broken into the grounds and held her sister for ransom.

That day had ended in blood.

She was certain there'd still be a smear of old blood, darkened over the years, along part of the wall. But she didn't want to look. That was from a previous time. A previous life, almost.

Her sister wasn't there anymore. Malora had died somewhere further north, in Porsenthia, after she'd fallen in with the wrong crowd and ended up just where their mother had said she would. A natural consequence of going against her wishes.

Calidra blamed herself. If she'd been a better sister, if she hadn't driven Malora away, perhaps she wouldn't have...

She gritted her teeth. She should be upset about the death of her father, not guilting herself for something that had happened years ago.

The villa was far too large for one woman to live in alone —even with the retinue of servants to cater to Furyn's every whim. Calidra wondered if her time away had softened or sharpened her mother's temper.

As they flew above Fellwood, Calidra stared blankly at the opulent golden pillars and statues carved on the edges of the villa's grounds. A cold truth settled in her stomach. The same one that she'd had for years, and part of what had driven her away. Her family's wealth was false. So was the power that had grown from it.

They were no more fit to be Lairds than anyone else in Fellwood.

Sigya Malora, the people had called her sister. Blessed by

Chyram, the Spirit of Gold, whose shrine was nestled deep in the mountains. Chryam rarely offered any blessings to people—it only happened once every handful of generations.

Malora hadn't even been interested in joining his order, yet the dragon had selected her, out of everyone else, and given her a boon.

Calidra peered over the griffin's side. Dozens of people streamed into the streets, staring up in awe and wonder as they flew overhead, hands shielding their eyes from the glare of the sun. Griffins weren't exactly an unusual sight, but a *war* griffin probably was. She stared back at the many faces, hoping to recognise Jisyel or Fenn among the gathered crowds.

They circled as they descended, flying over much of Fellwood, but definitely drifting towards Calidra's home. She knew it was coming, but it didn't make it any easier. She could have a lifetime to prepare for coming home and she'd never be ready.

Once they were over the marble wall surrounding the grounds, the gasps and stares thankfully disappeared. Now, they were on private ground, where they wouldn't be gawked at. Calidra only saw a handful of staff dotted around, and a pair of them darted inside the moment they spotted the griffin, no doubt to alert her mother.

'I hope Lady Vantonen is here,' Amsel said.

'She'll be here,' Calidra replied, almost wishing there was too much wind again to hear him.

Hailathlyl brought them down in the middle of the gardens. It was the most logical place—the courtyard was narrow, lined with trees and flowers chosen for their aesthetic rather than practicality. Manicured lawns made up a significant part of the gardens, watered four times a day to keep the grass lush and green. Although tall hedges divided up the gardens into neat sections, there was plenty of space even for a griffin as large as Hailathlyl to comfortably land.

Landing was less bumpy than Calidra thought it would be, but by the time she'd managed to get out of the harness and stand on solid ground, she wondered if she'd simply lost all feeling from the waist down. Her legs stung as her nerves woke up again, and she shook out her feet, wincing as she did.

'That was quite the experience!' Varlot slapped Hailathlyl's side affectionately. 'Never in all my days did I expect anything like it! I have to hand it to you, Amsel. Your griffin is *astounding*!'

Amsel beamed at the compliment, and nudged the griffin with his full weight. 'You have a new fan, Hailathlyl! Guess there's some hope for the Porsenthians after all!'

'Perhaps.' The griffin sat down and began preening herself.

Varlot roared with laughter. 'Spirits take me, if only I'd had one of *them* in the war!'

Calidra wandered away from the others, just a few steps to get some feeling back into her legs and feet, massaging her arms and wrists while she looked around. The gardens were much as she remembered them. A few more plants. The trees had grown broader. One new statue in the corner. Nothing of any significance.

The flower gardens were on the far side of the lawn, white and blue and pink, bringing colour to the landscape. Beyond those were the tea gardens, sun gardens, and the water gardens, if her mother still had those. She could smell the fragrant teas even so far from them. Some were worth more per gram than gold. Trust her mother to keep her wealth after Malora had left.

Bees and insects buzzed happily in between the bushes, seeking out nectar, and a golden hummingbird darted out of view the same instant she spotted it. It was so calm, so peaceful, completely shut off from the problems of the world.

Archways of delicate silver provided a path between the tall hedges that lined each of the gardens, and Calidra peered through the nearest one. Her breath hitched at the sight of the vast, cream villa beyond. A single storey feat of architecture and beauty, funded by falsity.

Her home. She'd not seen it in eight years.

And, strolling down the white stone path straight towards them, was Furyn.

'Amsel. Varlot. She's coming.' Calidra dashed back to the others. Immediately, she brushed away the dirt on Varlot's cloak and almost went to do the same to Amsel before she stopped herself. 'S—Sorry! I just…She likes things tidy. Presentable.'

Varlot frowned at her, but she turned away, taking deep breaths to calm her fraying nerves. It didn't matter what they thought of her behaviour. It was too late now.

Quillaja, her mother's handmaiden, passed through the arch first. Tall and slender, with impeccable manners and a calm confidence that Calidra had always been in awe of, the Olmese woman had been at her mother's side for as long as Calidra could remember. Her cool gaze passed over them, taking in Varlot, Amsel, and even the war griffin without reaction. But her hardened exterior cracked the moment she saw Calidra. Quillaja gasped, eyes widening in shock, the smallest of smiles on her plump lips; then she recovered herself and slipped back into neutrality. Ever professional.

Calidra latched onto that smile and braced herself. Furyn walked five or six steps behind her handmaiden, so graceful she seemed to float, her long, red robes trailing behind her.

'I present Lady Vantonen. Welcome to Fellwood, friends,' Quillaja introduced, lowering her gaze and interlacing her fingers, holding them loosely in front of her. Words spoken, she stepped back, allowing her mistress to come forward and address them as she chose.

Varlot dropped to one knee and lowered his head.

Amsel inclined his head, crossed one arm over his chest, and bowed low.

Calidra stood stock still—a rabbit caught in the gaze of a fox—and did nothing.

'Welcome to Fellwood.' Furyn extended her arms, her long sleeves giving her the effect of having wings. Impressive as usual. 'It has been some time since we had a griffin rider, or a griffin as fine as this one, in my home. You are most welcome here, my countryman.'

Hailathlyl snapped her beak and purred loudly, her long, cat-like tail swaying from side to side.

Calidra ignored the sting of hurt at being ignored by her mother in the first instance. Then again, it would have been rude to ignore the guest.

Furyn gestured for Amsel to rise, then she considered Varlot. 'It is rare for a Porsenthian to come here. Rarer still on the back of a griffin, even one as famous as yourself.'

'Indeed, but these are strange times.' Varlot straightened up. 'Lady Vantonen. I am reporting here, as requested by the Laird. I have also escorted your daughter, Calidra. I'm sure we can discuss the additional fee for this extra task.' He produced a sheet of paper from his inside pocket and offered it to her.

Furyn plucked from within her robe a pair of seeing eye glasses on a thin silver chain and read the paper carefully. 'Varlot Keir himself. How interesting. I laughed when my husband said he'd contracted you. Why would a man of your standing bother yourself with the needs of Bragalia? And yet, here you are. *Such* a formidable fighter.'

'At your command.'

Furyn's gaze lingered on him. 'A wasted journey, I'm

afraid. My husband requested this contract, but as he has now passed, there is no longer any need for it.'

Varlot reddened. 'Surely there is every need! The youth of today *must* know how to defend themselves. Why, even Calidra can—' He cut himself off at the harsh look Calidra gave him. Was he really so desperate for coin that he'd react that way? What in all of Tassar had happened to this mighty general? A man who had evaded death for so long that his reputation suggested he was impossible to kill? Just how far had he fallen?

Amsel stepped forward, distracting everyone from Varlot's sudden outrage. 'My lady, might we go inside? There are urgent matters to discuss regarding the safety of the canton. Of Bragalia.'

Furyn nodded. 'Of course. You must both be tired. Please, go inside and take some refreshment. You are of course welcome to stay and rest for as long as you need. Varlot, I will see what services I might require of you once this urgent business with my kinsman has been taken care of. And, the... griffin?' She looked uncertain at the enormous creature.

'I will hunt and rest,' Hailathlyl answered.

Amsel stroked the griffin's silky feathers again. 'Thank you again, Lath. We'll patrol this evening.'

Varlot had been about to object, staring hard at Furyn, who met his glare with one as equally savage, when he coughed awkwardly and looked away. 'Very well. I'll rest and then we'll *talk*.'

Calidra swallowed, wondering when her mother would address her, desperate for some form of positive acknowledgement, but terrified at the same time of being in the centre of Furyn's notice. The internal conflict made her sway on her feet. Every time Furyn spoke, Calidra tried not to tremble.

Two servants, whom Calidra hadn't noticed lingering just on the other side of the archway, appeared silently to lead

Varlot and Amsel through the gardens and towards the house. Once Amsel was out of sight, Hailathlyl took to the air, blasting them with a gust of wind as she flew straight up.

Both Calidra and Furyn stared up her, and once the griffin had disappeared from view, Calidra realised she was alone with her mother. Quillaja, evidently, had followed their guests inside.

'Mother.' Calidra uttered the word as calmly as she could, but her voice shook.

'It's good to see you have not *completely* lost your senses.' All politeness had faded from Furyn's tone. 'Eight years. You never wrote. How was I to know you'd not been eaten alive on that disgusting island?'

Heat rose along Calidra's neck. So her mother was permitted to not bother writing, but *she* had to keep in touch? She knew mentioning that obvious fact would only cause an argument, so she swallowed the building rage and avoided the topic altogether. 'Is Jisyel here?'

A sliver of emotion coloured Furyn's cheeks. 'Excuse me?'

'Jisyel. Has she arrived? With a young lad, Fenn?'

'No-one has come here other than you and those men,' Furyn gestured towards the house. 'Why? Are you expecting more company? I hadn't realised I would be hosting so many people for you. Shall I ensure the good wine is brought up?'

Calidra ignored the barb as a stab of panic shot through her. Varlot had been sure, so very sure, that Jisyel and Fenn *would* be here. There was no need for her mother to lie about that. 'They should have made it here by now. We'll have to send out a search party. I'll ask Amsel, too, once he and Hailathlyl are rested. We have the household guard and horses in employment? They can head out right away, while there's still some light, then we—'

Furyn cleared her throat. It wasn't a loud noise, and Calidra saw the tightening of her mother's lips rather than hearing it, and her voice died. Her mother raised her chin.

'You haven't been here for eight years, and the moment you return—on griffin-back, no less—begin making demands of *my* household?'

'Jisyel is important to me.'

'I have no doubt. But there are other matters of greater importance. Now you're here, you can finally begin seeing to them. Come.' Furyn turned away.

'No.'

Furyn stopped in her tracks, her long, golden earrings swaying at the sudden halt in movement.

Calidra licked her lips. 'The Myr are back. That's what Amsel's here to tell you. Probably organising some sort of defence. They're in Bragalia now, mother. And Jisyel is out there. We were separated on the way to Fellwood. Fenn, too. I hurried home in the hopes that she would've made it here by now, but if you say she isn't here, then she isn't safe. She could be—'

'You hurried home...so you could see Jisyel?' Furyn's voice had quietened.

'Yes?'

'What about your father? The funeral? Is *that* not why you came back? You've never visited before, I can't imagine why you'd start now.'

'Of course I'm here for the funeral, too. But as I said, we were separated on the way and—'

Furyn whirled around, silencing Calidra with a glare. 'How *dare* you. I've lost both daughters and now my husband, and all you're interested in is some wretch from a cursed rock in the middle of the sea! What about your home, Calidra? Your responsibilities here? What about *me*?' She didn't raise her voice, Furyn rarely had to, and her words cut Calidra's resolve like a knife. 'If the Myr are on the move, there are more important things right now than this...this... fling of yours.' Furyn strolled back to Calidra and looked her in the eye. 'I have done you the courtesy of keeping your rooms as they were. I will no doubt be busy in discussions with the griffin-rider for much of the day. I'll have Quillaja run a bath for you, and get you out of those filthy peasant clothes.'

'But—'

'Not another word, Calidra. The funeral is tomorrow. I'll not have you disgrace me any further. Get inside and we'll discuss matters once the service is over.'

TRUE TO HER WORD, Furyn spent the rest of the day in her study with Amsel, Varlot, and the head of the house guard. She'd also summoned the most high-ranking officers from within Fellwood itself, and they'd sealed themselves away while they pored over maps and discussed information and potential strategies against the Myr.

Calidra had spent a while with her ear to the door, but it had been made of solid oak, and trying to catch any of the conversation on the other side was nigh impossible.

Just being back in her childhood home was enough to awaken powerful emotions that she'd long since buried. It was disorienting to walk the same hallways again, see the same rooms, the same people. Her father had rarely been home—he'd spent more time outside Fellwood than in it—but knowing he was never coming back, that she would never again hear his voice within these walls, was upsetting.

Quillaja had emerged from the study after a short while, and set to obeying her mother's orders. The handmaiden had led Calidra to the south wing of the villa, which she'd shared with Malora as a child, and immediately arranged for the large, brass tub to be filled with steaming hot water. To the bath, she added a number of different emollients and herbs, even petals from the flowers of her mother's personal bouquets. By the time it was ready, Calidra wasn't sure if she would emerge clean or cooked in a soup.

Following instructions in a daze, Calidra was dimly aware of her skin being scrubbed, her hair washed, and creams applied to her body. Personal grooming had never been something she'd prioritised, only doing enough to cover basic hygiene, never bothering with the oils and scents her mother adored, and jewellery was the furthest thing from her mind when she dressed.

But back home, under her mother's orders, she was washed and dried, dressed in fine clothing and pungent scents, and given gold and gems to adorn her hair and fingers—as was becoming of her position, Quillaja explained when Calidra had objected.

She'd hardly touched the broth that had been served for dinner. Every sip had been full of the typical Olmese "tang," a blend of six key spices her mother often requested. The pork was richly seasoned, flavoured with lime and pepper, one of Calidra's favourite childhood dishes, but she didn't have the motivation to finish it.

It was dark by the time Quillaja had finished with her, and her companions had yet to leave her mother's study. Exhausted after all the travelling, the emotional turmoil, and her fraught nerves with seeing her mother again, Calidra had no strength to protest any of it.

It was probably for the best. Her mother always demanded obedience, and Calidra meekly gave it.

She sat beside the enormous mirror that dominated one side of her room, staring at the reflection of the open window, and wondered where Jisyel was. Whether she was okay, or whether she'd ever made it out of the bay that night in Ballowtown.

Quillaja sat beside her, a selection of oils on her lap as she worked them through Calidra's face and hair. She'd set up candles and incense, and the heady scents lulled Calidra to the edge of awareness. Sleep wouldn't be far off, even though she didn't feel she deserved rest.

'What have I done...' Calidra murmured, giving voice to her thoughts. 'I left her. Left her.'

'Hmm?' Quillaja responded, stoppering one glass bottle and choosing another. 'Left her? Not at all, Calidra. You've returned to her now.'

She shook her head. 'I don't mean my mother. I don't care about *that*.'

'Calidra, you really shouldn't speak that way about Lady Vantonen.'

'She's my mother. I can speak about her anyway I wish.'

'Perhaps.' Quillaja said no more, uncorking another bottle and sending the zesty smell of jasmine lily floating into her room. One of her mother's favourite flowers.

Calidra pulled away. 'Not that one.'

'Do you have a preferred perfume? A Porsenthian fragrance, perhaps? One you've been using while you've been away?'

'None of them.'

'Now, now, there's no need to be so moody. You'll need rose, I think. And some lavender. It'll help you sleep.' Quillaja uncorked them and dabbed several drops onto her wrist. 'Hold still, please.'

Calidra had no energy to argue. Not after what she'd done. She'd left her new home. Had lost Jisyel and Fenn. Who knew where they were, or whether they were safe. Tears rolled down her cheeks, unbidden.

'It is good to see you back. Lady Vantonen didn't think you would return, but I had faith you would. You were always so very sensible, Calidra.'

'Mmm.' A non-committal answer. Calidra's gaze never left the night sky as reflected in her mirror. She didn't see the opulence of her rooms, the finery of the clothes she'd been dressed in. Didn't feel so much as a flicker of comfort at the idea of sleeping in a bed stuffed with goose down. None of it mattered without Jisyel.

'I have faith in Malora, too, you know. She always did leave things to the last minute, didn't she? Hah, it would be *just* like her to arrive a minute before the priests begin the service.'

Calidra blanched. 'M—Malora?'

'Yes. We last heard just under four years ago? Somewhere up in Porsenthia. Foxmouth, I think? I suppose she might not be able to get away. Very busy what with the baby and—'

'Baby?' Calidra stood up so quickly Quillaja was thrown backwards, her jars and bottles of oils and perfumes scattered along the heavy wooden floorboards. 'What are you talking about, Quillaja?'

The handmaiden was on her knees, frantic, grabbing open jars before too much of the contents spilled out.

'Quillaja? Malora...Malora *died*?'

Finally with all the bottles stoppered and disaster averted, the handmaiden straightened up, still on her knees. 'Is that what you think? Oh no, Calidra. Your mother disapproves, of course. You know how much she *hates* being proven wrong. But yes, Malora is alive and well. If you'd come home or written sooner, you'd know all about it!'

Calidra thought she was going to be sick again.

The handmaiden smiled broadly. 'In fact, you have a niece!'

THE WARNING

FENN

F enn was beyond certain his feet were going to fall off. They'd gone past aching discomfort into cold numbness, and now they were spasming; bolts of electricity danced across his soles with every step.

Whoever he'd been before he'd lost his memories, whatever he'd done, hiking had *never* been part of his life. It didn't help that his boots were slightly too big for him—the wardrobe back on the Isle of Salt hadn't offered much of a selection. By the time they were within an hour of the town of Vaelar, he had several blisters on both feet and it felt like the skin on the tips of his toes had been rubbed off.

Why did Bragalia have to be so full of hills?

It didn't bother Jisyel or Selys, and he envied their stamina. Both of them waited for him a few paces ahead. 'What is that tattoo?' Fenn gestured to Selys's bare arm. 'Saw lots of priests at the shrine with them?'

Selys glanced down at her arm, as if seeing the markings there for the first time. 'Everyone who joins the order has a mark applied to them. It's a lifetime commitment.'

'It's very pretty. We don't see many priests on the Isle of Salt,' Jisyel said.

'Kind of a way to show your...dedication?' Fenn asked.

'Exactly.' Selys held her arm up, where the coloured lines weaving across her skin glittered.

Fenn took the brief pause to catch his breath, hands on his thighs. Although they weren't particularly high up, the air felt thinner than usual, and breathing was difficult. A drop of sweat rolled down his nose and he wiped it away with a huff.

Overhead, a cloud shifted, allowing the sun to beam down brightly. Fenn turned his head, squinting away from the light, and his breath caught. A shadow-like creature, wandering across the plains towards them—perhaps a league or two away, it was difficult to tell the exact distance. Whether it was the same one from Ballowtown or a different one, he couldn't say. But it *felt* the same. Wrong. Evil. *Terrifying*. Light rippled around it, as if it distorted the air where it walked. His chest squeezed in terror.

'J—Jisyel!' Fenn called, unable to tear his gaze from the creature in the distance.

'What is it?' Jisyel hurried over to him, a half-eaten apple in one hand. 'Are you hurt?'

He pointed, not trusting his voice.

She followed the gesture and peered out across the Bragalian grasslands. Then frowned. 'What?'

'You...can't see that?' Fenn asked, quizzical. He'd not pulled his gaze from it—he'd already made that mistake once with Calidra—and the creature was *definitely* there. It lumbered along on an ungainly pair of legs, although not quickly, moving at a steady pace.

Jisyel's frown deepened. 'See what? What are you pointing at?'

Frustrated, Fenn said, 'I know you can't feel things, but surely you can *see* them? It's the monster that attacked us in Ballowtown! The shadow creature? Or, another one just like it!'

Jisyel took a few steps forward, as if it would somehow

give her a better view. 'Fenn, that's just the air rippling because it's hot. You see it all the time in Bragalia and Olmir. Sometimes it looks like water from a distance.' She put her hand on her hips and stared straight up, heedless of the sun's heat bearing down on them. After taking another bite of her apple, she shrugged. 'It's the middle of the day, those illusions happen—'

'It's *not* an illusion! It's the creature from before!'

'What's all the shouting about?' Selys hurried back to them, her glaive already drawn, the feathers tied to the shaft fluttering in the wind. 'Fenn?'

'Can't you see it?' He whirled around to stare at the priestess, desperate for her to see, to understand. 'There, right in the middle of the plains!'

Selys turned her head, curious, where he gestured. She wore the same frown as Jisyel, the tip of her glaive lowering. 'It's hot out. Sometimes the heat tricks the eye, makes the ground look like water or shadow.'

'Selys, please. I *can* see it. It's a creature of some sort. Of shadow. It has two legs, two arms that are long, kind of… kind of dragging on the ground behind it.'

The priestess narrowed her eyes, the scar over her right eye tightening in the movement. 'Wait a minute.' She looked, *really* looked, staring until her eyes began to water, and held her breath.

It reminded Fenn of when she'd inspected him outside her shrine. He saw her body stiffen. 'You see it, now. Don't you?'

'It's the Myr.' Selys's voice was a whisper. 'Or…one of their spirits. Neros save me, I think it's one of their death spirits.'

'That's not possible!' Jisyel gasped. 'If it's right there, why can't I see it? Don't joke about these things, Fenn! Selys! It isn't funny!'

Selys shook her head and took several steps back. 'It's no

joke, Jisyel. Fenn has been touched by the Myr. Perhaps that's why he can so readily sense their magic? And I...I just need to focus. Know what I'm looking for, to be able to see it. Thanks to my order. We're closer to spirits than most. Fenn's right—it's there. We need to get to Vaelar. We need to warn people!'

Fenn gulped, panic growing in his gut. Adrenaline flooded his body and drove away the aches.

Selys took the lead and hurtled off.

The trio ran.

FENN COULD SMELL the town before they reached it; an unpleasant mix of rotten food, unwashed bodies, and stale urine.

Limping behind Selys's furious pace, helped occasionally by Jisyel, he was beyond relieved when they were finally able to take a break within sight of Vaelar's gates. He could hardly believe the priestess had such strength and stamina, and was in awe of her confidence. Even through her obvious fear and shock at seeing the Myrish creature—she remained focussed and determined. He wondered what she'd be like if she needed to fight one of those things.

His feet throbbed with pain and every muscle in his legs screamed, but his headache was an even bigger distraction. It had steadily worsened the further north they'd travelled, and now it pounded with such determination that he could hardly keep his eyes open. Whether it was to do with another day on the road under the harsh Bragalian sun, due to his physical location, or because of seeing the Myrish creature, he couldn't say.

People had died because of it. *Were* dying. Pushing the unpleasant thought to the back of his mind, Fenn hobbled onwards. None of it would mean much if he died, too.

He wondered whether Jisyel was as hurt as he was, then recalled her own curse. *She* didn't feel pain. He winced, nearly losing his footing. He'd have to remember to tell Jisyel to check her feet. That's what Calidra would do, surely.

'I'll go inside and see if I can find out who's in charge. Get a warning out to the town watch before anything happens.' Selys hurried along the path to the town's gates, where she promptly disappeared into the crowd.

'We'll rest here for a minute.' Jisyel's voice was soothing. 'I see you're hurting.'

'I'm…I'm okay.' Fenn clutched his head with one hand, swaying on his feet. He didn't want to be more of a bother than he already was. Although the Myrish spirit had been some distance away, and was moving slowly, dread grew at the idea of it being so close. If it came to Vaelar…

'Fenn. Don't try and be like Calidra—she toughs it out and *always* suffers for it. You're limping. And I guess that headache hasn't eased, either?'

'It's worse.' He tried to shake his head, but that sent up another spike of agony. He took several deep breaths, riding out the pain. 'The Myr…'

'There's nothing we can do right now,' Jisyel said, sterner than she'd sounded earlier. He wondered if she was covering up her fear again, like when they'd washed up across the bay. 'Selys will get word out to the people who need to know. And *we* definitely can't do anything if you're about to collapse.'

He raised his head, ready to argue, then closed his mouth. She was right.

He sat on a large rock beside the path, massaging his forehead with one hand. Although outside Vaelar, Fenn could see it was a smaller settlement than Ballowtown, and yet his struggles were already attracting attention. A group of children, hands and legs covered in dirt, stopped their games and watched him, a few circling like stray puppies, hungry for scraps. One pointed, whispering to their companions.

Fenn winced and dropped his hand, not wanting to look as vulnerable as he felt.

Jisyel followed his gaze. 'Don't mind them.'

He held his breath as a particularly vicious wave of pain washed over him, then a cloud passed in front of the sun, and the severity lessened. He'd give anything for some relief.

After a few minutes, Selys appeared at the gates and made her way back down the path towards them, her lips pressed into a thin line. 'The watch laughed at me.'

'Oh no! But you're a priestess?' Fenn said.

'I know, but they told me to be quiet and to stop spreading lies before they arrested me.' Selys shrugged. 'I did what I could. Perhaps word will spread and people can make their own conclusions.'

'But why didn't they take you seriously?'

'You'll see once we get inside. There's some trouble in town.'

Fenn groaned.

'The pain is worsening?'

'Seems to be. Sun won't help,' Jisyel answered when Fenn was unable to.

'The sooner we're inside, the better. Vaelar's walls might only be wood, but they'll offer some shelter.' Selys wirled her glaive and gazed along the edge of town, as if assessing it. 'There are other lost souls here. They must've seen the same creature you did, Fenn. With the presence of the Inquisitors in Bragalia, the atmosphere is...frantic. People are afraid. Most of the lost souls have been locked up, but I hope people here are wondering if they're speaking the truth. Whether the Myr really have returned? It'd mean they'd be less likely to be taken by surprise in an attack.'

Fenn shook his head, despite the pain of the movement. 'What's so hard to believe? I know what I saw. And you're a priestess! Why won't anyone listen?'

Jisyel threw up her hands. 'Because Queen Surayo is in

power! The Iron Crown has kept this entire continent safe for *years*. She and Toriaken created the peace treaty five years ago. The Myr can't be here. They *can't* be! And especially not death spirits!'

'Best not to talk about it loudly, Jisyel, or you might be arrested, too.' Selys glanced around, checking no-one had heard Jisyel's outburst. 'The guards were pretty twitchy. In my experience, that leads to people getting hurt.'

'Jisyel might be arrested? For speaking the truth?' Fenn was on his feet again, hands balled into fists at the injustice of it. Dizziness immediately gripped him.

'It's *heresy*. If anyone asks, you saw a wild cat.' Selys's voice had dropped, gaze lingering on the children. 'Let's get inside and get some rest. Jisyel, you can see if Calidra and Varlot are here, and we'll be on our way soon—tomorrow morning at the latest. You need sleep, Fenn, don't argue. I can keep an eye out in case that spirit comes close to town.'

Selys put her glaive away, and Fenn wondered how good she was in combat. Varlot, Calidra, and Torsten had all fought off the spirit in Ballowtown. Did the priestess have a chance alone?

Jisyel smiled at the mention of Calidra. 'Good idea.'

Fenn said, 'If...if the town is busy, hopefully no-one will pay too much attention...to us.' His breath came in ragged gasps as the pain swirled.

'You're right. There are many injured, too. We won't stand out as long as we keep moving, and keep *quiet*.' Selys looped her arm under his and gave Jisyel a pointed look. 'Come on, Fenn. Let's keep walking.'

'Thanks,' he muttered, unable to muster any more enthusiasm.

Jisyel and Selys helped him limp along the path to the high, wooden gates surrounding Vaelar. They paused briefly beside the two gatekeepers, each showing their papers. A brief flicker of panic darted through Fenn as they chuckled at

Selys, but they waved them all through. Even if they weren't keen on what Selys had said, at least papers signed by the priestess were permissible to the guards.

He let out his held breath as they walked through the gates—and immediately into the bustling crowd, enclosed under overlapping sheets of fabric, which provided shelter from the sun. Just as Selys had said, the streets were heaving. Dozens of people congregated in the wide street, on either side of which vendors sold a range of goods. Fenn saw everything from balls of soft cheese in brine to the wooden sandals that most people here favoured wearing. One woman sold beads of jade that were identical to the one on Selys's glaive, save the dragon carved into it.

Those who weren't selling anything clutched what few possessions they could. One man even had a small herd of goats tied together, the rope loose around his waist. Children chased chickens, and anyone able enough carried sacks of food, clothes, and other supplies.

A line of plucked geese had been strung up above the awning of a building, under which several cooking bots bubbled away, smells amplified in the enclosed space. Fenn wrinkled his nose at the amount of garlic. Several dogs, so thin their spines showed clearly through their matted fur, sniffed for scraps nearby.

Fenn was drawn to a trio of people who were seated on a carpet against a backdrop of textiles. Tubs of spices lay open in front of them, their colours bright and rich despite the muted sunlight.

One of the Bragalian vendors, a woman, caught Fenn's eye and waved him over. She immediately began talking, but it was a language he didn't understand.

She must've noticed his confusion, because she paused, then swapped into another dialect. 'Black cumin?' She pointed to one tub full of dark seeds. 'Sumac?' Another tub that held fine, wine-coloured powder. 'Mountain garlic?'

Enormous bulbs filled the pot, and the woman picked one up. With one twist, she opened it, revealing soft, deep-brown flesh inside.

'Oh! Uh…that looks wonderful, but—'

At the far end of the busy street, a group of eight people were chained at the waist, their hands bound in coarse rope, while a uniformed officer stood guard beside them. Everyone was clearly afraid, but many of them seemed confused, too, with wide eyes and gazes that darted nervously around.

Pity rolled through him at the ragged sight. He shook his head apologetically at the spice seller, and hurried to catch up with Jisyel and Selys. As much as he wanted to speak to the prisoners—the other lost souls—to see what their experiences were, and how they compared to his own, he couldn't risk attracting the wrong attention. Teeth gritted together, he forced himself to continue down the street, away from the crowds.

Beggars huddled together at the end of the vendors' stalls or at the corner of arched buildings, most on their knees. Many raised their palms to him, pleading, and spoke in a tongue he didn't understand.

'Is…are the people poor here?' Fenn asked.

'Vaelar is at the junction of three cantons. There's a lot of traffic that passes through,' Selys explained. 'Plenty of opportunity.'

'Looks awful, not like opportunity,' Fenn replied.

'There has to be a healer somewhere here, right?' Jisyel squinted at the signs where streets crossed. 'Might be worth one having a look at you, Fenn? While Selys and I see if Calidra and Varlot are in town?'

He recoiled at the suggestion. 'No, no! I'm sure it'll pass.'

'Really? You can hardly stand up by yourself, that headache is so bad.' Jisyel poked his shoulder, making him sway.

'If my headache is due to the Myr, I don't want anyone taking a closer look at me. Not when everyone here is already so on edge. I'll rest, have some water. No need to make anyone else suspicious of me.'

Jisyel folded her arms. 'But you're hurting.'

'You ought to rest, too, Jisyel. I can already feel blisters on my feet. Yours can't be much better, even if you can't feel it.'

'He's right,' Selys approached them, 'other lost souls have already been chained up. We don't want to lose Fenn, too, and get him passed on to an Inquisitor.'

Fenn barely suppressed a shudder at the thought. Although it was better that they were somewhere they wouldn't stand out too much—not now they were inside the gates of Vaelar, anyway—the sudden increase in people made him uncomfortable. More eyes to look at him, more voices to report his presence.

'Come on. Let's see if we can find a quiet inn.' Jisyel darted off, expertly weaving through the gathered people.

Fenn gave himself another moment to steady his legs before continuing after her. What he wouldn't give for another hot bath—he wasn't sure his feet had much left in them. With Selys at his side—the glaive at her back helping part people—the pair of them hurried after Jisyel as quickly as they could.

Each street was busy, with thick smoke choking the air down one particular area. One street had no vendors at all, but was home to entertainers of various disciplines. Some people were carving stone, others painting directly onto the walls of buildings.

A robed man made dice appear and disappear, whether from his hands, a box, or the hands of willing audience participants. 'If you can correctly guess where the dice will show, I will split half of all donations received today with you!'

Several people yelled out suggestions, confident they knew the magician's tricks.

'Ah, close, but not correct! Come on, can anyone tell me? Show me? Or is Old Mithal's magic too powerful for you mere mortals to understand?'

Distracted, from following Jisyel, Fenn tried to think about how it worked, wondering if the man had a second set of dice already hidden. Selys joined him and tutted. 'This sort of thing is common near the shrine. Always trying to show off.'

'It is?'

'If he was a *real* mage, I'd be impressed. But I've seen so many of these charlatans before that it just bores me.'

'Oh.' Fenn tried not to let his disappointment show. 'What's the difference between him and a real mage?'

'Tenacity. And some luck.'

Another duo shouted down the street, attracting a large crowd of eager onlookers. Fenn paused to watch them, despite himself. One of the pair juggled a range of objects, cheered on by the crowd who suggested more and more elaborate options. Apples. Balls. Someone's sandal. He threw everything higher, until they grazed the fabric canopy above. A grey cat lounged on the floor beside them, watching with a faint air of boredom.

'Thank you for coming to yet another performance of the sleepless travellers!' said the second man, who held a tangerine as he addressed their rapt audience. 'Donations to Uncus the Juggler and yours truly will help our cause.' He held out a straw basket as people threw in coins, silver and gold glinting.

The juggler finished his routine, catching the items and bowing low. 'My colleague Sodah will be setting up the next performance in a few minutes—fire-breathing! You don't want to miss the show, believe me!'

Fenn gasped and began to make his way towards the duo, excited to see.

'Fenn. *Come on.* As much as I'd love to show you every Bragalian delight, we aren't here for sight-seeing.' Selys pulled on his arm, leading him out of the street. They caught up with Jisyel at a smaller promenade where the crowds finally thinned.

Fenn was disappointed, but his feet throbbed again, and he knew the priestess was right.

A large inn dominated one side of the road, while opposite, a grocers displayed boxes and crates of fruits and vegetables. Each building had a fabric awning that kept produce and doorways in shade. Dust rolled around the ground, and Fenn coughed with his next breath. Despite the heat, he was glad he could actually see the ground under his feet, and he leaned against the wall of the inn, grateful for the respite.

After a second of looking around, Fenn realised why this area was quieter than the entrance to town—the stocks were here. Three of them in the centre of a small square, upon a raised plinth, and one was occupied—a young man had his head and hands locked in the gallows. His hair was dirty, his forehead damp with sweat, and his clothes had the same level of grime as most of the beggars Fenn had seen earlier.

Several rotten tomatoes lay at his feet, their ripe juices steaming in the day's heat.

'He's not one of the lost souls,' Selys commented. 'I can't see anything wrong with him.'

'Maybe we can get some information?' Jisyel suggested.

'No, Jisyel! Don't attract—'

Before Fenn could finish, Jisyel approached the man and blurted out, 'What happened? Why are you locked up here and not with the others?'

Shocked someone was speaking to him, the man twisted

as much as his restraints would allow to get a look at her, then spoke haltingly, 'Por—sen—thian?'

Jisyel nodded.

'Water?'

Jisyel immediately pulled a flask from her bag and lifted it to the man's lips. Most spilled down his chin, but he was able to swallow down several mouthfuls. 'Not lost soul.' His accent was thick and difficult to understand. 'Threw potato. At. Inquisitor.'

Fenn was so exhausted he almost burst out laughing. If he'd been bold enough, *he'd* probably throw a potato at Torsten if he ever had the chance to.

'Where did the lost souls come from?' Jisyel pushed.

The man shrugged. 'Boat. From Segandis.'

'Are there Inquisitors here? In Vaelar?'

'No.'

'Are they coming here? To pick up the lost souls?'

The man grunted as he tried to think of the right words. 'Maybe? Soon.' He coughed again. 'Water? More water?'

Jisyel obliged, but after taking another drink, he didn't respond any further. She returned, head low. 'I thought he might have some useful information.'

Selys played with the feathers on her glaive as she thought, untangling them where the wind had bound them together. 'I think the people here are more worried about rumours of the Myr than anything else. Let's use that to our advantage. I'll get us a room inside and make some enquiries about Calidra and Varlot. From your descriptions, those two would definitely be remembered if they're here or passed through.'

Jisyel nodded. 'Fenn, you okay to stand?'

He winced as he pushed himself to his feet. 'I'm okay.' But his gaze was drawn back towards the town's entrance. To those lost souls who were chained up, awaiting an unknown fate for an unknown crime. Briefly, he considered going back there, asking them questions as boldly as Jisyel had asked the man in the stocks.

But he dismissed it straight away. That would surely be the quickest way to get himself arrested.

They followed Selys inside, and after showing the innkeeper their papers and coin, were led to a modest room nestled in the roof of the building. Thankfully, it was several degrees cooler, and Fenn found it far easier to breathe once inside.

From the window, the patchwork of fabric that had been the market's roof now became a floor of colour, dazzling under the sun. Four narrow beds had been pushed into each corner, and Fenn gingerly sat down on one. It creaked loudly as it bore his weight, but it wasn't uncomfortable.

'Was the...Myrish spirit heading towards Vaelar?' Jisyel asked both Fenn and Selys.

'Hard to say.' Fenn began unlacing his boots. 'It...was heading in this general direction. What else is nearby? Where else could it be going?'

'The Shrine of Chyram lies to the north. Segandis to the south. Clifton to the north-east. All large settlements,' Selys answered, resting her glaive against the wall.

'Fellwood is beyond Vaelar. Half a day's travel north-west,' Jisyel added.

'Sounds like a lot of distractions before it reaches Fellwood. If it's even going there.' One boot unlaced, Fenn started on the other, sighing in audible relief as his feet were finally free.

'Are you sure you don't know where it was going? You couldn't hear it or anything?'

'How could I hear it from so far away?'

'I don't know. It's Myrish magic. Maybe it could talk directly into your mind?'

'Jisyel, stop it. I have no idea. Yes, I guess I can see them, but I don't know any more than you, and that's the truth!'

211

Easing his boots off, he unwrapped his socks—one of which had stuck to a bloodied blister on the bottom of his right foot —and hissed in pain.

'Oooh. Looks sore.' Jisyel sat down one one of the empty beds.

Fenn nodded. 'Yeah, just a bit. You'll want to take a look at your feet, too. They'll be just as bad.'

'Oh, I'm sure it's fine. They don't hurt.'

Fenn laughed at that. 'Jisyel. We both know you wouldn't feel them even if they fell off!'

'Ah, Hassen's curse?' Selys asked, standing in front of Jisyel and studying her intently. 'I did wonder what he'd done to you. So unpredictable, that spirit.'

Jisyel glanced away with a barely concealed grimace. 'I *had* hoped to find a cure.'

'Well, you'd need another spirit of equal or greater power. Perhaps Chyram? Or Yakris? If you fancy a trip into Olmir?'

Jisyel shook her head. 'I *want* to find Calidra. We need to get to Fellwood. After that…then we'll see.'

A pang of sympathy rippled through Fenn as he looked at Jisyel. 'You really love that woman. Don't you?'

'I do. That's why I have to—we have to get to Fellwood. Quickly. If you and Selys are both okay here, I want to go back into town. Check the other inns in case anyone's seen her.'

'But your feet?' Fenn tried.

'They'll be fine. I've survived worse. Blisters will heal. I'll be as quick as I can and rest when I get back. Promise.'

Worry surged within Fenn. 'Please be careful, Jisyel. I don't think Calidra would forgive me if anything happened to you.'

Tears sprang to the corners of Jisyel's eyes at Fenn's words. Her bottom lip quivered. 'She has to be here. And… and if not, she'll be in Fellwood. Won't she?'

'Of course!' Fenn stood up to comfort her, but collapsed

to the floor at his first step, his feet too sore to bear his weight. He caught himself on the bed frame as he went down, and Selys grabbed his other arm a second later—her reactions were faster than he'd realised. 'I'm okay. Honestly!'

'Jisyel. Let me accompany you. Two pairs of eyes are better than one when searching.' Selys said, once Fenn had assured them he was okay.

He smiled at Selys, glad she'd offered. He would have offered, too, if he'd been capable of walking. They had to stay positive.

'Thank you, Selys. I shouldn't be able to get into *too* much trouble if you're with me!' Jisyel wiped away her tears and straightened up. She rummaged around in her bag again, then pulled out a pestle and mortar and a sealed drawstring bag that smelled heavily of herbs. She put it on Fenn's bed. 'Mash this up and put it over your feet. A good, thick layer.'

'The paste again?'

'Glinoc paste. It'll do wonders for those wounds. We'll be back as soon as we can. Sorry to leave you, Fenn, but I'm not sitting around waiting while Calidra could be somewhere nearby.'

He understood, and wondered whether Jisyel was too stubborn to be upset for too long. It could be true, considering she had a habit of keeping herself busy whenever negative emotions threatened to overwhelm her. 'Good luck.' Fenn nodded as Jisyel and Selys left the room.

ALTHOUGH THE RICH smell of the paste could have caused a headache on its own, the medicine did its job. When Fenn awoke early the following morning, all redness had gone, new skin had grown under his blisters, and his feet didn't ache at all.

Jisyel and Selys had returned just before dark. Despite wanting to warn more of the townspeople about the Myr, after seeing how the lost souls had been treated, they'd kept quiet.

Unfortunately, their search had borne no fruit.

There hadn't even been a sighting of people matching Calidra and Varlot's description.

Jisyel had been crestfallen, not even wanting dinner. Although Fenn knew she couldn't taste food anymore, couldn't tell when she was hungry or not, he couldn't remember the last time he *hadn't* seen her without a pastry or a piece of fruit, or some other snack close to hand.

With the mood sombre, they'd gone to sleep early, with a view to leaving for Fellwood early the next morning.

Fenn's stomach turned at the possibility that Calidra wasn't there.

If she wasn't there, Jisyel would likely want to make her way back to Ballowtown. But *he* would be right at the Porsenthian border. The answer to his own curse lay further north, if Selys was correct. Would he leave Jisyel to travel alone, and try to find a cure by himself?

Or would he put off his own questions and stick with Jisyel, until she was reunited with Calidra?

It ate at him, and he woke up several times through the night covered in cold sweat, his muscles trembling.

More than he cared to admit, his attention was drawn back to the other lost souls. The man locked in the stocks had said there weren't any Inquisitors in town. Who knew how long they'd stay in Vaelar, chained up, waiting for Torsten and his Inquisitors to visit and take them away.

If he'd not been fortunate enough to bump into Calidra and Jisyel, *he* would have been rounded up just like those other people. Had it been luck? Fate? Just a coincidence that he'd ended up on the Isle of Salt and not in one of these Bragalian settlements?

His mind whirled with the possibilities.

They dressed quickly and quietly, and he was hardly aware of his movements, so focussed was he on thoughts of the lost souls. Why had the Myr chosen them? Had that, too, been luck? Or had they been selected for a reason? Had he been plucked from his home? Chased away from his friends and family?

Or had he been alone? Like the poor beggars that lingered on the streets of Vaelar?

Jisyel had been separated from her partner. Calidra could be dead or lost. And yet here he was, bemoaning his own situation. It wasn't as if he had been chained up. He was free. With papers to travel. With friends who cared about him.

Another flare of pain tore through his head and his fingers trembled. He sank to the ground and wrapped his arms around his knees. 'Who am I?' It came out as a whisper.

Jisyel squeezed his shoulder, tighter than was necessary, but her sentiment was clear. 'It'll be okay.' She didn't ask questions, nor demand an explanation for his behaviour.

Selys, too, looked at him from her scarred face without the slightest hint of judgement.

He shuddered, waiting for the emotions to pass, for his trembling to stop.

Whatever had befallen him, he'd put it right. And then, when he knew more, when his curse had been lifted, he would come back and help the other lost souls. Just as Calidra, Jisyel, Selys—and even Varlot—had helped him.

Fenn gritted his teeth. Jisyel hadn't floundered, despite her obvious turmoil.

Selys was confident and steady, her strength coming from within.

He resolved to be more like them, and got back to his feet, unaided.

Whatever lay ahead in Fellwood, he would stand by the people who had stood by him.

Selys led them out of the inn and through the streets—quiet so early in the morning. An owl hooted somewhere in the distance, and the pre-dawn light bathed buildings and streets in shades of grey. By the time they reached the wooden gates, the sun was beginning to rise, bringing colour to the world. He wondered whether that same shadow would be on the horizon.

Again, they showed their papers to the guards, and were waved through without preamble. Vaelar was busy. Getting people out of it was the ideal.

Fenn spent a long minute scouring the countryside for any sign of the Myrish spirit, but thankfully, saw nothing. After confirming the coast was clear, they left Vaelar. Left the lost souls to whatever their fate might be, and Fenn's heart grew heavy.

13

THE FUNERAL
CALIDRA

It was the morning of her father's funeral.

Calidra couldn't pin down all the emotions that raged through her. They fought for dominance, and none stayed on top for long. Grief, strangely, didn't feature. The man, though never unkind to her, had been the Laird first, a father second. She could count on one hand the number of times he'd shown her affection. He'd hardly even been present for her childhood.

Malora, of course, had been the apple of his eye. She could do anything she wished, and Calidra was usually the one punished instead when Malora went too far.

Her mother's reception had gone exactly as she'd expected; cold indifference that could turn into raging hot violence at any moment. It was as if she were seven years old again.

She turned her head, hardly caring about the thick pillows and soft blankets. All expensive silks and cottons brought over from Olmir, and more exotic fabrics she couldn't identify imported from Ulnoth or Perion. A far cry from the cramped rooms she'd endured on the way here.

But none of it mattered.

217

Jisyel wasn't there.

Who cared that she'd made it back for the funeral? That she would now have a second chance at having a relationship with her family?

It meant nothing if she had to face Furyn alone. She'd have to go through it without Jisyel, who'd been the only reason she'd even considered coming home in the first place.

If she had any chance of getting a search party out looking for Jisyel, she'd either have to force her mother to help, or go behind her back. Either option would be nigh impossible.

The villa, vast and luxurious as it was, offered Calidra nothing but emptiness. Apparently in her years of being away, her mother had significantly reduced the household staff. Instead of the early morning bustle, the smell of brewing coffee, of cooking breakfast, the building was quiet.

Hollow.

Somehow, despite its vastness, its luxury, it was a shell of a home—perfectly reflecting her feelings towards the place.

It was possible Furyn had dismissed some of the staff today, but Calidra didn't recall seeing many people when she'd arrived. There was her brother to consider, as well. Paicha. He'd only been a toddler when she'd last seen him, and was often whisked away to accompany their father on one of his border skirmishes to introduce him to his responsibilities early on.

She sighed, laying her head flat on her pillow and staring up at the blank ceiling.

Somewhere in the house, Varlot and Amsel were guests. Probably being treated with more dignity by her mother than *she'd* ever received. Calidra wanted to stay exactly where she was all day. She wondered if anyone would notice, whether her mother would come and drag her out of her room, or if she'd send Quillaja to do it for her.

Glancing at the window, judging the hour by the brightness of the morning sun, Calidra sat bolt upright. Jisyel wouldn't sit here, wallowing. And Calidra had done enough of that on her way to Fellwood.

Now was the time to act.

Getting out of bed, Calidra dressed quickly, feeling more refreshed than she had in weeks. It probably had something to do with the oils and scents that Quillaja had spent so long putting into her, and although she'd never cared for such routines, their effects couldn't be ignored.

With confidence and focus, Calidra had one goal—to get to the household guard and set them to work. Her mother would no doubt be busy with last minute funeral preparations and greeting early guests, giving her a small window of time to act. With any luck, the search party would be out of Fellwood before her mother even noticed.

And if Amsel made an appearance, she could ask him to look from the air with Hailathlyl, speeding the search immeasurably.

She gently pushed her nails through her hair, impressed at how one night's rest and a handful of her mother's cosmetics had worn away all the travelling knots. At least she wouldn't look like she'd been dragged through a hedge when she came to order the soldiers who worked for her family. It had been years since they'd seen her last, and she needed to make a decent impression.

Technically they worked for her mother, but surely she could sway them? She just had to think of them like the port masters in Ballowtown, and refuse to take no for an answer.

Decision made, Calidra raised her chin, opened her bedroom door, and strolled out. Early morning light streamed in from the windows along the hallway. Good. A dry, clear day would make searching easier.

She quickened her pace, turning away from the kitchens and out through a side door into the dew-covered grounds. Their household guard had their own quarters on the far side of the gardens, and it was to this low building that Calidra hurried towards.

Goosebumps rose on her skin the moment she was outside. A fine mist wreathed the ground; it wouldn't be long before the sun burned it away and provided Bragalia with another hot day. No-one was outside yet that she could see. Her mother would probably be awake, she'd always been an early riser, but Calidra couldn't see her anywhere outside. Even Calidra herself was unhappy about skipping her morning coffee, but this was too important to put off until later. She might miss her chance.

The guardhouse was a long, single-storey building of grey brick with a steep roof of dark slate. Smoke rose gently from the chimney on its northern side, and all the windows were already wide open. Her mouth watered at the smell of cooking bacon, reminding her of her empty stomach.

A large red door dominated the front of the building, slightly ajar, the Vantonen family crest emblazoned on it. Calidra knocked once, more out of politeness than to wait for an answer, and pushed it open. Stronger smells of cooking washed over her as she strode inside, straight into the communal area. Several of the guards were sitting on a long sofa, three more tended to a spit above a fire, where half a spiced pig roasted, fat dripping onto the flames.

'Commander? You and your team are required for an urgent mission. Immediately.'

At her words, the relaxed morning atmosphere dissipated. The men and women in her mother's employ got to their feet—most were already dressed in uniform, a few even had pieces of armour equipped—and stood to one side as their commanding officer entered from a door at the back of the room, summoned by her sharp words.

Calidra didn't recognise him—he'd probably been a regular officer and been promoted while she'd been away from home. She was annoyed with herself for not even knowing his name.

The commander was broad and muscular, stubble on his chin, with lightly tanned skin and brown eyes that were narrowed at her. Physically, he was every bit as intimidating as Furyn. He clutched his helm in one hand, a red feather atop it signalling his rank. 'The Myr are attacking?'

'What? No. You need to get your horses saddled, ready for a search.' Calidra's voice wavered for a moment. She'd forgotten their commander had been in talks with her mother the previous day.

Two uniformed men darted out of the building at her words, scrambling to get their jackets buckled up and their helms on their heads.

'Miss Vantonen. Our orders are to provide defensive strategies to the grounds here and aid the Fellwood officers as best we can in the event of a Myrish attack. Lady Vantonen has said nothing about a search.'

'*I* am telling you about it. How many horses do we have?'

'None to spare for a search I'm unaware of, I'm afraid, Miss Vantonen.' There wasn't a hit of anger in his voice, if anything, he was more polite than before.

She straightened her back and put every ounce of her mother's tone into her own voice. 'You dare disregard my order? Shall I tell my mother that you have refused to do your job?'

Despite her performance, the commander was *not* like the Ballowtown port master. He didn't so much as look ashamed. 'You may tell Lady Vantonen whatever you wish. But as I understand, there is a potential Myrish threat on our doorstep and we must prepare for it. I'm sure you understand the safety of your family and Fellwood is our greatest priority?'

Calidra's eye twitched. 'Fine. Give me a horse and I'll go by myself as you are incapable.'

'You can't!'

'I'm not a prisoner. I can come and go as I please.'

'But the Myr? We are tasked with your safety.'

'Then come with me. Ten or twelve should be adequate for the amount of ground we need to cover. Get the horses saddled up and we can make decent time before it gets hot.' She was getting too angry to care about respectability. Jisyel had waited too long.

Without another word, Calidra whirled around and marched outside. She walked alongside the building to the vast stables beyond, where her family's horses were kept. Calidra had never been one for horse riding, but was sure she could pick out a suitable animal that would get her back to Ballowtown.

Already, servants were tending to them—providing feed and fresh water—and they gasped in shock as she stormed past. 'I want the swiftest horse here saddled. Good stamina, too. It's a fair distance I must cover, and quickly.'

'M—Miss Vantonen!' one girl stammered, backing away, her bucket of water dropped.

Ignoring her, Calidra strode to the nearest stable, horse tack hanging on a long nail, which she grabbed. The servant girl made a noise that wasn't quite a word, wasn't quite a gasp and Calidra spun around. She looked past the girl to see her mother approaching, the two members of the guard escorting her, thunder on her face.

With an exasperated sigh, Calidra stepped away from the stable, the bridle and reins clutched tightly, and faced her mother. She'd *make* Furyn order the guards. They would no doubt move quickly if the lady of the house commanded them.

As Furyn walked past the guard's quarters, the commander exited and followed her, flanked by three more officers. Gold draped over Furyn like clothing. At her throat, her collarbone, across her shoulders and down the length of her arms, spider silk-thin beads wrapped around her fingers in stunning contrast to her beautiful, ebony skin. Sunlight brought the gold to life; it flashed with every step.

Her two griffins slunk along beside her like enormous cats. While without the intimidation of Hailathlyl, they were still exquisite creatures, with fur and feathers of vibrant teal and purple, and brilliant golden claws bred for their aesthetics. Four feet tall and just as long, they wouldn't get any larger, but were strong enough to be a threat without proper control. They both stood to Furyn's left, their orange eyes fixed on their mistress, bejewelled collars shining.

Her mother came to a halt several paces away from Calidra, her narrowed gaze passing slowly up and down her daughter. It lingered on Calidra's hand, and her expression shifted into a sneer. 'Oh. This fuss must be for...Jenna?'

'Jisyel,' Calidra corrected through gritted teeth.

Her mother sniffed. 'Of course. I had thought you'd have come to your senses and left her on that cursed rock in the Salt Sea.'

Rage filled Calidra like an ocean swell, and she forced herself to keep a lid on it. She'd run out of time and patience. She needed her mother to see, to *understand*. 'Mother, you have to realise Jisyel could be dying! Don't you understand how important she is to me?'

'Is that the best you can do?'

Claidra gaped, unable to say anything in response.

Furyn spoke again, her voice calm and quiet, 'You really mean to behave like this? On *today* of all days? When your family is of greatest importance? You're worrying about some Porsenthian *peasant*?'

Calidra couldn't hold it in any longer, her mother's words piercing the armour she'd wrapped her rage in. Her anger burst in less than a heartbeat, a furious storm decades in the making that rose to spew every injustice and unwarranted desecration against her. 'You had nothing to say when

223

Malora ran off with a spirits-forsaken *thief*! Didn't he steal one of your emeralds? And you *allowed* that?'

Her mother's fury rose like a tide, matching her own. 'You will not speak to me like that in front of the servants!'

'I don't *care* about them! Tell me why you had nothing to say when Malora left? Made me think she was dead all this time! That what *I'd* said had pushed her to it! Do you even understand the guilt I carried? Tell me why you were happy to let her go, but *I* had to stay as your obedient puppy? Why you declared me unworthy of help when I finally left and found someone who cared, somewhere I could call home? Why am *I* the one being dragged back into this? Why are my wants shut down? Jisyel could be lying somewhere out there, dying, the Myr closing in, and *again* you're letting my dreams burn because it might look bad on the family!'

'Fellwood *is* your home! And you are the elder sister! *You* are the one who could inherit all this if only you stepped up!' Furyn gestured widely with her arms. 'Anything else is irrelevant!'

'All *this* is *false*!' Spittle flew from her lips, but Calidra was past caring about decorum. 'You let Malora take *everything* from that golden spirit. *You* grew rich and lazy off it. We're no better than the people you bring in as servants! *We* were servants! I remember a childhood of empty bellies and scraped knees, hard work for little coin, but fun and freedom, too!'

'Your childhood was a sham. Filthy mud puppy. It *became* glorious! When we moved here, you had tutors. The best in Bragalia! You no longer had to play with peasants and ruffians. We gave you—'

'I was forced into *your* dream! Yours and father's! I'd rather have had a childhood covered in mud, without a care in the world, than all this hogshit!'

'Stop that filthy language at once! Learned from the dregs

of society in Salt Ash, no doubt. Disgusting Porsenthians and their influence.'

Calidra had never sworn in front of her mother before. Tried to avoid swearing in general. But she was too far gone to care. 'Hog. *Shit*. This whole family is hogshit! It *reeks* of it!'

Furyn's eyes darkened, a shadow of burning anger so deep and violent that Calidra knew there was no coming back from it. 'I'll *not* have another word spoken against our family.'

'If you honestly think I'm going to spend another second here, with *you*, while Jisyel is—'

Her mother's slap across the face was laced with so much fury that it sent Calidra spinning to the ground. Even the griffins backed away with a low whimper, their wings fluttering.

'Not. Another. Word.' Furyn's voice was a hiss. 'You're back, finally. Your adventure ends today, Calidra Vantonen. And your responsibilities to this family, to our land, to helping protect everything we have built and stand for, begin *now*.'

JISYEL WAS USUALLY RIGHT about things, and wanted to see the good in people. She'd always been sweet and silly, too kind-hearted for her own good, but naive and reckless to the point she'd ended up cursed by her own forest spirit.

Calidra loved the woman, loved how she challenged her opinions and preconceptions on so many things. Even if she didn't agree with her most of the time, she would usually end up understanding another viewpoint. Jisyel was good at that.

But the one point they'd argued on and off about for the past eight years was Calidra returning home. Jisyel only had her grandmother left. No siblings. No parents. No cousins. She'd give anything to be able to see them again, but wouldn't get the chance until she, too, crossed over to the spirit world. She'd wanted Calidra to take the chance while she'd had it. Not regret turning her back on her homeland, not while her family lived.

Calidra had vehemently argued against it. She hadn't *wanted* to return, not after everything that had happened. Her sister was gone, fallen in with the wrong crowd, and very likely dead—until Quillaja had brought her the revelation that Malora was alive and well. And a mother, to boot.

Jisyel had started gently, talking about how nice it would be to fix the relationship between Calidra and her mother.

Calidra had been scared, of course. She'd made a promise to herself that she'd never return. She'd sworn it! There were too many bad memories, too much pain and sorrow. Wounds so deep they couldn't be healed.

And yet, slowly, over the years, she'd come around to Jisyel's way of thinking. It *would* be nice.

In fact, after everything they'd put her through, *they* owed *her* a repair of the relationship. By the time Calidra had left Meadowhill, she'd decided that she'd *make* her mother see. She'd *make* her help.

But as Calidra sat at the farthest edge of their family's grounds, where the grasses and plants grew wild, and the graves of old Lairds were marked with ornamental stone, tears streaming silently down her eyes, she knew Jisyel had been wrong.

Half the town had squeezed into the grounds for the funeral, all dressed in their finery. Many wore gold at their throats or wrists, but none were as impressive as Furyn. It was to be expected. Malora had been chosen by Chyram, one of the very few ever bestowed with the power to create gold. Who could create wealth from nothing.

Varlot had been offered a seat as an honoured guest, but he had continued to argue his pay, his face like a melted kettle, and refused to join. He'd stalked off into town, asking

226

to be summoned when Lady Vantonen wished to keep her word.

So Calidra sat between two soldiers tasked with keeping her in line in case she tried anything. Not that Calidra had the strength of will to even *think* about it. Not after earlier.

Furyn, herself, was closest to the casket, her son next to her. The casket had been painted delicately with the family crest: three white feathers, tipped with gold. Calidra stared at the lad—her eleven-year-old brother—and hardly recognised him. Paicha had just seen his third birthday when she'd left. Funny. She cared for him less than Jisyel.

Calidra shook her head, a grim smile plastered on her face. Family was more than blood.

Instead of spending the funeral grieving her lost father or comforting her mother, she spent it planning her escape.

Amsel, however, hadn't joined for the proceedings, but he hadn't left Fellwood, either. Ever on guard, he and Hailathlyl had taken to the air to patrol the town, and their shadow periodically passed overhead. It brought some small comfort.

Her cousin—if she really was related to him—would probably be her best way out.

Calidra spent the time plotting her next moves, as three priests from Chyram's Shrine performed funeral rites and recited their canticles. She was supposed to chant along with them, but she couldn't muster the strength after what had happened with her mother that morning. She'd need every last ounce of energy if she was able to get out of this situation in one piece.

When the service was finally over, the candles had been lit, and the casket had been buried, Calidra stood beside her mother and brother as townsfolk offered their condolences and well-wishes on their way off the grounds. She offered them little more than a smile, the most she was able to give.

She didn't bother to look at her mother, her brother, any of the household guards.

They were all against her.

Any chance at rebuilding what had broken had been shattered. Calidra took that hurt, that searing ache, and used it to fuel her next actions. There was no going back.

'Lady Vantonen.' The commander of the household guard approached, once the grounds had emptied and chatter had died away. 'There is another priestess at the gates.'

Furyn frowned. 'Why did the shrine send another? We have three here already, and the service is finished. All rites have been performed.'

'Shall I turn her away? She has a small retinue.'

Furyn considered. 'Very well. Let them in, Sekano. I will take my herbal mix in the tea rooms, and greet them outside shortly.'

Calidra watched him head off, emotionless. 'If there are no more people to impress, I will excuse myself, too.'

Furyn glared at her. 'You are dismissed, but do *not* leave the house or gardens. The Laird isn't an hour underground and you want to get away again. I think a discussion is needed, between us, Calidra. About your responsibilities and expectations. With the Myr on their way, we *must* unite.'

'Unite.' Calidra couldn't believe her mother's words.

'Yes. It means you do not show disrespect. It means you stand with me, and with Paicha.' She rested her hand on her son's shoulder, who looked as bored as Calidra felt, his gaze drawn to the birds singing in the trees, oblivious to the boiling emotions.

Calidra was almost sad they'd never had a real chance to get to know each other, but she couldn't give up any more of her life for a family that was no longer hers.

Jisyel was family. Bellandri was family.

Not whatever her mother had turned the Vantonens into.

'Yes mother.' Her voice was flat, emotionless. At Furyn's

curt nod, Calidra got to her feet and headed back to the house. She'd need to get to her room without being pulled aside by anyone, repack her bag, visit the kitchens and grab as many supplies as she could.

There was a chance she could make it back to the stables, but she didn't want to risk getting caught again. She'd wear a long shawl over her shoulders to hide her bag, and wait in a shady part of the gardens for Amsel and Hailathlyl to return. Then, she'd make him take her into the air again.

She had her dagger. If she had to threaten him, she would.

Calidra was done wallowing.

As she approached one of the side doors into the villa, movement across the grass caught her attention. Commander Sekano was marching through the gardens, three figures trailing him. The one in the lead didn't look anything like a priestess with a large glaive across her back, and if it weren't for the swirling green tattoo across her upper arm, she wouldn't have realised she was one at all. Calidra spent so long focussed on the priestess that she didn't notice the other two figures until they were almost out of sight.

The strength went from her legs.

'JISYEL!' Calidra's scream tore through the air, stopping Sekano and the others in their tracks.

She couldn't move, couldn't breathe.

In unison, they turned to face her, confusion furrowing their eyebrows at her shout.

Her gaze locked with the woman behind the strange-looking priestess, and tears fell again. Her eyes and ears burned, tears blurred her vision, and it felt as if the wind shrieked in her head—she couldn't hear anything other than her pounding heart. All of a sudden it wasn't her heart pounding, it was her feet—pounding across the grass as she sprinted towards them.

'Cal!' Jisyel's voice rang clear as a bell above the rushing wind.

Calidra didn't care about the other people with her, about Commander Sekano's obvious frown.

The only thing in the world that mattered was Jisyel.

The Myr could have descended upon Fellwood in that moment, and she wouldn't have cared. Jisyel was back, and there was no power in Tassar that could take her away again.

They crashed together in a tight hug—laughter and crying. Calidra could hardly believe it, hardly believe Jisyel was real. Jisyel's face was flushed, red from the sun, her hair was unwashed and greasy, and her clothes had seen better days, but she was *right there*.

'Your face!' Calidra ran her thumb gently over a slash across Jisyel's cheek. It was healing, and she hoped it wouldn't leave a scar.

'It's nothing, Cal. It's nothing.' Jisyel grabbed Calidra's face in both hands and kissed her fiercely.

Calidra tasted tears, the salt reminding her of home. Her true home. *Their* home. She laughed through her tears as relief flooded her, and wrapped her arms around Jisyel, pulling her closer, as if to make certain that she was real and not some apparition. 'Jisyel, you're alive. You're *here*!'

Jisyel didn't reply, simply kissed her more. Over and over, her hands trembling where they held Calidra's face. 'I knew you'd be here. I *knew* you'd be okay!' Jisyel's voice was a whimper punctuated by sobbing.

'I was trying to raise an army to find you!' Calidra rested her forehead against Jisyel's, taking steadying breaths as the jubilation washed over her. 'I couldn't...I couldn't bear the thought of you hurt. Swept away in the water. Dying somewhere, I...'

'Sshh, Cal. Don't do that to yourself. I'm fine. I'm here.' Jisyel stroked Calidra's cheeks, the motion somehow soothing.

Calidra choked down her next words. Jisyel was right. She didn't want to give her worst fears voice. She didn't know how long she spent with her eyes closed, resting against Jisyel's face, focussing on her breathing and the feel of Jisyel in her hands.

Calidra had been on the brink of running away to find her, of threatening violence if she had to.

And now none of it was needed. Now, Jisyel was back with her. Safe.

They could face anything together.

Calidra gasped, eyes opening. 'The Myr! They're in Bragalia, Jisyel. Olmir, too. You weren't hurt, were you?'

Jisyel shook her head. 'Fenn saw one just outside Vaelar. But it didn't come to town. Didn't come near us.'

'Good. Good.'

'But the thing that attacked Ballowtown? That was one of them…'

Calidra glanced to the blue sky above. 'It won't be long before they get here, from the way Amsel was talking.'

'Amsel?'

'Griffin rider. Varlot and I flew here with him. I thought…I thought you might be here already. And when you weren't, I…' Calidra trailed off. Something Jisyel had said clicked with her. 'Wait, Fenn *saw* one? Fenn?' She stepped back from Jisyel, taking in her surroundings for the first time.

Fenn and the priestess stood off to one side, in low conversation, Sakano loitering awkwardly nearby.

'He helped me out on the road, Cal.' Jisyel grabbed Calidra's hand, squeezing her fingers harder than was necessary. 'Don't push him to the guards or Inquisitors.'

It had been the furthest thought from Calidra's mind. 'Who's the priestess? She looks…peculiar.'

'She's a Priestess of Neros, her name's Selys,' Jisyel said. 'She gave Fenn new papers.'

231

'What for?' Calidra was instantly on alert.

Jisyel laughed. 'Relax, Cal. She's fine.' Then, Jisyel's expression soured. 'She...she thinks Fenn is Myr-touched. That's what's caused his...problems.'

'Hmm.' Calidra didn't want to jump to any conclusions, but with a Myrish threat on their doorstep, Fenn being tainted by their enemy in some way didn't leave her with a good impression. 'How has he been?'

'Absolutely no threat to me! Like I said, he *helped* me!'

Calidra thought back to Meadowhill. The sick elthian. 'No, I mean...his headaches?'

Jisyel looked at Fenn, saying nothing for several seconds. 'He says he's fine. Reminds me of *you*, honestly.'

'But...?'

'But they're getting worse. He could hardly walk by the time we reached Vaelar.'

Calidra recalled her first instinct had been to get rid of him. People could rarely be trusted, and he'd been a stranger. Some young lad turning up on the Isle of Salt without any knowledge of how he got there. Why *shouldn't* she doubt his intentions?

But here he was.

And he'd been with Jisyel this whole time. Had made sure she wasn't alone. Brought her back.

Jisyel's words rang in her mind. Fenn's headaches were getting worse. Calidra hoped the elthian in Meadowhill had been afflicted by some other illness. That whatever hurt her *wouldn't* affect Fenn.

She owed him enough gratitude to help him with whatever was wrong.

'He wants to head into Porsenthia. The Nethal mountains,' Jisyel added.

'What for?' Calidra couldn't think of anything interesting in that part of the world, save snow and being too close to the Iron Crown.

'Selys says it's where a Myrish construct is.'

Calidra thought, scouring her memory for why that place stood out. 'At the battle site? That old myth?'

'Apparently. It's not like he has much else to go by. With Selys's papers, he won't be handed in to any Inquisitors, but if they're after lost souls...they might override the word of a priestess.'

Calidra thought, trying to piece together the puzzle. If the Myr were really back, there was something wrong with the Iron Crown. There had to be. Queen Surayo and Toriaken had kept peace alive for five years—what had happened to break her armour?

And if Fenn's headaches were worsening, he could well be on a time limit.

The elthian had been terrified, beside herself screaming. The pain had been too much for her body. How long until the same would be true of Fenn? It didn't warrant thinking about.

Something cold crept down her spine and along her arms as the seriousness of events became clear. Even the Olmese were sending warning messages. War griffins and warriors.

The Myrish threat *had* to be real.

'Fenn?' Calidra called, grabbing his attention.

He looked up and grinned. With his bright blue eyes and dark brown hair, he didn't stand out, but there was something that had changed about the set of his jaw, the determination in his gaze. Even though it had only been a handful of days since Calidra had last seen him in Ballowtown, the young man seemed older, more world-weary.

'Thank you, Fenn. For keeping Jisyel safe.' Calidra looped her arm around Jisyel's waist, as if to emphasise her point. 'I'm sure it couldn't have been easy.'

'Cal!' Jisyel playfully pushed her.

'I'm glad I could help. Thank you.' Fenn began to walk the

short distance across the manicured grass towards them. His knee buckled and his eyes rolled back.

Selys, closer to him, reacted immediately—darting forward to grab him before he could collapse to the ground —but Fenn was already unconscious. The priestess pressed the back of her hand to his forehead. 'He's burning up.'

'Get him inside,' Calidra said, releasing Jisyel to lead the way. Worry gripped her.

What if it was already too late?

What if Fenn's time had run out?

14

THE QUEEN
TORSTEN

Eastbrook, as capitals went, was less a fortress, more a sprawling, overgrown city that spread down a gentle hill to touch the sea. Full of native Porsenthians and those who'd emigrated from other parts of the world, eager for the safety of the Iron Crown, it was a melting pot of different races and cultures.

All perfectly acceptable as far as Torsten was concerned— as long as they paid their dues and had the right to live there. He didn't see the point in protecting anyone who didn't—or wouldn't—earn their keep.

The city itself was far from beautiful. There were certainly other places in Porsenthia that were more breathtaking, with more dramatic scenery, but Eastbrook had swelled over the years, and it was certainly a force to be reckoned with. It sat under the cool sun, against the backdrop of the Nethal Mountains, the vast Lasseen Ocean to the east. A simmering power, always ready.

Built primarily of stone ored from the mountains, Eastbrook was a swathe of narrow grey buildings, punctuated here and there with splashes of white. Crooked streets and narrow alleys linked sections of the city together, and even though most buildings were several storeys high, the palace itself dwarfed everything. A castle of iron sat atop the city's highest peak, towers haphazardly bursting from its inner and outer walls, wide balconies open to the air above, snaking around the main building to offer Toriaken multiple landing points. Queen Surayo and the Porsenthian rulers of old called it their home. Although much of it had been built with the same stone, Toriaken had fortified it with iron over the centuries, creating towering peaks and jagged turrets that glinted dully. Toriaken had shaped the iron in ways no human hand could; it flowed in curves and waves that would only be possible with glass.

The sword and shield of Porsenthia, Eastbrook, was the only place where the people could catch a glimpse of the dragon spirit bonded to their queen. Where Toriaken himself flew.

It had taken another two days of hard traveling to reach Eastbrook from Tonmouth, during which time Torsten weighed up Miroth's information. He didn't know the level of danger the Myr presented, but it had to be more than he'd ever have considered before if they were sending out death spirits.

Perhaps Surayo's concerns weren't foolhardy after all.

The carriage rattled over the wide stone bridge leading to Eastbrook's south gate, the Lasseen Ocean at his back. Even though Eastbrook had been his home for a number of years, the dark iron shadow above it was foreboding.

They made their way along the wider streets of East-brook, horses' hooves clomping loudly on the stone roads. People stepped to the side to let the Inquisitor caravan pass, eyes drawn to each carriage in a mix of curiosity and fear.

Torsten had instructed their curtains be drawn for their entrance into the city. There was no need to provide the people with ammunition for gossip and rumour to fester. He pulled at the corner of his own curtain, peeking out of the gap to gather his bearings.

They were already at the south end of *Queen's Parade*, the main path to the palace itself. It wouldn't be long now. Although the angle of the carriage didn't allow him to see their final destination, he could already feel the shadow of iron across him.

He was back in Toriaken's domain.

A horn, low and keening, played as they passed through the outer gates to the palace grounds, signalling the Inquisitors' return. The call was taken up by another horn along the wall, and another, and another, at regular intervals, until the palace sang with news of their arrival.

It wasn't needed, really. Toriaken—and therefore Surayo—would know they were back, but those elsewhere in Eastbrook, who hadn't seen the carriages, would know Torsten had returned to the city. He wondered what secrets would be hidden, hurriedly squirreled away and out of sight, now that he was back.

Several soldiers met them outside the iron palace, and the more junior ranked among them saw to their horses, leading them away and to the stables. An enormous statue of Toriaken dominated the courtyard, built atop a fountain in the centre. With his wings spread, Torsten had often wondered whether the spirit could make the statue come to life.

'Well met, Inquisitors.' The captain on duty offered Torsten and Nadja a short bow.

'How is Eastbrook? Any news?' Nadja asked, stepping out of the carriage and stretching her arms above her with a long sigh.

'The city is well. Queen Surayo eagerly awaits your report.'

Torsten nodded. 'We'll attend her now. Nadja?'

They left the other soldiers to deal with their captured prisoners—Torsten was looking forward to returning to

237

them later to begin his investigations. He wanted to know what connected them all, what would drive so many to such deceit. But first, Queen Surayo awaited.

He and Nadja followed the captain up the enormous grey stone stairs leading to the palace entrance, glad to get moving again after so long in the cramped carriage. They'd not gone up ten steps when Torsten heard beating wings. Pausing, he whirled around to look for the cause of the noise. It wasn't the strong, stiff wing beats of Toriaken, but the beat of feathers. Feathers that did *not* belong to any bird.

'Griffins, sir?' asked the guard captain, squinting up into the sky.

Nadja frowned. 'We weren't expecting any Olmese dignitaries.'

'No,' Torsten assented. 'But they wait for no-one. Captain, get a welcome party assembled at once. Nadja and I will stall them.'

'Yes, Inquisitor.' The man darted off without hesitation, racing up the stone steps and into the castle itself, barking orders as he went.

'I don't like unannounced arrivals.' Nadja caressed the hilt of her sword, then placed her hands behind her back, her eyes never leaving the sky.

'Nor I.' Torsten didn't care for the Olmese, either. Their griffins were powerful creatures, and deadly even half-grown. They were instrumental in the rise of the Olmese dynasties, and were not to be underestimated. Torsten himself bore the scar from one creature across his midriff that often pained him in cold weather.

A high-pitched shriek accompanied the wing beats as the enormous creature flew into view, flanked by two others.

The same horn that had announced the Inquisitors' return sounded again, a higher, shrill tone that played twice in quick succession. Not quite a warning, but it made him straighten his back. He would be ready for whatever the Olmese wanted.

From what he could tell, the griffin in front was a third bigger than the other two, with glossy brown feathers streaked with cherry red. It swept low, circling the castle once in a wide arc, leading the others.

Even from such a distance, Torsten could see its intelligent eyes taking in the sight below.

As they descended, the carriages moved off, clearing space in front of the stone steps for the griffins to land. Several soldiers led the chained prisoners away, hoods covering their heads, and into the depths of the palace itself.

Torsten kept his eyes on the three griffins as they touched down. The two smaller ones were a mix of grey and cream feathers, but all three had vicious talons that could crush bone. Torsten absentmindedly scratched his old scar before heading down the steps.

Before he'd even reached them, the griffin riders had dismounted; a young woman and two men, both of whom were older than their female companion by a decade or two. Glancing around and adjusting their clothes, they peered curiously at the line of prisoners taken away.

Torsten quickened his step and cleared his throat.

Immediately, the largest of the griffins, the red-brown creature who towered over them, stared at Torsten with its beady, orange eyes. 'Do not approach, Inquisitor. That is close enough.'

Unsurprised by the creature's speech, Torsten halted several generous paces from the Olmese riders and inclined his head. 'Your arrival in Eastbrook is unscheduled.'

'War is rarely scheduled,' the female rider replied curtly. She unbuckled the thick leather gloves that reached her elbows and pulled them off. She was shorter than Nadja, with hair dark as pitch and a slim, athletic build. Her body was draped in the hardy travelling silks of Olmir—brown and red to match her griffin. With the addition of a golden torc around her wrist, revealed when she took off her left glove, Torsten assumed her to be one of their military caste; a fighter whose skills matched the strength of her war griffin. But he didn't know who she was—his role concerned Porsenthia more than anywhere else—and they'd had few dealings with Olmir in recent years. She said, 'We must speak with Queen Surayo at once, by order of King Orlen.'

Torsten bristled at the demand.

'The danger must be great if Lady Arbora has travelled here personally.' Nadja silently appeared next to him and evidently recognised the woman. 'It is an honour to receive such an esteemed warrior.'

At Nadja's words, Lady Arbora's expression softened. 'Inquisitors. I cannot speak of my king's message to any but the Iron Crown. If you would take me to Queen Surayo swiftly, it would be better for all of us.'

Torsten caught Nadja's gaze, and he gave her the smallest of nods.

Nadja beckoned her forward, and Lady Arbora's two companions followed—gently patting their griffins and unloading a large bag from each. The bags were heavy, from the way they staggered under them, but neither complained as they followed their Arbora up the stairs and into the castle.

Figures already lingered at the entranceway—a welcoming retinue.

Torsten watched as the three griffins took to the air again, sending feathers flying, then he marched after the Olmese. Whatever they had to say to his queen, as a Master Inquisitor, he ought to be there. It could well be an extra piece to the Myrish puzzle.

And if Lady Arbora was correct, and war had come, it meant they were all out of time.

LEAFY TREES and plants filled many of the wide, open spaces inside the palace, and enormous windows brought in plenty of sunlight as well as a cool sea breeze. Queen Surayo had tried to make her home more comfortable, adorning the iron walls with greenery and flowering plants.

Torsten wrinkled his nose at the peppery scents, but was used to it within a handful of breaths.

A serving girl swept up dead pine needles from under the branches of one of the fir trees Surayo had brought in. She crouched down, then sank to her knees as she reached under the branches to sweep the needles with a stiff brush. Her bare arms were red where the leaf litter touched her.

Without their spirit, the trees died quickly, and were constantly being replaced.

He'd never understood why the palace needed such plant life, with all the effort and constant maintenance it needed, but it was one rule that Surayo refused to accede.

Although Toriaken's shrine was built into the base of the Nethal Mountains, a magnificent building twice the size of most shrines, and five times the size of Miroth's, the Spirit of Iron also had a cathedral within the palace for those wishing to show the spirit and the Iron Crown homage. Even now, a large group of people gathered at the door which led to the cathedral, waiting to be admitted by palace staff and priests.

Not for the first time, Torsten was pulled two ways. The fire in his chest belonged to Miroth, the spirit to whom he was bound. But for the past thirty years, he'd served the Iron Crown; Queen Surayo, and by extension, Toriaken.

He carried swords imbued with both spirits, and had spent decades learning to push one to the side while listening to the other, then swapping again. It was a delicate balance that had often shortened his temper and patience. For now, he turned away from the door to the cathedral. Nadja and

241

the rest of the welcoming committee kept the Olmese dignitaries marching at a quick pace, and Torsten followed, unwilling to let them out of his sight.

Every step brought him deeper into Toriaken's domain.

He steeled himself, ready to face his queen and whatever news the Olmese brought.

They walked down corridors and across halls, garnering curious looks from the other staff on duty. With three Olmese, two Inquisitors, four soldiers, and a herald in the welcoming party, they were a strange sight strolling through the palace corridors.

None of the visitors spoke while they walked, which was uncommon. Most people were compelled to comment on the splendor of the castle or its strength as Porsenthia's armour —figuring out some way to barter favour with the queen or her Inquisitors.

But the Olmese offered no such flattery.

Perhaps they were less than impressed?

Or perhaps their reasons for being here were genuine, and would not permit time for commenting on Porsenthian architecture.

He dwelled on it as they ascended a final flight of stairs, to the suites where Queen Surayo met guests. Armed soldiers stood at attention on either side of the stairway and in the hallway beyond. Though a few glanced at them as they walked past, most remained stoic, awaiting orders.

In other palaces across the world, gold, silver, and gemstones would lavishly decorate the rooms and corridors in a blatant display of wealth. Here, iron ruled. It was everywhere, from the swords the soldiers carried, to ornamental trinkets dotted in every room. Each and every piece could be imbued with Toriaken's strength in a heartbeat. While some people might see the grey of iron as bland, even distasteful, they were walking down the literal jaws of the dragon.

The herald requested everyone wait in a comfortable antechamber before he scuttled off through a side door. After deliberating for a moment, Torsten followed him into the small connecting room which led to the queen's audience chamber. Here, there were no more living guards. Instead, there were several humanoid shapes standing motionless against the wall, covered in shadow. Each one had been created from a slab of solid iron, and each wore two iron swords across their back.

The Iron Guard, Queen Surayo's final defence against threats.

None of them had eyes, they didn't even have faces, which unsettled Torsten every time he saw them. They remained motionless as Torsten passed, and it meant that when they opened the final door to Surayo's chamber, the queen was already waiting, expectant.

Queen Surayo Fasse-Ferren, the thirty-eighth monarch of the Porsenthian Empire, stood in the middle of her audience chamber atop an enormous, plush rug which covered the flagstone floor. It had been stitched with intricate colours showcasing Toriaken's magnificence—every scale gleamed, just like the real spirit. A fire burned in the large hearth behind the queen, and sconces along the walls had been lit. The room was comfortable and warm against the chill of northern Porsenthia.

She wore a simple gown of maroon with a loose bodice—which complemented her dark brunette hair and lightly tanned skin—and fine threads of silver detailed Toriaken's form across the skirt and sleeves. Instead of gold, silver, or gemstones, her jewellery was simple, functional, and made of iron, much like the rest of her palace. Long earrings reached her shoulders, slender rings crossed several fingers, a thick necklace that protected her throat more than provided beauty, and the ensemble was finished with a diadem atop her head, a ruby pressed into its centre.

Mages were rare enough in their own right, let alone one who had been blessed by a spirit.

Toriaken himself lay in the chamber, mist wreathing his body, blurring his edges as if he wasn't quite there. He was nowhere near his full size—even semi-corporeal, he'd have filled the entire castle—and Torsten realised Toriaken had withheld the majority of his power for the sake of Surayo. He could stand with her, watch and listen with her, as befitted the dual rulers of the Porsenthian Empire.

Another three of the Iron Guard stood beside the hearth, their left sides glowing red from the roaring flames. They leaned on their swords, as silent as the iron they'd been created from.

Even if the palace of Eastbrook wasn't a fortress in the traditional sense, the queen herself certainly was invulnerable through her link with the Spirit of Iron.

The dragon eyed Torsten and the herald, saying nothing as smoke plumed from his nostrils.

Torsten sank to one knee, ensuring his head was not as low as his companion.

The herald said in a lilting voice, 'My Queen, we have an envoy from Olmir to see you. Lady Arbora and two of her retinue. She has said it concerns...war. They request an immediate audience.'

Toriaken rumbled, a low growl that sent vibrations through the flagstone floors, even through the rug atop it. Torsten's knee spasmed and he quickly straightened up to ease the discomfort.

'Send them in. You and the others may leave us. Torsten, stay.' Queen Surayo spoke in a quiet voice, yet her words were clear.

Scrambling to his feet, the man hurried to the wide double doors at the head of the room. He opened it and bowed low, his cape falling over one shoulder, as he waved the Olmese inside. Nadja followed them, then he and the others of the welcoming committee left, closing the doors behind them.

Torsten positioned himself at Queen Surayo's right, slightly further away from Toriaken's head.

The three Olmese bowed, arms across their chests, one knee bent slightly. Nadja remained by the door, watching proceedings impassively from her usual spot by the room's main exit.

One of the Omese men said, 'Most esteemed sovereign, it is our honour to be graced by your presence.'

'A shame you bring worrying tidings.' Surayo gestured for them to rise. 'Please. Enlighten me.'

Lady Arbora stood and took another step towards the queen, before restraining herself. 'This is the first time I've been to your capital city. To your palace. What you have here is truly magnificent, and Toriaken is as great as the stories say.'

Surayo inclined her head, acknowledging her.

Lady Arbora continued, 'And I am aware of your magic, Queen Surayo. I know you have eyes and ears the length of your country. I know the great Toriaken guards your Empire's borders. But your armour has failed. We are all in danger—the Myr have returned. Even now, they threaten Olmir.'

'I never vanquished the Myr,' Surayo replied evenly.

Lady Arbora's eyebrow twitched. 'You banished them from this continent. Although Olmir is not part of your Empire, we are allies. We benefited from the armistice. But these dark creatures are worming their way back. And they are more powerful than ever.'

Torsten snapped, 'Lady Arbora! You speak treasonous words. It'll incite panic among the people to spout such things.' He put a hand on the hilt of his sword, hoping she understood the severity of her words.

The Olmese woman raised her shoulders in a shrug. 'Perhaps it *should* incite panic. And while Porsenthia is our ally, we have our own king, Inquisitor. We may speak as we wish.'

'My Master Inquisitor is correct, though. The Myr were defeated, weakened after suffering irrevocable losses,' Surayo said, giving nothing away.

Lady Arbora replied, 'They will be at your borders within a moon's turn, perhaps less.'

'They cannot break the peace treaty,' Surayo replied, some of her irritation showing. 'All the artefacts which gave them power are gone. They cannot rebuild what they were in only five years. In five *millennia*, perhaps.'

'My queen is correct. You have no understanding of what she did to the Myr to reduce them so greatly. You are mistaken.'

Lady Arbora ignored Torsten and kept her attention on the queen. 'Queen Surayo, I would not come here unless the news was real, the situation, dire.'

'Surely you have had sightings? Reports of violent deaths? Disappearances?' It was the first man who had spoken, stepping forward again. His dark beard was neatly trimmed, and he had warm, brown eyes that pleaded with Surayo. Although his vocabulary was perfect, his accent was difficult to understand.

Queen Surayo turned to him. If it had been Torsten's choice, he'd have told the man to be silent. But Surayo was not Torsten, and she did not admonish him for speaking. She slipped into the Ordonis dialect she'd clearly recognised and replied.

Torsten could only pick out a few words here and there, but it was a confusing, nasal accent that he'd never had the ear for. He waited with growing impatience as Surayo and the man exchanged a few more words, the other two Olmese nodding along at their conversation. He'd never known if he'd been astounded or envious of Surayo's ability to speak more than one language, but he disliked being excluded.

Eventually, Surayo switched back into her usual, broad Porsenthian, and Torsten wondered what he'd missed.

Lady Arbora said, 'Whether you believe it or not, the reality is true. You helped protect Olmir once from this threat. As it has risen again, we will fight with you. And if you will not have us in battle, allow us to aid your people—keep them safe, as Toriaken once kept our people safe.'

'I agree to think on this. We acquired a number of arte-facts from our last conflict with the Myr. I shall have our most learned mages study them for any sight of change, anything that might explain the things you claim to have seen. Until we make our decision, you are welcome to stay as guests.'

It was a dismissal, one the Olmese understood the moment Surayo spoke.

'Might we patrol the skies with you, great Toriaken? That we might show you the things we have seen, the things we know?' Lady Arbora tried one last time.

At her address, the dragon raised his head. Behind them, the three members of the Iron Guard shivered, the move-ment almost incomprehensible, and Toriaken's image enhanced. In the blink of an eye, he shifted from mist to solid flesh—iron made living. 'I have sensed no footsteps such as the Myrish magic in my domain.'

'You accuse us of lying?' Lady Arbora gasped.

Toriaken snarled. 'Humans are so often afraid of things they see, of shadows in darkness. They run to us. Beg aid. If there is a plague in your lands, it is not Myrish. I would know.'

All three of the Olmese seethed at the response, but had the graciousness to hold their tongues.

Surayo waved one hand towards the door. 'It is a long way to have flown, even on creatures as strong as your griffins. Rest. Eat. We will speak again once I have conducted my investigations.'

247

Torsten hated the fact his queen gave them hope. The possibility that she believed the Olmese's ludicrous claims. Despite the truth of the matter, he considered it weak to show them that she could be bargained with. That she would listen and consider. As far as he was concerned, a ruler *had* to be firm. Especially as she was supposedly the Queen of Iron.

But he, too, held his tongue, unwilling to anger Toriaken or the queen. Not before he had all the facts for himself.

When the Olmese had left the room, and it was just Nadja, Surayo, Toriaken, and himself, Torsten shook his head. 'Was that wise, my queen? If there is even the *slightest* rumour that the treaty has been broken—'

'I will not risk losing our allies. Their warriors are renowned, as you well know. And I want to check the artefacts. Do whatever research I must.' Surayo walked to the fire, and Toriaken shifted back into mist that floated around the large room. 'I sensed a slight...tremble. The finest lines of my magic, agitated. It had been so long, and the sensation was so faint, that I thought I was mistaken. Perhaps I still am mistaken.'

'There is no Myrish threat.' Torsten stuck to his guns, especially with Nadja in earshot. He didn't know the extent of Surayo's magic. Didn't know how long before she knew for certain they had returned. But he was unwilling to be truthful, that he had knowledge through Miroth of the Myrish death spirit, until he knew whether they were dealing with a desperate few or a full scale invasion.

He needed more time.

'Who knows what lurks beneath the sands of Olmir. There could be some monster affecting them and, as the great Toriaken suggests, they are panicking over the worst-case scenario. No matter how unlikely it is.'

Surayo gently brushed her fingertips along the mantle-piece, the firelight making her glow. 'What have I missed...?'

Torsten decided to change the topic. 'The prisoners are in the dungeons awaiting investigation.'

'Prisoners?' Surayo turned back to him, her eyes glazed over as if she were far away.

Knowing her magic, she probably was. Surayo had once claimed to walk through the spirit world, Toriaken as her guide, to deepen her bond with the dragon and gain greater understanding of the Guardians of Tassar.

Torsten said, 'The lost souls from Bragalia?'

'Ah. Yes.' Surayo blinked rapidly, coming back to herself. Her gaze sharpened. 'Find out *exactly* what has happened to them.'

AFTER PAUSING ONLY to grab himself a plate of cooked chicken, which he wolfed down in a handful of bites, Torsten made his way to the palace dungeons, only one task on his mind.

It was far cooler down in the cells, which were shadowed and draughty. The dungeons themselves were in a block separate to the main castle, underground it in fact, buried within the foundations. Rarely were they empty, but even having this number of prisoners was unusual. All the lost souls had been locked up in one cell, in case they tried to influence or adversely affect any of the others already detained.

Taking the papers from the stack near the entrance, Torsten nodded to the gaoler. 'I will get to work. Please ensure I'm not disturbed.'

'Yes, Master Inquisitor,' the gaoler replied, unbuckling a large ring of keys from his belt. 'Shall I have food sent for you?'

'No need. But I'd appreciate *quiet*.'

After the gaoler bowed himself out, Torsten thumbed

through the papers, wondering where to start. None of the names meant anything to him, and he assumed the people on it would all share a similar story. He walked through the door and into the corridor leading to the cells, trying to work out some hidden meaning in the names. Some pattern he'd missed before.

By the time he reached the cell door, nothing had come to mind, so Torsten decided simply to start at the top and work his way down the list. 'Ashothka? Which one of you is Ashothka?'

One man, in his late fifties or sixties, got shakily to his feet. He was thin and wiry, and looked like he'd spent much of his life outside.

'Where are you from?'

'I...don't know, sir.'

'The journey back hasn't jogged your memory?'

'No, sir.' His fingers trembled where they clutched the bars. 'Please, some food? We weren't given much on the way and—'

'You'll come with me.' Torsten unlocked the door and pushed it open. A dozen frightened faces looked up at him, but none dared make a break for it.

Obedient, Ashothka exited the cell and waited, gaze locked on the stone floor.

Torsten grabbed the short chain that dangled from his tied wrists and led him along the front of the cell down another, narrow corridor. They walked for about a minute, their footsteps the only noise, until Torsten reached a heavy, wooden door. He unlocked it, and pushed Ashothka inside.

The room was vast, circular, and empty—save one small, wooden crate beside the door. As Ashothka wandered inside, looking around with wary eyes, Torsten crouched by the crate and rested a hand on it. Something within rattled around violently at his touch. 'If you don't know where you are, don't know where you're from...I suppose you don't know much about spirits, either?'

Ashothka whirled around, arms wrapped protectively around his chest. He said nothing.

'Hmm. Have you heard of Nestol?' Torsten waited for the flicker of fear to cross Ashothka's face. Irritatingly, the man remained perplexed. It faintly annoyed Torsten. He preferred it when his prisoners knew what was coming next.

He ran his hand along the top of the crate, almost lovingly, despite the frantic movement within which jarred it. 'Nestol is the Spirit of Pain. Well. Not a *true* spirit, but he might as well be. You should hear some of the survivors' stories.'

Ashothka backed up until he was pressed against the stone wall on the far side.

Torsten looked down at the crate, speaking to it more than Ashothka. 'Actually, it's an old Myrish spell, would you believe? Taken as part of the war against them. Queen Surayo, for her faults, is quite the mage. She could see the usefulness of a spell like this one. She gave it life. And I am able to use it. It's *very* effective.'

Ashrothka's eyes widened as he understood.

There was the fear. The panic.

Miroth's fire flickered in his chest and Torsten smiled, his thumb lingering on the latch that kept the crate's lid sealed. 'It's perfect for torture. *I* can break bodies. *Nestol* can break your soul. Can delve into the depths of your mind and pull out *every* last secret, even the ones you don't remember. Incredibly useful, wouldn't you agree?'

'Please. Sir! I don't know anything! I don't know anything at all!'

'Now, now. There's no need for all these dramatics. Surely you want to remember what you've forgotten?' Torsten felt the fire in his chest burn with a savage hunger, one he would enjoy satiating.

Ashothka sank to his knees. 'Please!'

Then, the echo of footsteps outside.

He stood up and turned, annoyed the gaoler had dared let anyone through after his strict instruction to be left alone. Ignoring Ashothka's panicked whimpers, Torsten exited the room and pulled the door firmly shut behind him.

He glared down the corridor, ready to rebuke whoever had disturbed him, when he recognised the sandy hair and Inquisitor's uniform. 'Sarron!'

'Apologies for disturbing you, sir.' The man was out of breath, and was a fair bit thinner than when Torsten had last seen him in Ballowtown. That felt like months ago. 'You asked me to report immediately.'

'No. no. This is a good place to talk.' After all, they weren't within earshot of anyone. 'What did you find out?'

'I followed Varlot and the Bragalian woman, Calidra. They stayed in Ballowtown a day, probably waiting for their friends. Varlot spent most of the time drinking wine in a tavern on the edge of town. On the second morning, they headed north, to Meadowhill. Varlot took part in a dice game at the Meadow Markets. You know, the travelling one?'

Torsten nodded, listening intently.

'He won twenty-five silver pieces, too. Stayed in Meadowhill two days as well. They were heading towards Fellwood, for the Laird's funeral, from what I could gather. Unfortunately, they beat me there by half a day.'

'How?' Suspicion rose. How could two people on foot gain such distance on Sarron?

'War griffin. An Olmese warrior picked them up just north of Meadowhill. I wasn't close enough to hear the conversation, but I kept going.'

Another war griffin. It seemed envoys had been sent to Bragalia as well as Porsenthia.

'I managed to catch the end of the funeral, the whole of

Fellwood turned up to it. And…I also managed to watch when they were reunited with their friends.'

Torsten scowled. He didn't care about the company Calidra kept. 'Who cares about their friends? What about *Varlot*? He's up to something and I need to know what it is. That's why I sent you after *him*!'

Sarron scratched the back of his neck, sheepish. 'Well, sir. Their friend? The lad they were with in the tavern. Fenn?'

Torsten nodded, his patience wearing thin.

'He's Myr-touched. They had a Priestess of Neros there confirm it. Reckon that's what's wrong with his memory. The headaches and fevers, too. The Olmese know something. They're gathering their strength, ordering borders defended and recruiting into their army.'

Torsten's anger boiled. Fenn. He'd *known* the boy was trouble. 'Does Varlot know? About the lad?'

Sarron shrugged. 'He was there. Guess he does.'

Torsten wondered whether Varlot knew that before, when they'd met in Ballowtown. Was that why he'd been so quick to jump to Fenn's defence? Had Varlot turned rogue? Was he in league with the Myr?

No. Varlot had fought alongside him, against the Myrish death spirit in Ballowtown. Not to mention his entire military history.

Then again, it could have been a ruse.

Torsten frowned. Varlot was a murderer. Capable of things no man should be able to. And damn near impossible to kill.

'Sir…?' Sarron questioned.

Torsten blinked, forgetting he was there. 'Go and rest with the others. And not a word of this Myr business, do you understand?'

'But shouldn't we—'

'Do you understand?'

Sarron sighed. 'Yes, sir.'

'Good work. I'll call a meeting of Inquisitors soon. Await further instructions until then.'

With a short bow, Sarron turned and headed back down the corridor, leaving Torsten alone with his thoughts. After another moment, Torsten opened the door and re-entered the chamber, to find Ashothka huddled against the wall.

He recalled Queen Surayo's question from earlier: *what had they missed?*

As Torsten looked down at the Bragalian, fear and confusion clouding the man's eyes, he sighed. Fenn had used forged papers. Was almost certainly one of the lost souls—the same as Ashothka. The same as all the other prisoners he had locked up.

They were Myr-touched.

It was connected.

Fire roiled in his chest as the realisation struck.

It *shouldn't* have been possible. After Queen Surayo's decisive victory five years ago, after destroying the last of the Myrish artefacts, there shouldn't have been any chance they could rise again. Certainly not in their lifetime, anyway.

Torsten's lip curled. His instincts were usually right; Miroth's senses were often part of that. And Torsten had developed the nagging feeling that Apollo *hadn't* done his job properly five years ago.

'Insolent blaggard,' he muttered under his breath. The thief was going to rue the day he ever deceived the Iron Crown.

PART II

Hope gone and dreams broken,
Scattered in the wind, unspoken.
Smother iron's endless sight,
Restore our voices unto light.

15

THE THIEF

APOLLO

One of the most northerly towns in Porsenthia, Foxmouth drew in tourists from across Tassar. It sat at the juncture of the Lasseen Ocean and the Polar Sea, and where those two bodies of water met, there was often incredible fishing.

Apollo had long stated that the inn he owned in Foxmouth, *The Grumpy Fisherman*, had been named for this very reason. But that wasn't the case at all, as convenient a lie as it was. There was little need to correct the hopeful visitors and customers, who mostly wanted to try their luck at netting a goliath marlin, coldwater tripletail, or perhaps the more elusive silverfins that densely populated the waters offshore.

He'd never been one for fishing himself, and had learned everything there was to learn about the fish native to Foxmouth and northern Porsenthia once he and his wife bought the inn on the western edge of town, right on the seafront. Business had boomed, chiefly due to the location providing an unrivalled sea view, but also because it was surrounded by a number of fine establishments; blacksmiths, tanners, bakeries, and fishmongers.

It meant the street was one of the busiest all year round, with a constant flow of people, and a constant flow of coin.

And, given the town's proximity to the Shrine of Tori-aken, many people wanted somewhere to stay within convenient travelling distance to pay their respects to the Iron Dragon. *The Grumpy Fisherman*, a modest inn, provided Apollo and Malora with a respectable income. Steady. Safe.

'Are you daydreaming again?' Malora's sharp voice cut through Apollo's thoughts.

He'd been staring out of the window at the Lasseen Ocean, a mug of tea gone cold on the sill. Usually it was his spot for wistful dreaming, but today, the waters were dark and rough, and he'd been afraid one of the large fishing ships currently out to sea might be swallowed up by Neros at any moment. 'Mal, would I?'

'You do every day. Sometimes hourly.' His wife thwacked him playfully across the back with a towel. 'What is it this time? Reminiscing heists? Poking fun at Inquisitors? Reliving your great escapes?'

'No, no.' He looped an arm around her shoulder and brought her in close. Kissing the top of her head, he kept his gaze on the sea. 'Neros looks to be in a foul temper today.'

'She's been in a foul temper for weeks, now. What's the problem?'

'You're the priestess. You tell me why Neros is upset.'

She huffed and pushed him away. 'I'm not a priestess, Apollo. You *know* that! Stop expecting me to magically understand any spirit that comes within spitting distance of the coast!'

Apollo grinned and grabbed at her waist, tickling with one hand and pinning her with the other. He knew very well she wasn't a priestess, and hadn't had any powers for years, but it was a guaranteed way to wind her up—which never failed to amuse him.

Malora giggled, feebly pushing away his hand. 'Stop! Stop

it, Apollo!' She writhed in his grip, twisting like one of the slippery fish their patrons were after, and escaped. 'Can you pay attention for more than five minutes?'

'Where's the fun in that?' Apollo leaned on the windowsill, admiring his wife. He picked up his mug and sipped it out of habit, screwing his face up at the taste of cold tea.

'I'm not sure whether *you're* the four-year-old or Renys is!' Malora sighed and shook her head, though she wasn't really exasperated with him. Not yet, anyway.

'Mal, I'm hurt.' He pretended to pout.

'Yeah, still not helping your case, Apollo. I need to collect our order from the butchers or we won't have much to feed our guests this week. I left Renys upstairs but please keep an eye on her in case she goes wandering off and ends up on the roof again? I'll be back in an hour.'

Malora was often busy with the running of the tavern. She was far more organised than he was, and usually arranged their orders to keep *The Grumpy Fisherman* in business. But in the past two weeks, she had thrown herself into it with more vigor than usual, filling every second of every day with tasks, and already this morning she looked more tired than usual.

Apollo tilted his head, playfulness evaporating. 'You could have gone, you know. It wouldn't have been a problem. I'd even have come with you.'

She stiffened. 'Apollo, why are you talking about *that* now?'

'I know it's bothering you.'

Malora's shoulders dropped. 'I think I'll feel guilty about this until the day I cross to the spirit world. Perhaps even then, it'll stay with me.'

'Mal...' Apollo stepped towards her and pulled her into a hug, close against his chest.

She allowed herself a moment of comfort before pushing him away. 'No. I made my decision. Too late to go back now.'

'Even so, a funeral is—'

'I made my choice, Apollo. There's nothing for me in Bragalia.'

He knew arguing with her would only make her upset, so he held his tongue and nodded. He wanted to tell her she could always change her mind and return to Fellwood. That she shouldn't work herself to the bone. That she didn't need to worry about their daughter getting up to mischief. That whatever was happening with Neros would soon pass. 'I'll keep an eye on Renys.'

Malora didn't quite smile, but she relaxed, the tension dropping from her shoulders. 'Thank you. I'll be back as soon as I can.'

'No rush.'

They employed two young lads to help manage guests during peak seasons, and also an old widower who had no home in the town. All three were working at the moment, so he had no need to go back into the crowded tavern and deal with more questions.

Apollo was a notorious man running a notorious inn. A scar ran from his left eyebrow to his chin, a sharp curve cut into his face by Queen Surayo's Master Inquisitor, so he'd always be marked as a thief. He should have died multiple times over, but he'd turned away from a life of crime after being pardoned by the Iron Crown, and had settled down with Malora to run the tavern. He'd named it *The Grumpy Fisherman* as a nod to an old ally of his—a grumpy man who had given his life to help Apollo and Malora. Another part of his past, his old life, that he'd turned away from.

Though he never spoke of the specifics, many new patrons saw his scar and immediately bombarded Apollo with questions he preferred to avoid.

So, despite enjoying a busy tavern and the company of travellers from across the country, he often kept out of sight.

Renys, thankfully, provided an *excellent* excuse for sudden disappearances. 'Sorry, I can't stay and talk, Renys needs feeding. Sorry, I'd love to answer your questions, but it's Renys's bedtime. Come back tomorrow, and if Renys doesn't need to be watched, we'll talk then.'

He watched Malora from the window, keeping an eye on her as she left the tavern, a shawl around her shoulders to protect herself from the biting sea wind, and made her way down the wide street without a look back.

Apollo rolled his shoulders and backed away from the window. Renys was quiet, which usually meant she was up to something. He paused to briefly glance through the crack in the door, checking on the patrons currently eating breakfast, then darted upstairs, taking them two at a time. 'Renys?'

Reaching the landing with a slight grunt—he'd definitely put on some extra "comfort" weight during these past few years—he looked around for his daughter. The family lived on the first floor above the tavern, a hotchpotch of crooked rooms and corridors that was more rabbit warren than livable dwelling. It was part of the reason why the tavern had been so cheap. But it also meant that Renys could be in one of two dozen hiding places.

Worse, the hubbub of noise and chatter from below drifted up, and the building itself creaked here and there, making it impossible for Apollo to guess where Renys was. He peered past doors left ajar and wondered why his daughter seemed in a constant game of hide-and-seek.

Something fluttered to his right, but it was just the curtain in the wind. In the room corners, spiders scuttled away from his gaze, hiding in the cracks in the walls, looking for somewhere dark.

Apollo dropped to a crouch, putting himself at his daughter's eye level. All of a sudden, cabinets and cupboards that he'd have overlooked before became prime locations.

Renys giggled from the room opposite.

He darted across the hallway to their bedroom on his hands and knees, hardly suppressing his own laughter at their game. 'Where's Renys? Is she in here?'

More giggling.

He saw her bare feet behind the wardrobe, just visible in the gap underneath. With a chuckle to himself, he shuffled away from the wardrobe—pretending to look under the bed, behind the desk, even under loose floorboards.

Each time he searched in the wrong place, Renys's giggles grew increasingly louder, as if she were having trouble remembering that her part of the game was to hide. Apollo tried to draw out the seek for as long as possible, but their bedroom was not lavishly furnished, and there were only so many times he could check the same place before Renys would no longer find it fun.

Apollo backed up to the wardrobe, still in a crouch. 'I guess Renys isn't in here…'

A loud guffaw told Apollo what Renys thought of that.

Quick as a flash, Apollo lunged behind the wardrobe, finding his daughter covered in dust, cobwebs in her frizzy hair, and laughing so hard she cried. He pulled her out, getting cobwebs on himself, and proceeded to tickle her.

She squealed with delight, tickling him back, her laughter so loud he thought it could light the world.

The two of them played on the bedroom floor, chasing one another around, and more than once, Renys used Apollo as her personal climbing frame. He was on his knees, Renys on his shoulders trying to tickle his ear, when her laughter abruptly stopped.

'Ren?' Apollo held both her hands high above his head, but he couldn't see her face. 'Are you okay?'

She made a noise, a sort of grunt she often did when trying to work something out.

Apollo turned, trying to figure out what had suddenly captivated his daughter's attention.

'No!' Renys yelled. 'The window!'

Apollo obliged, spinning back to face the window. It was slightly open, the curtains drawn back, and offered a fantastic sea view as all the windows of *The Grumpy Fisherman* did. At first, his gaze lingered on the water itself, wondering if one of the ships had finally been caught up in the spirit's terrible power. Although the sea was as choppy as it had been when Malora left, he couldn't see any of the ships had been damaged or were missing. 'Ren?'

She pointed, although he could only see the tips of her fingers. 'Scary lady coming here!'

Apollo stepped closer to the window and peered out, down onto the street.

An Inquisitor.

Her dark uniform was clean and shining, and the people on the street gave her a wide berth, several throwing cautious glances over their shoulders at her.

Scary lady indeed. Renys didn't know the half of it.

Keeping one hand on steadying Renys—the little girl quite happy on his shoulders—he walked over to his desk and pulled out one of the drawers. He rooted through the papers in there.

'What's that?' Renys asked, ever curious.

'Something your da needs.' One handed, he pulled out an old book, battered and with half its cover missing. He flicked through the pages until he reached one with a small tear at the top. Folded neatly inside the page was another leaf of paper—much thicker and of far better quality than anything they owned.

'It's different,' Renys commented from above, clearly watching him with interest.

263

'It is. It's from a very important person.'

'Mama?'

Apollo smiled. 'Well...to lots of people, she's more important than your mama.'

'Nope.' Renys's words were confident and allowed no argument.

Apollo opened the paper, gaze darting down the sentences written in a scrawl so elaborate it was a wonder anyone could read it. But the most important thing was the bottom, where the cream vellum had been signed by Queen Surayo and marked with the Iron Crown's signature.

That simple note had changed his life. Changed Malora's.

Hi grinned. 'You're right. No-one's more important than your mama.'

One-handed, he carefully refolded the queen's pardon and slipped it into his inside pocket. He returned to the window, but there was no sign of the Inquisitor. She had to be inside the tavern already.

'Come on, Renys. We need to go talk to the scary lady now.'

'Don't wanna.' It was more out of stubbornness than fear.

'I have to. You wanna wait up here?'

'No.'

Apollo grinned. His daughter was so brave, so fierce. 'All right, you can come keep me safe from the scary lady, then?'

Renys immediately laughed, squeezing his hand with her own. 'Yah, I keep the scary lady away!'

Although Apollo spoke lightly to his daughter, a small seed of doubt plagued him. He'd been free for the past five years. Had built a life with Malora somewhere new, where no-one knew him or his past.

But the scar on his face led many people to summon town officers and even Inquisitors when they passed through. One determined old woman had even brought a priest from Tori-

264

aken's Shrine and been laughed out of the tavern for her suspicions.

He was used to showing his pardon from time to time.

It was the first Inquisitor of the year, so he supposed he'd been due another visit. Renys had seen most of them. Yes, she'd been younger, but she'd never had such a strong reaction to the uniform before.

By now, all the officers of Foxmouth knew about Apollo's history and pardon, and aside from a few grouches, most bore him no ill will.

There was always something about an Inquisitor, though.

They were closer to the queen.

As if in response, his right thigh burned with sudden intensity. An old mark flaring up where the queen's magic had once touched him. He winced, dropping to one knee.

Renys gasped at the sudden drop, but he kept her safe. 'Da!'

'Sorry, Ren. Spent too long on my hands and knees. Leg's cramping up!'

'Da, why did you hurt your leg?'

'I didn't mean to!' He gritted his teeth. 'Come on. Scary lady will come upstairs looking for me if we don't move soon.'

'No!'

Apollo used the windowsill to pull himself up to his feet. His shoulders ached with Renys atop them for so long, but he had no intention of moving her. Firstly, she wanted to see. Secondly, the Inquisitor might soften at the sight of such a young child with him.

Some of the previous conversations with the queen's police had been rather aggressive.

He'd need to put out word again, remind townsfolk of his pardon. But that would come in time.

Gingerly, Apollo exited the room, crossed the landing, and made his way down the creaking staircase. Already, the usual hubbub of noise and chatter from the tavern had quietened.

Before he reached the bottom, one of the lads who worked for him, Michal, appeared. 'Apollo! There ya are! Got another of them Inquisitors here looking for ya!'

'I know, I know. I saw her from the window.'

'Want me to hold Ren?' Michal raised his arms, as if to take her from his shoulders.

'It's fine, she'll stay with me. Just keep everyone eating and drinking. Don't wanna sour the mood in there.'

'Mood's already sour, but I'll do what I can. She's standing by the door, not moving. Said no-one can come in or out 'til she's spoke to ya.'

Apollo groaned inwardly. Great. A jobsworth. He wondered if she worked with Torsten to have such a ridiculously blinkered view of rules. 'I'm coming.'

Michal nodded and hurried back into the main tavern. Apollo watched him go and saw the full tables through the open doorway. Just what he needed, another public talking down.

'Ready, Renys?' he asked.

'Time to fight scary lady!' she cried, far louder than he'd expected.

'Okay, okay. Just stay quiet while your da talks to her.'

She tapped him on the head twice, confirming her assent.

Apollo tested his weight on his right leg. His thigh twinged but there was no pain. He shifted Renys a bit higher on his shoulders, then followed Michal through the doorway. Most of the tables were full of his regulars, with a few patrons sitting at the bar.

Just as Michal had warned, the Inquisitor stood beside the door, one foot blocking it from being opened. She was tall and well-built, in the dark regalia of all Inquisitors, a silver dragon pin above her breast. The same dragon insignia was on the scabbard at her hip, a longsword sheathed within it from the size of the weapon.

Her head snapped up the moment Apollo entered the main tavern room.

'Morning, morning. Carry on!' Apollo waved to the patrons who nodded at his arrival. 'Get that tea down you! Makes for a good day's work.'

A few chuckles answered, the mood obviously too tense for any genuine laughter.

'Inquisitor. There's a table here for you if you'd like to sit down?' Apollo turned to her, scanning for any softening expressions. He gestured with one hand, the other held onto his daughter's. 'We've a special on roast ham this week, and the Horush cheeses are shipped over every—'

'I'm not here for breakfast, Apollo.'

Apollo had never appreciated being interrupted, and even with Renys atop his shoulders, the woman cut straight to the point.

'Well, as we're on a first name basis, would you care to introduce yourself? Or should I just call you Inquisitor?'

She plucked a small iron dagger from her belt and held it up. A ruby had been pressed into the hilt, glinting in the morning sunlight. 'I am Inquisitor Nadja. In service to Queen Surayo and the Iron Crown.'

The dagger was proof of her legitimacy. She was the real deal, not some foolhardy person trying to impersonate an Inquisitor.

'Nadja. Fine. If you're not here for breakfast, perhaps you've heard about the great fishing here in Foxmouth? Season's right for the silverfins, but if you're going to stay a few weeks, that'll put you right on time for—'

'Apollo Tamlin. With respect, I am not here to fish. We need to talk. If your responses do not satisfy me, you *will* be under arrest by order of the Iron Crown. Tell your patrons to leave.'

Something cold tore through his stomach and all sense of joking fled. 'I have the queen's pardon right here!' Apollo fumbled in his jacket and held it up.

'It's of no consequence. Please, Apollo. Do not make me use violence.' Nadja placed a hand on the sword sheathed at her hip. 'I cannot adequately explain the seriousness of my visit. You're lucky Torsten himself is not present.'

At the mention of Surayo's Master Inquisitor, Apollo's blood ran cold, rooting him to the spot.

'Scary lady, you go away now!' Renys yelled.

Nadja didn't flinch.

And Apollo hoped Malora would take a *long* time at the butchers.

16
THE DREAM
FENN

F enn was flooded with darkness so intense, he couldn't tell which way was up.

All his senses had left him. He couldn't see, smell, hear, or even *feel* the ground below his feet. Couldn't tell whether he stood or sat, or even if he was laying down. And yet the dreaded panic he would have expected to fill him in such a situation was missing.

He was oddly...calm.

Strangely, he couldn't even muster the curiosity for *why* he wasn't afraid. It was as if the darkness smothered him, cradled him. Within the darkness, he was safe.

Fire burned in his chest, keeping him warm. It was only a small flame, hardly more than a candle flickering, but it was enough. He huddled around it with whatever semblance of himself he could find. It helped to solidify his body in the void.

Slowly, so slowly he wasn't sure it was happening, Fenn became aware of his limbs. His fingers didn't seem to be connected to his hands, their edges blurring, as if he were made of sand and a vicious wind swept parts of him away.

Fenn opened his mouth, what he thought was his mouth, but no sound emanated from his throat.

'You are whole again.'

A voice spoke in his ear. No, in his mind. Again, there was no sensation of rising panic or fear, only a faint sense of cold. He accepted the voice much as he accepted himself floating in...wherever this was.

'You are on the edge.'

The edge of what?

'The edge of the spirit world.'

Fenn wanted to frown, but he wasn't sure he had eyebrows—even a face—to do that. That meant he had to be...

'So much confusion. So much death. You are all so very, very weak. Why do the dragons covet your worship?'

Something shifted in Fenn's peripheral vision. A light, so faint it was just the hint of pale grey in a wash of darkness, but it was consistent and solid. He moved towards it. Or was he pulled by it?

Light engulfed him. His body came into focus, a solid mass instead of whatever he'd been before, and with it, the sense of pressure on his skin, in his mind. Was he underwater? No, he could breathe.

He remembered what the voice had said—he was on the edge of the spirit world.

Did...did that mean he was dead?

'You live. Just. You are unconscious. Our magic brought you here, because you were too weak to withstand it. But something is holding you at the edge, keeping you from crossing. I wonder how long it will last.'

Fenn couldn't see a body for the voice that spoke. He tried to turn, tried to look, but his movements were sluggish, like he was trying to wade through honey.

'We...cannot control you completely. Something blocks our touch.' The voice was clipped. Frustrated. 'You are dying. We

*are too powerful. Humans are too weak. There has been so much
death in the pursuit of life. We have been dying, and now you are,
too.'*

As the words were spoken, Fenn noticed movement
somewhere below him. A vast line of people, their faces blur-
rex. Dozens upon dozens of grey bodies shuffled along, one
behind the other, heading to some unknown destination
deeper in the darkness.

Fenn swallowed. He had a good idea they were heading
into the spirit world.

He tried to get a closer look, to see where they went, to
see if he was right, but his body was held fast where it
floated.

'If you go, you will not come back.'

Fear washed over him, and Fenn suddenly didn't want to
look upon where the people walked. Didn't want to see the
spirit world. 'Why am I here?' His voice hurt and every
breath scratched his throat.

'You will become an echo soon.'

Fenn knew, though he couldn't have said how, that the
people marching to the spirit world were echoes. All the
people who had died. Died...at the Myr's hands. Or rather,
their magic. 'When?'

'We can stop this. We can help you.'

'You can?' Fenn remembered Selys had told him there
might be a way to lift his curse. Something Myrish. 'Why did
you curse me in the first place? And all the other lost souls?'

A brief hesitation. *'An accident.'*

He tried to suck in a breath, to calm the sudden excitement. He was getting answers! Finally finding out what had
happened to him. 'What did you do? Where did you find me?
Who was I?' Questions burst from him like a river bursting
its banks. 'Why am I dying? How much time do I have left?'

More hesitation. *'Something important to you is lost. But you
can retrieve it. Vermecio can help.'*

Fenn tried to whirl around, to find whoever spoke to him, to look them in the eyes. It would be easier to have a conversation if he could *see* whoever was talking to him. 'What can help? Please! Where are you?'

'Everywhere...'

'Show yourself!' As Fenn's body became more solid, and he became more aware of himself, more of his emotions returned. Confusion. Panic. Anger.

Some unseen force plucked him up, shifted him away from the pale grey light and the echoes of the living. Thrust back into darkness, Fenn's emotions were smothered again, his bubbling anger soothed. Idly, he wondered if he was closer to, or further from, death.

He fought the sensation—previously comforting—now it tried to trap him. To smother his questions.

Something whooshed in front of his vision, a shape darker even than the void around him. A creature of magic, it was difficult to pin down in the swirling dark. Thin, angled, yet somehow sinuous. It brushed his face, leaving it cold to the touch, as if it were made of ice.

Fenn knew then, with powerful clarity, that this thing, this *creature*, was one of the Myr.

Panic and regret seized him and his chest burned with every breath.

Again, the disembodied voice spoke, but Fenn's attention dipped in and out of focus as he fought to escape.

'...belonged to...
...stolen...
Memories, once...
...lost...only fear...'

Hope gone...
Scattered... unspoken.
Smother...
...unto light.

...soon...gate...'

ICE GREW AROUND HIM, its biting cold crept along his arms, his legs, and forced its way across his body.

The darkness grew, a physical presence, a weight on his mind that he couldn't fight. Shrieking wind filled his ears, blocking out any other words the creature spoke.

And cold. So much cold. He was drowning in wave upon wave of it.

Abruptly, the fire in his chest burned brighter and eclipsed everything else.

❊

FENN'S EYES SNAPPED OPEN.

Heat.

Burning heat.

With a gasp, he forced himself up, only to find several pairs of hands restraining him. 'Fire!'

'You were having a nightmare,' Jisyel said, her voice somewhere to his left.

'Seizure, more like,' Calidra corrected.

Fenn blinked, taking in the faces around him, trying to orientate himself. Jisyel. Calidra. Selys. He clutched his chest and took a few breaths, ensuring his throat and lungs worked. Slowly, the heat subsided.

273

'We thought you were dead.' Jisyel squeezed his left hand between hers, her grip so tight his fingers paled.

'Jisyel. Too…too tight,' he gasped.

'Oh! S—sorry, Fenn.' Jisyel released his hand and stepped back, embarrassed. 'Just…just wanted to make sure you really *were* here. With us. I mean, in your mind.' She broke away, cheeks red with embarrassment.

Fenn wanted to laugh, but the mix of cold and heat had left him shaky, and he was afraid his mind would unravel and fall apart again. Had it been a nightmare? Or had he *really* been on the edge of the spirit world? They had thought he was dead. So had he.

Selys would know.

But he wasn't sure he wanted to ask her, nor have anyone else find out what he'd just seen. They'd only just come to accept he was Myr-touched. If they discovered he'd been in the spirit world with a Myr, *talking* to one…They'd think he was somehow being manipulated by their magic. And maybe he was.

Maybe he *was* the threat they'd worried he could be.

Fenn struggled to work out what was real. He tried to recall the few words the Myr had said to him—something that could help restore his memories? That had been stolen? The Myr had called it Vermecio?

And then it had said something else. Something that had sounded a sort of chant, not dissimilar to the funeral rites Selys and the others had performed on the dead.

But it was more meaningful than that.

It had sent shivers up his spine, and actual chunks of ice had grown along his arm.

He clutched his stomach, trying to keep the contents in one place while his head whirled. 'What happened?'

'You collapsed outside. Been unconscious about four hours,' Calidra said, glancing out the window. 'We've been checking up on you every so often. But you started screaming just now. So we all came in here in case...Well, just to make sure you were okay.' Despite her firm voice, she looked worried—chewing her bottom lip, her gaze darting to Jisyel more often than before.

Fenn licked his lips, trying to piece together what had happened. What he'd just experienced. It eclipsed his joy at seeing Calidra again.

He, Jisyel, and Selys had finally made it to Fellwood. They'd had to fight their way through the crowds of people flooding out of the mansion where Calidra's family lived. Most of them had been at the funeral, and they'd arrived as the service had finished.

Thankfully, Selys had been able to use her rank as a priestess to gain entry.

Calidra had been there, safe and uninjured. If anything, she looked amazingly well.

And then...and then...

There had been darkness. All-encompassing darkness. And cold.

'Are you okay, Calidra?' Fenn gazed around. 'Is this...I'm in your house, right?'

Calidra folded her arms and shifted her weight. 'You're in my mother's house. Lady Vantonen. Although your welcome here is less than warm, I have to say. Do you think you can stand up?'

Fenn shivered as another memory surfaced. He was *dying*. He'd been worried at the possibility, and the voice in his head —the Myr, he reminded himself—had confirmed it.

It had also said Vermecio could help...Whoever that was.

'Fenn?' Jisyel sat on the edge of the bed and patted his arm. 'Your face is all red.'

'It's warm in here.'

'Welcome to Bragalia,' Calidra laughed. 'From what Jisyel and Selys were telling me, you're wanting to head north though. Right?'

He nodded, gently, in case the movement set off more discomfort.

'All the way to the Nethal Mountains in northern Porsenthia,' Selys said, speaking for the first time. Her glaive rested against the wall of the room. Fenn wondered how soon it would be until she had to use it.

'To the Myrish construct?' he asked.

Selys nodded.

'Does it...does it have a name?'

She shrugged. 'Does it matter?'

'No, I guess not.' He rubbed his hands. 'What about you, Calidra? The funeral? Did you make it here in time? Did you end up in the water, too? In Ballowtown?'

'Varlot and I were fine. And yes, I made the funeral. But, honestly, I don't know how long I'm going to stay here...I... there's one more piece of my family left. One more person I can try and reconnect with.' Calidra took Jisyel's hands in her own, a smile on her lips. 'My sister lives. Quillaja told me. Malora is in Porsenthia, in a town called Foxmouth. I have to go there. I have to see her, and make amends.'

'That's incredible, Cal!' Jisyel's face broke into a smile. It lasted a second or two before fading. 'But...but what about Fellwood? This whole canton? This is your home. The Myr are on its doorstep!'

'Mother will have things under wraps.'

'Malora isn't going anywhere. It took you long enough to get off the island! Now you're here, you should stay and do what you can to help. Now more than ever! Don't look like that, I'll be with you.'

Calidra shook her head. 'You don't know my mother.'

'We're talking about the Myr, Cal. The Myr. Whatever... whatever your mother thinks of you or me, surely she'll appreciate the extra help?'

'Jisyel...'

Turning his head away from the women, Fenn noticed a

uniformed guard standing outside the window, his back to them. The window was closed and made of thick glass, but he wondered if the man had been eavesdropping.

Following his gaze, Calidra snorted. 'I said your welcome was cold here. Mother's household guard is trying to keep me obedient, and it won't be long before she wants to get rid of the rest of you. She'll find some reason to be offended, or you'll do something that disrespects her, and she'll have you thrown out.'

'How...unmotherly,' Fenn muttered.

'You're telling me. Fenn, do you feel able to stand up yet? Get some food down you?'

Fenn shuffled to the edge of the bed and placed his bare feet flat on the wooden floor. His toes were sore from all the travelling, but after Jisyel's glinoc paste, they were already healing. With effort, he pushed himself to standing, arms held out to the side to balance himself. After a slight wobble, he straightened. 'I'm fine. And yeah, I could eat.' He knew he needed to stop dancing around the real issue, and asked, 'Is there...any news on the Myr?'

'The city watch has doubled bodies on the wall,' Selys said, leaning on the wall beside her glaive. 'We aren't under attack yet, but who's to say how long it'll last. You're Myr-touched, Fenn. Getting your memories back might help uncover information about what the Myr are up to, help our spirits prepare. The sooner we're able to find out more, the sooner we might be able to stop the attacks happening.'

Fenn swallowed. This was why Selys had agreed to help him. For the good of the world. For her dragon spirit, Neros. Whatever he learned could help against the Myr, could stop more people dying.

He closed his eyes, trying to recall his dream of the spirit world. Or whatever it had been. The Myr had done something to him and the other lost souls. But...but it hadn't worked? So many people had died. Something about their magic being too powerful?

And he wasn't out of the woods yet. He shuddered, remembering the freezing touch of the Myr.

He didn't know why he'd been picked. Perhaps he'd simply been in the wrong place at the wrong time. But he was here now, and there was nothing he could do to change what had already happened. The only thing he *could* do was take steps to change his future.

Fenn was determined to ensure dying wasn't going to be part of it. Not immediately, anyway, and certainly not by the Myr's hands.

Jisyel frowned at him. 'You could always come back to the Isle of Salt, you know. I'm sure gran wouldn't mind. And when it gets busier, I'm sure she could do with a strong back and an extra pair of hands!'

As much as that sounded lovely, Fenn shook his head. 'I might have people waiting for me. My own friends and family. I bet they're worried sick! I have to keep going.'

Calidra let out a sigh. 'I saw someone on my way to Fellwood. Another lost soul, like you. She was young, just a child.'

Fenn frowned. Why did Calidra look so worried?

'There was a woman looking after her. Said the girl's brother had died. And...and the girl was dying, too. Fenn. I don't know how much time you have.'

'Sounds about the same for the other lost souls who passed through the Shrine of Neros,' Selys said, speaking in a low voice. 'We should go as soon as you're ready to move.'

Before it's too late, Fenn assumed she'd omitted.

Hearing it from someone else made it real. Solid. His mind reeled with images from the dream—if it really had been a dream. He wanted to focus on the positives. 'When I get my memories back, I'll know where I'm from. If I have any friends or family. And even if not, nowhere will be safe from the Myr. I can't just bury my head. Besides, whatever we find out might help against the Myr. It's what Selys is banking on. Right?'

Selys nodded, and Calidra's gaze dropped to the floor. 'Calidra, you must remember the killings in the war? Our spirits are the only defence against the Myr. The only ones powerful enough to drive them away, at any rate. Speed is of the essence.'

'You're right. Perhaps you'll even get a pardon from the Inquisitors for helping out! If it helps against the Myr?' Jisyel had clearly latched onto the one sliver of positivity in amongst Fenn's admittance he was dying.

'That'd be a relief,' Fenn said. He winced as a sudden sharp pain stabbed through his chest.

Calidra unfolded her arms and scratched her chin. 'You know. I think it'd probably be better if you stayed one night.'

Fenn frowned. 'Why? We just said I'm on a time limit.'

'It won't mean much if you can't walk. Look at yourself. You're on the brink of collapse.'

She was right. There was no point in bravado when he needed rest. He glanced at Selys, worried he was letting her down, but she offered him a smile. Fenn sighed. 'Maybe you're right. But we should get on tomorrow. Early.'

Silence fell upon the room, and Fenn drifted back into his thoughts. Selys was going to go with him into Porsenthia. The priestess was just as determined as he was to get answers for her spirit. But it would leave them vulnerable, especially if Calidra and Jisyel were going to stay in Fellwood. He chewed his lip as he thought. 'What about Varlot?'

Calidra's eyes hardened.

'That axe of his would be useful if we're going north.' Selys commented, following his train of thought.

'Probably. But...' Calidra trailed off.

'But what?' Fenn asked, concerned.

'Well. If you're going north, Fenn, he'll probably want to

come along. I couldn't say why. Man's got problems and I don't know why he's so interested in you.'

'We all have problems, Cal,' Jisyel said, 'if the Myr are on the move, having someone who's *actually* fought them would probably be a good thing?'

'He's the former Porsenthian general, correct?' Selys asked. 'A man of his calibre would be useful if we were to encounter any Inquisitors. There's only so far my rank and glaive can get us.'

'I don't trust him,' Calidra said, her voice flat.

Jisyel laughed. 'You don't trust *anyone*!'

Calidra huffed and walked away, pacing the room. 'I know, but there's something about him. He's got a taste for coin, for a start. An unhealthy one. Wine, too.'

'Everyone has their vices,' Selys said.

Ignoring her, Calidra continued, 'And he still hasn't adequately explained why he's so interested in you, Fenn. Perhaps he *does* know you from...before. It might be a bad thing.'

Fenn sat upright in the bed, resting his back against the wooden headboard. 'I helped Jisyel on the road, and that made you trust me. Varlot helped you, and you trust him...less?'

'Everyone has a motive, Fenn. You've clearly spent too much time with Jisyel—you're as naive as she is!'

'Hey!' Jisyel stuck her tongue out.

Fenn thought about it. Other than their brief meeting in Ballowtown, he'd not spent any time with Varlot. If anything, the man had been kinder to him than Calidra had been, and he'd known him for less time. At least Varlot hadn't waved a dagger in his face and threatened to pass him over to an Inquisitor.

Although Torsten had done most of the fighting against the Myrish creature in Ballowtown, Varlot had done his part, too. Having him along with Selys's glaive would surely keep

280

them out of trouble if they were to be attacked. 'Where's Varlot now?'

'Probably in one of the gambling dens in town. Mother refused his contract to train Paicha. He didn't take that rejection particularly well. Stalked off in a huff,' Calidra replied, in a tone that told Fenn exactly what she thought of that.

'Selys, can you see if you can find him? Ask if he'll come with us into Porsenthia?'

Calidra snorted. 'Fenn, I don't think that's a good idea.'

'Why not? He helped me before. Helped you, too? And he's fought the Myr. If we get into trouble on the way...'

'Fenn...'

'I know you don't trust him, Calidra, but his axe is going to be handy on the road. If he doesn't have a contract anymore, do you want him lingering around Fellwood? Possibly causing trouble?'

Selys grabbed her glaive before Calidra could say anything more, the dragon-carved jade beads clinking together. 'Don't worry about it. I'll find Varlot. You get some rest.' With a nod to the others, the priestess exited the room.

'Cal, you've got to let your walls down sometimes.' Jisyel hugged her, burying her face in Calidra's shoulder. 'Not everyone is out to get you. Selys and Varlot are both good people. And whatever happens with your mother, I'm here. It'll be okay.'

Fenn was stunned. Jisyel was silly, sweet, and playful. He'd seen her afraid—of him, when Selys had mentioned the Myr—and serious when she'd searched for Calidra in Vaelar. But this was another side to the woman that he'd not known about. He'd always assumed Calidra was the one who kept Jisyel grounded, but it appeared to be the other way around. Calidra simply had a stronger, more dominant front that she put on in front of strangers.

He almost felt rude for watching.

The two women hugged, clearly taking comfort and

strength from one another. When they broke away, Calidra wiped her eyes and turned to Fenn. 'Stay in here and get some rest. My room is pretty apart from the rest of the house, so you shouldn't be bothered. Mother will have no intention of checking up on you, anyway. I'll be back soon with something to eat.' She kissed Jisyel on the cheek before heading out the door, making sure to close it behind her.

'Thanks for being with me, Jisyel.' Fenn rubbed his eyes, ridding himself of the last traces of tiredness. 'I don't know about Varlot, and I don't know what I'll find in Porsenthia. But I'm...I'm really glad you and Calidra were with me.'

Jisyel sat on the bed and looped an arm loosely around his shoulders. 'We spend too long alone sometimes. And you helped me when I was stuck. I don't think gran would ever forgive us if we stranded you.'

'What about the Inquisitors?'

Jisyel laughed. 'That was Calidra being Calidra. When it comes down to it, she's a softie, really. And she *does* care. Just takes a while to trust people.'

'I suppose her mother is part of why?'

Jisyel nodded and drew her knees up to her chest. 'I know it's scary, but we're doing the right thing. I think.'

Fenn tried to force away the memory of the Myr's icy-touch, and focus on what it had said instead. Jisyel was lost in thought, and he wondered if he should tell her. *How* he could tell her.

She'd managed to come to terms with him being Myr-touched, and was in the best mood he'd seen her in now they'd reunited with Calidra.

He looked down at his fingers, trying to figure out what to say.

In the end, Fenn decided it would be best kept to himself. He closed his eyes, allowing himself to lightly doze, as he rested for what could be the last time in a long journey to come.

17

THE EXILE

CALIDRA

Calidra woke early the next morning, just before the sun rose. She turned her face away from the window and reached for Jisyel. Instead of the empty sheets she'd dealt with the past few days, Jisyel was there this time. Warm and soft and *real*.

'Too early,' Jisyel muttered, when Calidra gently shook her awake.

Calidra grinned. She hadn't realised how much she'd missed Jisyel's morning complaints. 'Come on. You're the one who wanted me to wake you early. You wanted to see Fenn and Selys before they left? Or have you changed your mind?'

Jisyel lifted her head off the pillow, suddenly more awake than she'd been five seconds before. 'I do want to!'

Calidra shook her head. 'I'm happy to go north with them. Malora…I can't believe she's alive.'

Jisyel yawned. 'Come on, Cal. How bad can it be here?'

'Extremely.'

It was a complicated issue. Calidra knew Furyn had a point, and many of her arguments were valid. With the Laird gone, her mother would need help running the canton and keeping their borders safe—from other Lairds and now the Myr, not to mention holding off Inquisitor visits ensuring they were paying correct homage to the Iron Crown. The canton depended on its Laird, which meant they were depending on her, too. Now she was back, it *did* seem silly to leave again so soon.

But she wasn't sure she could bring herself to stay. Not after how her mother had behaved.

She'd only just got Jisyel back. She didn't want to start immediately dismissing her advice.

Calidra had just wanted to grab Jisyel and run, get away from the Myr. But Fenn had been too exhausted. Poor lad hadn't stopped trembling until late that evening.

The Myr.

Anyone in Porsenthia—or most of Braglia—would deny the possibility of the creatures.

But Furyn hated Porsenthians, including Queen Surayo. And she was more likely to listen to her Olmese kinsman than the Iron Crown's flat refusal to accept the Myr's resurgence. At least her mother had taken Amsel's warning seriously, and posted extra watches on the outskirts of Fellwood. There was no chance the town would be caught in a surprise attack.

Calidra could get used to sleeping in a decent bed again. But just in case things went south with Furyn and Jisyel, Calidra had packed a bag ready for a quick escape. Better to be safe than sorry.

'I think you're making this issue worse than it is.' Jisyel sat up, pushing the sheets off herself.

'My mother didn't bother with Fenn, and he passed out in the middle of her garden! She won't care for you, either. She *hates* Porsethians.'

'I don't mind.'

Calidra rolled her eyes. 'You're too stubborn for your own good.'

284

Jisyel giggled.

Calidra rubbed her nose against Jisyel's. 'Come on. Let's get you something to eat before we see Fenn and Selys off.'

AFTER GETTING breakfast from the kitchens—Calidra was sure to grab a large jar of pickles which she stuffed into her bag—she and Jisyel headed out into the gardens. She and Malora had always shared a jar of them whenever they'd left Fellwood. Although she'd never been a fan of her sister's favourite snack, it was a tradition between them, and she wanted to continue that.

The sun had peeked over the horizon and it was already a warm morning, but before they'd even crossed through the first gate, they heard Varlot shouting.

They shared a worried glance, and when Fenn appeared from the far side of the garden, eyes wide as he ran towards them, Calidra's heart thudded. Had her mother done something? Said something? Was everything already falling apart? Her mind whirled with ways to placate her mother.

Fenn skidded to a halt beside Calidra and Jisyel, panting. 'I'm pretty sure one of them is going to kill the other soon!'

'What? Who? Why?' Jisyel gasped.

'Last night, when Selys went looking for Varlot, she found him in a gambling den. I don't know more than that, but Varlot is *angry*.'

'That's a long time to be angry?' Jisyel frowned.

Fenn shrugged. 'He's still annoyed about it this morning. Was fine up until he saw Selys.'

Calidra cringed inwardly. Her mother wouldn't allow scenes of this nature at her home. She cared far too much about keeping up appearances. This sort of yelling would *definitely* anger her.

She didn't waste any time. Dropping her bag of supplies,

she bolted across the gardens and through the hedge gate Fenn had come through.

When she rounded the corner, she was glad that no weapons had been drawn.

Selys and Varlot were in the middle of a heated argument —although as she watched, Varlot was doing all of the yelling while Selys held her ground, stoic. The noise was already attracting the attention of her mother's household guard, with two of them hanging back as they watched the pair, uncertain. It looked like Selys and Varlot were in a competition over who could stare the hardest in between Varlot's furious words.

'Where is my mother?' Calidra asked the nearest soldier.

The man glanced at her, then turned his attention back to Selys, Varlot, and his colleague. 'Lady Vantonen is occupied at present. Several officers from Fellwood arrived late last night to discuss how she plans to keep the canton safe from the Myrish threat.'

That shouldn't have been surprising. And really, Calidra *should* be with Furyn. But her entire relationship with her mother was made up of cyclical interactions of arguing, screaming, punching, crying, and then feeling awful for days on end. That wasn't healthy at the best of times, and certainly not while they were trying to mount a defence against Tassar's greatest threat.

Varlot's tantrum was all they needed.

Calidra marched over to the pair, stepping between them with her hands raised. 'Okay, what's the matter with you two? Varlot?'

'Get out of the way, Calidra!' Varlot roared. He drew his axe, more out of frustration, Calidra thought, than any real desire to strike her. Calidra only had her dagger in her belt, which she unsheathed and held up. It was a long hunting knife, perfect for skinning rabbits, but would be woefully ineffective against the former Porsenthian General.

286

'Calidra!' Jisyel yelled.

'Threaten me with that axe and you'll regret it!' Calidra forced as much strength into her voice as she could.

'I'm not threatening *you* with my axe, I'm threatening that halfwitted priestess!' Varlot spat, sidestepping Calidra.

She stepped over to block his path again, but the bigger man simply shunted her out of the way with his shoulders. 'Varlot! *What* is the problem?'

'What's the *problem?*' Varlot glared at her before returning his attention to Selys, who stood stationary, arms folded across her chest, her glaive sheathed across her back. 'That woman stole from me is what's the problem!'

'I did no such thing.' Selys glared back, finally reacting to Varlot's accusations.

'Liar!' Varlot was furious—a vein bulged on the side of his neck and he squeezed the axe's handle tighter. 'You stole thirty-two gold pieces and forty-two silvers! I was up seventy-five and that was gonna to grow before you showed up! If you hadn't distracted me, I'd have won the lot! You made me lose, and that's as good as theft!'

'You would have lost that even if I hadn't showed up.' Selys argued back, unflinching from Varlot's furious shouting, and yet to raise her own voice. 'You were too into your cups to notice.'

Calidra shook her head. 'Is this anger really over a game of dice?' She could hardly believe it. The Myr were at their doorstep, Fenn had been unconscious for most of the previous afternoon, and instead of patrolling the town, gathering information, keeping an eye out for Inquisitors, or *anything* that would have helped their cause, Varlot had wasted away the entire day—and most of the evening—in a gambling den. Because he was upset at Furyn's rejection.

No wonder her mother hated Porsenthians.

'Are you done shouting? You're behaving like a child,' Selys said.

'I don't care what you think of me,' Varlot snapped.

'I am not here to judge.'

Her response enraged him further, and he jabbed a finger in her direction. 'Don't start with that holy nonsense!'

Calidra stepped back to stand beside Selys. 'Varlot, no-one's keeping you here. Mother didn't pay you. I promised you she would, and I'm sorry she didn't hold up her end of the bargain. But if you're that short on coin, why waste a day in a gambling den? You could have been looking for other contracts? Gone back to Ballowtown to find work? Wallowing in wine isn't going to help.'

She knew she was being somewhat hypocritical—she'd done plenty of wallowing herself on the way to Fellwood, but she'd always tried to be pragmatic, too.

Varlot snorted his indignation. 'Like you have any idea what you're talking about.'

'You *do* realise we are under attack? Couldn't you have picked a *better* time to go off and play?'

'You don't get to tell me what to do!'

Calidra shook her head. 'Of course not, but surely you have *some* common sense?'

'Now is the *best* time to play! You know how much money people are willing to part with in a crisis? On the eve of battle, you get rich. It's always the way. I would've been able to get so much—'

'Come on, guys, we're meant to be working together, not fighting!' Fenn hurried forward, both his hands raised in a peaceful gesture. He approached Varlot. 'There's no need to be like this! Selys is just trying to help! *I'm* the one who asked her to find you. I wanted to ask if you'd—'

'Fenn, stay out of this, lad!' Varlot bellowed, then turned back to Calidra. 'She distracted me. Made me lose all that coin. With your mother going back on her word, you've left me in a hole! Despite the Myr being at our doorstep as you have already warned us about. Your brother could do with

288

learning a sword art, otherwise he's not going to make himself very useful is he?'

Varlot was practically frothing at the mouth. Was he really so absorbed by the gambling that he reacted this strongly? Or was something else going on? She cast a worried glance at Jisyel, who shrugged.

'All right, that's enough.' One of the household guards drew his sword and held it up.

There was no reason why her mother wouldn't have perfectly competent, well-trained soldiers in her employ, but she doubted very much that the man would be able to stand up to Varlot—even if he was on the cusp of a blind rage. She didn't want to get between them again, as Varlot might well end up swinging his axe.

She'd always been unsure of the bigger man, could tell he had a bit of a temper, was easily frustrated, and clearly had an issue with money. But his prowess in battle wasn't something to be sneezed at, and she suddenly wanted to keep her distance. Yes, he'd helped her. Without him, she might not have ever made it to Fellwood. And if Furyn wasn't going to pay him, then she was indebted to Varlot even more. But her instincts about the man had been right.

'We're allies. There's no need for bloodshed. Put your weapon away,' Selys said. She'd not even drawn her glaive.

If it came to a fight between the priestess and the former general, Calidra honestly wasn't sure who would come out on top. Usually she would side with a priestess—anyone who had the boon of a dragon would be a formidable opponent, no matter how strong the person they faced was. But Selys was a priestess of *Neros*. The spirit who never blessed her worshippers.

Yet Selys had all the confidence of someone who knew they had the upper hand in a battle. She didn't flinch, even as one of the household guards approached Varlot and made to bat away his axe with his own, smaller sword.

'General! Stand down!' the soldier ordered, levelling his sword at Varlot.

Calidra couldn't stand for this. She had to do something before it spiralled out of control. 'Varlot, please! I understand you're upset but—'

'*What* is going on?' Furyn's voice cut through the cacophony.

Calidra's resolve twitched, and she grabbed hold of Jisyel's hand as she turned to face her mother.

Furyn approached, one of her griffins trailing her, more of the Fellwood soldiers at her side. She took in the scene with a cool gaze, then rested it on her daughter. 'Calidra. The company you keep is certainly creating a disturbance.'

Calidra narrowed her eyes. It was just like her mother to berate her for something that wasn't in her control. She nearly apologised, before catching herself. 'I was about to stop it.'

Furyn's eyes narrowed, then she surveyed the scene before her. 'General, is there some grievance you wish to bring to my attention?'

'You know full well my grievance, Lady Vantonen.' Varlot lowered his axe. 'If you'd kept your end of the deal, I wouldn't have had to spend all day trying to get more gold.'

Furyn's lips pressed together. 'Right now, my money will be put into the defence of Fellwood. We need to protect our borders and send out patrols to ensure we are not taken unawares by the Myr. I'm sure a man of your reputation can understand the importance of that?'

'I suppose your word means nothing.' Varlot's voice had quietened, but his anger clearly simmered. 'I travelled all this way. Even if you didn't want me to train your son, you should compensate me for keeping your daughter safe!' He gestured in Calidra's direction.

'I didn't ask you to do that,' Furyn replied coldly.

Calidra balled her hands into fists.

Jisyel's mouth dropped open in shock. Then she gathered herself and approached. 'Furyn. It's good to finally meet you. I'm Jisyel and—'

'And I don't have *time* for this nonsense.'

Jisyel blinked, stunned. 'Calidra and I have come a *long* way to see you! To help you with the canton. With the Myr!'

Varlot laughed and adjusted his bearskin cloak. 'You may not need them, but surely *my* skills are unquestioned? I've *fought* the Myr, the very enemy you're about to face!'

Selys, too, stepped forward, and gave a short bow, her tattoo in full view in the morning sun. 'Lady Vantonen. Will you not honour your word to pay Varlot?'

Calidra gaped at Selys. After the way Varlot had treated her, she'd not expected the priestess to stand up for the man.

In response, Furyn raised one hand and gestured with her fingers. Half a dozen more of the household guard came forward at her command, each one armed and armoured. Sekano wore his helm, the red feather waving proudly.

Calidra's heart sank. Furyn never did things for show. If she'd called her guard, she meant it. And she wasn't sure she wanted to stay and help her run the canton if it meant driving away her friends with a show of force.

Jisyel, however, was infuriated. 'You can't honestly mean to turn your soldiers on us? After everything Calidra's been through? It's been years!'

Furyn looked down her nose at Jisyel, a sneer curling her lip. 'She turned her back on this family and only came crawling back here out of obligation. She doesn't care about us, about the canton. Only her *trysts*. I don't need some Porsenthian wretch here. Nor a drunk general.'

'Drunk general?' Varlot roared.

Several of the household guards drew their swords in retaliation.

'How dare you...' Calidra whispered, hardly aware she was speaking.

'Excuse me?' Furyn looked at her daughter.

Calidra had cried enough over the past few days. She wasn't sure she had any more tears left in her. But her mother had pushed her to her limit, and it took every ounce of strength to keep her voice in check. 'You clearly don't need me, either. You've always wanted things done your way. Never wanted my help—only another person you could order around. I won't be pushed anymore!'

But Furyn wasn't listening. She was glaring at Varlot as her soldiers approached him. From her expression, her patience, too, had worn out. 'I've had enough. I have an entire canton to protect against the Myr, and I don't have time for your complaints. Get your things and get out of Fellwood. All of you. If you're still here in five minutes, Commander Sekano will personally escort you to the town gates.'

Calidra had wanted Furyn to scream at her, to argue her point. To show some love, some acknowledgement of the hurt she'd caused. But Furyn didn't care. She'd never cared. 'I came here out of a sense of obligation, yes. To face my responsibilities, and see if anything could be salvaged between us. But the way you treated me? My partner? There's nothing left for us. I thought it would be the case, but now it's clear.'

Calidra took hold of Jisyel's hand, expecting her to tell her to try again, to work it through. But Jisyel simply nodded fiercely, her eyes watering.

As Furyn's soldiers stepped towards them, Calidra lifted her chin. 'You don't want help, fine. I can find my sister, and I can do it with a clear conscience. I can't *believe* you convinced me she was dead all these years!'

Furyn glared at her. 'Calidra. You're too emotional and immature to have any part in running this household, let alone the canon. I thought you'd step up, but clearly I was wrong. Get your things and leave.'

Calidra stalked away from the others, tears blurring her vision, and picked up the bag she'd dropped. Somewhere behind her, Varlot was blustering. He'd been the only person to ever talk back to Furyn, and it was going about as well as she'd imagined.

Absolutely pointless.

Moving in a daze, Calidra grabbed whatever she thought would be useful. Clothes. Boots. Medicine. Food. Water. Bedding. Whatever she could get in the brief timeframe she'd been allotted, grateful she'd pre-packed most of it after wondering whether they'd leave early.

She'd never thought it would be *this* early.

Sekano watched her, then escorted her and the others off the grounds without a word.

At least her mother's outburst would get rid of Varlot. That was the silver lining to everything that had happened. Furyn didn't want the Porsenthian in Fellwood, and Calidra didn't blame her. Varlot's reactions had been overblown, bordering on violent.

'Well. That was...extreme.' Jisyel stared up the slope, where the villa sprawled out under the bright, Bragalian sun. Somewhere high above, Amsel and Hailathlyl soared.

Calidra shook her head.

'I should've listened to you.'.

'It's okay. With someone like Bellandri raising you, it's no wonder you didn't realise what my mother would be like.' Calidra wrapped her arm around Jisyel's shoulder in a loose hug.

Fenn and Selys stood off to one side, while Varlot paced along the now closed gates to the Vantonen home like a caged griffin.

Fenn said, 'Calidra. I'm sorry if...anything I did—'

'Don't worry about it. Even without you here, she'd have got rid of me soon enough.' Despite her hurt, Calidra now had clarity. 'This isn't a case of her being upset with me because I've done something wrong. It's her finding something wrong because she's upset. And I always upset her.'

'Calidra...' Jisyel hugged her tightly for a moment.

She stood back after their embrace, turning to Fenn again. 'It's fine. We should make the most of it. The path through the mountains is short, but tricky and steep in places. The sooner we head off, the better. My sister is in Porsenthia, so Jisyel and I might as well come with you as far as we can.'

'Thank you.' Fenn gave her an apologetic grin.

Calidra turned to Varlot. 'General. Again, I'm grateful for your assistance. If it wasn't for you, I wouldn't have made it here. But don't be upset. There'll be work in town. With the Myr so close, I'm sure plenty of people will want training, even a private guard. Someone of your reputation is bound to find coin more easily from that than in the gambling dens.'

She thought about the more affluent areas of town, some suggestions on where he might have more luck, when Fenn stepped forward.

'Wait, Varlot. Don't go!' Fenn held out his hand as if to shake Varlot's. 'Look, I know I can't pay you right now, and I know you've dealt with broken promises before, but...but you helped me in Ballowtown. Please consider helping me again? Once I know who I am? Once I have my memories back? I'll make sure you're paid. You might even get a reward for aiding in the effort against the Myr!'

Calidra cursed at Fenn's naivety. He'd definitely spent too much time with Jisyel.

Varlot frowned, considering.

'I need your help. Please?'

'Well. At least *someone* wants me around,' Varlot glared at Calidra.

'Make your decision, quickly. We've already wasted enough time,' Selys said.

Varlot huffed, then scratched his chin. He'd not trimmed

his beard during the journey, and it was already looking rougher than usual. After a moment, he seemed to arrive at a decision, nodding to himself before taking Fenn's hand and shaking it. 'Fine. I'll come with you. Not that I have much choice. I left the army for a reason, and I *don't* want to be in the front lines against the Myr when they're attacking towns again.' He rolled his shoulders. 'Selys. Priestess? You owe me for the money I lost yesterday. You'd better ensure I'm repaid.'

Calidra narrowed her eyes at his menacing tone, but Fenn was too happy to notice. She did *not* relish the idea of tiptoeing around Varlot's temper again.

Varlot clapped Fenn around the shoulder. 'All right, lad. And while we're on the move, I'll teach you how to properly swing a sword.'

CALIDRA HAD WALKED this mountain path many times with her sister. Fellwood was on the Porsenthian border, and quite often the two would make their way to Spindleford for a day trip. It served the best dark ale anywhere they'd found —far better than the weakened stuff served in Bragalia, where wine was preferred—and had spent many nights in the town in the woods.

This time, it was more than a trip for pleasure. There'd be no time to sit down, drinking ale, wasting away hours.

Selys led the group, Fenn behind her. Jisyel walked beside Calidra, and Varlot brought up the rear.

Calidra didn't like someone walking behind her—especially after Varlot's outburst that morning—but it made sense to have someone with experience fighting the Myr.

The mountain path was not as busy as it had been ten or twelve years ago, but there was always the threat of danger. Bandits used the tricky terrain and boulders to set up ambushes for unwary travellers—inebriated people made easy targets—and Calidra kept one hand on her dagger's hilt the whole time. Now she was on her way to find her sister, it seemed fitting that she still had her dagger after all these years.

Below them, the vast Spindle Woods darkened the ground beyond the line of mountains. The trees were particularly dense, the woodland dwarfing the forest on the Isle of Salt by some magnitude. Alnothen, Spirit of the Spindle Woods, was an ancient dragon worshipped for her love of life. Plants and flowers grew to enormous sizes within the trees, and people of Spindleford were forever begging the spirit's aid to boost their crop growth or nurture their gardens.

Alnothen was a kind spirit, a far cry from the mischievous trickster that Hassen was, yet Calidra remained on her guard. Even the most docile dragon had bad days, and she wasn't sure she had the energy to deal with more bad tempers after that morning.

She kept her gaze on Fenn, half-expecting him to stumble over again, but he was steady on his feet, even laughing with Selys as they made their way along the rocky path. 'Varlot is rough around the edges, isn't he?' Calidra muttered to Jisyel once they were ahead enough to be out of earshot.

'Hmm? I guess his retirement isn't going too well.'

'The fighting? Drinking? Gambling?'

Jisyel shrugged as she carefully peeled a small orange. 'Lots of people have those sorts of struggles. Think what he's been through. What he's seen? I wouldn't be surprised if half the fighters in the world end up in the same boat.'

Calidra didn't know if that excused his behaviour or not.

'Come on, Cal. Give him a chance. Especially after all the help he gave you! You said yourself you wouldn't have made it to Fellwood without him.' Jisyel's hands swung as she walked, as if they were on a gentle outing and not crossing into Porsenthia harbouring a Myr-touched fugitive from the Inquisitors.

Calidra frowned. Was she being too suspicious again?

She'd thought the worst of Fenn, and he'd not turned out to be her enemy.

After a while, Fenn doubled back to walk beside Varlot, the two of them talking together in low voices that Calidra couldn't catch. Occasionally, Varlot would bellow with laughter, which was much better than the rage he'd shown back in Fellwood.

'How old are you, Fenn? Twenty? Twenty-two? Ah, my boy would be about the same, now.' Varlot remarked as he adjusted Fenn's stances.

Fenn was a quick learner, trying out some basic footwork as they walked, dodging and evading pretend attacks.

He wasn't too bad for a beginner, but Calidra knew he wouldn't be able to defend himself if they needed to fight. She considered what she could add to Fenn's teachings, how—

'Griffin!' Varlot barked, calling everyone's attention.

Calidra whirled round in time to see Hailathlyl swoop into view with a high-pitched shriek.

'Calidra Vantonen!' Amsel called out from the back of the war griffin, one hand held to the sky. 'I wish you and your company safe travels as you leave Bragalia!'

Calidra raised her hand to him, mirroring the gesture. 'Thank you, Amsel. Please keep yourself safe!'

'Lath and I are made for war! We *welcome* the fight!' Amsel laughed. 'I will see you again, Calidra! The Myr don't stand a chance against my blade!'

'Or my talons!' Hailathlyl added.

With a final nod, the griffin arced in the air, her feathers deep purple in the bright sunlight, and then she was gone— heading back over the mountains towards Fellwood.

'Can't believe you flew on the back of one of them!' Fenn said, his mouth hanging open at the sight.

'Not "on one of them." On that *specific* one,' Calidra corrected.

'Must've been a thrill!'

Calidra couldn't stop the smile on her face at his child-like enthusiasm.

'It is a wonder,' Selys agreed. 'One day, I shall travel to the Shrine of Yakris. I hope to meet more griffins in Ordana.'

'Another shrine?' Fenn asked, as the group continued on, hopping every so often into a few of the steps Varlot had shown him. 'How many are there?'

Calidra kept an eye out not just on her own footing, but Jisyel's, too—the woman could trip over a rock the size of her head and wouldn't notice until her face hit the ground.

'Many,' Selys answered. 'The larger and more prestigious ones are built for more powerful spirits. But some formidable spirits don't have any worshippers at all. Paragos, is one. He is the spirit of a blizzard that blows eternally across a mountain range bigger than this one.'

'Hassen doesn't have a shrine either, but he *is* a baby, as spirits go,' Jisyel said.

'Correct. So there are far more spirits across Tassar than there are shrines,' Selys said. 'Of course, even the Myr have their own spirits, but there are no shrines to them. Not on this continent, anyway.'

Fenn ran a hand through his hair. Calidra wondered if he was already getting tired or simply overwhelmed by the deluge of information.

Thankfully, as they made their way further down the path, more trees appeared, granting them patches of cool shade. The living forest whispered, a thousand voices animated by magic.

'Could you imagine if the Myrish spirits were the same as the dragons? How many more there'd be if they had shrines?

Priests and priestesses? People worshipping them?' Jisyel gasped.

Fenn shivered. 'What if they do? Just…just not in Porsenthia? Or Bragalia?'

'Who knows what those creatures have in their home country.' Varlot adjusted his cloak. 'They have all sorts of spirits and creatures under their control. Maybe they have more being whipped up in their home country as we speak?'

That worried Calidra. Perhaps they'd spent the past five years rebuilding their numbers instead of licking their wounds. 'But…but the peace treaty?'

'Toriaken, strong as he is, is just one spirit. And Queen's Surayo's magic is good, but it's *nothing* against them. The Myr could have anything in their cities and we wouldn't have a clue. Not like you can check what's happening on the far side of the world.'

'You've been there?' Fenn asked, wide-eyed.

'Aye. Once, not long after I became an officer. I never left the boat, mind, but that was as close as I wanted to get. One of Surayo's earliest strikes against Ibeos—that's one of the Myrish homelands, on a continent in the Polar Sea—you could see their cities from the ship. Looked like everything was carved straight from obsidian. Could feel their magic even at a distance. Flying creatures, too, huge, monstrous beasts bigger even than Toriaken.'

Fenn rubbed his arms. 'Well, we might be seeing one of these beasts for ourselves, right Selys?'

The priestess nodded. 'Perhaps not as formidable as what they sent to war, but yes.'

'I wish you didn't have to,' Jisyel muttered.

'My choices are pretty limited. Not many Myrish creatures here that don't already want to kill us. And I don't fancy going to that city Varlot went to—even if we *could* get there.'

More trees erupted from the ground on either side of

them, many of the roots exposed on the awkward path, bleached white in the sun. They walked under shade more than out of it, though, and Calidra was looking forward to a mug of cold ale when they arrived—the only place she preferred to drink something other than coffee.

Mostly, she was glad some of the earlier tension had dissipated. Varlot was a loose cannon, but one they needed, she had to admit. Especially now they were on the edge of the woods, where the dangers would multiply.

She took in their surroundings, remaining vigilant. A few butterflies dotted the trees, pink wings gently opening and closing in the dappled sunlight. Large thorn bushes grew in the shadows between the trees, their vines full of red and yellow flowering buds.

If she concentrated, the light whispers of life grew loud. Trees. Flowers. Grasses.

It was like being on the Isle of Salt again.

Jisyel evidently had the same idea, because she spun around to grab Calidra's shoulders and pointed at the foliage with a wide grin. 'No bogs here!'

'Thank goodness for that!' Fenn laughed.

Before Calidra could respond, a shadow darkened the glade and the temperature plummeted. There was only one thing that ever affected the environment that way. Calidra grabbed Jisyel's arm, her other hand resting on her sheathed dagger—not that it would do any good.

And then the dragon was upon them, a loud bellow announcing her arrival. Her scales were a plethora of vibrant greens and yellows, somehow more vivid even than Hassen's. She was bigger than him, too, with a longer, serpentine neck and fins across her ridged back. Each of her horns was a rich, forest green that faded to black, and moss grew along her legs and lower body as if she'd ripped herself out of the ground itself. There were even several small red and white mushrooms growing in the shadow of her wings, and her tail ended in a large rock that could have been plucked from the bottom of a pond.

Calidra shouldn't have been stunned. She *knew* Alnothen ruled here—the spirit was kind, benevolent. This forest was far bigger than the one on the Isle of Salt, so it meant the spirit of that forest would be bigger and older than Hassen, but she was still imposing.

Calidra tried to calm her breathing. Most dragons cared about their domains more than anything else. She checked she'd not accidentally stepped on a flower or plant—that was the quickest way to angering a dragon—and thankfully there was no damage near that she could be accused of.

She stared up at it, wondering if she should go down on one knee or bow, but the dragon ignored her.

'Alnothen. Great spirit!' Selys extended her arms and bowed low, one leg stretched out behind her as she showed her reverence. Neros's tattoo was in full display on her left arm. 'We thank you for your welcome into your domain. Please allow us to pass through in peace.'

Alnothen tilted her head and watched Selys. *'You are one of Neros's watchers.'*

Selys nodded, still in her bow. 'We mean no harm to you or your domain, great spirit. I shall visit your shrine once we are settled, and offer your blessed ones words of peace.'

'My brother has touched you, sick one. I wonder why...' The dragon's wings flexed as she watched Fenn. Her movements were slow and considered, as if every step cost her a huge amount of effort—except her eyes. They darted between each of them with intelligent, calculated certainty. And they lingered on Varlot. She ignored Selys, and hissed at the former general. *'You. Porsenthian. Varlot Keir.'* Flames jumped between the dragon's jaws with every word she spoke. *'You remain unwelcome here, murderer of children.'*

Mist exploded from Alnothen's scales, blasting in all directions and covering the dragon in seconds.

Calidra covered her face and turned to Jisyel, holding her breath as the wind whipped up.

'Alnothen!' Selys's words were lost in the gust.

When the searing wind passed, Calidra peeked out from behind her arm, only to find the dragon had completely disappeared. A thin layer of frost laid upon the ground where Alnothen had stood only moments before. Tiny ice crystals had formed on the tips of the leaves nearest the spot, which were already beginning to melt.

The slow drip, drip, drip of water was the only sound other than everyone's staggered breathing. Silence had fallen over their group, and Calidra watched Varlot—waiting for the man's reaction to Alnothen's accusation.

Varlot let go of the handle of his axe, glaring at the spot where Alnothen had spoken. 'Let's go.'

18

THE INQUISITOR

APOLLO

As his patrons left the tavern, Apollo's heart sank. A familiar, creeping dread made its way through his gut—something he'd not felt for a good number of years.

It had once kept him alive. Aware enough of his surroundings and encroaching dangers that he was rarely surprised. Some sort of warning that kept him one step away from those who wished him harm, or had tried to kill him.

But this threat was standing beside the bar as if she were about to help herself to the bottle of vintage wine he'd brought in from Westbrook.

An Inquisitor.

Not Torsten. Not even a Master Inquisitor.

Just one of Queen's Surayo's run-of-the-mill spies.

She'd already disregarded his pardon. That bit of paper had always been more than enough to send other officers running—after all, who would disregard the queen's word? And yet she didn't look like she was going to budge on her stance.

A handful of patrons gave him a pat on the shoulder as

they walked past, Apollo assumed in encouragement. It didn't do much to lift his spirits.

He glanced past the last of the patrons out the open door, but there was no sign of Malora. She'd be gone a while. That was probably for the best.

Apollo had kept Renys on his shoulders the entire time, and though his arms ached, he had no intention of letting her down just yet. Somehow he felt it would be better to keep his daughter with him, just in case the Inquisitor wanted to try anything. He'd never trusted Inquisitors before, and he wasn't starting now.

Nadja remained motionless by the bar, arms folded, watching the last of the patrons leave. 'You two as well. This is a private matter which only concerns Apollo Tamlin.' She dismissed Apollo's workers. Neither attempted to argue back, and simply joined the others outside, where excited conversation had broken out on the street.

Apollo winced. More rumours. Just what he needed.

'The girl?' Nadja asked.

'I'm not letting her outside by herself. She stays with me.' There was no chance Apollo was going to let the Inquisitor force his daughter away. Renys herself had gone unusually quiet, and he wondered if she was picking up on his unease.

Nadja opened her mouth as if to argue, then thought better of it and shook her head. 'Please. Sit.'

Apollo couldn't believe he was being ordered around in his own tavern, but he did as he was instructed—sitting down at the nearest table, which had recently been cleared of breakfast. A stain of bacon grease darkened one corner. He gently lifted Renys off his shoulders and sat her on the dry side of the table, one hand around her arm. She gave a huffed groan of displeasure at coming down from the height of his shoulders, but she didn't complain, soon entertaining herself with an unused teaspoon.

He was grateful she wasn't crying "scary lady" at the top of her lungs.

When they were settled, Nadja crossed the floor and took a seat opposite him, the wooden chair scraping on the floor as she pulled it back. It was suddenly very quiet in the tavern.

Apollo couldn't recall a time where he'd ever sat eye-to-eye with an Inquisitor. Usually they enjoyed looking down on people, asserting their authority with a mix of intimidation and barked orders. It was refreshing to have one who was decidedly more...human. But it didn't mean he could trust her.

Nadja leaned back in her chair and spent a long, uncomfortable minute surveying him. 'Do you know why I'm here, Apollo?'

'Can't say that I do. Someone else report me for this?' Apollo pointed at the curved scar that took up one side of his face. Marked him as a thief.

'Actually, it *is* related. Master Inquisitor Torsten gave you that after he caught you trying to steal from Queen Surayo's palace.' It wasn't a question.

Apollo didn't need reminding. He gave a noncommittal shrug, more interested in keeping Renys entertained than having a conversation with one of the queen's snakes. He let his daughter hold his hand between hers, the little girl inspecting every knuckle, nail, and wrinkle with obsessive curiosity, the spoon forgotten. She turned his hand in hers, pointing out freckles and hairs as if she'd never seen them before.

When he didn't reply, Nadja continued, 'As I understand it, you would have been executed for that crime. But you weren't. You were given a way out.'

As the conversation turned, Apollo became more aware of his heartbeat. It wasn't that loud, was it? Would Nadja be able to hear it from across the table? He looked up at her, but she hadn't moved—still leaning back in the chair, as if they were having casual chat over tea. He decided saying nothing was his best course of action, so he gave a small nod, his attention drawn back to his daughter.

Renys grumbled, eyes drawn to the windows, but otherwise kept herself amused for the time being.

'Five years ago, you were given a pardon in exchange for carrying out a task. Would you care to confirm that?'

'I was pardoned, yep. You've seen the paper. You and all the other Inquisitors who come sniffing around here.'

'Queens don't pardon thieves unless there's good reason, Apollo. Especially not a man of your...particular background.'

Renys pulled on his thumbnail and he flinched. 'Ouch. Gently, Renys!'

She giggled, finding his pain amusing, and squeezed it again.

'Renys, stop it!'

'Apollo. The task you were appointed?'

'I did it, didn't I? That's what the pardon's for!' Apollo snapped, pulling his hand away from his daughter.

Nadja frowned and went quiet.

Apollo continued to appease Renys, aware a drop of sweat beaded on his forehead. How much did this Inquisitor know? She couldn't have had all the facts, otherwise she'd have come straight in with an accusation, wouldn't she?

And he was quite certain no-one would have travelled across the Lasseen Ocean all the way to Malnova. It was a distant country with no trade routes. There was no way they could *possibly* know. Surayo had to be clutching at straws. Something had made the queen nervous, and he was an easy target.

He swivelled in his chair, pulling Renys off the table and onto his lap, almost as if she were a physical shield. He wasn't going to let the snake intimidate him in his own home.

'Good location, this tavern.'

He looked up sharply at Nadja's change of tact.

'Foxmouth is a busy town. Always busy, isn't it? Ships coming and going, even from other continents. I suppose you must get a lot of stowaways?'

Again, Apollo shrugged. What did they think he was doing this time, harbouring fugitives? Whatever the queen thought he was up to, she was sorely mistaken.

'It's easy for people to cross Tassar for the right price, isn't it? Surely any captain is happy to earn a bit of extra gold? And even easier if it's small cargo.'

Apollo had no idea what she did or didn't know, and had no interest in playing games with the Inquisitor. 'Neros has been in a foul mood recently. Not much of anything coming or going, these days.'

'Is that so?' Nadja pursed her lips and raised her gaze to the window. 'We've had a lot of people turning up recently. Stowaways, you might say. And reports of attacks. Hamlets, lone travellers, that sort of thing. I'm sure you've had no such trouble in as busy a town as Foxmouth?'

Apollo shrugged again, unsure.

'Well you should count yourself lucky. There are even rumours whispering in the quiet streets that the Myr are back.'

Apollo almost choked. How could Nadja, an *Inquisitor* of all people, say such a thing? While not outright illegal, mentioning the Myr was more likely to clear out a tavern than a batch of bad beer. To even insinuate the ancient, magical creatures had returned was paramount to treason.

The Myr.

In the silence that followed, Apollo realised that one, single word held more sway over him than he'd first thought. Memories flooded. Freezing cold. Aching muscles. Trudging through snow, battling his way against a blizzard that blew eternally. The weight of the Myr's stolen cargo in his pack as he carried it to the farthest edge of the world. Even his queen was not above taking what wasn't hers.

His thigh twinged with remembered pain where the queen's magic had touched him, and Apollo gritted his teeth against it.

'Da? Da you okay?' Renys asked, looking up at him with wide eyes full of worry.

'Fine, Renys.' He smoothed her hair with one hand, turning her gently away from Nadja.

'You're a sly one, I'll give you that. There aren't many who can outfox Queen Surayo's magic, or a spirit like Paragos. I'm impressed,' Nadja said, more than a hint of pride in her tone. 'But let's stop dancing around the issue, shall we? I need a straight answer. And let me warn you—what you say will have implications that go beyond my actions at this table.'

'You wouldn't hurt—'

'Renys? No. But I'm not just talking about your family, Apollo. The implications will affect *all* of Tassar. So believe me when I tell you I need you to be truthful.' Nadja's easy stance had disappeared, and she straightened up in her chair, as business-like as she had been when she first entered the tavern. Any shred of kindness, of compassion, had gone— replaced by a cool mask of indifference.

A typical Inquisitor pose.

Renys murmured, a noise more than a word, and pushed her face into his chest.

'It's okay Ren. I'm here.'

'Apollo Tamlin. Most Porsenthians, even most Bragalians, would like to believe the Myrish threat is long gone. A past nightmare, only useful for keeping our children's behaviour in line. But what I have seen these past few weeks has brought that fact into question.'

Apollo went very still. Didn't trust himself to look up at her.

'Queen Surayo was thorough with her war. She'd ensured

the Myr had no chance of resurging. She'd *crippled* them. With their last iota of power gone, they could *not* rise again. And you were supposed to aid in that. Keeping peace in Porsenthia. Am I right?'

He said nothing.

'Would you like a moment to gather your thoughts?'

Apollo glared at her. 'She said something like that...' His mind whirled, trying to remember what Torsten and Surayo had told him so long ago. Another lifetime ago. Most of the details had been overshadowed by the joy that he and Malora had survived a task that was supposed to have ended in his death.

And he'd cheated it again.

'If the Myr *are* back, then the only loose end we have left is you.' Nadja let the threat hang in the air.

'I don't know what you're talking about.' Apollo raised his chin. 'I told you, there are fewer and fewer ships with Neros as enraged as she is. Foxmouth supplies a lot of food to Eastbrook. I suggest Queen Surayo worries more about these dwindling resources than the Myr who are nowhere near. Well, whatever's left of them.'

He remembered the palace in the freezing snow. The chanting. The pressure of Myrish magic. The artefact they'd returned...The spirit who'd spoken...

'Apollo. I said I needed you to be truthful.' The warning was clear in Nadja's voice.

'What're you going to do? Execute me here? In front of my daughter?'

'Only the queen may exercise judgement over life and death. We just carry out her orders.'

Apollo decided he'd go for blind confidence. It was all he had. 'If Queen Surayo was unhappy with what I did, if her magic thought I'd messed up, I'd be dead already.'

'The effects of your...failure...were not apparent until now.'

'Failure? I did exactly what I was asked! That queen sent me to die. Sent Malora to die! My friend Yorik *did* die there —alone and frozen, without any other soul in Tassar knowing what happened to him! And you Inquisitors have nothing better to do than to come sniffing around here looking for some rule I've broken so you can lock me up again. I've done my time. I wear the scar of my past—spirits know I'm not allowed to forget it—so you can go back to your queen and tell her that she's worrying about the wrong thing.'

'Da...' Renys whimpered at his raised voice. 'Where's mama?'

He wrapped both arms around her, soothing her as best she could. 'Hush Ren. Your mama will be back soon.'

'When the scary lady goes?'

'When the scary lady goes,' he repeated, throwing the Inquisitor a dark look.

'Apollo.' Nadja got to her feet.

He smirked. He'd wondered when Nadja would assume the position all Inquisitors did—standing over him to assert their authority. It was their default, regardless of personality.

'Do you have any *idea* what that artefact was? What you were sent to destroy?' Her voice had quieted to a whisper.

Apollo was incredulous. How could she happily talk about the return of the Myr, but that damned key was forbidden? There was no point in lying about it if she knew what he'd been sent away with. 'It was some key.'

'Not just *some* key. It was a powerful Myrish artefact. One that *needed* to be destroyed. That's why you were sent to Paragos.'

'Why didn't Surayo destroy it herself?'

'Her magic is nothing compared to the power of that key.'

'What about Toriaken, then? Nothing can stand up to that dragon!'

'Apollo, you don't seem to understand. Paragos, a wild

and ancient spirit that devours magic, was the *only* thing in Tassar that could have destroyed that key. Toriaken is bound to the queen. As formidable as he is, that limits him. And the fact that you are standing here, whole, leads me to believe Paragos did *not* devour that magical key as you were instructed to do.'

Apollo couldn't believe it. 'Damned spirit would've eaten me, too.'

'That's exactly why *you* were sent!' Nadja raised her voice, and Renys whimpered again. 'A lifelong thief who was bound for execution anyway. Paragos is powerful. Greedy. How could he resist a prize as that key?'

'Oh of course. That's why Surayo never sent one of you, isn't that right? Can't risk one of her *precious* Inquisitors dying, but some common thief? Sure. Who cares about me?'

Nadja shook her head. 'You were marked for execution. You were given mercy. A choice you should not have been given. And from the sounds of it, you squandered that choice. Another poor decision to add to your very long list of poor decisions.'

Apollo swallowed, trying to think quickly. 'Well, the key is gone. No-one's ever getting to it again, believe me.'

'I *don't* believe you. Neither does Torsten. Or Queen Surayo for that matter.' Nadja brushed down her uniform. There wasn't a speck of dust on it, but she was meticulous none-the-less.

'Look. I was told to get rid of the key. That's what I did.'

'No. You were told *specifically* to feed it to Paragos. You failed.'

'I didn't fail! Surayo's curse is gone!' He was on his feet now, Renys in one hand, the girl already on the cusp of tears. 'She gave me my pardon. I got my life back! Everything is over! Maybe the Myr *are* back? But I don't see how it's got anything to do with me! Maybe they've had something else secret this whole time? Ever think about *that*?'

'It's a possibility.'

Apollo hadn't expected the Inquisitor to agree. 'Well...go investigate *that*, then. Leave me and my family alone.'

'I'm afraid I can't do that.'

Apollo turned away from Nadja, backing up towards the bar. He always kept a longsword behind there—he wasn't brilliant with the weapon, but he wasn't going down without a fight. Especially not to an Inquisitor.

'Apollo. I was sent here to bring you to the palace, nothing more. But I was curious as to the circumstances of your freedom. Of your past. I wanted to know for myself what kind of man you were.'

'What kind of man I was?' Apollo snorted, taking slow steps, edging closer to the bar.

Nadja nodded. 'Yes. Though you may choose to believe otherwise, I care about the fate of Tassar. The people in it. Not just in Porsenthia, but beyond. If the Myr have returned, we will be plunged back into war. Back into that dark time where people feared the night, when people were slaughtered where they slept.'

Apollo took another step. He was within five paces of the bar, now. He, like most people, remembered a childhood of fear. Remembered the jubilation when Queen Surayo announced the armistice. The end of the terror.

'Surely you don't want Renys to experience what you and I have?' Nadja continued, unfazed by his movements. 'Throwing her back into a time where Myrish death spirits roam free? Where life is sucked from the very ground we walk upon? Where our dragons die?'

Apollo tightened his hold on Renys and darted behind the bar. Dropping to his knees, he put his daughter on the ground and grabbed the longsword. When he stood up again, Nadja hadn't moved. She didn't even look at the tip of the sword pointed at her.

312

'If *you* are responsible for that, Apollo? Then *you* will have to face the consequences.'

'I've had enough!' Apollo snarled. 'I have the queen's pardon. I've lived my life free for five years, and whatever is happening in Tassar is *not* my fault!'

Nadja sighed, almost sadly, and drew her own longsword. The blade gleamed silver; light steel with an edge sharp enough to cut clean through a body.

Apollo didn't need any help remembering that. He pushed it out of his mind and raised his sword. It was old, with one part of the blade chipped, but it was made of good steel. 'Nadja. I'm asking you to leave. We don't need to spill blood.'

'I'm not a common soldier who loves to fight. I've never relished drawing blood. I would also prefer it if we didn't. But, if I must, I will.'

Apollo flicked the tip of the sword towards the door. 'Then leave. No harm done. And I'll sit here, serve my patrons, live my life, and do the same thing the next time an Inquisitor comes snooping around.'

'I can't do that. I told you. I've been sent to bring you to Eastbrook. You've answered my questions, but it's Queen Surayo who wants answers.' Nadja crossed the distance between them in a heartbeat.

'Stay there, Ren!' Apollo stepped away from the bar, unwilling to be trapped there.

His daughter wailed, tears already dripping down her cheeks, her arms outstretched for comfort.

'Last warning, Nadja. Get out!'

'You don't want to add harming an Inquisitor to your crimes, Apollo.'

He raised his sword. He wasn't going back. There was no chance he'd allow himself to.

The tavern door banged on the wall, it was thrown open with so much force, and Apollo looked past Nadja to see

Malora standing in the doorway. She dropped the boxes of butcher's meat, her face stricken. 'Apollo!'

'Mama!' Renys raced out of the bar, leaping over Apollo's leg before he could snatch her up.

Renys was as slippery as a fish when she wanted to be, able to worm her way out of practically any hold. But she was upset, frightened, and confused.

And Nadja was faster. Quick as a flash, she scooped up the girl and rested her on her hip.

'No! Scary lady! Let go! No! NO!' Renys was furious, screaming at the top of her lungs.

'Let go of my daughter!' Malora had no weapon, but she strode across the tavern floor towards the Inquisitor.

'I'm not going to hurt her. And I wish it hadn't come to this. Malora Tamlin, I presume? I'm arresting your husband for high treason.'

'*Treason*? What are you talking about?'

In Nadja's arms, Renys continued to scream and thrash wildly.

'Put her down this second!' Apollo levelled his sword at Nadja. He couldn't slash at the Inquisitor without risking Renys, but he was certain he could drive the blade through the Inquisitor's throat. They could always move again. Find another port town. Maybe even cross the Lasseen Ocean into Olmir, where Queen Surayo's power couldn't reach them.

He'd always wanted to see the desert. Renys would be fascinated by the griffins there, too. And she'd probably love the warmer weather. Malora, being Bragalian—technically half-Olmese—would be more at home there than she'd ever been in Foxmouth.

Tightening his grip, he bent his knee, ready to thrust.

'For his failure to destroy the Citrine Key, therefore opening a path for the Myr to return,' Nadja said, still speaking to Malora.

His wife's mouth dropped open. That action made Apollo pause.

'It appears the Myr are back. The Citrine Key was one of their most powerful artefacts. If Apollo did not destroy it properly, then we are on the cusp of war. *That* is high treason.'

'Apollo…' Malora's anger was abruptly swept away.

Seeing her so afraid killed Apollo's resolve. He lowered his sword as he tried to think. 'Nadja. I told you, I got rid of the key. Surayo's curse is gone. I'm alive. Isn't that proof enough?'

'I'm not convinced. And if you've nothing to hide, then you've nothing to fear, either.' Nadja sheathed her own sword one-handed, then produced an iron fetter from her belt.

Apollo's chest tightened. His next breath wheezed, as if his lungs had forgotten how to work. 'But you can't! I did what was asked! Malora…Renys…'

Nadja handed the screaming child to Malora, who took her numbly.

He couldn't believe it. *Wouldn't* believe it. 'You're making a mistake.'

'That's possible. And if it is, I'm sure Queen Surayo will adequately compensate your family for any losses while you are away. If the cause is something else, you will be free to go.' She threw the fetter at him, which twisted and moved in the air of its own accord.

Apollo had seen it before—a practically failsafe way of trapping petty thieves. Toriaken's soul was in every piece of iron. Much like the Inquisitor's daggers, it was another tool in their arsenal.

Running only made it worse—he'd seen people break legs and shatter ankles if they tried to escape the bite of the dragon's iron—so he didn't move. Head hung, he watched as the grey snaked around his ankles, locking them together with a dull click.

Malora ran to him, Renys in one hand, and threw her other arm around him. She sobbed, tears falling freely down her face. 'No, Apollo! No!'

'Mal.' His voice was a whisper. 'I'm…I'm sorry.'

19

THE POISON

FENN

In the wake of the spirit, Alnothen, Fenn's emotions were all over the place. He bounced between shock and awe at seeing such an enormous dragon—it put Hassen to shame—and the accusation she had made about Varlot.

After the man had shouted at Selys that morning, Fenn knew the former general had a bit of a temper, but Varlot had also helped him. The first person to do so, willingly. Even Jisyel and Calidra had only helped him out of obligation, and Selys was doing so to help her own spirit.

But Fenn couldn't believe what Alnothen had said.

A *child* murderer?

Varlot was a strong man and a powerful fighter. But surely he hadn't crossed *that* line? He *was* a good person, wasn't he?

Fenn didn't know what to think. He knew what it was like to be regarded with suspicion. Even Jisyel, who was the warmest, most positive member of their entire group, hadn't wanted anything to do with him after Selys had announced he'd been Myr-touched. He'd not technically done anything wrong, and although she'd eventually pushed her fear to one side, it had taken her a while to come around.

He couldn't so easily forget the way she'd looked at him. The accusation and fear in her eyes.

It was much the same look Varlot was receiving from Calidra right then.

Had Varlot been the same as him? Not technically done anything wrong—or certainly hadn't any control over what had happened—and that's why the spirit hated him? Maybe it was a misunderstanding. An accident, perhaps, not something Varlot had done on purpose.

He didn't have all the facts, so he couldn't judge. It would be wrong to even try.

'Let's keep going,' Selys said, 'there's a long way to go before we can rest.'

Fenn could see she was eager to be off again, picking her way through the foliage, using her glaive to delicately push aside thicker vegetation. He didn't blame her for not wanting to engage with Varlot for a second time that day.

He hurried to keep pace with her, hoping Calidra would let the matter drop. He didn't spare her a look, keen to avoid yet another confrontation in the middle of the wilderness.

'The path here is overgrown and difficult to see. Watch your step, Fenn.' Selys indicated with the tip of her glaive at a growth of purple, thorny roots that criss-crossed the leaflitter. 'That is tanglethorn. Native to this forest. You do *not* want to get stung.'

Fenn immediately wondered what would happen if he did, almost reached out to touch it out of blind curiosity, but caught himself. But the warning had been clear enough in Selys's voice, so he kept his mouth shut and his hands in his pockets.

'Wait, Selys! I'm not going anywhere until *you've* explained yourself.' Calidra pointed her finger at Varlot. 'Child murderer? Really? Is that why you left the Porsenthian army? Or were you forced to leave when they found out what you'd done?'

'Calidra...' The last thing Fenn wanted was another argument. He'd been on edge in Fellwood earlier, and was only just recovering from the high emotions. He didn't deny there needed to be a conversation, possibly even an explanation, to clear the air. But now wasn't the best time.

'You don't have a clue what you're talking about.' Varlot didn't bother looking at Calidra. He followed in Selys's steps, his head down, gaze fixed on the ground.

'No? Then why don't you enlighten us!' Her hand rested on the hilt of her dagger.

Varlot whirled around, rage in his eyes. 'That's amusing coming from you! A woman who didn't even cry at her own father's funeral!'

Fenn saw the tremble in Calidra's lip, saw the stab of hurt in her eyes. She recovered quickly, as he knew she would.

'This isn't about my dysfunctional family. Look at *you*! A former general, one of the most decorated men in the world, and you're *washed* up! Nothing but a gambling alcoholic, now! And a murderer, to boot? Why else would the spirit of this forest tell you that you aren't welcome?'

It was a low blow, one equally as hurtful, and Fenn couldn't take it any more. 'All right, all right! Stop shouting! You're not making this any better. Both of you back off!'

'Alnothen is unhappy at your presence, Varlot. Let's not give her any more reason to be angered by us. We need to keep going,' Selys said.

Varlot lifted his face to the canopy above, eyes closed.

For a moment, Fenn thought Varlot wouldn't react at all, but after a long moment, he sighed. 'I told you about what I saw, didn't I? At the Battle of Marlrush?'

'The men you killed there? Yes. I remember.' Calidra folded her arms, her eyes narrowed.

'Many people died there. And in other battles. Not just soldiers, not just the Myr, but families and children, too. Alnothen abhors any who take life. It goes against everything that spirit stands for. It's no surprise I'm unwelcome here.'

'What a crock of hogshit.'

'It's okay, Varlot. I'm sure you had to do a lot of awful things. That's what war is,' Jisyel said softly, ever the voice of reason. 'Cal, come on. Is this really the best time?'

Calidra rolled her eyes, but didn't object.

Fenn had worked so hard to get Varlot to stay, to see that he *was* liked and wanted, and he didn't want Calidra to drive him away through her distrust. As much as she hated her mother, he thought they acted very similarly. 'Alnothen let us pass. She might not like Varlot, but we can keep going. Selys said there's a long way to go, so why don't we put our energy into getting there, instead of shouting at each other?'

'You *want* to travel with this man, Fenn? After what he's done?' Calidra scowled.

'I don't even know what *I've* done. He hasn't hurt me. Only helped. And it was the same with you, wasn't it?' Fenn said, certain he was doing the right thing. 'I'm not going to judge until I know all the facts. And I'm not going to find out anything if we stand in this forest shouting at each other!' After how he'd been treated before, he didn't want to make anyone else feel as unwanted as he had been made to feel. 'You were fine with him an hour ago. He's the same person now as he was then.'

Calidra bristled, but she let go of her dagger, leaving it sheathed in her belt.

Jisyel rested her hand on Calidra's arm and whispered something in her ear that Fenn couldn't hear. Whatever she said, it made Calidra relax.

Fenn gave Jisyel a smile, hoping she would understand his gratitude from it, then hurried over to where Selys waited. 'Let's go.'

The mood had become subdued, and Fenn was keen to get rid of the rising tension. Quite how he'd do that, he wasn't sure, but he wanted to do *something*. Most of them were here because of him. Even Calidra and Jisyel could have chosen another route to go up north.

He was considering what to say when Jisyel collapsed.

'Jisyel!' Calidra cried, sinking to the ground to haul the other woman back to her feet. 'What happened?'

'I don't know?' Jisyel gazed around, puzzled. The colour had drained from her face, and she was pale enough to begin with that it made her look ill. Her eyes drifted in and out of focus. 'Cal...?' Absently, she waved a hand in front of her face, half-reaching towards Calidra.

'Jisyel? What's wrong?' Calidra kept Jisyel at arm's length as she looked the other woman up and down, her frown deepening.

'Jisyel?' Fenn made his way over to the pair, wondering what had happened. Jisyel had been fine a minute ago.

Again, she waved haphazardly, her eyes not quite focussing on him as he approached. Jisyel leaned on Calidra, tried to take another step, then staggered. She let out a groan, more of surprise than pain, given her curse, and Calidra kept her from falling to the ground.

'Come on, woman. Pull yourself together!' Calidra looped Jisyel's arm around herself and led them along the forest path towards Selys and Varlot.

As they passed him, Fenn noticed the bottom of Jisyel's trousers were shredded. Blood trickled down the back of her calf. 'Wait!'

Everyone came to an abrupt halt.

He pointed at the jungle of thorns Calidra and Jisyel had just walked through. Selys had warned him about it not long before. A mass of foliage with wide, dark leaves and purple thorns that protruded along the length of every stem and branch. 'Is that...is that tanglethorn?'

'Spirits take me, I hope not!' Calidra passed Jisyel to Selys, then hurried back to where Fenn pointed. 'Those thorns are three inches long! How did you *not* see them? There's nothing wrong with your eyes!'

Jisyel giggled, unsteady on her feet. She leaned heavily on the priestess. Her face had turned pallid. 'Selys? You look so upset?'

The priestess pulled back from Jisyel's face. '*I'm* fine, Jisyel. Looks like *you've* been poisoned.'

'Don't worry. I'm sure you'll be cursed soon, too...' Jisyel trailed off, evidently confused.

Fenn wondered what the poison would do Jisyel. He doubted it would be pleasant. Already, her foot was beginning to swell up, her clothes stretching around her bloated calf.

'I can't believe it.' Calidra stalked up the path, rifling through her bag of belongings as she did so. 'I can make some more glinoc paste—'

'It won't be effective against tanglethorn. We need to get to Spindleford. There'll be an apothecary and we can get a proper antidote there.' Selys shifted Jisyel's weight, struggling a little with the limp woman. 'She'll have a couple of hours before the vomiting starts. Less time if she gets excited.'

'Here. Let me help.' Varlot stepped towards Selys and Jisyel.

Fenn was quite certain Calidra's eye twitched, but she didn't say anything. How could she? Jisyel had been hurt, and Varlot was easily the strongest of their group. It would be petty to argue when Jisyel's safety was on the line.

'Do you think it was a warning? From Alnothen?' Fenn asked, suddenly worried the spirit was showing her dislike of them. Hassen had enjoyed intimidating him, and he wondered if Alnothen was the same.

'No. It's just Jisyel being...Jisyel.' Although Calidra's words were harsh, she wouldn't take her eyes off the woman. She helped Varlot lift Jisyel, resting her gently over one, massive shoulder. Fenn didn't think Varlot needed help, but he doubted Calidra liked not having something to do. Especially where Jisyel was concerned.

'I must've been through these woods fifty times, and I've *never* caught myself. Not even after half a barrel of ale!' Calidra said, walking beside Varlot as he followed Selys.

'And you said *I* got too into my cups,' Varlot said to the priestess, who didn't look back at him, more intent on navigating their way through the forest. 'Half a barrel, Calidra. Impressive for someone half my age.'

'Flattery won't help you. I *still* don't like what you've been accused of.' Calidra didn't so much as smile.

Fenn grimaced at the bite in her voice, but at least she was on speaking terms. Like him or not, they needed Varlot. He knew Varlot could have chosen to be spiteful, or refuse to help—or worse, leave them in the middle of the forest—but he hadn't. He'd stayed with them, despite Calidra's harsh words. Which were undeserved, as far as he was concerned.

Fenn was sure to keep a closer eye on where he was putting his own feet, lest two of them ended up poisoned. Once, a thorn caught the top of his boot, but he felt it catch and took a moment to extricate himself before any of the poisonous barbs pierced his skin.

It must've been impossible for Jisyel, unable to feel anything, to navigate the myriad of vegetation.

There was a breath on the wind, life energy from the plants. Every leaf rustled with its own, tiny voice, and he vividly remembered Hassen on the Isle of Salt. That forest had been alive. Jisyel had told him any place where life energy gathered gave rise to a spirit. This was an enchanted woodland. A forest that had a life of its own.

It was Alnothen.

Fenn wondered whether all the voices were Alnothen's, or whether the spirit had given life to everything in the forest, and they all spoke with countless different voices.

Reaching forward, he placed one palm flat against the

trunk of the nearest tree, which appeared to be coated in scales rather than bark—like a pinecone. His fingers tingled and his chest tightened, but it passed after a few seconds. Once again, the sounds and voices of the forest were loud in his head, just as it had been in the forest of Salt Ash. It was loud, louder than anything he could envision. A crescendo of life.

Of magic.

Withdrawing his hand with a gasp, Fenn tried to catch his breath. The last time he'd felt this, he'd been touched by Hassen. He couldn't recall Alnothen doing the same to him, but he was in her domain, and she was a bigger, more powerful spirit.

Resolving to ask Selys about it later, he hurried to catch up.

By the time Selys slowed their pace, about an hour later—it was difficult to judge time when wandering through the trees—sweat stuck his hair to his forehead. 'We're there?' Fenn gasped, desperate for water but not wanting to slow their party unnecessarily while Jisyel was in danger.

Aside from a few groans here and there, Jisyel hadn't said much. Her quietness had worried Calidra, who'd tried to initiate conversation every few minutes, to no avail.

The trees on the edge of Spindleford thinned, but the town itself seemed to have sprouted between the trunks as naturally as the fungi. Every building was made of wood, with only minimal stone that Fenn could see. Many of the houses were covered in vegetation—from flowers, shrubbery, fruits, even a few small trees. Moss sprawled along the exteriors of almost every building, dressing each in a different shade of green.

Fenn nearly stumbled over his own feet as he stared, awestruck. Although he didn't remember anything about his previous life, he'd seen several villages and towns since his waking—from the stark but long-lasting Hogsbrook, to the vast, vibrant Ballowtown, and the crowded, chaotic Vaelar. Even Fellwood and the Shrine of Neros were completely different.

But Spindleford?

It was utterly magical.

After getting his bearings, he caught up to where the others had gathered outside a large building. A weather-beaten sign hung above the door, a faded bell painted in soft yellow, with words written in a language he didn't recognise or understand.

Varlot had stood Jisyel back on her own feet, though she was just as wobbly as she'd been before. Dark circles hung under her eyes like bruises.

'Malora and I used to come to this tavern a lot when we were younger. It's quiet, and we never had much attention,' Calidra said, one arm steadying Jisyel.

'Let me cover food and board,' Varlot said, 'least I can do.'

Calidra blinked in surprise, but nodded, clearly deciding it wasn't worth another argument.

'Fenn. There's an apothecary in town. It'll have a pestle and mortar on the sign.' Varlot reached into his inside pocket and handed Fenn a small drawstring purse. 'The locals will have something for tanglethorn. Get something strong for Jisyel.'

Fenn took the purse and nodded.

'While you get Jisyel sorted, I'm going to pay my respects to Alnothen. Make sure we've not offended her too much,' Selys said, sheathing her glaive now it wasn't needed.

'Pay respects to Alnothen...?' Jisyel repeated in a low murmur, swaying as if she were drunk.

'Not you,' Calidra sighed.

'But I want to go and see her...'

'Come on, let's get you inside.' Calidra steered Jisyel towards the door that Varlot held open.

Fenn saw a few curious faces staring out at them from

325

within. He peered inside, wondering whether there would be moss and plants *inside* the tavern, too.

'Fenn. The apothecary!' Calidra snapped.

'Oh! Right! Yes.' Fenn shook his head and turned away, hurrying down the main street, through the maze of buildings. There would be time later on for exploring and asking questions.

Although some wooden planks had been put down along the streets, the amount of weeds and grass pushing up through them made them pointless. He clutched the purse close to his chest and glanced at the building signs as he passed them, hoping to spot the pestle and mortar.

He passed a few people, most of whom hardly looked at him. Many wore clothes of brown and green, looking just as much a part of the forest as their houses and shops.

Then, he spotted it. Built into the trunk of a tree so massive all five of them could walk through it abreast, the apothecary had a fine plume of smoke rising from its chimney. He couldn't place the scent, but it was thick and pungent, and it felt like it burned his nose hairs.

A honeyseller had a small shop beside the apothecary, glass jars full of differently coloured honey that Fenn wanted to taste. He was particularly intrigued by a rich, dark amber honey—wondering how it would taste if the flowers it was created from were within Alnothen's domain—when he pushed his curiosity to one side and approached the apothecary. Jisyel's needs were more pressing.

'Hello? Excuse me?' Fenn called after a quick knock on the door. 'Do you have something for tanglethorn, please? A strong antidote?' He staggered into the circular building, the shape of which fit the contours of the tree. Heat slammed into him and he clutched his chest. Fine smoke swirled across the ceiling, a trickle of it escaping through the narrow chimney on the room's far side.

'Tanglethorn poisoning? Hmm. Yes, yes. One moment,' an

326

elderly voice called from the back of the room, behind a thin curtain, where Fenn presumed the expensive potions and antidotes were kept.

While the old man pottered about out of view, Fenn noticed the cabinets and wares splayed out. Curiosity got the better of him and he wandered over to take a closer look. Lined up neatly on a cloth of blue velvet were several round, glass bottles. An indeterminate liquid filled most of them, and each bottle was stoppered with a cork. He picked up the nearest one and peered closely at it. The liquid inside was thick and viscous, and it sparkled with an inner light easily seen through the glass.

It was dazzling.

If he peered closer, he could *almost* make out an image. A face, perhaps? He brought it close to his eyes, trying to work it out.

'Lad, you're poisoned, not blind. That'll be of no use to you.'

Fenn nearly dropped the bottle, he flinched so greatly at the sound of the man's words. He whirled around to find himself nose-to-nose with the apothecary, who looked none-too-impressed at his wandering hands.

'Blue rosewort.' He held up a small glass jar in his wrinkled hand. 'For tanglethorn?'

'Thank you!'

The old man pulled away before Fenn could take it, a frown deepening the myriad of lines on his brow. 'You don't *look* like you have tanglethorn poisoning. Hmm. You have *something*, though...'

Fenn was about to agree, that he'd been touched by the Myr, before he remembered what a terrible idea that would be. 'I'm fine. Really. I just need the...blue rosewort?'

'It won't help you. Lad, let me do my job! How is your sleep? Are you feverish?' He put the back of his hand against Fenn's forehead.

'No, no! No! It's not for me! My friend, *she* was poisoned by tanglethorn!'

The old man pocketed the rosewort and clutched Fenn's cheeks between his hands. Despite his age—the apothecary had to be in his eighties at least—his grip was so tight that Fenn couldn't move.

'Um...I...I really only need the rosewort...'

'Any spotting in your vision? Tingling of the skin? Loss of taste?' He pulled at Fenn's face, peering into each eye and prodding at his throat with his thumbs.

Fenn coughed and leaned back. 'Honestly! Just the rosewort! I have money!'

After another moment of inspection, the apothecary finally released him. 'Hmm. We are in close proximity to the deadlands. Sometimes they'll affect people. If you lose your sense of smell or taste, you *will* come and see me, won't you?'

Fenn gulped. 'Why? What happens?'

'Remnants of the Myrish magic killed the land just north of here. It can affect people too, if you aren't too careful. A bleeding sickness. Skin sloughs off. Bones crumble. First sign is always loss—'

'Okay, okay! I'll make sure to see you if anything changes. How much for the rosewort?' Fenn wiped his forehead, desperate to leave the hot shop and get the medicine to Jisyel.

The apothecary straightened, then pursed his lips and retrieved the jar from his pocket. 'Two silver. One spoonful mixed in hot water. Tea is fine, as long as there's no sugar. Every two hours until the sickness and confusion passes. She will sweat out the poison, so make sure there are plenty of clean sheets. The vapour can be toxic.'

Fenn nodded as he handed out the coins from Varlot's purse, snatched the jar of medicine, and darted out before he could be poked and prodded again.

Thankfully, he wasn't accosted by anyone else as he raced back to the inn where he'd left the others. His heart thumped as he thought about the apothecary's words. He'd spoken of Myrish magic close by. The deadlands. As afraid as he was by the man's warning, Fenn wanted to know more. According to Selys, there was nothing Myrish until the end of their journey at the Nethal Mountains.

Could this…could this be a chance to learn more?

Varlot waited for him outside. 'Good lad, Fenn. Well done.' He took the medicine and purse, checking both before heading inside with them. 'We weren't a minute too soon. Jisyel's started vomiting.'

'Poor Jisyel. The apothecary gave instructions, too.'

Both men entered the inn, and Varlot led them straight upstairs where they followed the sound of Jisyel's retching to their room. After explaining to Calidra everything he'd been told about the rosewort, she dismissed them both, telling them that Jisyel needed space to rest, and wouldn't appreciate a watching audience every time she threw up.

Fenn was only too pleased to get out of there, especially if what he'd been told about the toxic fumes was correct. When he returned to the street outside, he took a deep breath of fresh air. North. That's where the Myrish magic was.

He glanced over his shoulder. Calidra would probably want him to stick around, but there wasn't much he could do while Jisyel was vomiting. It would be a good chance to explore, try and learn more about where he was, and if any of it brought forth hidden memories.

He took a moment to try and figure out which way was north, then set off. The town wasn't that big. He was sure he'd be able to figure out the right way.

'Fenn? Where you off to?' Varlot called from the inn's entranceway.

'Um…' He paused. 'Just, you know. Stretching my legs?' It was a pitiful lie.

Varlot raised an eyebrow. 'Stretching your legs…? After being on the move all day?'

'Yeah...?'

'Fenn, you need to work on your lying.' Varlot folded his arms and grinned. 'Look, I don't care what you get up to. But don't go too far. It'll be dark soon and these trees make it very easy to get lost.'

'You...don't mind if I explore the area a bit?'

Varlot shrugged. 'You're your own man. I don't care what you do. Just pay attention so you don't get hurt, otherwise we'll have two people vomiting all night.' He jerked his thumb over his shoulder. 'Calidra's right about the ale here. When you get tired, come join me for a drink, yeah?'

'Sure.' He was about to head off when he saw Varlot stare into the forest, his gaze longing. He'd never seen that look on the man before. 'You okay?'

Varlot blinked and looked down at Fenn. He pursed his lips. 'You know, Fenn. I envy you.'

'Why?' How could Varlot envy being cursed by the Myr?

'Sometimes all I feel is...bitter regret. You know. 'Cause you're alive and they ain't.'

Fenn wasn't sure what to say. He wondered if Varlot meant his brothers-in-arms, or the child Alnothen had accused him of killing.

Varlot shook all over, as if a sudden chill had taken him. 'Never mind. Come see me for that drink later.' He turned and went back inside

Fenn watched the doorway a while longer, in case Varlot came back outt. After waiting, he hurried off, beyond eager to get away and have his own space for once.

He'd been surrounded by people from the moment he'd awoken. Hassen, first—he was never going to forget that dragon—then Calidra, Jisyel, Varlot, Selys. Even Torsten had tried to chain him up.

This time, being alone was less terrifying.

He wandered through the meandering streets, not paying attention to where he was going, just letting his feet carry him in whatever direction they chose. He wanted to see the remnants of the Myrish magic, but he also wanted to just take the time to explore. To see what was here, and whether any of it would jog his memory or at least become mildly familiar.

Fenn realised that Spindleford was larger than he'd first thought—a patchwork of buildings and gardens, all growing where the trees gave them space—but was less populated than anywhere else he'd been so far. For its size, he hardly saw anyone.

Several covered bridges linked sections of the village together. All were made of wood, mostly covered by moss, vines, and trailing plants, as if the bridge was as much a part of the forest as the trees were. They were charming, and Fenn dragged his fingers along them as he crossed each.

When the trees suddenly fell away and dry, open land sprawled out before him, it was a shock.

The sun was well on its way to setting, casting orange hues across the landscape. Whatever ground he could see in the low light was dry and cracked, as if all life had been sucked out of it. There wasn't even the smallest hint of a weed.

His chest burned and his fingers trembled, and Fenn sat down on a small patch of greenery on the very edge of the treeline, waiting for the ache to subside. It did, eventually. It took until an inky sky blanketed the land and the broken moon had risen before he'd properly recovered from it.

Fenn knew the trembling was getting worse. But there wasn't much he could do about it except trust in Selys and hope that whatever awaited him in the Nethal Mountains was genuine.

If not...? If not, he didn't know what he'd do.

Vermecio. That's what the Myr had told him could help. It had to be the name of the Myrish construct Selys was leading him to. Would it know he had been Myr-touched? Would it consider him one of them?

Would it even matter?

He sat there for some time, contemplating everything. His companions. The dragons. The Myr. His own mortality. His stomach growled and he took a breath, steeling himself for the pins and needles that would most definitely race along his limbs after being sat down for so long, when a high-pitched wail caught his attention.

Fenn looked around, but couldn't see anyone.

He stood up, worried auditory hallucinations were going to join his tremors, fatigue. and chest pains, when he heard it again. This time, it was clear—it came from the dry lands ahead.

Fenn stayed in the shadow of the trees and peered out as the biting sting of his legs waking up began to grow.

Who would be wandering those lands at night?

'Please help me!'

He gulped. It was a woman's voice, though he couldn't see her in the low light.

'My child! Someone? Anyone?'

More wailing followed, and Fenn's blood ran cold. He squinted, trying to discern movement in the shadows ahead. She sounded close.

'Please! She's dying....'

Fenn massaged his calves, trying to get the feeling back into them. Everything was numb from where he'd been sitting. He didn't want to race to her aid only to trip over at the first step and humiliate himself. He'd be of no use at all if that happened.

Then he saw her.

A shaft of moonlight cut through a cloud, illuminating a pale-skinned woman wandering through the deadlands. Her hair was raven-black and reached her waist. He couldn't see what she wore, but assumed it was some dark material because it was difficult to make out much detail. Her mouth hung open in a scream, her eyes red with tears.

Something about her was unnerving. Was it the way she moved? The way her jaws hung open in a perpetual scream? He couldn't quite place the feeling. Maybe it was just Calidra's suspicions rubbing off on him.

'Help me. Help my child!' the woman repeated, another sob punctuating her words.

'Fenn! What in the name of Neros are you *doing* out here?'

He whirled around to find Selys several trees away, racing towards him, glaive out, a dark streak of blood across the tip of the blade. 'Selys? I was—'

'This is the edge of the deadlands! Surely even with your curse you can feel how dangerous it is?'

Fenn lowered his head as she scolded him. 'I was just looking. I wasn't going to go *out* there!'

'Oh, really?' Selys came to a halt beside him and glared out at the dry land beyond. 'Because it looked to me like you were getting ready to run down there.'

He scratched his nose to stall while he thought of an excuse. Lying wasn't his strongest suit—Varlot had that right —so he opted for the truth. 'Okay, I *wasn't* going to. Honestly! But then there was a woman out there. All alone. She was calling for help and I thought I should—'

'Where?' Raising her glaive, Selys stepped past him and held her ground, gaze scouring the length of the cracked lands.

'She was...she was there a second ago...' Fenn couldn't see her now. Even if the woman had run off, she'd been close enough that he *should* have seen her.

'Fenn...'

He swallowed. 'It...she...it wasn't another of those shadow creatures. It was a woman! She was crying! Looking for her child!'

Selys lowered her glaive when she couldn't see anything,

then turned to him. She patted his shoulder with one hand. 'Fenn. This place is known as the deadlands. You can see there's no life here. Nothing for spirits. Nothing for us.'

'What happened?'

'It's the site of a battle against the Myr. One of the biggest in history. It's said their remains still hold power. They are creatures of pure magic, Fenn. What you saw might have been part of it. These tales aren't limited just to ships and sailors.'

'The apothecary said something like that...' He stared out at the empty plain. 'What I saw was definitely a woman.'

Selys shook her head and gave him a small, sad smile. 'The Myr are our greatest enemy. They are creatures of pure magic, in direct opposition to the magic of our spirits. They feast on us in any way they can. Some create beasts of war and violence. Or creatures of stealth.'

'The death spirits?'

'Yes. And others. That "woman" is often an omen. If she sees you, you're marked for one of their attacks.'

'She didn't see me.'

'For your sake, Fenn, I hope not. It seems Tassar itself is conspiring to see you dead. And why wouldn't it? You're tainted by the Myr. So please, stick with us, and don't make it any easier for them.'

20

THE SHRINE

CALIDRA

As far as Calidra was concerned, vomiting was the worst affliction of sickness a person could endure. The very act of it was beyond repulsive. And *why* did it have to come out through the nose, too?

She rubbed Jisyel's back and held her hair as she retched up every morsel of food she'd consumed over the past day or two. Then, it had turned to bile—an awful substance that turned Jisyel's voice scratchy and rough.

It had been three hours of sickness, another hour of retching, and now Jisyel had to endure sharp hiccups and the foul-tasting medicine. But it was working. After the second dose, Jisyel had more colour in her cheeks, and by the third dose, she was no longer puzzled. Calidra was just glad Jisyel could finally have a proper conversation.

She refused to acknowledge the fact that Varlot had carried Jisyel all the way through the Spindle Woods to the town, paid for their room and board, *and* paid for Jisyel's medicine. She refused to give it any thought at all.

Once the worst of her vomiting had passed, Jisyel had taken a cool bath and rinsed out her hair, which had considerably improved her mood. Her foot had swollen, her skin stretched and sore, but the bath had helped. For the past thirty minutes, she'd been tentatively sipping water, a thin blanket wrapped around her shoulders.

'Here. Something easy to eat.' Calidra put a bowl of red grapes on the table in their room.

'Thanks.' Jisyel picked a few of them, the biggest in the bunch, and popped them into her mouth.

Calidra also ate some. She'd not had much of an appetite, but knew it would be better to have a handful of the sweet fruits than nothing at all.

After she'd eaten less than half, Jisyel shoved the bowl away.

Calidra scowled and pushed it back to her. 'Don't be childish. Eat them all, not just the big ones.'

'I don't like the little ones.' Jisyel eyed one as if it had done her a great insult by simply existing. 'They're not as sweet.'

'Jisyel, you can't even *taste* the difference!'

She pouted, unwilling to eat the smaller grapes. 'I *remember* I don't like them.'

Calidra shook her head. 'You need to eat. Especially after what you've been through today. Come on, or I'll make you have some of those pickles I brought for Malora!'

With a long sigh, Jisyel did as she was told. She chewed methodically, slowly, without satisfaction. After she'd eaten a few more, she sighed. 'I'm sick of this.'

'I can imagine. But hopefully the medicine will have put a stop to it. It's been a few hours since you last—'

'No. I'm sick of *this*.' Jisyel gestured to herself.

'What?'

Jisyel grabbed Calidra and kissed her on the lips. 'I'm sick of not feeling *that*.' She pointed to the grapes. 'I'm sick of not tasting those.' She lifted her swollen foot—it had been wrapped in a linen bandage—and scowled. 'I'm sick of not feeling *anything*!'

336

Calidra took her hand and gently squeezed her fingers. 'Jisyel...'

'I know it's my own fault. I *know* I was stupid. Reckless. I should never have joked around with Hassen. Even a young spirit like him...dragons are too powerful.'

'I wasn't going to say it was your fault...'

Jisyel put her hand on her face, hiding herself as tears fell down her cheeks. 'Stupid spirits! Stupid me!'

'Jisyel. It'll be okay,' Calidra said. It was the default thing to say when someone was upset. When you could do nothing to fix it, but be there for them and offer a hand of support and comfort through the distress. 'I know it's been a tough day. Everything with my mother this morning, then Varlot... And now the tanglethorn.'

'No! It's not that!' Jisyel got to her feet and ran both hands through her hair. 'It's this stupid curse. Three years I've put up with it. Three years I've ignored how much hogshit it is!'

Calidra knew Jisyel preferred to put on a positive face and pretend things were better than they were. But she hadn't realised Jisyel hated the curse quite so much.

'Fenn is doing something about...about whatever's happened to him. I stayed on the island and kept on at *you* about going back to Bragalia. I'm such a hypocrite!'

'You always like to put others first, Jisyel.'

She laughed, but it was joyless. 'I know. Have to make sure gran is okay. Guests are okay. *You're* okay. Fenn's okay.' She waved her hand vaguely in the direction of the window. 'What happened to me was punishment for being stupid. I understand that. My problems aren't as big as yours. Or Fenn's. Or anyone else's!'

Calidra stood up and crossed the room to her. She wiped away Jisyel's tears before wrapping her arms around her. 'Your problems are *just* as important as everyone else's! You know that, Jisyel. Don't think you are any less!'

Jisyel shook as she cried. Calidra knew it was probably

a mix of stresses, including what her body had been through—emptying its entire contents in a handful of hours would be enough to drain anyone's energy—but she also knew Jisyel had been holding onto her sadness for a while.

She'd always evaded conversations about Hassen or the curse he'd inflicted upon her. Always laughed it off like nothing serious, as if there was nothing in all of Tassar that could get to her. But the truth was the opposite.

Jisyel *hated* it.

Hated the lack of touch, of taste. Of anything and everything physical.

And worst of all, she hated being a burden. It was why she never spoke about it, never acknowledged it was even there.

Calidra squeezed her tightly, trying to impart some comfort, some reassurance that she was loved, that she was important beyond all measure, regardless of what she thought of herself.

Jisyel quietened, but kept her face pressed into Calidra's shoulder. She sniffed. '...Pay respects...to Alnothen...'

'What?'

'That's...what Selys went to do. Didn't she say that?'

Calidra thought back. Honestly, she hadn't paid much attention to the priestess. Not when Jisyel had been on the verge of vomiting, unable to walk or talk. 'I think so. Alnothen's shrine is deeper in the woods.'

'I want to go there. I want to ask Alnothen for help.'

Calidra didn't think the spirit would be interested in talking to someone who travelled with Varlot, not after the accusation she'd given him. 'I'm not sure that's the best idea...'

Jisyel wiped her flushed face clear of tears. 'I want to. Maybe Alnothen can help? She could get rid of what Hassen did? When have I ever had a chance to approach a powerful spirit before now?'

338

'Jisyel, you can hardly walk. The swelling hasn't even started to come down—'

'I don't care. I'll hop the whole way there on one foot if I have to!'

Calidra shook her head. Stubborn as she was, Jisyel was even more so. She couldn't remember a single argument where she'd won, not after Jisyel had dug her heels in. Jisyel already had that look in her eyes.

She glanced out the window. It was starting to get dark.

Going to the shrine was a terrible idea, but she couldn't let Jisyel stand this close to a spirit powerful enough to potentially help, and not act. She'd stayed on the Isle of Salt for so long, looking after Bellandri—and then herself—without ever taking the chance to do something about her own curse. It had only been three years, but they had taken their toll on Jisyel. 'Well, you'll need help. Be typical you catch your other foot on another growth of tanglethorn, and I can't carry you the whole way. I'll see if Fenn is around. Or if Selys is back.'

Jisyel smiled, and Calidra's heart lightened at the sight. 'Get your cloak on. I'll go and find Fenn.'

'Thank you, Cal.' Jisyel half-hopped, half-jumped forward and threw her arms around Calidra.

'Don't thank me yet. Alnothen might not even want to talk to you.'

'Maybe not. But I'll have tried.'

CALIDRA STALKED BACK through the darkening streets, furious. *Where* was Fenn? Why was he out and about, wandering around Spindelford when he'd been Myr-touched?

What if someone knew what he was? Called for an Inquisitor?

She couldn't find any trace of him in town, and the

apothecary hadn't offered much help either, which had fuelled her frustration.

It had also taken her far longer than she'd wanted to look for Fenn. Selys hadn't returned either, and Jisyel was eager to get going. If they waited any longer, it would be too late to go. Strolling around in the Spindle Woods in the dark wasn't something Calidra wanted to do with a poisoned Jisyel on her arm. Calidra knew she was strong, but she couldn't do that by herself.

It left only one option.

And Calidra wasn't sure how much more of her pride she could swallow that day.

Alnothen hated Varlot. If she asked him to help, the spirit would probably outright refuse Jisyel's plea. But she didn't have any other options. If Varlot didn't help, they wouldn't be able to go at all.

She gritted her teeth, reminding herself this was for Jisyel, and entered the inn. She spotted him quickly enough in the small crowd.

Varlot was hunched over a large tankard of ale, wearing his bearskin cloak, at the far end of the bar. He'd kept his hood up, too, despite the warmth of the room, and Calidra wondered whether he was trying to hide himself.

She crossed the threshold, picking her way between the few patrons eating their dinners, until she reached his side. There was no need for small talk. 'Varlot. Jisyel needs to go into the woods. Can you help her walk?'

Varlot glanced up at her, then returned his attention to his mug. 'What's she going into the woods for? She needs to take a piss, there's a latrine out back.'

Calidra fought to keep her eyes from rolling. 'Actually, she wants to speak with Alnothen. I can't carry her the whole way.'

'What makes you think I'm going back out there? You heard what the spirit said. Ain't exactly a warm welcome.'

'Alnothen is a spirit of life and creation. She won't hurt you.'

Varlot shook his head. 'Maybe so. But it ain't gonna be pleasant for me, I can tell you that. And if she's been throwing up her guts all afternoon, probably best she don't go for a late night stroll either.'

Calidra couldn't agree more, but she was doing this for Jisyel. What *she* thought was best didn't factor into it. 'I know. But she has a curse. And Alnothen might actually be strong enough to lift it.'

'What makes you think the dragon will even listen?'

'She probably won't. But there's a chance she might, and that's enough for Jisyel.'

Varlot took a large swig from his mug, downing it in a single gulp. 'Woman got herself cursed. Tripped over tanglethorn. You try and get her out of that mess, I don't want no part of it.'

Calidra seethed. 'I know you're only here for Fenn, though I don't have any idea why, but could you be a bit less petty?'

He shrugged and let out a belch.

'You know what, Varlot? I think you're just an angry, bitter man who has done some awful things. There's no need to take it out on me.'

'How *dare* you talk to me like that! After everything I did for you!'

'For which I'm grateful. But helping me doesn't give you free pass to behave like a...like a...wild hog!'

Varlot's hand went to the handle of his axe.

Calidra didn't flinch. 'What? You're going to hurt me because I said something you didn't like? Is that what you do to people who don't fawn over you?'

'You're one to talk! Always waving your dagger around!'

'I defend myself. For someone who's always moaning

about being alone and unwanted, you ought to treat us better.'

Varlot went still. 'Excuse me?'

Calidra narrowed her eyes. She knew she was suspicious of everyone, but the fact he'd agreed to come with them after wanting to head off had set alarm bells ringing. She didn't trust him. Didn't trust what he wanted with Fenn. 'Just because you helped Fenn against Torsten, you think you can guilt him into keeping you around? I know your true colours.'

'*You* were going to give him to the Inquisitors!'

'I was. I made a mistake. Something *I'm* willing to face, unlike you.' She was aware of people in the tavern staring at them, but she didn't care.

'Wait. Varlot? *Varlot Keir?*'

Varlot withdrew as a man named him.

'By Alnothen, it *is* you!'

Calidra frowned at the short, balding man, who'd crossed from his table over to them. 'Do you mind? I'm trying to have a private conversation and—'

'Death brought you back again, did it?' the man continued, pushing past Calidra. 'Have you even visited your wife and son? Hmm? Or are you straight back to the bottom of a bottle?'

Varlot huffed and shook his head, clearly angry but unwilling to take the bait.

'Hmm? Why don't you show some respect!'

Varlot stood up and towered over the man. 'Why don't you go back to your dinner before things get messy.' His voice came out as a low growl, and Varlot's warning was clear.

The man shrank away, though his glare remained, and he shuffled back to his table, where his companions watched in stunned silence.

Varlot said, 'Calidra. Get Jisyel. Let's go.'

Her shoulders dropped in relief. She knew it was a risk, but she didn't know what else to do. Tell Jisyel they couldn't go? That she'd missed her chance because she'd been poisoned and was too sick to walk unaided?

Calidra wondered why the man had spoken so harshly to Varlot, but she didn't have time to dwell on it. She had no idea when they might next find another spirit—or shrine—that could help Jisyel.

For three years, Jisyel had put up with Hassen's curse. But speaking to a spirit would have meant leaving the Isle of Salt —something Calidra hadn't wanted to do. It was her own selfish fear that had kept both of them on the island, and Jisyel had always played off her curse as if it didn't bother her. She'd probably just accepted it, as Calidra had accepted she was never going to have closure with her family. It had been enough that as long as they were together—even on the island—nothing could hurt them.

Calidra hadn't realised how upset the curse had made Jisyel. How much Jisyel hated it.

And she was going to do what she could to put it right. They needed to see Alnothen while they could.

She followed Varlot out of the bar and towards the wooden staircase that led up to their rooms.

She'd been a little in awe of him when they'd first met. He'd been kind, generous, and willing to help. When people had been thrilled the former general had been in their presence, he hadn't belittled them. He'd even ignored the looks from women, when many others would have revelled in the attention.

That man had been angry, but perhaps he had lost someone in the war and blamed Varlot for it.

Perhaps Alnothen had been mistaken.

'Jisyel should be ready now. I'll help her down the stairs, then we'll go?'

Varlot nodded, and Calidra darted up. She knew it was

343

probably a stupid decision, but there was no way she'd be able to carry Jisyel all the way there and back by herself. Even though Alnothen had said she despised Varlot, she was a spirit of life and nature. Killing people wasn't something Alnothen had ever done. It was a calculated risk.

Pausing halfway to the top, she turned around and faced him. 'Thank you.'

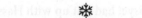

VARLOT KEPT TO HIS WORD, and Jisyel leaned heavily on him as they made their way through the forest. Small torches had been lit along the way, showing the narrow stone and wood path that led deeper into the trees—which thankfully had been cleared of all roots, including tanglethorn.

Calidra had wondered whether Jisyel would change her mind once she realised how difficult the trek would be, but if anything, she became more determined with every step. It didn't take long before Jisyel got into her rhythm of walking, and Varlot was more patient with her even than Calidra would have been.

Guilt grew in the back of her mind, much like it had after Fenn had proven not to be a threat as she'd first assumed.

Moths and biting flies swirled around the flames lighting the path, and Calidra spent most of the journey angrily waving them away. They passed several people on their way back to town from the shrine, but Selys was not among them.

Calidra had expected to see the priestess, but she supposed there was more than one path to the shrine, and it was possible they'd missed Selys while she'd been looking for Fenn or speaking with Varlot.

Strangely, Calidra had never bothered to visit the Shrine of Alnothen before. She and Malora only ever came to Spindleford for recreational reasons. Even Malora, who had been blessed by Chyram, had never bothered to see the shrine. Malora had never been a fan of the trees—or more specifically the insects that lived within them—and they'd always kept to the edge of the Spindle Woods whenever they'd visited.

Calidra could see why.

'As much as I can't stand this place, at least we're safe from the Myr here,' Varlot muttered.

'Safe? How can you be so sure?' Calidra asked.

'Alnothen,' he replied simply, as if that explained everything.

Trying to ignore her growing frustration, Calidra asked, 'Alnothen? How does the spirit make any difference? We were near Neros's shrine in Ballowtown and Meadowhill, and we were attacked.'

'We're *in* her domain. Dragon spirits have powerful magic,' Varlot shifted Jisyel, who clutched his arm as they walked, 'especially in their domains. Deadlands can't encroach any further south because Alnothen is too strong. Their magic can't cope with hers.'

Calidra knew about the deadlands, the area that had been drained of life following the Battle of Marlrush. She'd never realised the Myr could have drained more land had Alnothen not been present to stop their magic.

'Why don't the dragons just get rid of the Myr? If they're that strong?' Jisyel asked.

Varlot strugged, the action causing Jisyel to stumble. 'I think they've been trying to. But kinda hard to wage full scale war when you're bound to a forest or a lake somewhere.'

'Toriaken can fly anywhere in Porsenthia though?' Jisyel hiccuped. 'Maybe further?'

'Well, he's bound to the Iron Sword, ain't he? He's got more freedom than most in that way.'

Calidra thought about it. She knew dragon spirits were

locked into their domains. It was what they *were*. The source of their power. She'd never considered how limiting it could be, too. As far as she was concerned, it had just meant something else to watch out for whenever travelling through somewhere new.

'Any respite from the Myr is good enough for me. Fenn needs to keep moving, and if we can have even one night safe, that's a win,' Calidra said. If the Myr really were coming back, if they were launching a new invasion, perhaps hiding in Spindleford wasn't such a bad idea, if Alnothen could keep the forest out of danger.

Bellandri would be safe on the Isle of Salt. There'd never been a Myrish strike on the island. Not in living memory. That was certainly one benefit to being on a spit of land on the edge of the world. But if she and Jisyel were on the mainland when more fighting broke out? Flocking to hide under Alnothen's wings might be one way they could stay safe. Malora, too. And her family.

She was considering how she'd convince the others to listen to that idea, when Varlot broke her train of thoughts, muttering under his breath. 'What are you talking about?'

'Nothing.'

'Really?'

He sighed. 'Been years since I last came this way. My wife was bonded with Alnothen.'

Calidra hadn't known that. 'Was? She's…a priestess, too?'

'Alnothen blessed her. Was more of a curse, though.'

Calidra could understand that. Malora had been in a similar situation.

'What happened?' Jisyel asked, her voice shaky but stronger than it had been in hours.

'Shrine's a minute or two away. You two can make it from here.' Varlot let go of Jisyel, who clutched a tree for support.

'What? If it's so close, can't you help us the rest of the way?' Jisyel asked, her knees trembling.

'I'm not welcome.'

'Varlot. Don't let us down now, not when we're so close.' Calidra shooed away another biting fly and stalked back to him, annoyed he'd also evaded another of their questions regarding his family. 'I can just about see the shrine through the trees. It's not far!'

'Then you'll be fine on your own. I'll wait here and help you on the way back. I can't imagine you'll be in there very long. Foolish to even ask the damned spirit.'

'Varlot!' Calidra snapped, her voice rising.

'Look. Alnothen isn't my biggest fan, and you wanna ask her for a favour. You think having me there will *help* your chances?' He walked off the path and sat down on a fallen log, careful not to squash any of the mushrooms clustered on top.

'Please come with us? I don't mind if you're there. I'm sure the spirit won't mind either?' Jisyel pleaded.

'You're an idiot if you believe that,' Varlot said.

'I don't appreciate you speaking to Jisyel like that. After what she's been through, you're refusing?' Calidra wouldn't allow anyone to speak to her or Jisyel in that manner.

Was Varlot stepping aside because he truly didn't want to hurt Jisyel's chances? Or was he afraid of what the spirit might reveal? Alnothen had named him a child murderer. Would she divulge more secrets? Is that what kept him at bay?

She gritted her teeth, angry with herself. She was always looking for a reason not to trust people, and he had brought them this far already. She needed to be less bitter. More softly, she said, 'Alnothen is the spirit of this forest. She already knows you're here. What difference does a handful of steps make?'

'A lot.'

Jisyel trembled slightly. It had been a mistake to go on such a long walk before she'd properly recovered. But they

347

were here now, and it would be silly to go back to town without trying to beg the spirit's help.

'Come on, Jisyel.' She offered her arm, and Jisyel hopped between the tree and Calidra.

Perhaps they'd be lucky and find Selys still at the shrine. Having a priestess on their side would surely strengthen their plea.

With a final dark glare towards Varlot, Calidra led Jisyel down the last section of path and to the vast courtyard outside Alnothen's Shrine. More torches hung from the sides of the building—which had the largest tree Calidra had ever seen in her life bursting *through* it.

Or perhaps bits of the shrine had simply been built around the tree?

It was made up of disparate parts—a small building over roots, a steep-roofed chapel to the south, even a towering spire—all with dozens of individuals lingering around them. Most were people from Spindleford, Calidra assumed, as they wore a similar garb of browns and greens, woven from natural fibres. A small burial ground lay just beyond the tree-line, tearful visitors coming and going in a slow, silent march. Flowers in a myriad of colours cascaded down the walls of the shrine, bringing brightness to the clearing and filling the air with a light perfume.

Calidra heard many people begging for aid or blessings—hoping for a successful harvest, an easy birth, for distant relatives to be safe.

'We should find one of Alnothen's priests.' Jisyel stared up at the vastness of the shrine and the tree which burst from it, her eyes round in awe. 'They'll be in robes.'

Calidra couldn't see any priests or priestesses, but they may have been inside.

She was about to take a look, when the ground trembled, and she clutched Jisyel's hand. Around them, people also held onto each other, trees, the shrine itself, whatever they could reach.

'A quake?' Jisyel gasped.

But it wasn't. Calidra felt *something* moving underground. A presence so powerful she couldn't mistake it for anything other than what it was: Alnothen.

With a deafening roar, the dragon spirit burst from the ground in an explosion of light and fire. Her wings spread over them, throwing everything under a blanket of shadow, her head tilted back as she bellowed her fury. Orange flames leapt from her jaws and columns of fire spread upwards. The canopy caught, but the leaves didn't burn. They crackled, swallowed by the flame, smoke pluming from the foliage. Then the fire was gone, and each leaf was bigger and brighter than before— vibrantly green, with every budded flower now in full bloom.

Those at the shrine gasped in awe.

Calidra almost screamed in terror—Alnothen's golden gaze was fixed on Jisyel and herself. Alnothen may have been a spirit of life, nature, bounty. But she was a dragon. A predator. An ancient creature of magic. And her rage washed over them like her fire over the leaves.

Coming here had been a bad idea. A *terrible* one.

'Cal…' Jisyel whispered.

'Varlot Keir. I warned you once that you were unwelcome. Do you forgot my blessed one lays in the ground here? Her child? By your actions?' Alnothen's voice boomed.

Summoned by the spirit's voice, Varlot appeared in a gap between the trees, sheepishly making his way along the wooden path, hands behind his back, his head bowed low. 'Alnothen…I was not…'

'You were aware. You could not forget the blood on your hands, as I cannot forget it. I see it now on you, rivers of red dripping from your fingers. Where you walk lies death. It has always been your true nature.'

Calidra slowly backed away, dragging Jisyel with her. If Alnothen wished to berate Varlot, she had no desire to attract the spirit's attention.

Varlot lowered his head even more. 'I am not here for your forgiveness—'

'*You* cannot *be forgiven for such desecration!*' More fire from Alnothen's jaws. It set the forest floor alight, weeds and grasses growing taller in seconds.

Calidra felt the heat of it singing the air, but there was no pain.

Unfazed, Varlot continued, 'I brought these two. Jisyel asks your help.'

Calidra hated him for turning the dragon's gaze off himself, but couldn't blame him. She'd have said anything to get the dragon away from her if she were in his shoes.

Alnothen's long, sinuous neck turned, and her eyes locked with Calidra's. A crown of moss coiled around her eyes and horns, with thin red growths spurting from it. After a moment of study, the dragon shifted to face Jisyel. Pulling her massive body through the trees, through the shrine itself, Alnothen approached the pair, her nostrils flaring. Her body flickered, transparent and then visible again. '*You have my brother's scent on you.*'

Jisyel looked the dragon squarely in the eyes. 'I'm from the Isle of Salt. Hassen cursed me. Please...please...can you expel it? I can't feel anything physical. If I'm burned. Cold. Hungry. Can't feel the touch of someone else.' She looped her fingers through Calidra's, providing a united front. 'Three years, I've suffered. I have been punished enough! Please free me!'

Again, the dragon considered, and the clearing seemed to hold its breath. The fires along the forest floor died down with a crackle, and the final few flowers bloomed around them.

Nothing else moved. No-one spoke. Varlot stared from across the clearing, his mouth hanging open.

'I could remove my brother's touch. His power is far inferior to my own.'

Calidra's heart skipped a beat.

'But I would want you for myself.'

'W...what?' Jisyel stammered.

Alnothen snorted and flexed her wings. *'You ask me to interfere. I want something in return. And as Varlot took one of my blessed, he can give me a new one.'*

'What? I didn't mean for that!' Varlot said, straightening up. 'Jisyel came here on her own.'

'Wait, wait. Stop shouting!' Jisyel yelled. 'Alnothen...what would it mean?'

Calidra wondered that, too. It was another reason she wished Selys was with them. The priestess could explain. Maybe even bargain.

But the idea worried her. If it was anything like what had happened to Malora, Calidra would refuse *for* Jisyel. Giving up control of your body, having people beg for help, was an awful experience. And with so many people at Alnothen's Shrine, there would no doubt be a long queue demanding aid for stupid things like wanting their pumpkins to grow. She squeezed Jisyel's hand, hoping she'd feel the warning. She'd be trapped under the spirit's claw.

'I would gift you some of my power. You would help my people. Fight my enemies.'

Jisyel turned to Calidra. 'That doesn't sound too bad...'

'No, Jisyel! I'll bet Alnothen would expect you to live here forever, too.'

'Of course. My blessed must stay with me. Help the forest grow. But after a time, you could spread my word throughout Tassar. My power would rise to greater heights, and so would yours.'

It left a bad taste in Calidra's throat. 'Jisyel, you wanted

351

the curse to be lifted, and you wanted to go back to the Isle of Salt. None of this—'

'If you return to Hassen's domain without his touch, he will be most displeased. He would curse you again. Something more powerful. More lasting. This is why I do not wish to interfere... unless you become mine. Then nothing can curse you again. My protection is great.'

Panic rose. Calidra didn't want to lose Jisyel to some forest spirit. She took back everything she thought about Spindleford being safe. The fact that Jisyel was even *considering* the spirit's request showed that she didn't understand the dangers. 'Jisyel. No. Don't be silly. It's not worth it for that.'

Jisyel stared at the ground, one hand interlaced with Calidra's, the other balled into a fist.

'Jisyel?' Calidra asked. Her voice carried a note of pleading. She couldn't lose Jisyel so easily, so quickly. She couldn't!

'Why not take me, instead.' Varlot's voice cut through the quiet like a knife.

'Why would I take you, murderer?'

'If you want payment for help? Take me. I'm from Spindleford. Two of your blessed are dead...because of me. I know they're there in the burial grounds.' Varlot stared into the dark trees. 'You won't kill me. So take me. Use my strength. And heal Jisyel.'

'You life is worth less than nothing, Varlot. So full of violence. You should be in the ground feeding my forest, where your rage can no longer fester and pollute my followers.'

The barbed insult was devastating. Even Calidra winced, and it hadn't been aimed at her. Nor could she believe that Varlot had tried to step up.

The man's shoulders sagged, all defiance leaving him, as if his strength had died in that moment, thanks to the dragon's tongue. 'I...I wasn't in my right head back then. And I've changed. I ain't done anything else wrong since.'

Alnothen snarled. '*Yes. You were ill. Yes. You may have changed. You may never do it again, as you promise. But what you did was unforgivable.*'

Varlot stared towards the burial ground, saying nothing.

Calidra followed his gaze, wondering who Alnothen accused him of killing. Then it twigged. Varlot had said his wife was blessed. If she was dead...because of him...It would explain Alnothen's abhorrence at his presence.

But *two* blessed? Was the second one...his son?

'*Leave this place.*' Fire enveloped the spirit as she spread her wings again, then leapt into the air. In the moonlight, Alnothen's green scales appeared black. Ripples of silver light bounced off her horns and vegetation growing along her body, then she was gone, lost in the night sky.

Jisyel sank to her knees, tears streaming down her cheeks, her chest rising and falling rapidly.

Calidra crouched down beside her, giving her all the time she needed to recover. There was no point in pulling her back to her feet, not after that. Calidra wasn't sure her own heart would ever recover from the intensity of that encounter.

Varlot walked past them, his eyes unreadable. 'I'm going to the burial grounds.'

'Varlot.' Calidra stopped him with a single word. 'Tell me honestly. Are...are your wife and son buried there?'

'...Yes.'

'Did...did *you* put them there? Was Alnothen right about you?'

Varlot said nothing, continuing down the path and into the trees, swallowed up by the darkness.

Apollo ignored the stares.

Most, he knew, were simply curious. It wasn't every day an Inquisitor marched someone out of Foxmouth in irons. He couldn't blame them for wanting to see what was going on, see who was accused of wronging the queen.

But nestled among them were other, more malevolent eyes. People looking for an opportunity. Some way they could take the misfortune of another and turn it to their own advantage.

Apollo was certain Malora and Renys would be fine. They had good staff. Loyal patrons. Had been a pillar of the town for the past five years. But he wished Malora still had the power of a dragon spirit on her side. Something a little sharper to keep the more prying eyes away.

He had no idea what he was walking into. He had his pardon, regardless of Nadja's dismissal. And he no longer had Queen Surayo's curse upon him. That had been lifted when he'd returned to the palace after his successful trip.

It should be enough to prove he'd done what had been

asked, and that he couldn't be accused of causing whatever trouble was growing in Tassar.

If the Myr *were* back, he could understand the queen's fear. If he were in her shoes, he'd have pointed fingers, too. Not that Apollo had known what the Citrine Key *truly* was. What it was capable of. But that *wasn't* his fault. The queen hadn't bothered to tell him.

Perhaps she should have told him more than just where he was going and what task he had to complete. Perhaps *then* he'd have shoved that key down Paragos's throat.

And yet, cold guilt squatted in his gut, growing inch by inch as the minutes ticked by, the discomfort so great that it made walking difficult.

He was grateful Nadja had left Malora and Renys alone. He had no doubt that if Torsten had been the one to visit him, he'd have brought the entire family back to the capital in chains as an example to any would-be wrongdoers.

His mind wandered back. Five years ago, Queen Surayo had sent him away to the distant country of Malnova with an artefact she'd stolen from the Myr in her latest conquest. Sent him to feed that thing to a dragon so massive it would give Toriaken a run for his money. Feeding the spirit the key without being eaten himself simply hadn't been a possibility.

So what if the queen had wanted him to throw his life away? He hadn't.

But if he'd known what the key truly was? What would he have done differently? He'd never have been able to marry Malora. Never have met Renys. He shook his head, the movement small so it wouldn't attract attention.

Nadja marched him through the streets, heading steadily south. Apollo looked up every so often to gather his bearings, and paused when they crossed a small square—the scent of melting sugar and butter thick in the air. 'Inquisitor Nadja. Have you tried the fudge here? Honestly, it's quite something else. Foxmouth might be known for fishing, but the locals know the *real* treats. If you—'

'Have you forgotten the irons at your wrists and ankles?' Nadja whirled around. 'You could be hanged for what you've done!'

'All the more reason to have something tasty, first. I'll even pay! I have a few coins in my pocket. You'd need to get them and—'

'Apollo. If you carry on like this, I'll have to gag you.'

He closed his mouth. Nadja wasn't playing around. But it had been worth a try. And the fudge really *was* delicious.

He'd have to figure something else out. Apollo had cheated death so many times throughout his life that he'd be damned if he was going to lose everything for some stupid misunderstanding. Especially not with Malora and Renys waiting. He'd worked far too hard to build the life he had.

They reached the town gates, and Nadja nodded to the officers on duty. Apollo kept his head down—although he was sure even if they didn't recognise him, the gossip would travel through Foxmouth quickly enough that everyone would soon know he'd been taken.

Apollo stopped again, frowning at the empty road beyond. 'No carriage?'

'I travel light.'

'Do you know how difficult it'll be for me to walk the whole way to Eastbrook in these?' He gestured to the fetters around his ankles, which while lenient, did not allow him to take a full stride.

Nadja held up her hand for him to wait, then nodded to one of the officers on the outside of Foxmouth gates. The young man disappeared into a large stable for a minute, before returning with two horses in tow—one chestnut, the other piebald.

Apollo shook his head. 'Can't ride one of them with—'

'Will you stop complaining, Apollo? I've been more than

merciful with you. I'll remove the irons around your ankles so you can ride.'

Apollo's mind whirled. He knew northern Porsenthia, had grown up there and spent a considerable number of his adult years in the area. If he got away from her, there would be places he could lay low for a while. He'd get a message to Foxmouth and meet Malora and Renys later on.

He just had to escape from one Inquisitor—who had given him a strong pair of legs to flee on.

'I see those eyes of yours calculating,' Nadja said. She took the reins from the officer and handed one to Apollo. 'The horses are tethered together and respond to this.' She pulled out a small, silver whistle that had been tucked into her uniform. 'One blow on this, and they return to me. So don't get any ideas and make your situation worse. I'm not above binding you completely in iron and throwing you over the horse's back. Or even dragging you along in the dirt behind it.'

Her words didn't dissuade him. Apollo raised his eyebrows in mock surprise. 'Inquisitor, I think you'll find I've been nothing but obedient since you made it clear I wasn't going to win an argument against you.'

Nadja frowned, gently patting the neck of her piebald, then pulled herself up and into the saddle. She gave herself a moment to adjust the reins before straightening up and taking out her iron dagger. With a flick of the tip, the fetters on Apollo's ankles slackened, then broke apart—leaving one bracelet of iron around each ankle, but they were no longer joined.

Apollo considered darting away, but the sensation passed as quickly as it appeared, and he clambered up the side of the chestnut mare and into his own saddle. It was awkward, but the irons around his wrists gave him enough movement to steady himself and clutch onto the reins.

The moment he was seated, Nadja flicked her dagger

again, and the irons tightened, locking his wrists to the horse's reins. The chestnut mare shook her head and stamped one foot as Nadja looped more iron along the tether between the two animals. Apollo watched in amazement as the grey matter moved like fat drops of water along the line. It solidified, the thin coat of iron now binding both horses— and their riders—together.

Satisfied, Nadja turned her piebald away from Apollo and nudged her forward.

Obedient, Apollo's mare followed.

He was trapped. Potentially walking to his death. Apollo remembered the sensation before—a freezing blizzard, the palace in the snow, and the Myrish creature within. It had been terrifying, had made his legs numb with fear. And the creature had been *happy* the key was returned. Happy when Yorik, the grumpy fisherman, had died. The man whom Apollo had named his inn after.

He fought the nausea that rose in his gut at the memories.

Even he and Malora had barely escaped that place with their lives. The Myr—or the palace, he'd not been sure which —had sucked their energy from them. Even their very breath. It had only been by a miracle that they'd made it out.

If that was what was coming? More Myr? More of their creatures?

He wouldn't stand for it.

Escaping that death trap had made him pledge that his time of thievery was over. He'd offered Malora the life she deserved. He'd been true to his word ever since, fulfilling his promise to her to the letter.

And they had Renys, now. He couldn't imagine life without her. Whatever happened…whatever calamity befell Tassar, he had his daughter. Wasn't her life worth more than all the gold in the world?

Apollo twisted in his saddle, as much as his restraints

would allow, and stared back at Foxmouth as they walked away from it. Malora. Renys. He whispered, 'I'll come back soon. I promise.'

NADJA LED THEM WEST, along the rocky paths through the base of the Nethal Mountains. She kept her tight-lipped approach, refusing to rise to Apollo's repeated attempts at conversation or distracting her.

Even though Apollo considered himself a man of patience, he eventually tired of trying to engage with her and slipped into contemplative quiet after an hour or two of travelling with nothing but the clop of the horses' hooves to accompany them. They didn't travel quickly. The horses barely went above a gentle walk, trotting only when they overtook a small caravan of traders heading the same way.

He'd not expected to travel into the mountains, and wondered if the trickier terrain would make it easier to escape. He couldn't outrun a horse on flat ground, but over a steep, rocky incline? Perhaps he had a chance.

Apollo resigned himself to a quiet journey, keeping his eyes and ears open for any opportunity to get himself out of the situation. He had more chance of getting away from a single Inquisitor somewhere on the road than in an entire palace full of them—Torsten included—not to mention Queen Surayo herself.

If they didn't like what he said, he was unlikely to leave with his head. Just the thought of it made him shudder.

He was hardly aware of where they were going, just that the mountains rose up on all sides as Nadja led them down a path that cut right through the enormous rocks. The first iron ores had been built here several hundred years ago, and where Toriaken had been discovered, a shrine had been built to the glory of the dragon. Over the years, as Toriaken's power and worshippers had grown, the shrine had been added to. Now, it was the largest of any shrine on the whole continent—a tourist attraction in its own right, with crowds of people flocking to northern Porsenthia for a glimpse of the dragon, or to beg his aid.

It was silly, really.

Shortly after Toriaken had been discovered, some Bragalian mage had managed to bind the dragon's soul into an iron sword and claim his power. He had become the first king of Porsenthia, the first to wear the Iron Crown. Queen Surayo was simply the latest in a long line of descendants to use the dragon's power in the same way.

It meant that all the hopeful people begging for help might as well be talking to stone. Toriaken's loyalty lay solely with the Porsenthian ruler, and nothing else.

Apollo had always found it amusing that the rulers of the Porsenthian Empire—and the reason it had been able to grow so vast in the first place—was because someone, a Bragalian no less, had seen an opportunity and taken it.

Really, they'd been no different to himself.

Nadja took them deeper into the mountains, and they kept a constant pace for most of the day. Apollo soon realised she was taking them directly to Toriaken's Shrine. Strange. Was the queen going to meet them there? Surely not, if she was preparing for war.

It was possible they'd take a boat downriver, through Westbrook and into the larger Eastbrook—the Porsenthian capital. Perhaps travelling through the foothills and plains would give him more opportunities to escape. By taking him through a handful of settlements, he wouldn't have a moment to get away, not with so many officers to keep an eye on him.

Apollo huffed, aware he sounded like his daughter, but not particularly caring. While atop the horse, he could do nothing but go where Nadja directed it.

'Behold! Toriaken's greatness!'

Apollo glanced up at the loud voice. A bearded priest stood atop a boulder by the side of the road, arms held high as he shouted to a group of gathered people. His long sleeves flapped in the wind, revealing a collection of iron jewellery on his wrists. His left arm bore a silver tattoo that reached his elbow, sinuous and twisting.

'The bastion of the great spirit's power!'

Apollo rolled his eyes. Nadja ignored the priest.

Several people within the group shuffled forwards, partly to get out of the way of the two horses, partly to get closer to the priest.

'Please help! My son has gone missing!' a woman cried, on the verge of tears. Her silk cowl looked to be of fine material, but her unkempt hair and haggard appearance reminded Apollo of thieves in the town of Horush.

'Your son ran away from home!' someone replied, elbowing the woman to one side. 'I need Toriaken's blessing! My wife is going to have our baby any day now! I need a safe delivery!'

Apollo leaned forward in his saddle, curious.

The woman shoved the man. 'He may have run away, but his friends haven't heard from him in weeks! He wouldn't abandon them! Something's happened to my boy, and I need help to find him!'

'Please, calm yourselves!' Again, the priest's voice carried over the cacophony of noise. 'Come with me to the shrine. Bring your tithes. If you are generous, Toriaken may bless you.'

Apollo snorted. He knew shrines relied on donations. It was how they were built, how they gained worshippers, and how the spirits' powers grew. But Toriaken was different— he was already bound to Queen Surayo. He wasn't a wild spirit, free to bestow curses or blessings upon whomever he wanted. Not that these desperate people realised.

361

Then again, they probably hoped having their name ascribed to a large donation to Toriaken's Shrine would put them in the queen's favour. If the crown even noticed. Apollo wondered whether he should have made a few donations over the years. He might be in less of a mess.

Unwilling to listen to the priest, the man and woman continued to shove and push each other, until the woman was sent sprawling on the ground.

'You aren't going to stop that? Breach of the peace, isn't it?' Apollo asked Nadja. If she was busy dealing with the kerfuffle, he might be able to get away. He glanced at his surroundings—plenty of places he could hide.

The Inquisitor glanced over to the scrap, but continued onwards. 'My job is to bring you to Eastbrook. Nothing more.'

'Oh, really? I've lost count of the number of times Inquisitors on *other business* took time out of their day to question me.'

'Perhaps you were in the middle of a theft?'

'Nope. I'm always just wandering down the street, minding my own business. But you let *that* happen?' Apollo jerked his chin towards the fight, even though Nadja wasn't looking at him.

'If you feel you have been served some injustice, you ought to report it.'

'Yes. This right here is injustice!'

Nadja sighed. Clearly she didn't think Apollo deserved a reply.

He wanted to get away from the Inquisitor. If he made it to the palace, he'd be in hotter water than he already was. Worse, he wasn't as fit as he'd been five years ago. Nadja could certainly outrun him. He'd need to be clever, strategic. Choose his moment wisely.

It would be the only way.

Toriaken's Shrine appeared to grow from the mountain-

362

side itself. Apollo had seen it only a handful of times, and always from a distance. Up close, it was astounding. Easily as grand as the palace itself, the shrine was a myriad of towers and high walls, fashioned from mountain stone and iron combined. Several entrances were carved into the shrine at ground level, all doors open, allowing a constant stream of people in and out. Aside from a handful of beggars, most people were dressed in their finery, as if they were meeting royalty, not visiting a place of worship.

Several musicians sat along the walls, playing on stringed instruments and woodwind pipes, entertaining the gathered crowds and occasionally accepting a coin or two.

Above the shrine, the Nethal Mountains' snow-capped peaks were bright in the sunshine.

He shivered in the bitter wind. 'Why are we here?' Apollo asked, head tilted back as he tried to spot the tops of the tallest towers.

'The river passes close by and runs all the way to Eastbrook.'

So he'd been right about their route.

It would pass through Westbrook, a town where he'd spent several years of his youth and where he often bought wine for *The Grumpy Fisherman*. He was sure he could remember enough of it to hide away for as long as was necessary. He stared at the shrine as he and Nadja passed in front of it. The road was wide and well-maintained—at least some of the donations weren't going directly into the queen's pocket—and the people here weren't interested in gawping at him.

He'd always planned on bringing Renys to the shrine, once she was a bit older. She'd probably spend the entire day finding nooks and crannies to hide in, and would certainly try and climb up the towers to reach the roof.

His stomach sank. If he didn't get away soon, he'd never see her again, let alone bring her on a day out. They'd have to get out of Porsenthia. Get away somewhere the Iron Crown couldn't follow.

Unless he could convince the queen of his innocence...

'Please, can you spare some food?'

There were so many beggars at the shrine, so many people asking for help, that Apollo ignored the young man at first.

'You see him, Apollo? You've caused that.'

Nadja's voice caught his attention. Apollo looked where she pointed, where a young, disheveled man on his knees clutched at a priestess's robes. 'I don't know where my family is. Don't...don't know where this is.'

Apollo's heart lurched at the sight. The young man couldn't have been more than fifteen or sixteen, with fair hair and skin. It didn't look like he'd eaten in a while. 'How am I responsible for some beggar?'

'He's one of the lost souls.'

Apollo narrowed his eyes. They were past the front of the shrine now, heading west. Already he could hear the roar of the falls where they plunged into the river. Nadja didn't change the horses' pace, and Apollo swivelled in his seat to watch.

The young man coughed, flecks of blood spattering along the priestess's cream-grey robes.

She stepped back from him and scowled. 'You are tainted!'

'Please!' Again, the young man shuffled forward on his knees, and reached for the priestess's robes—only to be pushed to the ground. 'I'm...I'm so scared. I was told...in the town on the river...they said I could come here for help. That you would help me!'

'We help those faithful to Toriaken and the Iron Crown.' She smoothed her robes. 'You are beyond help, lost one.'

He wailed, a noise so raw that Apollo couldn't bear to hear it. The man slumped to the floor, his body jerking.

'Nadja. You should do something!'

'It's not my mission.'

'But he…is he dying?'

Nadja pressed her lips into a thin line and shook her head.

The man's fit overcame him, his body rigid as his limbs thrashed about. He let out a howl of anguish, hands clawing at his own face, nails drawing blood.

Apollo turned his horse and urged her over to him. But the chestnut mare got no further than five or six steps, before Nadja held him fast. He glared at the Inquisitor. 'What are you doing? We have to help!'

'No, Apollo.' Nadja backed her own horse up, pulling Apollo's with her.

He could see her lip tremble, her fingers shake where she held the reins. Did she want to help? 'I know you have orders, but this is a man's life! What if he—'

'He is one of the lost souls. Torsten believes they are traitors to the crown.'

'Traitors?' Apollo couldn't believe it. He looked down. His wrists were bound but his feet were free. With considerable effort, he heaved himself to the side, swinging his leg up and over the horse's back, and tumbled to the ground. Letting out a groan, he got to his feet and sprinted across the courtyard —past all the people who stood and stared at the seizing man and did nothing—uncaring about Nadja's shouts to him.

Apollo skidded to a halt beside the man. His jerking movements had subsided, but blood ran down his cheeks, and his whole body trembled.

'So…cold…'

'It's okay, you'll be okay.' Apollo knelt down beside him, bound wrists on the man's shoulder, hoping he would feel reassured. 'A doctor will be here soon.'

Again, the man moaned and coughed. More blood trickled down one nostril.

'I'm Apollo. I'm here with you,' he said, trying to impart as much comfort as he could. 'What's your name? Where are your family?'

'I don't know! I don't know! It's all gone...I...I can't remember anything!' His words dissolved into unintelligible grunts. His skin was almost grey, with dark patches under his eyes as if he hadn't slept in some time.

Without his memories, the man was lost. Truly lost. He understood now why Nadja and the other Inquisitors were referring to them as lost souls. And he was dying. How was that possible?

'It's okay. You aren't alone.' Apollo didn't know what to do. He looked around at the faces gathered, expressions a mixture of shock and disgust.

Another tremble from the man. Another hacking cough.

Apollo tried to inject some humour into his words. 'Were you poisoned? You don't look too well, I'll be honest. Not after what you've done to your cheeks! Does anyone here have any glinoc paste?'

The crowd murmured in low conversation, but no-one rushed forward to aid him. No-one offered help. Not even the priestess.

'Apollo.' Nadja's voice cut through the conversation. She remained atop her piebald, her iron dagger clutched. 'You can't do anything for him.'

Apollo ignored her. Was this the work of the Myr? Was *he* responsible for this man's pain? Terror? 'He'll be fine! He needs to rest.'

But even as he said it, he knew it wasn't true. He'd seen many people die. From battle wounds, starvation, from disease. He knew the lad didn't have long left, but he refused to let him die scared and alone, when at a shrine of all places, he should receive care and compassion.

Nadja, to her credit, allowed Apollo to sit with the man as he died.

Once his breathing quickened, his death wasn't far behind. Nadja spoke with the priestess who'd lingered nearby, told her to have a burial mound raised by order of the queen.

Wordlessly, Apollo clambered back onto his horse. He didn't have the mental fortitude or the strength in his legs to run away. Not after what he'd just encountered. He was amazed that Nadja wasn't as heartless a creature as he'd first thought—she'd done that young man a kindness, and Apollo hoped he'd be able to find his way to the spirit world while in the shadow of Toriaken's Shrine.

Nadja told him again that if he'd lied about the key, that man's death was on his conscience.

Apollo didn't need her to tell him that.

He kept his head down and stayed quiet as they approached the river, where a boat waited.

Soon enough, he'd have to face the queen.

22

THE MEMORY

FENN

Fenn woke up several times throughout the night, afraid that if he fell into too deep a sleep, he'd end up at the edge of the spirit world and come face to face with the Myr. Every time he drifted off, he jerked awake again, unable to rid the sensation of cold insects crawling across his skin. Although he was quite certain it was his sleep-deprived mind playing tricks on him, he couldn't shake the feeling of something cold touching his flesh. By the time the sun rose the following morning, he was exhausted.

They were heading north today, across the deadlands and further into Porsenthia, Selys constantly pushing them to keep going.

Just the thought of it made him shudder in a way it hadn't before the previous evening.

Selys had assured him that the deadlands would be safe if they travelled through the day, but Fenn couldn't stop thinking about the woman from the previous night. Or had it been a Myrish creature?

Whatever it had been, he didn't want to go anywhere near the place.

Perhaps he was simply taking Selys's warning more seriously, but he wasn't sure.

Thankfully, his headache had subsided, and he was able to get himself washed and dressed in relative comfort, despite his growing sense of unease.

If Jisyel hadn't recovered, he doubted she and Calidra would be coming. But when he made his way downstairs, he found both of them already up and eating breakfast—a large plate of creamy mushrooms which smelled heavily of mustard, a chunk of seeded bread, and a bowl of sliced green fruit that he didn't recognise.

The two of them already had their packed bags under their table—able to head off at a moment's notice. Fenn shouldn't have been surprised. Calidra wanted to get to her sister as quickly as possible, and why shouldn't she? If *he* knew he had a sister, knew where she was, he'd probably have travelled all day and night to reach her.

Calidra was chasing answers just as much as he was.

Already, half a dozen patrons were dotted around the tables, eating quietly and talking in low voices. He paid them no mind and approached Calidra and Jisyel's table, stifling a yawn.

'Fenn. You're up early.' Calidra nodded at him, both hands wrapped around a large mug of steaming coffee.

'Have you seen Selys or Varlot?'

Calidra shook her head. 'Haven't seen Varlot since last night. Maybe he's at the shrine?'

'He...went to the *shrine*?' Had he misheard?

Jisyel nodded, her cheeks reddening as she ate another mouthful of breakfast.

'And spent the whole night there?'

'It's possible.' Calidra took another sip from her mug.

He sat down at their table and peered at their food. It was unappetising, especially as his stomach had been in knots all night. 'How're you feeling Jisyel?'

'Much better. Foot aches a bit, but I can walk on it now without hobbling!' Jisyel smiled at him through a mouthful of mushrooms. 'That medicine worked wonders. Thanks again for getting it for me.'

If Jisyel was eating, she was definitely on the mend. But Calidra's words about Varlot being at the shrine worried him.

Alnothen had *warned* Varlot he wasn't welcome—the man was going to get himself hurt or worse. And Fenn needed him. What was Varlot *thinking* going to the dragon's shrine?

Fenn wondered if it had anything to do with Alnothen's accusations.

He sighed. He'd been patient ever since Calidra and Jisyel had brought him to Bragalia. He'd begged for help, pleaded not to be left to fend for himself. Selys was helping her spirit more than him, he knew that, but the priestess might also be able to lead him to answers. Varlot was the only one who seemed to be there for *him*. Who wanted to make sure he was okay, and recovered his memories.

So why was Varlot doing something stupid like going directly to Alnothen and putting that journey in peril?

Fenn would have left the area as quickly as he could, if the roles were reversed. Yes, he was curious, but even he understood a clear warning when he saw one.

He glanced at the door, considered going into the woods himself to find Varlot. Then again, he probably *shouldn't* race off without Selys. If she came in to find him gone again, she'd likely pin him to the ground with her glaive. Although he wanted to laugh at the image, he was too worried about Varlot to even let a smile grow on his lips.

'I hope you aren't thinking about running off again,' Calidra warned.

He tried to push his face into the epitome of innocence. 'What? Why would you think that?'

'We could've done with you last night. Where did you go off to, anyway? I was looking for you for ages.'

Fenn wasn't sure what was wrong with having some time by himself for once. Plus, Varlot had essentially given him permission to go. 'Just exploring the town.'

'Fenn. It isn't safe for you to be wandering around.'

He shrugged. 'Why not? There's no-one here. No Inquisitors.'

'But we're in Porsenthia now,' Jisyel said gently, 'there's more risk of you being spotted by an Inquisitor. We're in the seat of the Iron Crown's power. There are more of them here than in Bragalia.'

Fenn frowned, frustrated. He wasn't a prisoner. He wasn't doing anything wrong. 'I'm *fine*. What did you need me for, anyway? I didn't think there was much I could do to help, the state you were in, Jisyel.'

'Yes but what if an Inquisitor had strolled into town and arrested you? None of us would have known,' Calidra said.

Fenn huffed, his frustration rising. 'I'm not a child, Calidra! I know I'm Myr-touched. None of you let me forget it. Is it so bad for me to look around when we had a few hours to spare? What if there was someone here who knew me? I might've found a friend or relative?'

'And how likely is that? Everywhere you've been has been new.'

Before he could retort, Selys opened the inn door with a bang and walked inside, every step creaking on the wooden floor. 'Good morning,' she greeted, joining them. 'Everything's packed and ready to go, save your personal effects. Glad to see you're looking better, Jisyel.'

'The apothecary had decent medicine.'

Selys nodded. 'Good. And not a moment too soon. We ought to get going as soon as you've finished. Come on, eat up, eat up.'

Fenn turned to her. 'Is something wrong?'

'Alnothen is...unhappy.'

'Yeah, I guessed that when we got here. But why rush off now? Varlot isn't even—'

'Varlot is the one causing her...irritability. Alnothen is kind, with patience beyond most spirits. But trust me when I say we shouldn't outstay our welcome.' The priestess's gaze lingered on the doorway, as if she expected something terrible to follow in behind her at any second.

'If Varlot is the one causing it, shouldn't we wait for him?' Fenn asked, unwilling to race off again after he'd worked so hard to regain Varlot's trust. It felt like their group was constantly on the verge of splitting up, which made him uncomfortable. He didn't care for raised voices, high emotions. It reminded him of being helpless—like he'd been in the bog on the island; against the Myrish spirit in Ballowtown; against Inquisitors and others afraid of lost souls— afraid of people like him. 'We should all leave at the same time, shouldn't we? We got here together, we should go together.'

'I have no doubt Alnothen's fury will lessen when he's gone. But while she's angry, we should make ourselves scarce. And we'll want to make good time across the deadlands.'

At the mention of their destination, Fenn's stomach turned. He'd been curious about the Myr, desperate to learn more. Now? Now, he was just as afraid of them as everyone else. And he couldn't shake that feeling of ice growing across his skin.

Had it just been from seeing that woman the previous night?

Fenn shook the worry away and lifted his chin. He had to take a stand. 'I don't want to go without him.'

Selys raised an eyebrow. 'Fenn, you don't know what the wrath of a spirit is like. It's not something you want to experience. Not as bad as corrupted spirits, mind, but their anger is as terrifying as it gets.'

Fenn shook his head. 'I *do* know what it's like to be alone, though. To have people think the worst of you. I'm *not* going without him.' He refused to budge on this, and ignored Calidra's stare—though he thought it was one of incredulity rather than annoyance.

Selys held his gaze for a moment. 'Fenn, I want peace as much as you do. But I'm ready to leave. We need to reach the Nethal Mountains as soon as we can. We *have* to find out what we can about what the Myr are doing. Only you can help me with that, and we've already realised you're short on time. We need to leave, now. Even Jisyel is ready to go.'

'I'm not going without Varlot. I barely managed to convince him to come with us in the first place!'

Selys sighed, more in frustration than resignation. 'What you might find out in the mountains, Fenn, is greater than one man, or one friendship. We're talking about the *Myr*. About all of Tassar. *That* is more important than anything else. The dragons are the Guardians of Tassar, spirits of life, of guidance and protection. Without them, we are *nothing*.'

Fenn understood what she was saying. Knew that if the worst happened, he'd not only lose his own life—a looming threat that he'd done his best to ignore thus far—but the Iron Crown would lose vital knowledge that could protect them against the Myrish resurgence. 'Give me an hour. Please.'

The priestess huffed and pulled out her glaive, inspecting it. With a quick movement, she smacked the flat of the shaft across his shoulder. 'Fine. But no longer. If I have to push you the whole way there with this blade, I will.'

He yelped in surprise. Clutching his shoulder—it only stung a little—Fenn nodded. 'I'll get my things.'

He stood up and headed back upstairs. After re-securing his pack as soon as he reached his room, he stared out the window, at the strange bark on the trees and the lush foliage that surrounded the inn.

Varlot. What was he *doing*?

Fenn couldn't leave it. He had to do *something*. Hurrying downstairs again, he raced through the tavern on the ground floor, and out the main door before anyone could stop him.

Cool and fresh, the morning air was a welcome relief, and the large canopy above only let in thin streaks of sunlight. The shrine shouldn't be too hard to find. He cast his gaze around—there were more people up and about now than there had been yesterday afternoon or evening. Most came from a deeper part of the woodland, where there were fewer buildings. Many were farmers or gardeners who wore long, knee-high boots and carried baskets of fruit and vegetables under their arms.

Fenn was about to head off, when one man stood out among the crowd of people. 'Varlot!'

The former general glanced up at the sound of his name being called. His eyes were red, his skin sunken around his cheekbones. 'Fenn? That you, lad?' His voice was rough.

'Varlot! Were you at the shrine all night?'

'What makes you say that?' Varlot approached him slowly, a stiffness in his limbs that hadn't been there before. He didn't look Fenn in the eye.

'Calidra said you'd been there. Selys wants to head off. But we can wait an hour if you haven't had time to rest?'

Varlot shrugged, and a small tuft of brown fur fluttered away from the edges of his cloak. 'Been up three days without sleep before. This ain't a problem for me.'

'But...you *do* need to sleep?'

'Don't worry about it. I didn't sleep last night, so I'll sleep another night instead.' His tone was sharper than usual.

'If you're sure?'

Varlot rummaged around in a bag slung over one

shoulder and pulled out a short sword sheathed in leather. 'Got this for you. Might have to use it, places we're going.'

Fenn caught the weapon in both hands as Varlot threw it towards him, and stared at it in wonder. 'For me?'

Varlot grunted in reply. 'Told you I'd teach you how to swing a sword.'

It took Fenn a moment to remember his voice. 'T—Thank you!'

'Ah. There you are.' Calidra said from the entrance to the inn. She looked Varlot up and down once, her expression dark. Her gaze flicked to Fenn, and to the sword in his hands, but she said nothing.

Fenn was relieved at that, though he could have sworn she took a breath as if she *was* going to say something.

'Heard Selys wants to get going? Deadlands'll be horrible to cross, but I guess it's the quickest way up through Porsenthia.' Varlot said, some of his old strength returning to his voice, though he still sounded annoyed. 'You don't wanna bump into whatever the Myr left behind at night.'

Calidra pursed her lips. 'No. Good thing we have you and Selys with us.'

Fenn let out a sigh. He didn't know what Varlot had done all night, but from the sounds of things, they'd have a long day of walking ahead of them. He could ask his questions then.

ALTHOUGH FENN HAD ALREADY SEEN the deadlands, they were astonishingly different in daylight than they had been the night before. Under the cover of darkness, the place had seemed quiet, magical. Like someone deep asleep, their breaths the only movement.

Under the harsh sun, however, it was intimidating. And

now he was at the edge, about to step out onto it, a significant portion of his courage left him.

Fenn hadn't realised—perhaps he'd not *seen* it—but a fine, shadowy mist clung to the cracked ground like dew clung to grass. The shadow had grown thicker the closer they travelled to the edge of the trees, and with it, a deep sense of foreboding. He was amazed he'd not seen it the previous night, but he supposed shadows were impossible to see in the dark.

Selys didn't comment, so he didn't mention what he could see, just in case it pushed everyone over the edge from tension into outright panic. Besides, the priestess was already frustrated with him, and he didn't want to irritate her any further.

They were silent as they left the shelter of the trees and walked out onto the arid landscape, as if collectively holding their breaths. The hard ground crunched underfoot, his presence agitating the shadowy mist. It felt paper-thin, as if his foot could go through it at any moment—swallowed up by an enormous hole.

A shiver ran up his leg, but the ground held.

Letting out a breath, he crept forward, several paces behind Selys and the others. With every hesitant step, his sense of dread grew, and the eerie fog thickened. His heart pounded and he clutched his chest, trying to stay in control of his breathing. It felt like a small fire burned there, and it was now fluttering in panic. More shadows flickered in and out of his vision, disappearing as soon as they appeared. They reminded him of the echoes from his dream.

The sensation of ice on his fingertips grew.

'Fenn. Keep up!' Calidra called, already some distance ahead.

He'd been standing in one spot for longer than he'd realised.

Goosebumps rose along the flesh of his arms despite the

warmth of the morning, and he exhaled slowly. The dry, cracked ground was pale under the intense sun, reflecting light and sending rays of it bouncing through the mist. There were no rocks or trees to offer shade, or to break up the landscape, and he felt more vulnerable even than when he'd been stuck in Hassen's muddy bog.

They were still within sight of the trees. He hoped Alnothen would be calm now they'd left, but there was no sign of the enormous forest spirit, so he turned away and continued onwards.

Calidra and Jisyel both seemed off. It took him the best part of an hour to put his finger on why—Jisyel was subdued. Instead of bouncing along and chattering away happily, she was withdrawn.

Something had to have happened that night at the shrine with Varlot. The former general, too, was quieter than usual. That, Fenn had put down to lack of sleep. But now he wondered whether something more impactful had happened while he was staring out at the deadlands.

'You could have stayed, you know,' Calidra said to Jisyel.

'What, and let Fenn and Selys head off? What if they bump into Inquisitors?' Jisyel replied.

On hearing his name, Fenn hurried to catch up with them.

'You know what I mean.' Calidra's tone was sharp.

Jisyel said nothing for a while, not meeting Calidra's hard stare. 'Do you regret leaving?'

'Do *you*?'

'I don't know. It...it didn't feel right to stay. With Alnothen so...upset.'

'Fenn, watch your step!' Calidra snapped.

Fenn had been so keen to hear their conversation that he almost missed the crack across the ground. He caught his foot on the lip, stumbled across it, but regained his balance before he toppled over.

Calidra kept her gaze on him while he righted himself, and Fenn felt his ears reddening in embarrassment. She'd obviously seen him trying to listen in.

He slowed his pace, letting the two of them get a bit of distance, before continuing on.

Selys led them through the deadlands with a surefooted-ness that kept Fenn from freezing up in fear. There was something so *visceral* about this place, something so ancient and deadly, that it was an effort not to race away in blind terror. Whether that was an after-effect of seeing the Myrish creature, or this place simply had that effect on people, he didn't know. No-one said anything as they walked—even Jisyel was as tight-lipped as Calidra, her usual joyous nature subdued.

His new sword bumped against his thigh, the movement uncomfortable, but he had nowhere else to attach it other than at his belt. Feeling its weight made everything more real, every imagined danger more intense.

Once or twice, he saw more of the humanoid shadows burst across his vision, only to disappear again a moment later. Were they echoes? Were they his mind playing tricks on him? 'No-one else is here, are they?' Fenn called out, the mist swallowing up his voice.

'No.' Selys didn't look back, but she grabbed her glaive and held it ahead of her. 'Did you see something?'

Fenn gulped, wondering if his association with the Myr was the cause of his visions. He'd not seen a death spirit—he was sure of that—just echoes of people. Somewhere behind him, Varlot drew his axe, the noise setting his teeth on edge.

'We shouldn't be here.' Varlot grunted, quickening his pace to walk beside Fenn.

'It's dangerous?'

'Bad luck is what it is. You *don't* visit battle sites. Too much death.'

Fenn could deal with bad luck. He wasn't sure he could

deal with the Myr. He knew he should expect contact with them—after all, he was walking straight towards one of their constructs—but where before he had been excited at the prospect of learning more, at finally discovering answers, he was now afraid.

He dug his fingers into his chest, distracting himself from the pain of it.

Selys and Jisyel had said dragon spirits were created wherever there was an abundance of life energy. Forests. Mountains. Lakes. But a battlefield was the opposite—it was a site of death.

He wondered whether that was why the place felt so ominous? Because it was so far removed from everything the dragons spirits were: life. The Myr themselves had sucked all life from the area—there wasn't a single plant, grass, or weed in sight for leagues around them.

'And there's no Iron Dragon to fight with us, this time.' Bitterness laced Varlot's voice.

'We don't need Toriaken. We have you!' Fenn grinned, doing his best to be reassuring through his discomfort. 'And me, too. It's good to not be completely defenseless now,' he said, his sword an awkward weight at his hip. He'd yet to use it and he hoped he wouldn't have to.

Varlot smiled and shook his head. 'You're a good lad, Fenn. Whatever you find out about yourself, I hope you know that.' He put his hand on Fenn's shoulder and squeezed gently, genuine warmth in his smile.

The moment Varlot touched him, Fenn's vision flared into life. All at once, the half-seen shadows rushed into full focus—living, breathing people wearing armour from head to toe. Most brandished swords or axes, but there was a line of men on horses holding lances at the farthest edge of the deadlands. Hundreds of them. No. *Thousands*.

Mouths were open in a wordless scream, lips moved to portray instructions, but Fenn couldn't hear a thing.

Suddenly, they were moving, a flagbearer waving his standard high and proud—The Iron Crown. It was the same insignia on the Inquisitors' uniforms, and on the back of the gold coins Fenn had seen before.

Dust and grass were thrown up underfoot as the waves of soldiers charged ahead, fury etched in every line on every face. Above them, the sky was a white mist which coalesced into black arrows. Countless lethal blades fell, and terror rained down.

Fenn shivered, watching, waiting. The Myr—for they could be nothing else—appeared on the edges of the deadlands, the first of their number falling to the arrows raining down upon them. They were a solid wave of cold shadow on the horizon. Grass wilted at their every step, lightning crackled, announcing their advance with flashes of blue and white.

Fenn's fingers twitched with the remembered touch of ice.

They bore no weapons, wore no armour, no clothes, no boots. They had no flags, no horns announcing their arrival. They moved as one—a single entity made up of a thousand, thousand parts. Every golden eye was fixed upon the waves of Porsenthian and Bragalian soldiers.

'Fenn? Speak to me!' Varlot shouted in his ear.

He'd collapsed, the hard ground digging into his back. His chest burned so much it was difficult to breathe. Fenn coughed, blinking as the vision faded. Only Varlot, Selys, Calidra, and Jisyel were there.

There was no army. There were no Myr.

Varlot offered him a hand up.

Fenn took it, grateful, only to be thrust back into the centre of the vision. Images flared outwards, bright and vibrant, their colours blurring together as if he was looking at them through water. It was later in the battle, now. The Myr had made their advance, and everything was chaos and motion. Fenn was glad he couldn't hear them, couldn't *feel* them. Blood coated the ground in deepening puddles, rivulets of crimson saturating what was left of the grass. Fire raged across the battlefield, gorging itself on the fallen.

One of the Myr approached Fenn—no, a man to Fenn's left—its gaping jaws open wide, revealing circular rows of teeth flashing in the fires. It shuddered, clawed hands outstretched, and the man dropped to the ground like a sack.

Fenn could *see* the lines of magic pouring from the Myr's fingers like a burst water pipe. It crawled over the Porsenthian armour, piercing flesh through the cracks, driving the life from his body. It was happening all across the field. People dropped to the ground, armour ineffective against the Myrish magic.

And beyond the waves of Myr were their spirits. Hulking monstrosities swarmed the battlefield, appendages bursting from their bodies to ensnare any who were unfortunate enough to be close to them. A man was decapitated. A woman was disemboweled. Blood rained down in an eternal deluge.

He trembled.

Another wave of Posenthians charged forward, their sheer numbers overwhelming the Myr. Blades were driven into flesh. Magic, once so effective, vanished as the Myr died. They pushed the Myr back in a surge of power, only for one of their number to eventually fall. Throwing themselves into the gap, the Myr and their spirits fought back, driving their aggressors away—splitting them up and picking off the isolated fighters.

More arrows rained down, bringing death by the hundreds.

Fenn wasn't sure he was breathing anymore.

Then, a darkness so complete Fenn thought he'd lost his sight, encompassed everything.

Fire blasted down in a column larger than any tree in the Spindle Woods, blindingly bright. He closed his eyes, but his vision had whited out.

If he'd been there, he was sure he'd have heard the dragon's roar. Felt the heat of the spirit as it grew near.

Seconds dragged past. He squinted, then gaped, at the sight of the dragon. Toriaken, Spirit of Iron, had arrived at the battle on wings so massive that Fenn couldn't see where they ended. Every scale was solid grey, dull, save where his flames made them glow orange and red.

Toriaken was too high up for Fenn to make out any details of the dragon's eyes or face, but his presence alone had changed the atmosphere of the battle. His fire did the rest.

The Myr didn't burn so much as *explode* in Toriaken's breath. Chunks of smoking flesh scattered, blasted out after impact. Many of their appendages were bladed and sharp, impaling those unlucky enough to be within the path of their death. Their spirits died in much the same way, every limb torn apart and disintegrated in the dragon's fire. Black smoke rose from the charred corpses, filling the sky with ash and blotting out the raging fires.

'Fenn!' Calidra grabbed him by the shoulders, steadying him as he swayed. 'Fenn, can you hear me? Say something!'

Dimly, he was aware of a thin line of drool trickling down his chin. Hurriedly, he wiped his face with the back of one sleeve and coughed again. 'Calidra?' She drifted in and out of focus, everything else outside his immediate view was dark.

'I'm here. Spirits take me, I don't know what's going on with you, but we have to get out of here.'

He tried to nod, but his headache surged back into life with such fury that he nearly blacked out. There was ice on his fingers again, slowly creeping up his forearms. Again, his chest tightened, a ball of fire driving the ice back.

'Do not lose focus.'

382

He blinked at the voice in his mind. He hadn't heard it before. It wasn't the Myr.

Had Varlot said something, and he'd just been too confused to understand it?

Calidra shook him roughly. 'Fenn. Come on. I don't want Varlot to carry you. Both times you've collapsed after he touched you. Spirits only know what's going on.'

Fenn leaned on her and took a shaky step forward. Thankfully, no more visions of battle accosted him. He could hardly believe the sky was still there, so vast were Toriaken's wings. It put Alnothen to shame, and that had only been a vision.

No. A memory.

He glanced at Varlot, who followed a few steps behind Calidra.

'Varlot? You were...is this where...where the Battle of Marlrush was fought?' Fenn's voice trembled.

'It was.'

'I saw it. I saw the Myr. Toriaken. All the people who fought...'

'How is that possible?' Calidra asked, not breaking stride as they continued across the dry lands. She dragged him more than led him, but he didn't care.

Selys paused, looking around intensely. 'I feel the remnants of the Myr here. Their magic is so strong. It's kind of...lingering.'

'So the people in Spindleford *were* telling the truth?' Calidra said, 'I thought it was just superstitious nonsense.'

Jisyel clamped one hand over her mouth. 'But...but the Myr aren't here now, are they?'

Selys turned to Fenn, as if he had the answers. 'I don't understand your...bond with the Myr. Whatever connection you have with them goes beyond a superficial level. The sooner we reach the Nethal Mountains, the better.'

'Keep going, lad. Come on. You're stronger than you think.' Varlot patted him on the back as he walked past.

Abruptly, Fenn was thrown back into the chaos.

The battle was over, dead bodies piled up in a smoking ruin. Torn flags and broken shields littered what was left of the grass—most of which had dried and withered, if it wasn't already drowned in crimson.

Varlot—or a younger version of Varlot, his face streaked with blood—knelt beside a heavily bandaged man. Blood seeped through the linen across his abdomen, viscera spilling out. He was missing both eyes, his face torn wide open by monstrous claws, leaving little more than gore from his nose down. His teeth seemed too bright against the red. Varlot clutched his hand. His lips moved, but Fenn couldn't hear. This, like the other visions, was absolutely silent.

Many living were doing the same—speaking to those dead or dying, clearing away the ruined corpses, setting up a perimeter in case their enemy returned. On the far side of the battleground, Toriaken had landed. His bulk was that of a mountain, and hundreds of armoured men and women had gathered by his feet, tiny against the dragon spirit.

But Fenn's gaze was drawn back to Varlot. The man whose hand he held had passed away, his fingers going limp. Fenn's heart ached for another loss.

Someone approached, the movement attracting Fenn's attention as Varlot turned his head to look.

There was no mistaking the man's face. Even without the uniform, and dressed in the same armour as Varlot, Fenn recognised Torsten.

Suddenly angry he couldn't hear, Fenn watched as the two men exchanged words. Varlot got up from his knees to look Torsten in the face. From their body language, it was clear they were having some sort of dispute. Torsten pointed with his index finger towards Toriaken and the battle site.

Varlot gestured to the dead man on the ground below him. His hands were covered in gore.

More gesticulating.

More anger.

Varlot removed his helm and drew his weapon—the same axe he wielded now, with a snarling bear carved into the handle. Fenn didn't remember seeing that before.

Fenn expected Torsten to retaliate. To draw his rusty blade and aim it at Varlot, burn him where he stood. But he didn't. He leaned backwards, a smirk plastered on his face. He said something under his breath, his lips barely moving, and Varlot stopped in his tracks.

Varlot's shoulders slackened and the axe fell from his fingers. A defeated man. A broken one.

Fenn shuddered back to consciousness. It appeared that only seconds had passed—no-one was staring at him or trying to rouse him. Varlot walked ahead, now, his axe clutched tightly. The handle was different to the one Fenn had seen in his vision. Instead of dark brown, the bear carved into it, the handle was flat, black, and unadorned.

'Come on, lad. You ain't dead yet.' Varlot called over his shoulder.

Fenn wondered how much death Varlot had seen and caused.

He wondered what Torsten had said on the battlefield.

And as the final images of the vision faded into dark mist, Fenn wondered how much time he had left.

23

THE DECISION

CALIDRA

I t had taken them a day to cross the deadlands, and
another half day to reach Tonmouth, a large town on
the edge of the Salt Sea. The night they'd spent in the
deadlands, in the shadow of Marlrush Fortress, was one that
would haunt Calidra, it had been so eerie. Combined with
Fenn collapsing—and the realisation he was experiencing
memories of the battle through visions—she couldn't get out
of that place quickly enough. Now they were in Tonmouth,
she realised how easy it would be to get a boat from here and
just sail south, straight back to the Isle of Salt. Straight back
to Bellandri and her inn. Where it was safe.

Where there were no Myr—real or in memories.

After all, she'd done her duty and returned home for the
funeral. Her mother didn't want help running the canton.
And if Jisyel wanted to go back home, she'd let her of course.
She half-expected her to board the next boat south. Bellandri
would be expecting them back by now, anyway.

But *she* couldn't. Not just yet.

Even though Jisyel and Bellandri were her family, she had
to find her sister. Someone she'd believed dead…It had been
close to a decade since she'd last seen her. They'd been close

as young children, but Malora's blessing by Chyram had thrown everything out the window. The gold Malora had been able to create had elevated their family from simple groundskeepers to Lairds of the canton—able to buy their way in by hiring more and more mercenaries to join their cause.

Malora had always been the favoured child. More obedient than Calidra, she'd had a stronger relationship with Furyn. And because she'd created the family wealth, been responsible for every bastion of power they had, Furyn had allowed her to get away with far more.

Including dating a thief.

Worse—a *Porsenthian*.

Calidra had been furious when her mother had permitted it. She'd fought Malora over her stupid choices, over everything. All the falseness. They'd ended up arguing even more than she'd argued with her mother. Calidra had screamed at Malora to leave, if she loved that thief so much. If she was so sure he was right for her.

And Malora had left to "throw her life away," as Furyn had claimed.

Calidra never saw her again.

Furyn had confirmed she'd received word of Malora's death some time later.

If Quillaja hadn't said anything when Calidra had returned home, she'd still be none the wiser. And the fact that Malora *hadn't* returned to Fellwood proved she was no longer under their mother's thumb. That alone made Calidra even more excited to reunite with her sister and make amends. They were finally free. Both of them.

She looked at Jisyel, wondering if *she* was going to return to Alnothen. Removing the curse was something Jisyel was desperate for. Calidra wondered if she'd been selfish by asking Jisyel not to take up the spirit's offer. They'd spoken about it briefly in the deadlands, but everything had been so chaotic that they hadn't had time to address it again. She knew they couldn't tiptoe around the subject forever. 'Have you considered going back home?'

Jisyel glanced up. 'Of course I've considered it. But I'm coming with you, you know. I wasn't there when you saw your mother again. I *will* be there when you see your sister. Besides, I want to meet her!'

Calidra hadn't realised she'd been so tense until she let out a breath of relief. 'I'll...get a bird sent back to Bellandri then?'

'Definitely! Can't have gran worrying!'

'I can't wait to sit down.' Fenn yawned, stretching both arms above his head and attracting her attention. He had dark circles under his eyes. His skin was paler, his face more gaunt. He'd been yawning a lot, and his movements were more sluggish than before.

He was beginning to look ill.

She didn't know if that was due to his experience in the deadlands or simply how long it had been since the Myr had touched him. His trembling certainly hadn't improved. And when he'd come back to them after his vision, lines of terror had been carved onto his face.

The lad was dying, just like the little elthian had been.

Calidra would be terrified if she was in his position. It was impressive how hopeful Fenn remained throughout his ordeal. He took a lot of strength from Selys, and even more from Varlot, and that friendship seemed to be enough for him.

Perhaps that's what happened when you no longer had memories. No guilty past weighing you down. He had flickers of frustration that showed through, and that was to be expected. But he was a good man. Jisyel always had an eye for good people, too, and she'd taken to Fenn from the first moment they'd spotted him. He'd stayed to help Jisyel, had done what he could for them. Pulled his weight.

He could easily have cut them off and travelled alone. It had put him in a good light, and to see him so shaken was unnerving. 'You look like you could do with a few days' sleep, Fenn.'

'No time for that, Calidra. There's some way to go, yet. I'm just glad we're in the right country, now,' Selys said. The priestess hadn't needed to use her glaive during their journey, which had been a relief. If anything, she'd been more likely to turn it upon Varlot than on any bandits or Myrish spirits. 'Wait here while I check out the town.' She had a habit of scouting ahead and making sure their route was safe. She'd said she was responsible for them, being the one who'd suggested heading north.

Dust from the deadlands caked their clothing, and Calidra wanted to get rid of its stink. It was dirty. Tainted.

Calidra herself had a choice on how to proceed. Tonmouth had a large port, with ships sailing up and down the Porsenthian coast. Larger vessels would sail around the northern coast, through the Polar Sea, before docking in Foxmouth. Although the distance was much greater, it would be faster than travelling on foot.

But travelling on water did *not* appeal.

Selys and Fenn would be taking that ship, getting off near Nethal, right on the doorstep of the old battle site. While the site wasn't as large or formidable as the deadlands, there was a good deal of superstition about the place. After seeing Fenn overcome by visions in the deadlands, she wasn't sure it would be a good idea for him to go there.

But what else was he to do?

Try to get himself comfortable while he waited for death?

She'd grown fond of him during their journey, and she knew Jisyel considered him a friend. If Calidra was honest with herself, she didn't want to see any harm befall him.

After Fenn's last collapse, Varlot had kept his distance, the former general trailing behind the group, more sullen than usual.

'It has to be something to do with the fact that Varlot has been here before, fought the Myr here. There's a connection between his experiences, the Myrish magic, and Fenn. It's as if they've left a marker in the soil of what transpired, and only Fenn knows the language to read it,' Selys had explained after suggesting Varlot stop grabbing Fenn by the arm or shoulder. 'Physical touch must be what triggers it.' It meant that she, Calidra, or Jisyel had to help Fenn whenever he stumbled—which he'd been more prone to after drifting in and out of consciousness so often.

'Was it intentional?' Varlot had asked, concerned. 'What the Myr did to Fenn and the others? Some way of getting back to Porsenthia? Attacking us when we thought the threat was over?'

'Who knows. I don't claim to understand the Myr or their intentions,' Selys had replied.

'If the lost souls can see Myrish magic, read the Myrish language, as you say, ain't that something we should be worried about?'

No-one knew. But whether it was intentional or a side-effect of whatever the Myr had done, Calidra hadn't been sure Fenn would even make it *out* of the deadlands. Credit to him, he persevered, mostly without complaint. He had a steely determination that hadn't been present before— certainly not that she'd seen on the island or in Ballowtown.

The moment they left the deadlands, the colour returned to his cheeks. But he looked far worse now than he had even when she'd discovered him at the bog on the Isle of Salt. She glanced over at Jisyel, who had made her way to the large yew trees that grew outside Tonmouth, standing in the shade of their needle-like leaves.

Tonmouth was set high, with sheer cliffs dropping down into the Salt Sea below. Calidra turned her face to the breeze, savouring it. If she closed her eyes, she could imagine herself back on the island. A place where she only had Hassen's tricks to deal with, rather than Myrish spirits combing the land. Where things had been simpler.

Where her *real* family was.

She joined Jisyel under the tree.

'Glad we're out of that awful place,' Jisyel said as Calidra sat down next to her. 'Poor Fenn. He looks as bad as I did when I was poisoned.'

'He does. Except there's no antidote for him. What if Selys is wrong?'

Jisyel's gaze dropped. 'Don't say that.'

Calidra obliged, but it didn't stop her thinking about it. Their shadows lengthened as minutes dragged past and the sun began to set.

Fenn had been utterly reliant on them since they'd found him. Now, he was putting his faith in Selys. And even then, Selys was travelling on a guess. Assumptions usually ended up with things going wrong, but there wasn no-one else he could turn to.

Calidra had tried to tell herself that she only cared about Jisyel and finding her sister. But if she was honest, she had to admit that she cared about Fenn's plight, too.

'Inquisitors in town.' Selys made her way back to them.

At the priestess's words, Fenn joined them in the shade. Varlot, too, headed over to them.

'Doesn't your word count for anything here?' Fenn asked.

'It does. But I don't want to take any chances. The lost souls have spread to Porsenthia. The town guard is rounding up anyone they deem suspicious for questioning.'

'Just like in Vaelar?' Fenn asked.

Selys nodded. 'Yes.'

'This is Torsten's hometown. Likely the Inquisitors stationed here were hand-picked by him,' Varlot added.

Sweat rolled down his forehead and he sat on the grass with a heavy grunt. 'You best watch yourself, lad.'

'Can't we skirt round them? Go to another town?' Fenn asked.

'We'll take a ship the rest of the way.' Selys turned her gaze to the Salt Sea beyond the edge of the cliff. 'We shouldn't bump into any Inquisitors there. And it *is* the quickest way to Nethal.'

Fenn absorbed the information with a short nod, then he turned to Calidra and Jisyel. 'Do we...do we say goodbye here, then?'

'Goodbye? What for?' Jisyel asked, eyebrows furrowing.

Fenn blinked. 'Calidra—you hate water, right? You aren't going on the ship, too?'

Calidra frowned. He was quicker off the mark than she gave him credit for, despite how unwell he was. She couldn't be angry with him for pointing out her weakness, though. Her fear of water was what started so much of this mess— she wouldn't have needed as much convincing to return to Bragalia if she'd not been so afraid of that damned crossing. 'Well, we haven't decided yet.'

'Wait a minute,' Selys interrupted. She stared back at the town wall—a block of stone that roughly encircled Tonmouth. 'Varlot. You said Torsten was born here?'

'Aye.'

'Interesting...'

'What is?' Calidra asked, wondering what in all of Tassar could be interesting about the Master Inquisitor and where he had been born.

'I never realised his loyalties could be torn. It explains some of his more brash behaviour,' Selys muttered, pacing, one finger thoughtfully scratching her chin.

'What are you talking about, woman?' Varlot snapped.

'He has a sword, doesn't he?'

'All officers of the Porsenthian army have weapons.' Varlot brandished his own axe. 'This is mine.'

'No, no. I mean…a personal sword?'

Varlot tilted his head back as he thought.

'He has a rusty sword, doesn't he?' Fenn added, voice raised in excitement. 'I mean, I remember seeing a patch of rust on it.'

'It threw fire out the tip, back in Ballowtown,' Jisyel said.

Varlot shrugged. 'All Inquisitors work for Queen Surayo. She's bonded to Toriaken. They use iron artefacts to use Toriaken's power, too.'

Selys shook her head. 'Ah, but was that the iron dagger that Torsten used to throw fire? Or was it his personal sword?'

'I don't understand what you're getting at.'

The priestess grinned. 'There's a spirit here, quite a young one, of a lake just north of this town. Miroth, is his name.'

Calidra connected the dots. 'You mean…Torsten might be blessed by that spirit?'

'Surely someone would have noticed that by now?' Jisyel said.

'Yes. Or they mistook every act of spiritual power as Toriaken instead. After all, Inquisitors are known for that fire trick,' Selys said. She'd stopped pacing. 'If Torsten is bonded not to Toriaken, but to *Miroth*…His motives could be different to Queen Surayo and the other Inquisitors.'

'You mean, he's doing his own thing? And not for the crown?' Jisyel asked.

Selys nodded. 'Miroth, and many other young, weak spirits, are often overlooked. It's rare to notice their power unless you follow an order, like I follow Neros. Or perhaps are blessed yourself, and even then, you need to be looking for it.'

Jisyel picked away some of the tree's needles from her

cloak. 'Does it really matter who Torsten follows? We don't want to bump into him *anywhere*.'

'If he is actually a priest of Miroth, he should be watched more carefully than before. He might not act as the Iron Crown does. Or as it commands,' Selys said.

Calidra shrugged. Better to be far away from Torsten than watching him closely. 'Torsten isn't in town, is he?'

'I don't know. I only gave the gates a cursory glance and saw Inquisitor uniforms.'

'He'll be back at the palace by now, I expect.' Varlot leaned back on his elbows, a strand of grass between his lips. 'I wouldn't worry, Fenn. You got this far okay.'

Selys sighed. 'This area is quiet enough. Why don't you set up camp here, have something to eat and save the coin we have left. I will go and visit Miroth's Shrine.'

Calidra saw Jisyel stare at Selys. Did she want to ask Miroth about her curse, too? 'Jisyel?'

'Hmm?'

'I want to check the ship schedules.' Calidra got to her feet. 'Then we don't need to worry about running into Inquisitors in town or Torsten being tipped off to Fenn being here.'

'Wait!' Jisyel leapt to her feet and wrapped her arms around Calidra's shoulders. 'Be quick, okay? I'm starving!' She kissed Calidra on the cheek before letting go.

'You can cook, you know. It's not that hard to boil water and fry some vegetables.'

'I know, but when you make it, it tastes so much better!'

Calidra rolled her eyes at Jisyel's giggle, then headed up the path behind Selys, one hand already in her pocket for her own papers to show the guards at the gate. She'd given Jisyel the opportunity to speak about Miroth or talking to the spirit, but she hadn't mentioned it at all. It was a relief.

She glanced back once, seeing Fenn and Varlot in conversation in the shade of the tree. She'd been wrong about both of them. Fenn hadn't been a threat. And whatever killing Varlot had done in the past, he'd protected them ever since joining. It was clear he was still badly affected by what he'd done.

She chewed her lip as Selys reached the gate a few steps before she did.

'Priestess? I've never seen a priestess dressed like that.' Only one gatekeeper was on duty—a stocky woman with a frown so severe Calidra wasn't sure she was capable of any other expression.

Selys wasn't bothered by her brusque manner. 'Easier to travel like this.'

'Travelling late, aren't you?' The gatekeeper scrutinised Calidra's paper with the same intensity as she scrutinised Selys's. Her armour was much too big for her. 'Wait. Vantonen? You're that Laird's daughter! What are you doing in Tonmouth?'

'I'm allowed to travel wherever I wish.' Calidra put as much arrogance into her voice as she could muster.

Selys folded her arms. 'Is something wrong?'

'Lots of rumours going on about trouble in Bragalia.' The guard hadn't taken her gaze away from the papers. '*Bad* rumours.'

Calidra decided to humour her. She shifted her weight to one hip. 'Such as?'

'All sorts. Lost souls. Murders. Rogue spirits…the Myr.' The last word came out as a whisper.

'You *dare* claim the Myr are back on the continent?'

The guard seemed to realise her error and shoved Selys and Calidra's papers back to them. 'Of course not! They—they're just rumours! Like I said!'

Selys frowned at her. 'Because it sounded *very* much like you were suggesting they'd returned. You mean to say you doubt Queen Surayo words? I'm travelling to Miroth's

Shrine this evening. Shall I tell your town's patron of your thoughts?'

'My faith in the Iron Crown is absolute!'

'Then perhaps you should consider your words before you voice them.' Selys gave her a curt bow as she took her papers back from the gatekeeper.

Calidra followed suit, adding, 'We'll both be back through here tonight. We're staying on the edge of town. I do expect a smoother passage on our return.'

The woman's lip twitched, but she didn't object. 'Be swift. We lock the gates at full dark.'

'Thank you,' Selys said.

Calidra had no intention of thanking the woman after that appalling treatment, but Selys was welcome to her polite manners. 'I'll see you soon, Selys. Please be careful.'

'Oh, spirits don't bother me. It's people I only ever have issues with!' Selys cackled, one hand resting on her glaive. The priestess had never been anything other than unfailingly polite, determined, and in control. Utterly resolute in her decisions and confident in everything she did.

Calidra wasn't sure she wanted to ever bump into her when she was in a foul mood.

Though the streets were beginning to darken as dusk fell upon the town and the broken moon rose to the north, there were plenty of people around. Inquisitors, as Selys had warned, appeared to be out in force—she'd counted half a dozen before she'd even made it within sight of the docks.

When she passed through the large market square, most of the shops had closed for the evening—linen cloths and blankets covering up their stalls—though there were plenty of people milling around. Numerous fountains provided a constant, musical ring of water that she was sure comforted many people of the town.

It just set Calidra's teeth on edge.

'...trade's gonna dry up with the Myr coming back.' A woman let out a snort of frustration.

'Don't worry. The queen will get rid of them, just like before,' replied a man with a nasally voice.

Calidra slowed her pace as conversation from a trio of vendors drifted over to her. She didn't want to be rude and listen in—she'd chastised Fenn enough for that—but the mention of the Myr gave her pause.

'The queen has exaggerated things, you know. The Myr aren't that bad. I used to have a farm out near Hillsbrin. We saw the Myr more than we saw Inquisitors,' a second man replied. He was tall, with broad shoulders and a broader gut. 'It was fine. They only came every few months. Bit of a shock to see some of our best lemon trees dead in the morning and a few years were tough, but it wasn't that bad. None of these massacres like the Inquisitors keep saying.'

Calidra loitered near the fountain, despite the noise of constantly trickling water bringing swathes of discomfort and irritation.

'Things might've been fine for *you* Johan, but for the rest of us, the Myr were devastating!' The woman rested her hands on her hips.

'Like I said, Surayo will look after us,' the nasally man replied.

The bigger man, Johan, shook his head and slapped his thigh. 'You town folk are too stressed. Get some beer in you and enjoy the natural course of life, that's what I say! And keep all profit without some distant queen taking it from you!'

The woman glanced up and Calidra hurried on quickly. She didn't want to be caught eavesdropping. Her heart pounded as she left the square, making her way through the twisting streets and towards the edge of land.

Regardless of what the law said about speaking of the Myr, people were discussing their possible return openly.

Built against the sheer cliff face, Tonmouth Docks were easily as large as the Ballowtown port, just spread over more area. Several large boats floated in the bay, the last of the day's gulls soaring overhead, looking for scraps.

Keeping a watchful eye overhead, she approached the wooden scaffolding that had been fitted to the cliff edge. A narrow, rather rickety staircase led down to the water. It would be a harrowing descent.

Calidra peered at the noticeboard pinned to one of the larger wooden beams. It was a schedule of ships departing and arriving, along with destinations, journey durations, and costs. There was a note about the ships travelling to Foxmouth reminding passengers that the journey's length was always subject to Neros, Spirit of the Lasseen Ocean. If the spirit was in a good mood, it meant smooth sailing. But if she was in a foul mood, it could add days, even weeks, to the voyage.

Calidra had to hope Neros was content. She didn't want to wait any longer than she had to.

She glanced up as the wooden stairs creaked and a heavy-set man pulled his way up the last few steps and onto the path. He wore a thick, woolen jumper underneath an oilskin jacket, and a leather jacket that reached the back of his knees on top of that. He surveyed her for a moment with beady brown eyes, a long smoking pipe clenched between his teeth. 'Careful, lass. Winds can blow a person clean offa this cliff. Last one fell, we had to pick up bits of guts in a bucket before the gulls got to him.'

Calidra backed away immediately, pulling her cloak more tightly around her shoulders.

He scanned the noticeboard, then tapped his hat. 'Captain Kifil. You planning on travelling far?'

'Foxmouth.'

'As far as that, eh? I wouldn't go if I were you. Fishing ain't worth it, no matter how good they pretend it is.'

Calidra furrowed her eyebrows, ignoring the comment about fishing. 'Why not?'

'It's near Eastbrook, isn't it? Lots of trouble being stirred up there. Seen griffins and all sorts in the skies. You'd think there was another war on.'

She folded her arms. She wasn't going to come this far and be dissuaded by a superstitious sailor. 'My sister is there. It's important I get to her sooner rather than later.'

Kifil scratched his chin—clean-shaven, which Calidra found odd for a ship captain—and grinned. 'Well any coin is helpful in these times, I s'pose. Inquisitors are arriving all the time. After Torsten was here last, who knows what trouble's coming to land. Hah. Might be better to stay at sea for a while.'

The thought didn't fill Calidra with much confidence. But surely if there was trouble in Foxmouth just by virtue of being near the capital, it would be better for Malora to get away. They could sail back here, and keep going, all the way to the Isle of Salt. Back to Bellandri—back to safety.

Or as safe as things *could* be with Hassen's tricks. She half-expected the entire island to be an enormous bog by the time she and Jisyel made it back there.

She looked at the noticeboard. Ships left for Foxmouth every other day, with the next voyage leaving the following morning. 'Are you sailing there?'

'I am. Ain't got much choice! No sailing, no money.' Kifil laughed and wiped his eyes. 'I've sailed the Lasseen Ocean for years. Salt Sea and Polar Sea are much better. No spirits to play with you.'

'You used to sail the Lasseen Ocean? To...to other continents?'

The captain nodded. 'More money, of course. More risk. Lost too many good sailors. Packed it in for good about five years ago. Didn't want no more to do with those distant places.'

His words reminded her of what Varlot had said about the Myr. Their homeland was on a continent far to the south. Had this captain seen something?

No. She was jumping to conclusions again. Plenty of ships sailed the Lasseen Ocean, even now. There was no way he would have any insider knowledge or be part of whatever was happening with Fenn and the other lost souls.

'Ship leaves right before lunch. Let's hope for a fair wind so you can see your sister, eh?'

Calidra nodded, too wrapped up in her own thoughts to answer verbally.

Kifil chuckled as he walked past her, most likely heading for his own warm bed—probably a stiff drink or two before. 'It gets plenty cold up north. You'll want to wrap up warm.'

She nodded again, gave him as much of a smile as she could muster, then he was heading into the darkening streets. The sun had almost set, creating bars of red and orange across the Salt Sea.

Fenn had first seen one of those Myrish creatures when they'd crossed the Salt Sea. Would she see one, too? Calidra peered out across the water, the waves and ripples dizzying when she focussed on them for too long.

The Myr. Lost Souls. *Curses.*

If she and Jisyel had stayed on the island, she'd never have known about any of it. Wouldn't have had to deal with her mother, either.

But as she stared out over the water, she realised she'd never have found out about Malora. Or her child. An entirely new part of her family had appeared, when another had firmly closed the door on her.

Whatever lay ahead, at least she had Jisyel. At least she was doing what *felt* right—running towards her dreams instead of away from them.

And whatever awaited in Foxmouth, she'd be ready.

24

THE TRAP

APOLLO

The palace was more intimidating than Apollo remembered it. When he'd last been here, just over five years ago, he'd been getting his pardon from Queen Surayo. The mage queen had removed the curse she'd put upon him—she'd been able to tell where in the world he was, and no doubt inflict an instant, grisly death had he disobeyed her command—and just being in the shadow of the enormous building made his thigh twinge, where the queen's magic had touched his skin.

Maybe curses never really went away.

He couldn't shake the sight of that lost soul writhing in pain, as if their own skin was poison. And if *he'd* had anything to do with that...if he'd really, truly messed up by not feeding that blasted key to Paragos? Perhaps he didn't deserve the freedom and the life he'd built with Malora.

The thought was an unwelcome weight that roiled in his stomach like a sickness.

A horn blew loud and clear, announcing their arrival. Nadja raised one fist high to the sentry atop the massive iron gates, and they slowly opened to reveal the palace beyond.

Although adorned predominantly with iron in the same way Toriaken's Shrine had been, the palace was less magnificent. To Apollo, it was just another prison.

The courtyard was busier than Apollo had ever seen it before, with numerous troops assembling in the vast, sandy grounds that filled the inner keep. A dozen guards stood at attention around the palace perimeter, and more patrolled in twos or threes. Several chariots had been prepared, waiting along the length of the wall, where horses were being outfitted in plates of ceremonial armour. Apollo spotted several Inquisitors, their dark uniforms standing out in a sea of grey and white armoured soldiers.

After everything Nadja had told him—he didn't think this Inquisitor *could* lie—and after everything he'd seen, it was clear things were changing in Porsenthia if Surayo was amassing her military.

A high-pitched shriek caught his attention, and, alarmed, he glanced over to the far side of the courtyard, where three enormous griffins paced in a large compound, their huge talons churning up dust with each step. The biggest one had feathers of cherry-red, and a beak that looked like it could snap a person in two—armour and all.

Apollo flinched at the sight of the fearsome creatures. He'd never seen one before, and to be thrust so close to them was almost more than his nerves could take. He turned in his seat, but his chestnut mare hardly broke her stride, following Nadja without being distracted.

If griffins were here, saddled griffins, that meant there were Olmese here, too.

Things were more serious than he'd allowed himself to believe.

Nadja reined in her horse, the piebald whickering gently at her command. Two guards were already making their way towards them, having approached the moment they passed through the gates. Both carried spears and wore full armour,

402

which clinked as they hurried over to them. While they bowed respectfully to Nadja, Apollo couldn't help but notice one guard sneer at him, his disgusted gaze lingering on the scar across Apollo's face.

He was used to it, but on Queen Surayo's doorstep—the place he'd tried to rob once, which had earned him the thief's scar in the first place—it felt more ominous.

Apollo kept his head down while Nadja gave her orders, then he was getting off his horse. He groaned at the ache in his legs, and patted the animal affectionately as he dismounted. 'What now?'

'Ordinarily, you'd be kept in a cell until such time as Queen Surayo summoned you. However, she has been eagerly awaiting your arrival, and we will see her presently.' Nadja flicked her dagger, the iron around Apollo's legs rejoining. She once again brushed down her uniform, getting rid of stray hairs, dust, and grime picked up. Even her hair, which she'd maintained with careful combing throughout their journey, wasn't allowed to be messy or out of place.

Another member of the palace staff approached them—a stableboy from his muddy apron—and took the horses' reins from Nadja. He was young, with long, flaxen hair that had bits of hay sticking in it.

'Make sure they're well-rested.' The Inquisitor rubbed the muzzle of her piebald. 'They did well.'

'Of course, Inquisitor.' The young lad bowed low, his hair covering his eyes.

Nadja took hold of the iron chain dangling from Apollo's wrist. 'Come on, Apollo. Your queen awaits.'

He followed, obedient. They'd spent so long on the road that he knew he should have a failsafe excuse ready by now. Some argument to challenge the queen's questions. But he had nothing. Only the growing sense of guilt for what was happening to Tassar.

If he was the cause, Surayo would have him hanged immediately.

Even now, he couldn't see a way out of his situation. More guards were posted at regular intervals from the bottom of the enormous stone stairwell all the way to the top, where it led to the palace's main entrance. He stared at the back of Nadja's head as she led them up the steps. Would she let him send a message back to Foxmouth? Or would she just be notifying Malora of the queen's justice after the event?

The thought of never seeing Malora again rattled around in his mind like a maelstrom. Never seeing Renys again. Hearing her laugh with delight at one of his silly pranks.

His left knee buckled and he dropped to the ground with a crack.

Nadja stumbled, pulled down by the chain she gripped, but she didn't fall. 'Apollo!' She wound the chain around her hand and heaved him back up. 'You've been good this whole journey. Don't start getting any stupid ideas now. It's far too late for that.'

Apollo staggered onto his feet, but his knees were weak. It was too much. How in all of Tassar was he going to get himself out of this mess? Nadja was right, it was far too late. 'I slipped!'

She narrowed her eyes but didn't berate him. 'Mind your step. I'll widen the fetters.' Pulling out her dagger, she flicked the tip towards him. Immediately, the iron reacted, melding like water, and lengthening Apollo's permitted stride.

He knew he needed to keep an eye out for exits, threats, places he could hide. But the walk up the rest of the stairs and through the grand halls passed in a blur. The guilt was overwhelming. Crippling. Apollo was vaguely aware of plants and greenery within the palace walls, of guards stopping to stare at him, of the oppressive pressure that filled the air. Conversations died down as they passed.

404

His breathing grew shallow. 'Nadja. I don't suppose there's time to send a bird home? Let Malora know I'm here safe and sound, hmm?'

'No. Queen Surayo awaits.'

He pulled at his wrist restraints, but they were as immovable as they had been back in Foxmouth. 'Nadja, would...you send one? In case...I can't?' He didn't want to give it words.

Nadja shook her head and quickened her pace.

When they passed through narrower corridors, where living guards were replaced by the Iron Guard, Apollo focussed on his breathing. He was in the eye of the storm now.

One pair of the Iron Guard, each on either side of the corridor, moved as they passed, falling into step and marching behind them.

Apollo turned to look, walking backwards so he didn't end up being pulled by Nadja, fascinated and horrified by the queen's unnatural soldiers. He'd seen them before, of course. When he'd broken into the palace, when the queen had put her curse on him, and when she'd removed it. They'd just stood silently in the queen's rooms before. They unnerved him as much now as they had then, especially when they moved of their own accord, and he turned back with a shudder.

Clearly Queen Surayo wasn't taking any chances with him this time.

Eventually, Nadja came to a halt by a wide door made of dark rosewood. Apollo found it peculiar. Every door within the palace's innermost sanctum had been made of iron. He wondered why the queen had opted for a rosewood door that led to her personal chamber. If that was where Nadja had brought him.

'You will show deference to Queen Surayo at all times.'

Apollo didn't reply.

Nadja didn't knock, but they waited in front of the door

for several seconds before Apollo heard a heavy click as it was unlocked. It swayed forward without so much as a creak, and Apollo was once again in the presence of Surayo, Mage Queen and Supreme Ruler of the Porsenthian Empire.

She was alone, save her Iron Guard. There wasn't so much as a handmaiden in sight.

Apollo swallowed. Whatever was to be discussed, the queen didn't want anyone to hear.

Nadja stepped inside, giving Apollo's chain a short, sharp pull to force him in behind her. The Iron Guard followed them into the circular room, one on either side of Apollo, keeping just outside his peripheral vision. It put him on edge, which he supposed was the point.

Queen Surayo herself was seated in a throne made of rosewood—the same as her door—raised on a small altar and surrounded by open windows, the sea beyond a vibrant blue. There were no lit sconces, no fireplace, no tapestries on the walls, nothing that would suggest this room was where Surayo met with people. A dozen of her Iron Guard stood motionless at the walls. Ever silent. Ever watching.

'My queen. I have returned with Apollo Tamlin, as you requested. He was obedient and quiet, and gave me no trouble during our journey.' Nadja dropped into a low bow.

Surayo tapped the back of her right hand—the closest she ever got to applause. It was a sure sign of her acceptance.

Apollo remained standing, though he lowered his head in a sort of half-bow. After Nadja had come as close to praising him as she would get, he didn't want to squander that by being disrespectful. He knew it would probably be better to hold his tongue, let Nadja do all the talking, but he couldn't—not when his life was on the line. And ever since he'd been a boy, Apollo had covered up his nerves with talking and humour. 'Queen Surayo, I hadn't thought we'd ever meet again.'

At his words, Surayo's sharp eyes turned to him.

Her look reminded him of Malora, she had the same brown eyes—pools so dark he could lose himself forever in them—and he remembered Surayo was just another person.

She might be known as the Iron Queen, but she had a heart. Emotions. Feelings. She *had* to.

'I had hoped never to see you see you again, thief.'

'Well, you gave me a pardon. I thought that was the end of our professional relationship. I could live my life, have my family.'

'You are here because the threat is greater than your family's importance. I would assume my Inquisitor has already told you this.'

'She did. But—'

'Be silent! Your queen speaks.' The Iron Guard trembled with barely contained movement.

Apollo cursed inwardly and bit his tongue.

'If my Inquisitor has told you this, then you understand the gravity of the situation. You were sent to Malnova for one specific task—to feed that magical artefact to Paragos. Did you complete this task?'

'The key is gone!'

'Did you complete this task?' Surayo repeated, slower.

Apollo pursed his lips, remembering the Moonlight Palace. The Myr. The Spirit of the Eternal Blizzard that claimed dominion over the area. 'Paragos certainly...has *control* of the key, now.' If only the queen had *told* him what he was carrying. He wouldn't feel so much damned *guilt*!

'Well, the veracity of your claim is in doubt.'

'I'm afraid my questioning ended up in much the same way.' Nadja placed her hands behind her back. 'A silver tongue, this one. Perhaps a few days in the cells will loosen it.'

'I should have expected nothing less.' But Surayo didn't sound angry—she sounded contemplative. 'There is more than one way to get the truth from a person, Apollo. You must be aware of this?'

'Are you going to curse me again? *Force* me to talk?'

Surayo laughed, genuine amusement breaking through her stoic exterior for a moment, before she controlled herself again. 'I would not waste magic on you. Not when there is another war to prepare for. No. Torsten will get the truth from you.'

Both Apollo and Nadja reacted in the same moment.

'The Master Inquisitor? But Apollo is under my authority! I should be the one to question him. Two days in the cells, and I'll have every answer you desire, my queen.'

'No, Nadja. He is under *my* authority. And Torsten will be the one to get an answer out of you, Apollo. Torsten is far more efficient in these matters, you understand.'

'Get your answer?' Apollo shook his head. 'You have your military back in training, you've added more soldiers to your patrols. The lost souls that are out there are dying. You *know* the Myr are back. What difference does it make how or why? Shouldn't you focus on fighting them? If you're so sure I'm to blame, why not let me stand and fight. I've a family to protect.'

Surayo smiled, the motion small. 'And give you yet *another* chance to destroy things? To sabotage me and slip away for another few years?'

He glowered.

'I believe *you* are the cause of their resurgence, Apollo. You have caused my peace to go up in flames after five years. Have caused my people to die. If it is found that you did as I had asked, you will be acquitted of all charges, of course.'

Apollo's throat went dry.

'But I doubt that's the case. And if we find you guilty? You shall suffer the consequences and be hanged as a traitor not just to the Iron Crown, but to Tassar. You are the cause of the people's suffering. The lost souls now. The casualties of the war to come. That's all on *you*.'

He couldn't believe it.

There was always more than one way to achieve a goal, and he'd managed to get rid of the key! The fact her curse had been removed showed he'd done what had been asked. And how was he supposed to know what could happen if he hadn't completed the task in the specific way she'd wanted? 'If you kill me, it won't change anything!' Apollo was shouting, now. 'You'll still have the Myr coming for you!'

'What's it going to be, Apollo? Will you admit right here and now that you didn't feed the key to Paragos? Or will Torsten have to force it out of you?'

'The key is gone! I got rid of it! That's what you cursed me to do. Surely you can see—'

'I'm bored of listening to him. Nadja. You have my leave to go. Take this man to the lower cells via the western stairs. Torsten will be waiting for you. I will have my answer soon enough.' At the queen's words, the Iron Guard drew their swords as one, tips pointed at Apollo.

It was the end of his discussion with Surayo.

Nadja's fists shook, but she didn't argue, simply dropped into another bow. 'Yes, my queen.'

AN IDEA BREWED as Nadja led him away from the queen's chamber. Apollo couldn't stand Torsten, but the Master Inquisitor was prone to bouts of rage—his temper often got the better of him. An angry man was easier to escape from than the cool calmness that Nadja exuded.

It would be his only chance.

He'd have to bet on Torsten's nature remaining unchanged over the years—the man loved languishing in his authority and drawing out punishments. His death wouldn't be quick, if

Torsten had anything to do with it. And Apollo needed to use every extra second the spirits chose to give him.

'I appreciate you sticking up for me,' he said. He'd never tried to garner favour with an Inquisitor before, and didn't think Nadja would even entertain the idea, but he wanted her to know he appreciated that small kindness. Perhaps she would send word to his family.

'I was not "sticking up for you," I was relaying facts.' Her voice was clipped. She'd definitely been blindsided by Surayo's command, and was seething about it.

'Even so, I appreciate it.'

She grunted. Then said, 'You're welcome.'

Apollo soon began to recognise bits of the palace as Nadja took him towards the cells. When he'd been arrested last time, he thought he'd die there. Perhaps he still would, and his death had simply been deferred for a few years. 'Nadja. We both know what Torsten's like. He's going to kill me, isn't he.' It wasn't a question.

She didn't reply.

'Nadja. Be honest with me.'

'I don't know. Only Master Inquisitors may work in the lower cells. But…it's likely. If you're guilty.'

He had to convince her to tell Malora. He held Nadja's gaze. 'Then would you send a bird to Foxmouth? Tell Malora? Tell her to get out of Porsenthia with what's happening? Please?'

Again, Nadja said nothing. 'Through here.' They'd stopped outside a large door in the middle of a quiet hallway. She pulled on the handle and heaved the heavy metal door open.

Apollo didn't push his luck. He'd asked her twice now. He had to hope his plea would sink in.

A narrow staircase greeted Apollo on the other side of the door, leading down to a dark lower level. No torches had been lit, and he did *not* want to venture down into the unknown shadows.

'Here is where I leave you,' Nadja said, her voice quiet. She had her dagger in hand, and with another twist, the fetters around his wrists and ankles melted away.

Apollo whirled around, but she was already blocking the gap in the doorway with her body. 'As Queen Surayo said, Torsten will be waiting for you. If you are innocent, I will personally escort you back to Foxmouth on a carriage pulled by the swiftest horses in our fleet. But if you have lied to us, to all of us, then I will not grieve your death.' She closed the door, the slam reverberating down the stairs. Then the noise of a deadbolt locking it into place signalled his escape closing.

He waited in the darkness for a long while, steadying his breathing. When he was quite sure Nadja would have left, he tried the door handle—but it was locked shut and wouldn't move, no matter how much force he put into it.

With nothing left to do, he made his way gingerly down the steps, hands touching the walls on both sides, guiding himself down. If he lingered too long, Torsten would no doubt come looking for him, and he'd be on the back foot.

He couldn't allow that.

The stairway led deeper than he'd thought, plunging him into absolute darkness. Apollo didn't want to breathe, as if any tiny sound might alert some terrifying monster to his presence. When the stairs ended, the narrow corridor continued. Apollo followed the walls along, feeling for any breaks in the stone, for any doors or windows. Although the stone was rough, there were no weaknesses that he could feel. Nothing crumbled away, and he couldn't detect any gaps.

His heart thudded in his chest. This was just like Torsten, wanting to throw his victims off guard.

A low moan echoed. It sounded very far away. He froze in place, holding his breath, straining to listen.

Another moan.

Apollo couldn't tell if it was the first voice again or a second.

When nothing approached, he continued on, more cautious than before. A scream punctuated the moaning, and it set Apollo's teeth on edge. There were people here, hurting.

He quickened his step as much as he dared but didn't call out.

Finally, light illuminated the end of the corridor, revealing what he'd felt—a narrow stone hallway, no doubt built in the bowels of the palace—and it ran past a single wooden door.

Apollo could keep going. The corridor was illuminated more brightly further ahead, but the groans of pain were coming from behind the door. He tried to walk past when a particularly loud shriek pierced the air. It sounded like a woman. A young one. Perhaps only a girl?

He hesitated, lingering outside the door, desperate to race down the hall and try and find some way out of the palace, but unwilling to do so while people were hurting. 'Come on, Apollo. Don't be stupid. Don't be stupid...'

A breath of cool wind kissed his face from the corridor's end. A chance at freedom.

Another scream.

Apollo gritted his teeth. He'd already made his decision. He knew he had.

There was no gap around the doorframe to peer inside, to get an idea of what he was about to walk into. He thought it was better that way.

Apollo took a breath and grabbed the handle. With one twist, he was inside. The door locked behind him, and he immediately regretted his action.

Torsten stood in the centre of the circular room, illuminated by wall sconces. He held his own Inquisitor's dagger high, which had no doubt locked the door the moment Apollo entered, a grin of deep satisfaction splitting his face.

All around him were numerous people in varying states of distress. Some clung to each other, sobbing silently. Others had pressed themselves against the stone wall—smooth in this room—eyes wide in terror. Many were bleeding from superficial wounds on their faces or arms. Several groaned or writhed around, while others shrieked in abject terror.

But worse than those in obvious pain were those who were slumped over, expressions vacant, mouths hanging open. They were alive, true, he could see chests rising and falling, but there was...nothing there. No light in their eyes. As if whoever they were had been cut out of their bodies.

'Ah. Apollo Tamlin. I was wondering when you'd turn up.'

'Torsten...What have you done? What are you *doing*?'

'Getting answers.'

'You're *torturing* them!'

One man, maybe five or six years Apollo's senior, crawled over to him on his hands and knees. He clutched Apollo's boot with a wrinkled hand, fingers covered in blood. 'Get away...While you can...'

Torsten chuckled. 'They truly are empty-headed vessels. I do wonder how the Myr did this. I've not seen it before... some magic that has taken their senses and thoughts from them. It would be most useful to have access to this power. To use it for our own needs.'

Apollo's eyes widened at the realisation. This man, all the people in the cell, were lost souls. He crouched down and took the man's hand in his own. 'It'll be okay.'

'If this is what the Myr are unleashing, we have a new fight on our hands, Apollo. Could you imagine if whatever they've done to these people they do to our soldiers? Our guards? Imagine forgetting how to fight. We'd be annihilated in seconds.'

'Why torture them?' Apollo squeezed the man's hands, terrified what Torsten would do.

'I must be thorough. I'm sure you can appreciate that.' Torsten sheathed his iron dagger at his belt and strolled past Apollo and the man, heading for a wooden box beside the door that Apollo hadn't noticed. 'It's better I have someone like you, Apollo. *Much* more interesting when you actually have your presence of mind. I can find out so much more.'

'Torsten...' Apollo glanced around while the Inquisitor busied himself with the box. The door to the room had been locked, but if he could get the dagger off Torsten, he had a chance. It was too late for the people already in here, and it killed him to admit that.

But if he could do something about Torsten, he could ensure no-one else fell to his torture.

Nadja had removed the irons from his wrists and ankles, allowing him to make his way down the stairs. And he was going to use any advantage he could get.

Apollo charged across the room, leaping over two youths sprawled on the floor, and barrelled towards Torsten. The Inquisitor lurched backwards, and Apollo grabbed hold of his sleeve. Once a thief, always a thief. His quick hand found the dragger, fingers grasping the hilt.

Then, Torsten's elbow crunched into his nose, and he was thrown backwards, the dagger skittering across the stone floor.

Searing pain exploded across his face, and Apollo clutched his nose with one hand. Blood coloured his fingers. He'd not expected the Inquisitor to react so quickly and cursed his luck.

'None of that, Apollo.' Torsten readjusted his uniform where Apollo had forced it down. But Torsten didn't go for his dagger, he remained near the wooden box, sliding the top off to open it. Whatever was inside hissed loudly.

'Apollo. It's been too long since I was able to use this to its fullest effect.' Torsten withdrew a creature, no larger than the palm of his hand. It was thin, with milky, translucent flesh. It had no eyes, nose, ears, or any other distinguishable features, and reminded Apollo of a maggot. The creature hissed again, writhing against Torsten's touch.

'What...What do you think you're doing?' Apollo staggered to his feet, his vision flickering in and out with the intensity of the pain in his nose.

Of the few people in the cell who were conscious, many screamed and backed away from Torsten and the thing he held.

'Allow me to elucidate for you.' Torsten smoothed his hair with his free hand.

Apollo stood his ground, annoyed with himself for letting Torsten hit him so cleanly. The dagger was out of reach, over to his right, near the stone wall. He didn't know what this creature could do, how fast it was. Darting to the iron dagger might speed up his own demise, so he remained in place, braced and ready to act.

'I am going to peel back the layers of your mind, one by one, and see what dirty little secrets you have tucked away. Nestol will aid this.' Torsten approached him, taking slow, measured steps. He smiled down lovingly at the creature he carried. 'My queen and I believe you are to blame for the Myr. You may well have shaken the people's belief in the Iron Crown. Apollo, that's unforgivable.'

Apollo backed away a few steps, not turning away from Torsten. Blood ran freely down his face, and he had to breathe through his mouth. 'Maybe you should be outside training with the others? Making yourself more useful. I saw griffins. Even the Olmese are here, then? And you're hiding away here, still setting ants on fire?'

Torsten's smile darkened. 'It doesn't matter what you say, Apollo. I've wanted to show the world your truth ever since I caught you in the palace. That scar was a good start.'

'And what if I offer to join the fight against the Myr? I'm handy with a blade.'

'What, and deprive showing the world of your treachery? I think not. I'm going to enjoy discovering every single secret of yours. You have a wife, don't you? Does she know about your sordid past? What kind of man she's chosen? Someone who opened the door for the Myr's return because of his own selfishness? Laziness? Or was it plain arrogance that you didn't think you'd get caught?'

'Okay, Torsten? I'm gonna need you to remove your head from your own backside for two minutes and listen—'

Torsten threw Nestol at Apollo's feet. It moved lightning-quick, faster than a striking snake. It clamped down on Apollo's boot, anchoring itself to him. Appendages burst from its body, eight—no, ten—legs crawling up him. More appeared as it moved.

He flinched, scrabbling at it, to no avail. Apollo darted across the room as the worm-like creature clambered higher —over his waist, his torso—and picked up the iron dagger. He plunged it into Nestol's milky flesh. He cut a gaping hole into it, but there was no blood, no thrash of pain. The creature split where the blade cut it, and it knitted its flesh together on the other side, all the while continuing to clamber up higher and higher.

Apollo cut and slashed, looking for a weak point. He drove the tip into the creature's legs, but nothing affected it.

'Now, Apollo Tamlin, we shall discover the truth of what you did.'

The creature's white flesh reached his throat, and it slowed, as if working out where to go next. In his panic, Apollo hadn't realised the cold in his limbs where the creature had touched him. Even through his clothes, his boots, it felt like ice formed across his skin—numbing him and rooting him to the spot.

Nestol wrapped around his throat, its body elongating into segments, and the uppermost blade-like appendages pierced his forehead.

Apollo screamed.

PART III

Open soon will the gate,
Your suffering within doeth await.
Revenge is our key to start,
And life's fate shall be Death's art.

PART III

25

THE GAMBLER

FENN

A strong easterly wind drove the groaning ship through the cold Salt Sea. Bigger than the schooner that had brought Fenn from the Isle of Salt to Bragalia, and definitely older, *The Duschtet* had four enormous masts and a crew of eighteen that were kept busy in the choppy waters—constantly adjusting sails and clambering up and down rigging.

Getting through Tonmouth to the docks had been somewhat harrowing. He'd been terrified an Inquisitor would spot him, but the others had insisted on sending messages to friends and family before they boarded. Calidra, Jisyel, Selys, and even Varlot had all spent several long minutes in the dovehouse just after first light. Fenn, of course, had no-one to write to. No-one to send his well-wishes.

Jisyel had asked him if he wanted to add a note to her letter to Bellandri, and, flustered, he'd not been able to think of anything on the spot. Jisyel had smiled and said she'd tell her gran that he was doing well and would hopefully regain his memories soon. She also said he'd promised to visit her once everything had settled down.

Her kindness touched him, even though he wasn't sure he could keep that promise.

Several pigeons nestled in their roosts had maroon feathers, which Jisyel explained were birds exclusively used by Inquisitors. Just seeing them made him more nervous, and he ushered the others away the moment they were done.

It hadn't taken long to get onto the ship. Calidra seemed to have a passing familiarity with Kifil, the captain of *The Duschtet*, which sped things up—the captain was as eager to get going as they were. There weren't any passengers other than their small group, either. Kifil had said most travellers were put off by the recent attacks on towns and villages, preferring to stay at home and protect their loved ones. Even though the Myr hadn't been overtly mentioned and there'd been no official word from the Iron Crown, the appearance of lost souls in Bragalia had already started to snowball rumours. Gossip had spread like wildfire, even to the point the town guard had spoken openly about it.

Although people had faith in the Iron Crown, the deaths couldn't be ignored. Especially now it didn't seem like Porsenthia was immune from the attacks that had begun in Bragalia.

Fenn had been relieved once the boat had lifted anchor and they'd pushed out and away from shore. One step further from Inquisitors. One step closer to answers.

It didn't take long for Calidra to look like she was suffering with tanglethorn poisoning—her skin quickly lost its lustre and although she spent most of her time in the middle of the ship's uppermost deck, she was close to vomiting within an hour of setting sail. Jisyel kept her company, sitting with her the whole time, offering soothing words and rubbing her back, and they talked in low voices. Selys loitered by the ship's prow, staring out over the water ahead, her glaive clutched in one hand as if she expected to be accosted by a sea monster.

Varlot, more sour than usual, had gone below decks before they'd even left Tonmouth and had refused to come out, bellowing at anyone who came near that he wanted to be left alone. He'd also sworn to take his axe to the next person who told him he needed fresh air, and the crew gave him a wide berth after that.

Fenn wondered if Varlot was seasick, too, and trying to hide it. The man hadn't been himself since leaving Spindleford.

The cool air was helping his own headache, but he had far less energy than the previous few days—fatigued so greatly that nothing alleviated it—made worse by the trembling fits that were only a cough or sneeze away. More voices echoed in his head whenever his attention wandered, usually a mixture of words he recognised and sounds in a language he didn't know. They kept him from restful sleep, and were with him every time he closed his eyes for more than a few seconds.

And ever-present was the intense burning in his chest. It had been growing hotter over the past few days, and he wondered if it was his body's way of warning him that death was near.

'Are you sure I'll find answers in the Nethal Mountains?' Fenn asked Selys, joining her near the ship's prow. He moved unsteadily along the deck, the swell of the ocean waves threatening to send him flying every few steps. He grasped the handrail and caught his breath, annoyed at how off-balance he was becoming.

Ahead, the waters of the Salt Sea were cold and black.

'No. But it *is* my best guess,' she replied, turning away from the sea to look at him. She studied him with a frown. 'Your face.' She reached out to brush a finger against his cheek.

Fenn hadn't looked in any of the mirrors on the ship, but he knew his skin was ashen from what he'd been able to catch of his own reflection in the water. He didn't look healthy. 'This thing...this construct? If it can remove the Myr's touch...will I survive?'

'I don't know, Fenn. But you have a Myrish curse upon you. If the construct is powerful enough to remove it, perhaps all you'll need is rest. With the curse lifted, your memories should return. And hopefully your strength, too.'

He nodded, more to himself than to her. If the construct couldn't help—or wouldn't—he was certain he'd only be days away from dying, and he'd be back on the edge of the spirit world...

His fingers twitched, then started to tremble.

Fenn clutched his hand and squeezed, trying to force the tremors away, but they were already working their way up his arm. His shoulder weakened, numbing, and he sank to the floor with a gasp. He leaned his forehead on the railing and peered out at the water through the gaps, focussing on his breathing.

'You must keep going, Fenn! While there's still breath in you.' Selys rested her glaive against the railing and crouched down beside him, one hand on his shoulder. Softly, she said, 'Hold on. It won't be long until we're there. This is a good ship.'

'I know. It's...' Fenn bit back a whimper of pain. He tried to cover it up with a joke. 'It's just the movement on the water. Think I've caught Calidra's seasickness!'

The priestess didn't find his words amusing, her expression as serious as ever, and Fenn looked away, unable to hold her gaze. In truth, he was terrified he was going to join the other echoes sooner rather than later. It had been only eight nights since the bog on the Isle of Salt. He wasn't sure he'd last another week. The fear was utterly crippling when he thought about it. Determined, he pushed it away, forcing himself to think about the journey, the sea, his companions, the burning in his chest—*anything* to keep his mind distracted.

'I won't tell you it'll be okay, because I don't know. And I don't want to lie to you.' Selys steadied him as the ship rocked. She was perfectly comfortable on the water, and he remembered Jisyel saying she'd grown up somewhere famous for pirates. 'But you *have* to be strong, Fenn.'

'I know. I'm trying.'

'Neros is troubled. I feel her discontent. Her fury.' Selys looked out over the water. 'I sent word to the shrine, although I'm sure the other priests there will have felt it, too. We must ready ourselves.'

'What for?' It was a silly question. He *knew* the Myr were coming. After what he'd seen and felt, it was irrefutable.

'Stock up on supplies and provisions for the sick and injured. There'll be many in the coming weeks if the Myr are not stopped. They may bring more curses with them, too. Perhaps different to what they did to you and the others.'

'If they're coming back, why bother cursing me? And all those other lost souls?' The question had been circling his mind for days. 'If they're strong enough to come back now, to send death spirits here and attack people? What's the point of cursing a handful of us to lose our memories and die?'

Selys leaned back with a sigh. 'Who's to say why the Myr do anything? It must be connected, but I couldn't say how or why. Perhaps it was their first strike against us, testing our defences, our reactions. Perhaps they have a base somewhere hidden in Bragalia or Porsenthia, and you were cursed to forget it so you couldn't reveal their location to the Iron Crown. Perhaps they *tried* to kill you, but were too weak, and left you and the others cursed instead.'

He winced again and dropped his gaze.

Softly, the priestess added, 'Perhaps you were just unlucky.'

Fenn was desperate for answers, but above all else, he wanted to know *why* this was happening to him. Why *he'd* been picked and left to suffer. Once his curse had been lifted, once he was no longer in danger of dying, he would have time to learn more—including finding his family. He wondered whether he had a partner. Friends. People who cared for him. Worried about him. Who were searching for him, even now.

As he struggled back to his feet, Fenn also wondered if the opposite could be true—whether there was no-one out there. Perhaps *that* was why the Myr had cursed him? Because there would be no-one to search, and no-one to mourn his passing.

Vermecio. That's what the Myr in his dream had named the creature that could help.

Why would the Myr suggest he go to it if it couldn't do anything? The Myr in his dream—vision, whatever it was— had been frustrated at the deaths.

It had wanted him *alive*. Fenn was certain of that.

Whatever the Myr had tried to do, why they'd touched all those people, it had to be for a purpose. But the people they'd cursed had been too weak to survive, and when they'd crossed over to the spirit world, they'd done so as echoes.

He remembered when Selys and the other priests and priestesses of her shrine had been performing burial rites. She'd told him they'd given each person a gift, a trinket of sorts, so when they crossed over, they'd know who they were. She'd said entering the spirit world lost and confused was a terrible fate.

Fenn swallowed, holding himself steady as the last few tremors passed. He rested his elbows on the wide handrail. Some of the spray hit his chin, the taste of salt strong. Selys, too, stood up. She stared ahead, but her gaze drifted to him every so often.

He looked away. He didn't want pity.

426

Or was she frustrated he might die before she got her answers? It was a dark thought.

Another ocean swell threw the ship up and he slid on the wet deck, only managing not to tumble over by gripping onto the rail. He could see why Calidra hated the water.

Fenn rubbed his eyes and tried to rid himself of his growing frustration. He only had to wait one day until they stopped on the coast near Nethal. One day before he'd say goodbye to Calidra and Jisyel, maybe for the last time.

One more day until he got his answers—whether he liked them or not.

FENN SAW the shadow before Selys did. It reminded him of his journey to Ballowtown, and his stomach lurched at the sight.

This time, Calidra didn't ignore him or accuse him of making it up.

Selys confirmed the sighting, although he was sure Calidra believed him even without the priestess's second opinion.

The shadow hovered over the mountain like a thundercloud, swirling around the top of one peak in particular. Just seeing it made Fenn's mouth run dry, but none of the crew noticed. No matter how busy they were hauling in ropes and manoeuvring the ship, he was certain they'd spot an enormous shadow looming overhead.

'Best not to worry them.' Selys shouldered her bag, ready to disembark. 'We're hoping to learn what we can to *avoid* conflict. Sailors will panic, and gossip spreads across the sea faster than anything else.'

'So you're saying we shouldn't warn these people that you can see an enormous shadow above the mountain?' Calidra scowled. 'If I was on the cusp of being attacked by the Myr, *I'd* like to know!'

'But they might not be.'

Calidra folded her arms. 'You're putting a lot of faith in this *thing* you're going to see. What if nothing's there? Place is more myth than reality.'

'I can see the shadow. So can Fenn. There's something Myrish there, that's beyond doubt. Whether or not it'll give us answers is another question entirely.' Selys wasn't backing down.

'You're risking the lives of thousands, *millions*, on this!'

'The construct has been there for decades. Its presence is nothing new. In fact, I imagine any priest or priestess worth their salt has already seen the shadow. But it's dormant. Not an active Myrish threat, otherwise everyone would know about it by now.'

Fenn's head pounded with their raised voices. He'd wanted a peaceful goodbye, not another argument. 'Please, stop. I've had just about enough of this fighting!' Another flare of pain spiked through his chest and he clutched the front of his tunic, nearly dropping to one knee.

Selys and Calidra turned away from each other, both looking sheepish.

The ship carefully approached a snowy beach, difficult to make out in the low dusk light. Fenn couldn't wait to get off the ship—travelling this way for more than a few hours certainly disagreed with him. He blinked, realising he'd been staring at his destination for some time. 'S—sorry! Got a lot on my mind.'

'Of course you do.' Calidra nodded.

Before anyone could say anything else, Varlot barged his way past the working crew from below deck. His eyes were red and he reeked of stale wine.

Fenn couldn't believe it. They were on the final leg of their journey, and he'd picked *now* to drink so heavily his

428

steps were erratic, as though he might fall over at any moment. The ship had docked. Wasn't even moving anymore. There was no excuse for his unstable steps. 'Varlot? How…how much have you had to drink?'

Varlot ignored him.

Fenn glanced at Calidra, who shook her head angrily. He hurried after Varlot and reached for his arm, slipped and missed, grabbing the edge of his bearskin cloak instead. 'Varlot! How are you going to fight in that state? You're going to—'

Varlot shoved Fenn backwards. With seawater covering much of the deck, Fenn slipped and went flying. He cracked his elbow on the large wooden planks, the sensation so excruciating that it brought tears to his eyes.

'Varlot, what are you doing?' Jisyel leapt to Fenn's defence. She helped him back to his feet, glaring at Varlot all the while. 'Calidra hates being on water too, but she doesn't behave like *that*!'

Fenn grimaced as he accepted Jisyel's help. This was not how he'd envisioned his goodbyes to be.

'You're falling over like a newborn foal. Protecting you will be impossible if you can't even stand on your own two legs.' Varlot's voice was rough. 'I ain't holding your hand.'

'I wasn't asking you to hold my hand,' Fenn muttered.

'Never mind. I'm sure the mountain snow will sober him up quickly. Come, we have to keep moving,' Selys said.

'Step aside, step aside!' Captain Kifil strolled past, a barrel held on one shoulder.

Calidra stepped back, out of his way. 'You're getting off the ship?'

'Dropping off supplies, Calidra. Be on our way in a few minutes, so don't get too comfortable.'

Her face split into a grin. 'Right. I'm getting off this boat, too.'

'You are?' Fenn asked, daring to hope she was coming with him.

'I'm not staying on board a second longer than I have to. Besides, having solid ground underfoot will help this nausea.'

'A few minutes ain't gonna help your sickness,' Varlot muttered, but Calidra didn't listen—she'd already followed the captain and a handful of his crew off the gangplank. Fenn heard her sigh in audible relief, and hurried after her, Jisyel, Selys, and Varlot following.

'We're on a tight deadline. Be back on board before we set off again. Horn'll sound twice when we're about to leave, and we won't wait for you,' Kifil said, giving Calidra a stern gaze. When she nodded back, he continued on to speak with the few people that worked at the tiny docks.

Varlot frowned deeply and folded his arms. 'Bit silly to risk missing your ship just for a minute or two of solid ground, ain't it?'

'It's more than that. We're also saying...goodbye.' Calidra offered Fenn a thin smile. Her skin was somewhat sallow, her legs wobbly, even on dry land.

They were some distance from the nearest town—Nethal, for which the mountains were named—but there was a small outpost that had no doubt grown after ships docked here over the years. It was a collection of ramshackle buildings, built mostly of wood, and covered in snow, a short distance from the water. Mountains surrounded them on all sides, and Fenn shuddered to think how much of a trek it would be to travel into Nethal.

Several snowy paths led up into the mountains, a few leading to more buildings—possibly homes or inns that he could only see by the lights in their windows—but it was getting too dark to see much beyond that.

Lanterns had already been lit, marking out each building with a halo of soft, yellow light. It made the shadows darker, somehow more ominous. And of course the Myrish shadow loomed above the mountain like a waiting storm. It reminded him of the shadow-like mist across the deadlands, if slightly less oppressive.

None of them were in any rush to get to the outpost—even Selys hung back, happy to give Fenn the time for his goodbyes.

Calidra stood with her arms on her thighs, taking deep breaths. Jisyel rubbed Calidra's back, then looked up at Fenn. 'There's not much time...'

Her words meant more than one thing. She and Calidra were bound by the ship's departure. He only had as long as his body held out for. From his raging headache, that time seemed less and less.

Jisyel clutched her arms. 'It feels strange after all this time to be going different ways, doesn't it?'

'Yeah. You'd better keep a close eye on Calidra. I know she's not a fan of water.' Fenn tried to keep his tone light-hearted, but he knew he sounded resigned.

Jisyel giggled. 'Oh, silly. Cal will be the one looking after *me*, you should know that!'

He scratched the back of his head. 'Just keep each other safe, okay? And...and, well, I guess...This is goodbye.' He didn't know what to say without it coming across as awkward.

'Fenn!' Jisyel wrapped both arms around his shoulders, squeezing tightly. 'Thank you. Thank you so much for everything!'

He was surprised by the gesture, by the warmth in her voice, and squeezed her shoulders. 'You helped me, too. Far more than you realise.'

As Fenn hugged her, he saw Kifil and his crew make their way back to the ship, and he was surprised at how fast they'd been.

Jisyel stepped back and wiped her eyes. 'I know, but... We've been through a lot. You've *got* to come back to the island once you have your answers. I'm sure gran would love to see you again. And your family, you have to bring them, too!'

He knew she meant well, but the words stung—they pointed to an uncertain future. If he didn't have anyone, he wasn't sure he *could* go back to the island empty-handed. Despite his worry, her seemingly endless optimism was a refreshing change from Selys's stark realism. 'Thanks, Jisyel. Look after yourself, won't you?'

'Fenn.' Calidra watched him carefully, as if afraid he might collapse at any moment. 'We *will* see you again. I'm sure.' She stepped forward and hugged him with the confident surety that she always held herself with, even though she'd been on the edge of throwing up shortly before.

Shocked by the hug—he'd not thought he'd be deserving of one from her—Fenn grinned. 'I really hope so. And good luck finding your sister. Be careful out there. Who knows where the Myr or their spirits are.'

'Don't worry. Nothing's getting past me.'

A horn blew from the ship. A warning they were getting ready.

'Fenn? It's time to go.' Selys pulled her thick, fur-lined gloves on, then turned to the others, 'Calidra, Jisyel? I pray Neros favours you for the rest of your journey through the Polar Sea and into Her domain. May She bring you good fortune upon the water.'

Jisyel also hugged Selys, though Calidra shook her hand. Neither raced off to the ship despite the horn blow.

Varlot let out a grunt—though of soreness or frustration, Fenn couldn't tell—and pushed his way through the snow. 'Where are they? We weren't late?'

'What are you talking about?' Selys asked, her voice clipped. 'Varlot, you ought to stay off the wine if you want anything you say to make sense!'

'Be quiet, woman. I'm trying to *look*!'

432

Fenn pinched the bridge of his nose. This was *not* what he had in mind when he'd asked the former general to come along with them. Calidra had spoken poorly of his habits—gambling and drinking—and now Fenn could see why. 'Varlot, I'm counting on you. We both are. Who knows what's waiting for us on the mountain. Maybe have some water and—'

He cut himself off as a pair of uniformed men approached from one of the buildings on the edge of the outpost. Inquisitors. Already, his fingers were shaking.

'Inquisitors? Here?' Jisyel had been starting to make her way to *The Duschtet*, hand in hand with Calidra, but they whirled around at the Inquisitors' approach.

'You two should get back to the ship. We'll be fine.' Selys rested her hand on Fenn's. 'Relax, Fenn, it'll be okay. Just get your papers ready.'

'Halt right there!' One of the men barked, slightly further ahead than his colleague. 'No-one comes in without an inspection!'

'I am Selys Ioran, Priestess of Neros, on a pilgrimage for my spirit.' She gestured to Fenn. 'This is my apprentice. He and I—'

'By the spirits, I don't believe it! Londa! Londa, hurry up will ya? The bloody pigeon was right! It really *is* Varlot Keir!' The Inquisitor laughed, now jogging towards them, one hand resting casually on the hilt of his sword.

Calidra and Jisyel loitered nearby. 'If you need my word to help against them…We aren't in Bragalia, but I speak with the Laird's voice.'

Fenn gaped. The Inquisitor had *known* Varlot was coming?

'Wow, the years ain't been kind to ya, Varlot,' Londa said, catching up with his colleague. He was the shorter of the two men, with a stocky build and broad shoulders. They both wore fur-lined cloaks and heavy boots, and moved easily through the snow.

'Londa. Barlen.' Varlot nodded to the two men, then clasped their hands in greeting. 'I shoulda known you two would get stuck at this outpost. Have you been here since the war?'

Barlen laughed bitterly. 'Uh-huh. Pretty sure my arse has frozen off. Good thing we get a nice, cosy carriage to Eastbrook for a bit.' His gaze fell upon Fenn, and he sneered.

Varlot grinned broadly. 'Aye, and some decent wine I hope, too? Nothing worse than a dry journey to Eastbrook!'

'What is all this hogshit?' Jisyel shouted.

Fenn looked from Varlot to the two Inquisitors. They knew each other, clearly. Perhaps they were even friends.

'If you're done with your familiarities, perhaps we can get going?' Selys made her way past the three men, dragging Fenn along with her.

'Selys, you can get on if you've business to attend to for your spirit,' Londa said, stepping aside so he no longer blocked the path for her. 'But the Myr-touched traitor comes with us.'

'Nonsense. He's no traitor. He's my apprentice,' Selys replied.

Both Inquisitors chuckled. 'Unfortunately, he's being taken from your care by order of the Iron Crown.' Barlen pulled out a sheet of parchment from inside his cloak and opened it up. 'A writ for every lost soul found. They're to be brought to the capital immediately. No exceptions.'

'I think you'll find the duty of a priestess is *above* Queen Surayo's desires.'

Her words killed their laughter. Barlen returned the writ to his pocket and stepped forward, towering over Selys. 'Look, priestess. I don't care what you think, I got my orders. Varlot here has given us a good tip. Gonna get well paid for

434

this, and that's the end of it. Now, run along, before you get yourself arrested, too.'

'On what charges?'

'On the charge of pissing me off.'

'Varlot? *What* is going on?' Calidra snapped, dagger in hand as she stalked towards them.

Shock and fear rooted Fenn to the spot. The two Inquisitors were armed. They knew who he was. And Varlot had been the one to tell them. His voice broke. 'Varlot? How *could* you?'

'Lad, it's nothing personal.' Varlot didn't look at him. Didn't look at any of them—just kept his gaze on the Inquisitors.

Fenn drew the sword Varlot had given him and raised it up. 'After I trusted you! You were *helping* us!'

'And for what? I do honest work for honest money. And after everything I've been through? Everything I've done for this country? After what *I've* lost?' He shook his head, his lip curling. 'I helped you, Fenn. Thought I was doing the right thing, you know. Thought after everything, I was where I was supposed to be. That good things would *finally* come my way.' He snorted. 'Instead, I get that Bragalian woman accusing me every two seconds, I get the priestess taking my coin, and I just wonder what's the point.'

'Varlot…' Fenn whispered.

'That's no excuse to betray Fenn to the Inquisitors!' Calidra yelled.

'Calidra! The ship!' Jisyel called.

Varlot stepped away from Calidra and gave her a dark look. 'But just like everything else, it was for *nothing*! I've bent over backwards for you all, done everything you asked and more, and what do I get? Fuck. All.'

Fenn lowered his sword slightly, guilt creeping in. He had kept Varlot there on the promise of money—a promise he knew full well he might not be able to keep.

Varlot's voice softened to a growl. 'I'm done with having everything thrown back in my face. I carry on as I am, and I'm just wandering from town to town, drinking myself to death. Alnothen was right. I *should* be buried in the ground.' He rested his hand on his axe. 'This way, I'm helping my queen again. My country! This way gives me a new chance. A shot at new life. It gets me back to where I should've been before...' Varlot sputtered, trailing off.

'Before what?' Fenn seethed.

'Before he killed his wife and infant son,' Selys's voice was flat. 'Alnothen had you banished for what you did, didn't she? The lives you took. Were you thrown out of the army for that? Or did you have enough conscience to leave before they found out?'

Varlot reddened. 'You have no idea what you're talking about, woman!'

'It isn't my place to judge, I've already told you that. But I now see your true colours.' The priestess glared at the two Inquisitors standing beside Varlot. 'You know what Fenn and I must do. Go back to the capital if you must. See if it cleanses your guilty conscience more than your actions thus far. Do *not* impede us. *We* are helping the queen. *You* are acting as selfishly as you ever have.'

Varlot glowered.

The horn blew twice.

Fenn gazed at the ship. Calidra and Jisyel would have to run. He could run, too. Leave Varlot, forget Selys's idea, and get away while he had the chance. There would be some other Myr he could get to. Or perhaps another way to this one that didn't involve going through Varlot and a pair of Inquisitors hungry for gold.

His stomach turned.

'Don't you go getting any ideas, lad,' Barlen growled, following Fenn's gaze. 'We have authority to stop that ship, even *if* you run for it.'

Even in the short distance from the ship, the sound of creaking chains as the anchor was slowly hoisted up echoed loudly. He had no doubt the Inquisitors could stop the ship. He couldn't let that happen—it would stop Calidra from finding her sister. 'Calidra, Jisyel. You need to go.'

'But look at what's happening!' Jisyel gestured towards Varlot and the Inquisitors.

'I know. But there's no time. I'll be fine.'

Calidra looked at him for another second, then up at the ship. She shook her head and sheathed her blade in a huff. 'Varlot, you're a bastard. I don't care *what* you've done for your country. Fenn deserves better.'

Jisyel tearfully pulled at Calidra's sleeve, and the two of them sprinted back to the ship, kicking up snow.

'Last chance. Step aside and let a priestess of Neros and her apprentice through.' Selys stood beside Fenn, her stance wide. Ready to fight.

Varlot watched Calidra and Jisyel leave, his face growing redder by the second. He drew his axe and batted Fenn's sword away as if it was a minor inconvenience. 'I was a *general*. Your word means nothing! Londa. Barlen. You want your gold or not? I ain't going back to the queen empty-handed.'

Fenn stepped back as the Inquisitors drew their swords. He couldn't believe it. He should have listened to Calidra. Should never have trusted Varlot after what he'd been accused of doing.

Selys pulled out her glaive and twirled it once. 'We need to get away, quickly,' she whispered, her voice so low Fenn could barely hear. 'We run for the mountain on my signal.'

He didn't nod, didn't want to move. His heart thundered in his chest and his headache pounded with the rolling emotions. He wasn't sure his legs had it in them to run—but he had no choice. If he didn't, he'd be taken away.

Torsten's cruel gaze lingered in his mind. There was no

way he would allow it.

Varlot, Londa, and Barlen surged forward as one. An axe and two swords against a glaive.

Selys moved faster than Fenn would ever have thought she could, her glaive a blur of silver flashing in the dusk. Crack. It knocked a sword away. Crack. Skittered along the edge of Varlot's axe, sending sparks high into the air.

One of the swords went flying, and Londa raced after it, clutching his bleeding wrist.

Selys planted her foot down and drove the tip of her glaive into the small of Barlen's back. He writhed away at the last second, the hooked blade slicing into his cloak.

'Assaulting an Inquisitor, that's what you're gonna be arrested for, priestess!' Barlen fumed. 'Even your spirit won't be able to save you from *that*!' He shot forward, his sword slashing across her shoulder.

Selys didn't reply, didn't even wince as the steel cut into her flesh. Her every movement was methodical, calculated. She spun in place, whirled her glaive around, and slammed the butt of it into Barlen's exposed temple. He dropped to the ground like a sack of potatoes.

Fenn's hope soared. He could hardly believe she'd taken on all three of them and come out victorious—without badly harming any of them, either. He was in too much shock to grin, but relief flooded him as the immediate danger passed.

Varlot stood with his feet wide apart, panting heavily. He held his axe high, ready for Selys to attack him. His own cloak had been sliced a few times, but he wasn't injured.

'Fenn and I are going now.' Selys said, though she turned her head to check whether Londa had retrieved his sword yet and was returning to the fray. She lowered her glaive. 'Varlot. If you have any heart left. Don't follow.'

Varlot sputtered, but nothing intelligible came from his lips.

She grabbed Fenn's hand. 'Run.'

26

THE CHASE

APOLLO

Darkness surrounded him. Apollo was naked save the chains that wound along his wrists, ankles, and torso. They locked him to the ground, digging into his flesh but not quite drawing blood. He could stand but not take a step. He could pull on them, twist them, but they would not break. No matter how much strength he forced into his limbs, he was trapped.

There was no light to disrupt the darkness, and he felt no hunger, fatigue, nothing that would indicate the passing of time. He didn't know if he'd been there ten seconds or ten years.

There was only pain.

Relentless, unending pain.

It pierced his skull like a hot knife; searing ice driven into his forehead and left there to fester. He could just about open his eyes against the agony, but he was so lost in darkness that it didn't matter.

'You understand why Nestol is called the Spirit of Pain?' Torsten's amused voice floated in the air, an indeterminate distance above Apollo's head.

At the mention of the creature, Apollo saw it. The thing

439

had attached itself to his body, clawed limbs digging into his skin as it held itself in place on his chest. Its flesh was milky and translucent—a worm-like creature with no discernable head, hardly even alive. Just the sight of it filled him with a repulsion so great he bent the chains around his ankles trying to get away. But the metal held him fast, and the creature sank its blade-tipped appendage into his forehead once again.

Apollo was barely able to breathe.

It wasn't a worm or maggot. It was a leech.

Memories raced through his mind. Sights, sounds, smells. The Iron Guard in the palace, motionless beside the queen. Griffins in the courtyard, pacing up and down on their massive taloned feet. The dying man outside Toriaken's shrine, blood pouring down his cheeks. His own plans to escape Nadja—looking at potential hiding places in the mountains, thinking of the hidden paths he knew to be there. His wild, panicked thought of moving to Olmir with Malora and Renys, where the Iron Crown couldn't follow. The scent of sweet, buttery fudge in Foxmouth.

More images flashed past, ever faster. Places he knew, had been. *The Grumpy Fisherman*. Customers ordering sardines for breakfast, the rattle of cutlery in a dozen hands. Early morning fishing with Renys on their little boat, her laughter lighting up the dawn. Late nights with Malora in his arms, moving together, skin against skin, the taste of her...

He twisted his head away, biting his lip to keep from screaming.

He couldn't let Torsten see. Couldn't let him know every detail of his life.

The creature on his chest grew heavy, its swollen body pulsing as it plucked his dreams and secrets and fears and desires from him like a mosquito growing fat from cow's blood. It drew everything from his mind, carving deep into it, leaving no thought unturned.

Apollo writhed, trying to get away, but the chains kept him locked in place—his mind an open feast for the creature Torsten had unleashed.

His memories went further back, careening through the years in a matter of seconds. Renys's birth. Buying the dilapidated tavern. Seeing Neros burst forth from the seafront in Foxmouth in a rare appearance. Sailing back across the Lasseen Ocean, wounded and bloody, but alive. Paragos's Eternal Blizzard. A Myrish spell chanted...

Apollo screamed and pulled back, forcing all his strength into the movement. His mind was laid bare, stripped of every wall, his every hidden thought ready to be pulled from him.

'No!' The scream burst from his throat, fuelled by agony and terror in equal measure.

An enormous explosion threw him to his knees. Sharp pain laced through his arms and legs, grounding him to reality, and the darkness faded as if sucked away by a wind he couldn't see.

When he opened his eyes, his breathing haggard, Apollo found himself back in the circular room. Dead and dying people were all around him, their dark blood staining the stone floor. He looked around, bleary-eyed, trying to get his bearings.

Torsten and the creature were both gone.

Looking down at himself, he was almost surprised to see he was still fully dressed. There were no chains around him, either.

Apollo stood up straight and was immediately accosted by a wave of dizziness. The pain of his broken nose returned, intense, but the blood on his face was sticky and drying. He'd been there a while.

He took several breaths, waiting for his vision to focus. Where was Nestol? How much had that *thing* seen? Taken?

Wiping the sweat from his forehead, Apollo remembered Torsten had taken the creature from the wooden box beside the door. Determined, he staggered across the small room to peer down at the source of his pain. His nose throbbed with every step, but the intensity of what he'd been forced to experience was already fading.

He frowned. The box had been resealed, its lid locked in place.

Apollo whirled around, only to find the iron dagger gone. Torsten would have needed it to unlock the door which was—

He blinked. The door was ajar.

He couldn't believe it.

Another explosion tore through the building and threw him to the cold stone floor again. He braced against the impact, saving his teeth from chipping. Dust and pebbles fell from the ceiling, covering his hair in a layer of white. *What* in Neros's name was going on?

Something terrible. It had to be.

Torsten never would have left mid-torture, otherwise.

He could get out, steal a horse and get back to Foxmouth as quickly as he could. Grab Malora and Renys, and get away. Olmir was a good idea. Probably the best one they had.

Apollo was about to race off when a thought struck him. He peered back through the doorway at the wooden box that held Nestol. It held whatever images and knowledge it had plucked from his mind. There was no chance he was going to allow the Iron Crown access to *any* of it.

It needed to be destroyed.

And fuck it. If it screwed with Torsten, all the better.

Apollo picked up the box. He'd half-expected the thing to be nailed to the floor, and thanked whatever spirit had decided to bless him with some luck. Box wedged under one arm, the creature within hissing but unable to get out, Apollo elbowed the heavy door open and peered out into the gloomy corridor.

He couldn't hear anything, nor see anyone.

442

He glanced back at the other prisoners Torsten had tortured. Some were alive, but in varying states of shock. Most would be dead within hours. 'I'm sorry. If I can get help, or someone to come back for you, I will.'

Even though none seemed aware of his presence, let alone his words, it was necessary to acknowledge their suffering. With nothing else to say, and time likely against him, he exited the room and raced down the corridor towards the light.

His booted feet pounded on the stone floor, and it didn't take long before the first splints of soreness shot up his legs. Apollo ignored the twinges. He could rest when he was free.

The long corridor brought him into a wide room with barred cells on either side. He took a moment to glance around the eerily quiet dungeons. It was confusing. Why weren't there any soldiers on guard or patrolling the halls? What *had* that explosion been?

Silver glinted in the corner of his eye, and he grabbed one of the short swords in the racking against the wall. It was dull, with a chip along the edge and clearly in need of repair, but at least he could defend himself.

With nothing to lose, he raced down another hallway, past a series of doors. One flew open to his right. He didn't look, just kept running. Anyone could be an enemy here.

'You! Stop right there!' A deep voice bellowed.

Apollo would have laughed, said something sarcastic over his shoulder, but he was too shaken after what Torsten had done. He wasn't going to stop for anything, not after that miraculous escape.

'Halt in the name of the Iron Crown!'

Again, Apollo ignored him, darting down another corridor and sprinting for all he was worth. Footsteps chased him, getting closer with every step. He couldn't outrun him.

The sing of metal whistling through the air made him

falter, and Apollo whirled around, bringing up his own sword to meet the blow before it struck his back.

He'd never been good with a sword, and certainly was in no condition to fight after escaping torture. Apollo's arm went numb the second both swords collided, the vibration drawing the strength from him. He managed to keep his grip and stepped aside, narrowly dodging the next blow.

His opponent was a well-built man, tall, with a grizzled mustache. Although he wore a steel breastplate, he didn't appear to be of high rank, nor an Inquisitor. 'Drop your weapon and cease this!'

'Not a chance!' Apollo panted, staggering back, willing some strength back into his right arm. He was running out of energy, fast.

With a roar, the man charged forward, sword levelled at Apollo's throat.

Adrenaline coursed through him. It was now or never. Apollo grimaced and darted forward, ducking at the last moment and driving his knee into the man's groin. He kicked out, sweeping the man's legs out from under him, and the soldier sank to the floor with a groan, his metal armour crashing loudly against stone.

Heart thudding at the attention that noise would attract, Apollo picked a direction and continued down a new corridor until he reached a short staircase. A slight breeze whispered from the top of the stairs, and it was enough for Apollo. It *had* to be the right way to get out of this spirits' forsaken deathtrap.

He shoved the sword through his belt loop and leapt up the stairs, forcing his legs to keep working.

A door greeted him at the top, angled steeply and built into the low stone ceiling. He shoved it open with his shoulder and stepped out into the cool, evening air, breathing heavily.

The scent of damp fur and straw hit him. Water flowed

444

somewhere out of sight. Horses whinnied. And in the distance, shouts. The ground was smooth flat stone, well-maintained with only a few weeds jutting out between the cracks. 'The palace courtyard?' Apollo gasped aloud, not quite able to believe his luck.

Nestol thrashed around, violently slamming into the sides of its box, and Apollo adjusted his grip. He'd not been able to stab the thing to death. Whatever it was, there *had* to be a way of killing it.

'Stations, people! Get arrows on those battlements! I don't want an empty wall in sight!'

Apollo crouched down, hiding in the shadow of the wall as a group of bowmen ran past, their weapons drawn and helmets firmly on and secured.

Fuck.

The palace was under attack.

He didn't need to guess by what.

Apollo followed behind the bowmen until he reached the end of the wall and peered out into the courtyard. Everything was chaos. Officers barked orders. Soldiers scrambled to obey. Weapons and shields were brought forth, and the horns atop the gate blew out their high-pitched warnings.

To his left, the three griffins were in their compound, flapping their wings and letting out their own cries.

Icy fear lurched in his gut. They could fly. Would be faster than any horse. Perhaps he could convince one of them to help...

Apollo didn't allow any time to talk himself out of it. He darted across the courtyard, praying his legs didn't give out on him, and approached the low wooden fence that surrounded the three huge griffins.

'The Myr are drawing in!' One griffin roared as he approached. It was the biggest of the three, with a mixture of brown and cherry-red feathers that appeared closer to black in the dusk. It raised itself onto its rear legs, its front talons flailing in the air as it flapped its wings. 'Where is my Lady?'

'I don't know, but I have to get out of here.' Apollo leaned back to avoid being savaged by the griffin's talons.

'We must ready for war!' Another high-pitched shriek, and this time the other two griffins joined in the cry, the noise deafening so close.

Something bright tore across the sky, lighting it up as if it were the middle of the afternoon. Apollo whipped around to stare—just in time to see a fireball hurtle across the walls of the grounds and slam into the palace wall. Stone crumbled, chunks of it crashing to the ground with another ear-splitting explosion.

Again, the griffins cried out. More bodies appeared from side doors, many in uniform, most with drawn weapons. No-one paid Apollo any attention.

The biggest griffin was nearly twice as tall as he was. But the other two were a fraction of the size, their shoulders just under his eyeline. He gulped. This was the biggest risk he'd taken so far. 'I need to get this thing destroyed. It's of Myrish origin.'

'Why do *you* carry it, Porsenthian?' the griffin snarled, stretching its wings out and lowering its head—its hooked beak mere inches from Apollo's face. In the low light, the griffin's orange eyes glowed like embers.

The intensity of its gaze almost stopped Apollo's breath in his throat, then Nestol thrashed around under its arm. 'Can you kill it?' He didn't know whether the creature would be able to move quickly once he opened the lid, but a griffin had more chance of putting an end to the creature than he did with his chipped sword.

'Of course.'

That was some confidence from a creature who'd not even seen what Nestol was, but Apollo didn't have time to argue. The entire Eastbrook military was gathering, and Torsten was already out. He could be spotted any second.

'If you're sure? Be ready, it might move quickly.'

In response, the three griffins growled, talons raking up the dirt as they readied themselves to pounce.

He had no idea what to expect, but was certain the griffins would be quicker to respond than he would be. Unlocking the latch of the lid, he gritted his teeth. He had no idea if he was doing the right thing, but he couldn't let this creature continue to exist. Not after what it had taken from him.

With shaking fingers, Apollo slid the box's lid open.

Nestol hissed like an angry cat, the sound somehow more insidious.

'What is this?' asked the cherry-red griffin.

'Something that has to be killed!' Apollo crouched low, blocking Nestol's escape with his body.

Fat on Apollo's memories, the worm-like creature wasn't as nimble as it had been when Torsten had set it on him. It writhed in the low light, body glistening as if covered with a translucent sheen of mucus.

It rolled out of the box and flopped wetly onto the ground, body pulsating.

The large griffin struck, its beak slicing directly into the creature.

Apollo grinned as the sound of flesh tearing meant the griffin had hit its mark—but his joy was short-lived. Much like when he had struck it with a blade, Nestol simply peeled apart and knitted itself back together. 'It won't die!'

Enraged, the griffin shrieked, slashing with its talons and gouging deep lines in the courtyard ground, but Nestol was impervious.

'There's gotta be some other way.' Apollo shook his head.

Two more fireballs streaked across the night, lighting up the entire courtyard again.

Nestol hissed and curled up.

Apollo reached forward, grabbed it, and threw it back into the wooden box with a shudder.

'They come!' one of the other griffins snarled, 'from the sea.'

Its words sparked an idea. 'That's it! The sea! We can drown this thing!' Apollo locked the lid and hopped over the low fence surrounding their compound. 'Please. Can you fly me there? I'll drop this into the water and drown it!'

The large griffin tilted its head, contemplating. 'If it does not drown?'

'It'll be in Neros's domain. If anything can kill it, that spirit can. And it'll be away from the palace and Torsten.'

'The Master Inquisitor had this?'

Apollo nodded. 'There's no time! Can you fly or not?'

The griffins turned to one another, communicating in clicks, squawks, and trills. They seemed to come to some sort of decision because the cherry-red one raised its head again. 'Olvalthar will fly you. We will wait for our Lords and Lady. The Myr approach, fly swiftly.'

Olvalthar lowered his head to the larger griffin, glossy cream and grey feathers shining in the firelight. 'And you as well. I will destroy this Myrish creation and return to fight with you!'

Apollo didn't hesitate, despite how enormous the griffins' talons were up close. With Olvalthar's help, he threw himself onto the griffin's back, awkwardly hanging onto the box the whole while. The griffin had been saddled, and there was a handrail, too, but the beast was larger than a horse, ungainly, and far less comfortable.

Without waiting, Olvalthar leapt into the air, wings beating powerfully.

Although the wind rushed past his ears with a scream, Apollo was able to peer over the side of the creature to the palace courtyard below. It was dark with gathered bodies, their cries along with the warning horns adding to the cacophony. Parts of the palace were aflame.

Apollo gritted his teeth. Getting to Foxmouth on the back of a griffin would only take a couple of hours. He needed to figure out how to convince the griffin to take him. He held on tight, trying to come up with a convincing idea.

'Look to the sea.'

Apollo did as the griffin told him, and his mouth went dry.

It was difficult to see the Myr at night—their true forms were mostly shadow—but he remembered the feel of the air when they were near, the cold, biting pain that accompanied them. It was the same icy presence that had been in that palace in Malnova. The same freezing terror he'd felt growing up whenever they'd raided.

They were on the horizon, coming from the east. In the low light, they merged into one dark shadow that floated just above the sea—heading straight for Eastbrook.

Every so often, a ball of fire would be hurled forward. Many missed the target, falling short and landing in the seawater. Others crashed into the cliffs, sending chunks of rock falling down. But some hit their target—the palace itself.

His heart thundered as Olvalthar sped over the palace walls, over Eastbrook, and above the Lasseen Ocean. Any other time, he would have loved the rush of the experience. Wanted to bring Malora and Renys on a flight on griffin-back.

But the rapture was pushed away by the growing malaise.

The Myr were *back*.

And he had been the cause of it. The catalyst that had allowed them to regain some of their power. He didn't fully understand it, but he knew it was something to do with the key.

Fuck. He needed to get to Malora and Renys and get them

to safety. There was no time to lose with the Myr approaching Eastbrook.

'Kill the creature!' Olvalthar's screeching voice was faint in the wind.

Trying not to look over the edge now they were so high up, Apollo double-checked the latches were secure, then threw the box over the griffin's side.

It plunged into the water with a splash—Apollo had wondered whether he should try and dash it on the rocks, but Olvalthar had flown further out than he'd anticipated. It was now in Neros's domain, and out of Torsten's reach.

Whatever happened, even if Torsten was able to catch up to him, he would know nothing. Even if he was the cause of the Myr's resurgence, his family would be safe. *They* were more important than anything else.

'It's done.' Apollo coughed, his throat dry and nose burning in the rushing wind.

The griffin nodded and banked steeply, wings spread wide to allow the turn.

Apollo held on tight. He needed to get away. Right now.

Directly ahead lay the city, and Apollo's breath caught. Toriaken was *rising* from the palace turrets. Apollo had never before seen The Spirit of Iron so close, and the dragon dwarfed the city of Eastbrook when he unfolded his wings.

Something that enormous, that powerful, shouldn't be able to *move*, let alone fly. He was a mountain of iron, the Myrish fire bouncing harmlessly off his dull scales, and he let out a deafening roar. The noise was so loud that Olvalthar dropped several feet in the air.

Apollo gripped the handrail lest he was thrown off by the force of the dragon's awakening.

Olvalthar veered off to the left, away from the path of the incoming dragon—who was heading straight for the Myr on the horizon behind them. It wasn't a moment too soon, because Toriaken took to the sky with an enormous leap.

A hurricane blasted across them, several of the griffin's feathers sent flying in the wake of Toriaken. The dragon moved faster than Apollo would have expected a spirit of his size, but the griffin was small, nimble, and managed to evade being caught directly in Toriaken's winds.

The dragon's enormous tail whipped past them—a solid slab of iron that could crush fortresses with a single swipe. Apollo flinched as Toriaken soared overhead, goosebumps rising on his arms, and the griffin again was thrown off course.

Shrieking, Olvalthar spiralled in the air, wings frantically beating to stay aloft and heading in the right direction.

Apollo held back a scream of terror as dry land rushed up to meet them.

The griffin let out another squawk, spinning in the air again as the last of Toriakan's wind hit them. Opening its wings, Olvalthar gained some altitude, soaring high up and above the wake of the dragon's passing.

Faded colours flashed past as the griffin struggled to control its spin—green fields, dark green forests, a line of blue water, the grey and brown of Eastbrook, a line of steel water on the horizon.

Then the colours were more vibrant as if lit up by the sun.

Olvalthar righted, but the griffin's head was low—it was clearly stunned. They were losing altitude fast, even though the griffin's wings were extended as if gliding.

Apollo turned to face the sea, towards the sudden brightness that had lit their surroundings. 'Olvalthar! Fire!' But his warning was too late, and the griffin was too weak. The Myrish fireball—one of several that had been hurled towards Toriaken and the town—tore through the sky toward them.

He grabbed the griffin's feathers and twisted, hoping to get the creature to react, to dive out the way or turn. But

Toriaken's power had been overwhelming, and Apollo couldn't get Olvalthar to respond.

He looked over the side and cursed. Even with his vision spinning, they were too high up. He'd risk death if he jumped.

With one final prayer to any spirit that would listen, Apollo braced as the Myrish fire slammed into them and sent the pair crashing to the ground.

27

THE SEA

CALIDRA

'I hope Fenn is okay.' Jisyel was wrapped in a thick, fur-lined cloak to stave off the chill of the Polar Sea, and the wind was biting, but she looked out at the water, as if pulled by it.

Calidra suppressed a shiver. 'Come and sit down.'

Jisyel turned away with a sigh, her face pale in the cold wind—not that she noticed.

Calidra's stomach lurched every time the ship crested a wave, and she'd been huddled on the deck in the centre of the ship for the past hour. It was the only place where her sickness was tolerable. 'Fenn will be fine, I'm sure. Selys is with him. That priestess won't let anything happen.'

'But Varlot *and* Inquisitors? What if—'

'Stop worrying.'

Jisyel pouted. She made her way over to Calidra, slumped down on the deck beside her, and threw her cloak out to cover both of their legs.

Calidra savoured the wave of warmth from the thick material, and rested her cheek on Jisyel's shoulder. She couldn't see much from sitting on the deck, but she could just make out the tips of icebergs as they floated past. They groaned like old wood, the noise echoing across the flat, empty sea. It gave her goosebumps.

She'd never been so far away from home before. Never been so far north. And she wondered how Malora had ended up somewhere so cold.

Calidra tried to time her breathing along with the ship's rocking. Some way of keeping in control of the nausea that fought for dominance. She laced her fingers through Jisyel's hair, absentmindedly playing with it while the haunting sound of creaking icebergs reverberated.

'Fenn looked ready to collapse.'

'Jisyel…' Calidra didn't want to control what Jisyel talked about, but they were on a ship in the middle of the Polar Sea. Whatever had happened, whatever *was going to happen*, there was nothing they could do about it. 'Talking about Fenn will only make you feel worse. We can't do anything from here.' She smoothed Jisyel's hair. 'I know you're worried.'

Calidra had *known* there was something off about Varlot. She'd had put it down to her own silly suspicions driving her thoughts. Perhaps a tinge of jealousy at the man's strength and control. But after seeing how he'd reacted? What he'd done to Fenn? She'd been angry that she hadn't pushed her concerns harder.

She should have forced him to leave when they'd been in Fellwood. Yes, he'd helped her, but that didn't give him a free pass to take advantage of Fenn. Probably to line his own pockets, too. She wrinkled her nose at the memory.

Had they not been reliant on *The Duschtet* to reach Foxmouth, they'd have stood with Fenn and Selys. And there was no telling what might have happened had she and Jisyel stayed.

Not for the first time since they'd set sail again, she wondered whether finding her sister really was more important than keeping Fenn safe. Her sister could wait another few days in blissful ignorance. Fenn's life was on the line right now. And if Selys was to be believed, it affected all of Tassar, too.

Again, anxiety grew in her gut. Had she done the right thing? Was she looking after the right people? Would her decisions today affect her poorly tomorrow?

'If your sister is blessed by Chyram, would she...would she...' Jisyel trailed off, as if realising what she was asking after the first few words had already escaped her lips.

Calidra sighed. She didn't want to think of Jisyel as another beggar, desperate for the help of someone favoured by a spirit. It had been close to ten years since she'd last seen Malora. Just knowing she was *alive* was overwhelming—let alone a mother—and the thought of asking her for help hadn't even crossed her mind.

'I don't know, Jisyel. We didn't exactly part on good terms. She might not want anything to do with me.' That, too, had been a possibility Calidra had staunchly ignored. She'd thought she could salvage some sort of relationship with Furyn, and that had gone out the window. What if that was the case with Malora, too?

No. Surely her sister would welcome her with open arms, much like Calidra would, if their roles were reversed.

Neither of them had behaved amicably when they'd been under Furyn's oppressive control. She wanted to focus on the positives. The possibilities. She kissed Jisyel on the cheek, hoping to keep her spirits up. 'But, maybe she'll know someone who can.'

Calidra shivered as the cold wind skirted around the back of her neck and her sense of dread grew. What would be waiting for them in Foxmouth?

SHOUTING WOKE Calidra in the middle of the night. Confused, and sure she was still dreaming given her unfamiliar surroundings, Calidra swung her legs off her bunk and rested her bare feet on the scratchy wooden floor.

It took her a few seconds to remember where she was. Although *The Duschtet* was a large vessel, the passenger quarters they'd been given were cramped, and only had room for single beds. Jisyel slept in the bunk above her, and Calidra scrambled up the ladder to shake Jisyel awake.

'Whassmatter...' Jisyel mumbled, turning away from Calidra to face the wall.

'Jisyel, get up. Something's wrong.' She peered out the small circular window in their room. The sea was rough, with sharp waves and plumes of foam bursting from them, but the sky was dark. They were some way off dawn. And yet her heart thudded as if someone had drawn a blade against her.

More shouting sounded above their room giving voice to her unease.

Where were they? It was too dark outside to make out any detail. There might have been land in the distance, but everything was a mash of black and grey, and it all blurred together alongside the churning sea.

Then, in the distance, cannon-fire.

'Jisyel! I think we're under attack!'

Calidra's words roused Jisyel, who half-fell off the top bunk, and landed heavily on the floor. 'Has the ship been hit? Are we sinking?'

'I don't know. But I can hear cannons.' Calidra pressed her face against the window, looking for any indication of what she'd heard.

Something exploded outside—much closer than the cannon-fire had been—and more orders were shouted from on deck.

'Jisyel, get dressed. Quickly.' Calidra pulled her own boots on, hopping on one foot in her haste. She grabbed a thick shawl and wrapped it around her shoulders, careful to tuck it into her collar and protect her neck from the cold.

Jisyel helped her fasten the toggles on her cloak, and then the two women were racing out of their cramped quarters and up the ladder to the main deck. Oil lanterns had been lit since sundown, and they burned low, throwing much of the deck into elongated shadows.

'Get those harpoons primed!' Captain Kifil bellowed. 'Load the cannons! Quickly man, move those legs! Unless you wanna take a swim tonight!'

Calidra put a hand across Jisyel, stopping her in place before a pair of crewmates charged into her.

'Are we under attack?' Jisyel called out.

Kifil glanced over at her. 'No. *They* are.' He strode past, taking a longsword from one of his crew, and brandishing it high. 'We're gonna have to keep clear of the islands. Don't want a rock to rip our hull apart before we have a chance to help!'

Calidra and Jisyel hurried over to the side of the ship. Now they were out in the open, where the dawn sun had begun to cast a thin, fiery light on the horizon, Calidra could see they *were* near land. Without a map in front of her, she couldn't tell exactly where in Porsenthia they were, but there was a settlement on the coast ahead. It was a large town, nestled up against the sea. Far to the east, the mountains rose up from the ground like enormous, shadowy ghosts. Fenn and Selys were somewhere in there, on the far side of the mountain range.

The settlement *had* to be Foxmouth.

And the bay beside the town was full of ships blasting cannons at the horizon. Calidra clutched Jisyel's hand.

'Why are they fighting?' Jisyel asked, scowling at the naval battle underway.

There had to be close to fifty ships on the water, of various sizes. Most were fishing vessels rather than warships, but they were all armed. As she watched, one ship lurched as it fired another cannon out into the pre-dawn gloom.

She couldn't see what they were shooting at. 'What's happening? Captain?'

But Kifil was too busy to answer her.

One of the crew, a lad of perhaps seventeen or eighteen hurried past, carrying a length of rope. Calidra grabbed him by the sleeve, and he yelped in fright. 'Who are they fighting?'

The lad turned to her, bloodshot eyes watering. His mop of hair was messy, his uniform crinkled, as if he'd recently been dragged from bed. 'Can't you see? It's the *Myr*.' He pulled out of her grasp and raced off towards Kifil's shouted orders.

Jisyel shook her head. 'That can't be right!'

'Why not? There were Myrish spirits in Ballowtown and walking across Bragalia.'

'But we're in Porsenthia! We're near *the Iron Crown*!' Jisyel gripped the ship's handrail. 'The queen kept us safe!'

Calidra joined her, and looked up past where the ships were firing. She wanted to see the Myr for herself and understand what they were all truly up against. If they were attacking Foxmouth...

Her heart skipped a beat and she pushed the anxious thought away. Malora would be fine. There was a veritable armada between Foxmouth and the Myr on the horizon. And as the ship sailed closer, she could hear raised voices in the brief lapses of cannons.

'Fire incoming!' Jisyel screamed.

Calidra looked at the horizon in time to see a fireball charging through the sky, leaving a plume of thick smoke in its wake. Three more appeared alongside it—cast from a huge shadow that floated above the sea.

'It's them...' Calidra whispered, not quite able to believe what she was seeing. This wasn't the same as an individual spirit in Ballowtown, or even the one that had attacked her and Varlot outside Meadowhill.

This was the Myr *rising*.

Her mouth fell open.

On the horizon, several mounds floated towards them. If she didn't know any better, she'd have thought they were hills or mountains. They were dark, shadow-like, and growing as they came closer. They were coming from the south, lit up by the slowly rising sun, and it was in this flash of yellow-orange light that Calidra could tell the shapes were not features of some distant landscape. They were creatures. Living creatures of pure magic. Crackles of light flashed across their bodies every so often.

And they were heading towards Foxmouth.

More cannons shot towards the mass of the Myrish creatures. Several slammed into the shadowy spirits, but it didn't dissuade their slow, consistent approach.

'Jisyel...'

'Wait, we can't possibly fight them!' Jisyel shouted, stepping back from the side rail. 'We need...we need Toriaken! The queen! We need the army! A fleet of warships!'

The Duschtet groaned in the water as Kifil put his crew to oar. Waves churned under the hull as the ship cut through the cold waters, heading straight for Foxmouth and the other vessels already protecting the town.

'We should get away! Get help?' Jisyel yelled, but none of the crew paid her any mind, too busy with their own tasks.

Panic and chaos built in equal measure. 'Jisyel, we can't leave Foxmouth. Even if we wanted to!'

'Why not? That's the *Myr*! Just *one* of their spirits almost killed us all in Ballowtown!' Jisyel gripped Calidra's arms.

'My sister lives in the town! She has a daughter, as well. Young. They're in danger!'

'But...but...' Jisyel's eyes were wide with fear. 'We...we can't fight them!'

Calidra chewed her lip. Jisyel wasn't wrong, but she couldn't leave Malora and everyone else in Foxmouth to be destroyed by the Myr. She understood why Kifil was adding his own firepower to the battle.

But if she and Jisyel stayed, they'd be in danger of being ripped apart, too.

'We need to get a rowboat. Get to Foxmouth ourselves. Find her, and get out.' It was a ridiculous plan, but it was the only thing Calidra could think of at that moment.

The Duschtet was a large enough vessel, and she'd seen four rowboats secured to the ship's sides. 'Come on, Jisyel. Help me release one!' Calidra darted away, her stomach churning at the movement, the terror, the stress. She grabbed one of the ropes tying the nearest rowboat and began unknotting it. It was stiff with salt, and had probably never been undone before. She gritted her teeth as the fraying material bit into her fingers.

'Shouldn't we ask someone first?' Jisyel stepped aside as more of the crew barrelled past, racing back and forth along the deck with supplies and weapons.

'I think the captain has his hands full at the moment. And if we don't get off right now, we're going to end up in the middle of the fray.' Calidra loosened the first knot and moved to the next. 'Come on, help me!'

'But...'

'Jisyel! Captain's probably forgotten about us! He's going to be doing what he can to keep his crew safe and defend Porsenthia against the Myr. I'm not a soldier and neither are you. We shouldn't be here in the middle of it!'

Jisyel hesitated a moment longer, conflicting emotions raging across her face, then she stepped forward and started on one of the other knots.

Another explosion sounded right beside them, and Calidra covered her eyes from the sudden flare of brightness. The Myrish fire was nearly upon them. They couldn't have been more than a few minutes from the edge of the ships outside Foxmouth.

They were going to get blown to pieces.

Before she had a chance to unsecure the knot, *The Duschtet* lurched as its own cannon-fire joined the other ships.

Calidra lost her footing as the ship swayed, the sudden drop forcing bile into the back of her throat. She coughed and spat it out overboard, wincing at the acrid taste. She *couldn't* lose her focus, not now.

Then she heard the Myr's hissing.

It was an insidious noise, somehow low enough that it rippled through her chest, and high enough that it set her teeth on edge. The sun peeked over the horizon, bathing Foxmouth in warm, pink light. It was enough to show the Myr in their full horror, too.

There were dozens of them. A hoard of Myrish creatures each nine or ten feet tall. Many were humanoid in appearance, others were more like animals—all covered in swirling smoke. Their amber eyes were chips of light in their dark bodies, and they set upon the ships with fury.

One ship, a single-masted sloop, erupted in splinters as one of the Myr's attacks blasted its hull in a direct hit. The crew screamed as they went up in flames, orange fire roaring high as it licked up the mast. 'Abandon ship!'

Calidra staggered back as the heat surged over them. The fire was intense, like nothing she'd ever felt before. 'Jisyel, stay clear!'

'The ropes!' Jisyel pushed forward, untangling the knot to release the rowboat.

'You'll burn!'

Jisyel didn't reply, too focussed on the knot. Her fingers were bright with heat as the flames soared ever higher, close enough to touch.

461

Another fireball careened past—high over the gathered ships—and slammed into Foxmouth itself.

Calidra gasped, racing to the other side of the deck to look at what damage the Myr had done to the town. Already, a plume of black smoke rose from where the fireball had landed. She couldn't tell from this distance, but it looked like it had hit a cathedral of sorts, somewhere in the middle of town where it sloped up towards the mountains.

More buildings were catching fire as the Myrish attack ate through stone and wood alike.

Again, *The Duschtet* lurched as it fired cannons—three in quick succession. The waters of the Lasseen Ocean slapped against the ship's hull, sending spray into Calidra's face where she peered over the edge.

She staggered back, the taste of salt making her nausea worse. 'They're already attacking the town!'

'Last knot!' Jisyel called back.

Calidra ran back to her, and together they finally released the rowboat. It dropped like a stone, landing in the water below with a splash. She glanced around the deck, in case any of the crew had seen. But they were too engrossed in their own tasks, following their captain's orders to fight back rather than flee.

Another explosion rippled through the bay, the waters bubbling violently as more flames tore through the air. Three more ships had been lost, and several parts of Foxmouth were on fire.

'We have to get off now!' Calidra cried.

'Shit, we can't. Our stuff is in the cabin!' Jisyel shook her head. 'We won't last long without our food and clothes!'

Calidra bit her lip to keep from cursing. They didn't have time for any of this. The Myr were upon them. If they didn't go now, they wouldn't make it at all. 'We'll come back for it!'

'What if the ship goes down?'

'We'll get more! Jisyel, come *on*!' She couldn't believe she was doing this. Stepping into a tiny row boat and dropping into an ocean in the middle of a battle. If it wasn't for her desperate desire to survive overwhelming her fear of water, she'd never have reached this decision.

Calidra could barely hold her tears back as she saw more and more of Foxmouth blasted to pieces. She could hardly see the town at all underneath the black smoke.

Jisyel ran to her and clutched her hand. 'Cal...'

'On the count of three, okay?'

'One...'

'Two...'

A deafening roar cut through the shouts of battle, the raging fire, and the groan of splintering wood. Underfoot, the waves swelled again, bigger than ever before, and Calidra and Jisyel were thrown to the deck floor as the ship tilted violently backwards. Screaming, they grabbed onto the mast before they slid past it, as boxes and barrels and everything else unsecured on deck rolled away.

'Hold on!' Jisyel called, eyes squeezed shut as the ship continued to tip further and further back.

Crewmates slid backwards, trying to grab anything they could reach before they were flung off the back of the ship and into the sea below.

Calidra gasped. *The Duschtet* was almost vertical and groaning with the forces pressing against it. Her legs dangled as she and Jisyel gripped onto the ship's mast, but already, her fingers were weakening.

Green light surged upwards, throwing smaller ships into the air as it burst from the water with a thunderous snarl.

Jisyel's grip failed, and she dropped away from the mast with a scream.

Calidra reached for her without thinking. She grabbed Jisyel by her wrist, wincing at the pain lacing through her arms as her muscles stretched. 'Jisyel!' She looked down. Jisyel's free arm flailed along with her legs. Beyond her, the back of the ship appeared mere inches from the churning sea. Another crewmate slid past, grabbed for the rail, slipped, and plunged into the water.

'Cal! You can't hold on forever!'

She gritted her teeth. Her fingers grasped the ship's mast, but they were already beginning to slip. 'I'm *not* letting go!' *The Duschtet* was easily three hundred feet long. Maybe more. A drop like that wouldn't necessarily be fatal.

A second flash of fire lit up the sky as the Myr attacked again.

The ship juddered as fire exploded against the exposed underside. Something blew apart, and burning debris fell down around them, streaming smoke.

'Jisyel! I'm...I'm going to let go.' She couldn't believe she was saying this. Couldn't believe she was preparing to throw them both into the sea. 'Are you ready?'

'It doesn't matter! Let go before you lose all your strength for swimming!' The wind blew Jisyel's hair in all directions, her skin paling in the cold.

Calidra *could* swim. But it had been many years, and she wasn't even sure she could remember how. She'd have to. She'd have to force it. Somehow.

Jisyel looked back up at Calidra, and screamed.

Gulping, Calidra turned her head to see what had scared Jisyel.

Neros, Spirit of the Lasseen Ocean, filled the air with her bulk. Water sluiced down her vibrant scales and steam rose from her open jaws. Calidra realised with another wave of nausea that the spirit had *pushed* the ship up as she'd risen from the water, and sent other smaller vessels flying.

The dragon was sea-green and blue, with fins connecting each vicious-looking spine that ran along her back, her attention fixed on the approaching Myr, with no regard to the chaos she'd caused on the surface of the ocean. She roared again as the Myrish attacks slammed into her. More fireballs headed for Foxmouth in a torrent of magical energy, distant explosions ringing across the water.

Calidra winced. Her fingers and wrists burned with pain, and the effort of holding on any longer was too much.

She let go.

The two of them plummeted.

Calidra was too afraid to scream as the dark waters rushed up to meet her faster than she'd realised. She didn't even have the time to take a breath or brace, and then she plunged into the water. The shock of the cold bit deep into her, along with the terror of what was on the surface.

She squinted one eye open, unable to see much more in the murky darkness than bubbles and the occasional flare of light where a burning ship sailed somewhere above her.

The impact had numbed her arms, and most of the strength in her fingers had gone—she couldn't even unclench her fist.

Where was Jisyel?

She couldn't see anything, couldn't make out any details, and Calidra thrashed as panic rose.

Something grabbed her by the collar. Looking up, ready to fight, she pulled away. But she couldn't see in the darkness, and whatever had grabbed her was stronger than she was.

Her chest burned as she realised her breath was running out, then she was being dragged up towards the surface.

With a hacking cough, Calidra burst through the water, her eyes stinging from the cold and the salt. 'J—Jisyel?' She couldn't see in the darkness, let alone recognise anyone.

'Are you okay?' Jisyel gasped, her hands running along Calidra's body. 'Are you bleeding anywhere? Hit anything on the way down?'

Calidra struggled to tread water, and held herself back from clutching onto Jisyel. That would be a quick way for them both to drown. 'I'm...okay...' Her teeth started to chatter.

Overhead, Neros bellowed her fury and sent a spew of flames towards the pack of Myrish creatures, now locked in combat with the armada of fishing vessels and merchant ships. Many were little more than burning husks, their sails torn or aflame.

'We need to get away from that.' Jisyel pulled Calidra, swimming away from the carnage in the water.

Calidra didn't argue. Didn't have the energy to. But she couldn't swim quickly, and lagged behind Jisyel after a handful of strokes. She couldn't do much more than focus on her breathing, try to keep her panic at bay, but it was winning.

Something cold and numb twisted in her gut, and made every moment slow and difficult. She couldn't feel her fingers, her arms. Even her legs moved like she was swimming in honey. Calidra slipped below the surface, water rushing into her nose.

She pushed up again, coughing as her nose and throat burned. 'Jisyel!' She meant to shout, but it came out as a whisper. Calidra coughed, trying to keep her head above water.

A shadow fell upon her and she turned as much as she dared, hoping the fires had been extinguished, that no more people needed to get hurt or die.

With a low, ear-splitting groan, *The Duschtet* capsized, and a wave of freezing water washed over her.

28

THE RIDDLE

FENN

Fenn's exhaustion was overwhelming. If anything, the journey across the sea had drained his already weak limbs of whatever energy they had left, and coupled with the tense stand off against Varlot and his Inquisitors—and his and Selys's subsequent flight from them—his body had been pushed to breaking point.

His fury at Varlot's betrayal was the only thing fuelling him on through the snow.

He'd *trusted* the man. Vouched for him on more than one occasion. Even when Calidra, someone whose word he trusted, had spoken against Varlot, Fenn had been certain of the man's honour.

He'd been desperate not to lose the *one* person who hadn't wanted to use him for his own, selfish reasons, that he hadn't seen the warning signs. Even Selys had only come with him because of her spirit. Calidra and Jisyel hadn't wanted anything to do with him at the start, and had suggested palming him off to Inquisitors at the first opportunity.

Varlot had stood up for him—against Torsten of all people—had been the only one to treat him like his own person during the entire journey.

What a kick in the teeth that had been.

And priestess or not, the next time Selys came across Inquisitors, she'd likely be marched away in irons for what she'd done. Her faith in this Myrish construct had to be as strong as her faith in Neros if she was willing to risk that.

Fenn was driven by something deep inside that he couldn't place, and his head throbbed in time with his pulse, so painful he could hardly think straight. Every step was agony on his weak body, but he was too close now to quit. Especially after Selys had fought off Inquisitors for him.

He wrapped his arms around his shoulders, glancing back at her. The priestess, for once, wasn't leading them. She'd dropped a short way behind, and they were relying on his ability to clearly see the Myrish magic to figure out where they needed to go.

Although the wind on the mountain was biting, the snow wasn't especially deep, and they were able to make good progress despite the low light. It hadn't taken more than a few minutes before the outpost disappeared from view, and even the Polar Sea was nigh indistinguishable.

Unfortunately, Selys hadn't escaped the battle against Varlot and his Inquisitor friends unscathed—she bore a wound on her shoulder from one of their swords. Although it was only a shallow cut, he blamed himself for the injury.

It had stopped bleeding after an hour or so of walking, and she didn't grumble about it.

Fenn took solace in the fact there was no chance of being followed so high into the mountains. Selys's display of fighting prowess had knocked the Inquisitors back, and even Varlot had been surprised. He'd hurled vitriol at them as they'd run, but he hadn't followed. Probably too drunk, now that he thought about it. But Fenn clutched to the possibility that there was still *some* good in the man, that he'd been backed into a corner and hadn't seen any way out.

It was probably naive—he'd definitely spent too much time with Jisyel—but he could hope.

And no-one else was going to come anywhere near the mountain. It was the site of an ancient battle against the Myr, according to Selys, and viewed with a good deal of superstition by people across Porsenthia and Bragalia.

Fenn wondered whether everyone was actually somehow aware of the Myrish presence, but only he—and those like him—could actually *see* it. He supposed it didn't matter. Once his curse was removed, he'd be just as blind as the rest of them.

Yet, his mind and body were conflicted. The freezing ice that caked his limbs was at odds with the burning fire in his chest. It was as if he was a puppet on a string, pushed and pulled by forces outside of his control or understanding. But as long as it led to answers, he didn't care. As far as he was concerned, the Myr had got him into this mess, and the Myr would get him out of it.

Darkness had long since enveloped them, and visibility had dropped so much that Fenn could barely see the shadow wreathing the mountain. But he didn't need to see it. His body knew exactly where to go, and the path to get there.

'Do you think it'll be much longer, Fenn?' Selys called up to him. 'I'm afraid…my knees are beyond my years.'

He didn't look back. 'We're close. Can't you feel it, too?' His sense of the Myr was so strong it was a physical weight. It was a wonder everyone in Porsenthia couldn't feel it—and this was an old construct that wasn't even a threat.

He dreaded to think what the Myrish homeland would feel like.

Shuddering, Fenn pulled his cloak tighter around his shoulders and continued on. Nearly there. Then, he'd be safe. He'd have his answers.

And he could finally begin his journey home.

469

'Selys, how did you learn to fight like that? It was incredible! Do you get people trying to steal from the shrine a lot?'

'Oh. From time to time, I suppose.' She waved her hand dismissively.

'And you need to be able to take on three attackers at once?' Fenn coughed, the effort of speaking more than a handful of words already too much for him.

'I wasn't always a priestess, you know. Before I joined Neros's order, I was part of a warband.'

Fenn stumbled. 'A what?'

Selys helped him up, wincing as she moved her shoulder, the movement causing it to bleed again. 'I'm from Segandis originally. That's a town in southern Bragalia, on the edge of the sea. Spent half my time on boats and the other half defending them.'

Fenn coughed again, his breathing raspy.

'I'll...tell you the story another time. Focus on where you're going, Fenn. That's more important.'

He continued on for another handful of minutes, following the growing pressure around him, until the steady incline levelled out. The mountain continued to rise above him into the darkness, but the pull had eased. 'We don't have to go any higher.'

'Thank Neros.' Selys joined him, her breathing heavy. Blood trickled down her right shoulder from under the makeshift bandage she'd tied around the wound.

'You're bleeding.'

She wiped it away. 'I'm fine. Let's keep going.'

He swayed in a sudden gust of wind, and braced against it. His knee buckled and he dropped into the snow. He was almost out of time. With a grunt of effort, he got to his feet and pushed forward into the growing pressure, heart thudding. They were getting close. 'Vermecio...'

Then he saw it. A cave—its entrance half-obscured by thick snowdrifts.

'In there?' Selys asked, creeping forward.

He didn't reply, just stared. It was the place he needed to go, where the invisible pull was strongest. Where he'd finally see the Myrish construct.

He let the pull carry his feet, navigating around the rocks and boulders that littered the cave entrance. Selys used her glaive to check the path before every step, using it to avoid pitfalls or slippery patches hidden under the snow.

Giant chunks of ice sat just within the cave's mouth, glinting dully in what little light reached it.

Fenn sucked in a breath as he crossed the threshold. The oppressive pressure filled the air inside, making it difficult to breathe, and he took a moment to steady himself. Ice climbed up the walls like moss, and countless frozen stalactites hung from the vaulted ceiling.

Selys joined him in the cave's mouth and took in their surroundings with wide eyes. She made a gesture with her fingers across her forehead and murmured Neros's name under her breath. 'This is it, Fenn. The answers we seek.'

He was impressed at how confident she was. Her certainty hadn't wavered even for a second throughout their whole journey. 'I'm ready for them.' Fenn picked his way deeper into the cave, following an icy tunnel as it led into the mountain. The shadowy mist he'd been following swirled along the floor, dissipating with each of their footsteps, and Fenn realised writing had been scrawled in fine ink along the ground itself. Glancing around, he noticed the same writing on the walls, too, much of which was under the ice. There were letters in dozens of languages, but he only recognised one word: *Vermecio*.

'Do you see this writing, too?' Fenn asked, not daring to raise his voice above a whisper.

Selys frowned. 'There are lots of languages here. Some of these are old.' She brushed her fingertips against the wall, and a few of the letters flashed blue for a heartbeat. 'Holy languages. I recognise a few letters from the books in the shrine.'

'Can you read them?'

She peered at a section of writing closely, running her thumb under a line of text. 'Some sort of guardian, maybe? A name, I think? Ver...ver...vermecio? I don't understand.'

'Let's keep going.' Fenn wasn't sure why he didn't want to tell her about what he already knew—his encounter with the Myr on the edge of the spirit world, or the fact he'd been given the construct's name as a place he could find answers.

Something about holding that knowledge made him uneasy. Like he was doing the wrong thing.

Selys nodded, following him deeper into the tunnel, her footsteps carefully placed. She kept her glaive out, ever-ready.

Fenn rounded a corner, navigating between thick pillars of ice, and entered a wide chamber. The ceiling was so high that he wasn't sure there *was* one—the walls stretched upwards endlessly, and thick, shadowy mist filled the space above his head.

They'd found the construct.

The large chamber wasn't quite circular, but it was roughly round, with a floor of icy stalagmites, their tips as sharp as the ones that dangled from the tunnel's roof. Water dripped down the frozen walls, and Fenn's breath misted in front of him.

And at the far end of the chamber, Vermecio waited.

The creature had the maned head of a lion, with powerful clawed limbs attached to a vaguely humanoid body. Three pairs of wings were tucked tight against its side, each folded like the wings of a giant bird. Two thick, curved horns jutted out from its chin. It sat still as stone, unmoving. Waiting. Mist poured from the creature's body. Its hairless skin rippled, shifting colour every few seconds—silver, black, purple, blue—and it stared at them with three lidless eyes. Each was a different colour—one red, one white, one gold.

Fenn found its unblinking gaze more unnerving than the construct's bizarre appearance.

It didn't look like any of the Myrish spirits he'd seen before, and he wondered just how different this construct was in comparison.

They both held their ground at the chamber's entrance, neither willing to take the first step inside. It was a place of ancient magic, where the Myrish creature had dwelled untouched for centuries. Selys had said it was no threat, but standing before it, Fenn had his doubts.

Most of Vermecio's limbs were encased in ice, contributing to its lack of movement. But its head turned, its neck creaking as it moved, and Fenn was reminded of the statues he'd seen outside Neros's Shrine.

'H—hello?' Fenn called out cautiously, once Vermecio's gaze fell upon him.

'You have arrived.'

A shiver ran down his spine at the creature's words. It spoke in monotone, which somehow made it more eerie than if it had spoken with a human voice.

'What *are* you?' Selys entered the chamber, the tip of her blade held high.

'I am a bastion.'

'Of power?'

The Vermecio shook its head, the movement slow. *'Of our collective memories. Thoughts. Knowledge. But I was created in haste. I have not the strength I should.'*

Fenn didn't like the sound of that. 'You're a Myrish construct, aren't you? I've been cursed by the Myr. I'm dying.' He approached Vermecio slowly, his legs threatening to give out with every step. He couldn't afford to slip over now, he doubted he'd be able to get back up. 'Can you remove the curse?'

The lion head turned as Fenn approached, the noise reminiscent of stone grinding against stone. Again, its skin shifted colour, ripples of gold running through dark purple. Light flashed, and more smoke poured out of its body, leaking from its skin like water. *'I saw you cross the site of our last great defeat. Where the Iron Dragon sent so many of us to the spirit world.'*

'How could you possibly see that from here?' Selys asked, incredulous.

'I see through our mists. Our magic marks our passing.'

Fenn shook his head. Everywhere that dark mist had been, Vermecio could see? He thought about it. That made the mist essentially a gravestone for the Myr.

It made sense. Many Myr had died in the deadlands and the mist had been thick there.

He stood in front of the creature and looked up at it. Vermecio sat at eight feet tall, an imposing creature that seemed to be made more of stone than flesh. 'Wait, wait. You *saw* me cross the deadlands?'

'That is the name which your people gave the area, yes.'

He thought back to the place, to the smoke wreathing the ground, and the visions he'd had in that awful, dead place. 'Is that a bastion, too? How many are there?'

'No. There are only three, of which I am one.'

'Where are the other two?'

'I...do not have that knowledge. I am weak. Created in haste. I have not the strength I should.'

Fenn frowned at Vermecio's repetition. It sounded like himself—knowing it *should* remember more, but unable to access those memories, that knowledge. Selys had said it was a construct, and Vermecio itself had said it had been created, and yet Fenn sympathised with its plight. 'Why did the Myr curse me? And all the others? So many of them have died!'

'Our time is now.'

He shared a glance with Selys, who raised her shoulders in a shrug.

She tapped some of the encroaching ice with her glaive. 'What does that mean for Tassar? "Our time is now?" What are the Myr planning?'

'I...do not have that knowledge. I am weak. Created in haste. I have not the strength I should.'

Fenn's scowl deepened. He wasn't sure if Vermecio was truly alive or not. Had it all been for nothing? Selys had been so sure he'd find answers here. Had left her shrine on that assumption. This was *supposed* to be his solution. His memories. Even the Myrish voice that had spoken to him on the edge of the spirit world had said as much.

But the construct seemed...broken.

The realisation sapped any hope that had built on finding the cave.

'This thing must be some sort of spell,' Selys said, giving words to his own thoughts. 'Some way of preserving knowledge over the years. It doesn't really have its own consciousness. We'll have to think of specific questions to ask it and get our answers that way.'

Fenn turned back to it, stared at its strangeness, and focused on its multi-coloured eyes. It was time to see if his journey had been worth it or not. He placed his hand flat against the creature's nose. It was strangely smooth, and as cold as the ice in the cavern. 'Can you see the Myr's touch on me? See how it weakens me?'

'I see.'

'Can you remove it?'

It went quiet, and Fenn didn't know if it had run out of ability to talk, or if it was just considering.

'Vermecio?'

'You...know my name.'

Fenn ignored Selys's curious glance and focussed on the creature in front of him. He tried to keep the pleading tone

475

from his voice, but he was on his last legs. Perhaps naming the creature would make it obey. Even now, the edges of his vision dimmed as the cold mountain sapped his strength. 'I was told you could help me. I'm going to die otherwise!'

'Perhaps...you can help me, also.'

Although the request surprised him, Fenn didn't hesitate. Didn't care to ask for details. If he didn't agree, he wouldn't live much longer. 'I will, if I can.'

'Fenn!' Selys called.

He raised his other hand towards her, gesturing for Selys to stay out of the conversation. Even if it was a poor decision, it was his decision to make. *His* risk.

Perhaps he wasn't so different from Varlot after all. He'd been backed into a corner with no way out, and as much as he pretended he was okay, Fenn didn't want to die.

His chest squeezed with sudden tightness, fire burning within him as he focused on the Myrish construct. 'Please, Vermecio.'

'I...can try. I have not the strength I should.'

Fenn straightened and pulled his hand away. It was enough for him. If Vermecio couldn't, he might well die on the mountain. 'Then try.'

'Fenn...' Selys stepped over to him. 'If this...if this doesn't work? Will you forgive me for dragging you out here? I can see...I can see how weak you are. This trek was too much for you. I could tell even on the ship, and I forced you to keep going when you should have rested.' She cupped his cheek in one hand.

'Selys, if it weren't for you, I'd never have had *any* hope to hold onto. Whatever happens, you have my thanks.'

She chewed her lip, her uncertain gaze drifting between Fenn and Vermecio. 'Fenn, you...you don't even know what it wants. What if the cost is too great?'

'If it doesn't work, I'm dead anyway.'

She nodded, her expression grim, and stepped back. 'May Neros bless you, Fenn. I hope this works.'

He put his hands behind his back and raised his chin. 'I'm ready, Vermecio. What do I do?'

'Sit.'

Fenn did as instructed, with some effort, sitting cross-legged on the floor, in between two enormous spears of ice. Before he'd taken his next breath, the pressure in the chamber intensified. The writing on the floor flashed bright blue underneath him, and Vermecio let out another plume of swirling mist. He couldn't move, couldn't so much as shift his gaze or open his mouth. It felt like his body was filling with ice, rooting him in place, and he let out a startled grunt.

A moment later, the thick, swirling mist passed through him. Ice covered every limb, all the way to his fingertips. The fire in his chest thrashed around.

It was like being on the edge of the spirit world again, where his edges were blurring away, and the fire was the only thing he could focus on. His breath caught, and the same darkness as before lined his vision, the same sense of *nothingness*. What remained of his strength faded, his head spun with sudden dizziness, and he fell forward into the void.

Much like when he'd been on the edge of the spirit world before, there was no fear. No pain. There was only peace. A sense of contentment. There was nothing to him anymore. No body. No mind.

Fenn half-heartedly wondered where the other echoes were, whether he would join them as he crossed over, or whether he would simply…vanish.

He'd been a fool. Calidra would certainly say so if she could see him now.

But he'd *tried*.

His throat tightened and he breathed. Fierce, freezing air filled his lungs with a gasping breath, and he opened his eyes.

'Fenn!' Selys's voice sounded distant.

He sat up, and with his next inhale, energy surged into his arms and legs. The next breath brought the world into focus, every colour bright and vivid, and Fenn sprang back to his feet in wonder. He clenched and unclenched his fists, amazed at the strength in his arms. His head felt lighter than air, and his muscles no longer twinged in frustration.

He was *alive*. Truly alive.

Vermecio had *done it*. It had chased away death.

'Fenn! Are you okay? Say something!' Selys appeared in front of him, a wide grin on her face, her blue eyes dancing in the reflected light of the ice cave.

'Selys! It's gone! The pain!' He spun around in a circle, arms held wide. If it came to it, he was sure he could race back down the mountain and outrun a dozen Inquisitors if he had to. Fenn burst out laughing, the rapturous joy too overwhelming to keep inside.

One thing remained, despite the pain lifting: the fire in his chest. It burned away merrily, somehow brighter than before. Strange, he'd thought that was a marker of his weakness, of being close to death. Why was that still there?

'Can you tell me what happened, Fenn? Where were you attacked by the Myr? What did you see? Tell me everything!' Selys asked excitedly.

Fenn shook his head, trying to focus. 'Oh! Yes, of course.' He rubbed his eyes, thinking. He cast his mind back, over the past few days, to meeting Calidra and Jisyel on the Isle of Salt.

Coming face to face with a dragon spirit.

Before that, he'd been...he'd been...

A dark fog settled in his mind, masking everything beyond the muddy bog in the forest.

'No...' His joy slipped away like draining water. 'No, it...I can't...No!'

'Fenn?'

He clutched his head with both hands and sank to the floor. 'No! No! NO!'

Selys was with him a moment later, her arms wrapped around his shoulders. 'What's wrong, Fenn? Whatever happened, whatever you saw, we can work through this! We can—'

'No!' He wailed. 'They're still gone. There's *nothing* there!' Fenn rounded on the construct, fear and rage charging through him like a furious storm. 'Vermecio! My memories were taken by the Myr! Why didn't you restore them?'

Again, the bastion considered, more smoke pluming from its limbs. *'I cannot.'*

Fenn went numb. He couldn't believe it. After all this time, after everything he'd been through to reach this place. None of it had mattered. His eyes burned with the threat of tears.

He'd been such an idiot.

'But, help me, and I will be able to.'

Startled, Fenn studied the creature, but there was no way to gauge any emotion from it. Defeated, he shook his head. 'Really? What do you want?'

'What I ask in return? Nought but a trinket.'

He frowned, waiting.

'A sliver of gold. A blade you cannot fight with. A bow from which an arrow cannot fire. Bring me this token, and I will have the power to restore your memories, Fenn.'

His heart pounded as Vermecio spoke his name. And what did any of it even mean? 'You want...three things?'

'Only one.'

Selys tapped the tip of her glaive on the ground, her gaze distant. 'It must be some sort of riddle?'

Fenn's eyebrows knitted together as he tried to think through the waves of emotions cascading through him. His hopes had been crushed before, and he didn't know if he could stomach it again.

Gold. Blade. Bow.

But…not weapons? He folded his arms, pacing the chamber, his breath misting in front of his face. 'A blade…you can't fight with?'

'It wants one thing, correct? Is the blade part of an object?' Selys suggested.

'I should have known this wasn't going to be as easy as just getting here and having everything answered.' He dragged his fingers through his hair as if it would give his mind a boost of thought.

'A bow, but you can't shoot an arrow from it?' Selys continued to tap her glaive. 'I have no idea.'

'I have to figure it out. Because…because once I bring it to you, you'll be able to restore my memories, right?'

Vermecio turned all three eyes on Fenn. Its mouth pulled back in a crooked grin, exposing several large, gleaming canines. The first emotion it had shown since they'd arrived. '*Yes.*'

'How do you know you can trust what it says?' Selys said, studying the construct.

'It restored my strength, didn't it? I'm not in any more pain.' It was a mild lie. The headache, fatigue, and weakness had gone completely. But the burning in his chest remained. He could cope with that. And if nothing else, the construct had certainly chased away the looming death. That was a bigger relief than he could put into words.

He leaned against the wall, heedless of the cold seeping through his clothes, and thought. Faded light trickled in from the tunnel, and he wondered how far off they were from dawn. They should probably get some rest—he couldn't remember the last time he'd slept properly.

Fenn closed his eyes and exhaled. He was expecting voices in his head again—the Myr whispering to him, telling him to find Vermecio—but he was greeted by only silence. The peace was more than welcome—it was utter relief.

Selys screamed.

Fenn jumped and saw the priestess collapse. 'Selys?' He crouched by her, holding her up by her good arm. 'What's going on?' he asked Vermecio, but the construct hadn't moved.

The priestess gasped, tears streaming down her cheeks. She could hardly breathe, sucking in tiny mouthfuls of air. 'It's...Ne...ros...Her...her fury...'

Alarmed, Fenn backed away. They were nowhere near the Lasseen Ocean. It was *leagues* away. 'Is something happening with the spirit?'

'She...she...' Selys writhed, her limbs jerking. She balled her hands into fists and hit the cave floor, sending up small plumes of icy dust.

'What can I do? Selys? Selys! Talk to me!'

But she didn't seem to hear him.

'*The dragon of the sea,*' Vermecio said.

As if summoned by the construct's words, light flared from Selys's body, throwing gold and pink across the ice in the cavern. It burst from her skin, her hair, her eyes.

Fenn's own chest burned with more frenzy than before, and he clutched it, sinking to one knee as a multitude of powers filled the cavern. 'Selys!'

She slowly got to her feet, fingers trembling as light pulsed from their tips. 'I...see...Neros...'

Fenn stood beside her, one hand holding onto the priestess in case she fell again. His own aches faded to a low thrum. 'Are you okay?'

She looked at him through glowing eyes. 'Fenn. You are... I can see...' Selys picked up her glaive and held it out to Vermecio. The blade glimmered in the light she threw off. '*That* should be destroyed.'

'What? Wait! This is the *only* thing that can help me!' Fenn stood in front of her blade, blocking her strike against Vermecio. 'What's with the light?'

481

'Neros has chosen…Neros has blessed…' Selys shuddered, her grip on her weapon loosened, and it dropped to the icy floor with a loud clatter. She slumped forward, her hair covering her face.

Fenn kept a wary eye on her, not quite daring to move.

When Selys straightened, the movement was awkward, jerky, as if something pulled her body to move in their own way. *'This is a bastion of the Myr.'* She spoke with a voice that was not her own, deeper, more resonant. *'The enemy.'* Selys raised a finger and pointed to Vermecio. It no longer trembled, instead sending forth sparks of light. *'Our most ancient enemy. They are here again. In my domain. Approaching. They will only become stronger. It must die.'*

Fenn drew his sword. 'Selys…?'

Selys cocked her head at him like a bird. Her eyes were blank and unfocussed. *'Why has my little brother touched you? Protection from their influence, perhaps?'*

'Selys, what are you talking about?'

'My priestess will carry out this task. The Myr cannot continue to taint Tassar. All of their bastions must be destroyed. It is the only way.'

Fenn's mouth hung open. Selys was…Neros was speaking *through* her. 'This construct has been here for *centuries* and done nothing. It's only a spell, you told me so yourself! And it's my *only* hope of getting my life back. Learning who I am, where I'm from! You *can't* destroy it or I won't get those answers!'

'It is unfortunate. But one life does not matter when all of Tassar is at stake.'

'What are you talking about? You wanted those answers too!' Fenn screamed with panic, hardly aware of his own voice rising.

The light disappeared with a crack, and Selys fainted.

2 9

THE HUNT

APOLLO

A rock digging into Apollo's back was the first thing that woke him up.

The second was the tickle of a feather just under his nose.

He opened his eyes with a groan and stared straight up at a tangle of green leaves. It took him several seconds to figure out he was looking at a tree canopy, and from the unpleasant dizziness when he moved, he realised he'd hit his head *hard*.

Through the leaves, a dark cloud loomed overhead, bathing him in semi-darkness. Apollo shivered, not wanting to get caught in the rain. It was an absurd thought, but the first one that came to mind.

He sat up and awkwardly reached for the rock under his back. Wincing as he pulled it out, he realised in horror that his left arm was covered in blood.

Shooting pains raced through his legs as he got to his feet, and he gasped when he looked at where he'd fallen. The tree behind him had been torn in half. What was left of the trunk was splintered—jagged edges sharp as blades stuck out in all directions. Leaves and vines had been shredded, and debris littered the woodland floor. Whatever plants grew in that spot had been flattened. 'Spirits take me.'

His neck twinged as he turned his head to get a better look at his surroundings. 'Getting too old for all this…' There was no sign of the griffin, although there were a slew of cream and grey feathers in among the leaflitter. The sight reminded him of when a local cat had caught a gull one morning, leaving nothing but feathers and a smear of blood just outside *The Grumpy Fisherman*.

He hoped Olvalthar's fate had not been so grim.

'Olvalthar?' Apollo called, shakily taking a step forward and clutching his bleeding arm. On closer inspection, there was a deep line gouged across his bicep—probably when he'd crashed into the tree, there were bits of bark and dirt studded around the wound—and it stung.

He'd be in trouble if he didn't get out of here quickly.

If *he'd* survived the crash, the griffin had to as well. That creature was three times the size of him and built for battle. With another groan from his battered body, Apollo turned in a gentle circle, trying to follow the path of destruction while figuring out whether his legs worked properly.

Olvalthar couldn't be far.

As he moved gingerly through the woodland, Apollo struggled to come to terms with what he'd seen from the griffin's back only minutes before. The Myr. Here, on the edge of Porsenthia.

The queen and Nadja had been right. What *had* he done?

He'd thought it had all been about escaping his own death sentence. Starting a new life. In reality, he'd opened the door and unleashed the Myr back upon the world.

Shit.

So much for living the rest of his life in a quiet seaside town. He'd have to face the Myr again. Everyone would.

Renys would have to deal with that freezing terror for the first time.

Apollo gritted his teeth. He *had* to get them away. He *had* to get back to Foxmouth.

The Myr attack on the palace had been a terrifying shock, but it had bought him a window of opportunity—and he wasn't going to waste it.

At least Torsten would be too busy defending Eastbrook to be on his tail. He didn't want to think about what Torsten might do to Malora and Renys if the Inquisitor somehow reached them before he did. He doubted Torsten would be as forgiving as Nadja.

Apollo took a few more shaky steps, his knees weak and trembling. If he could find the griffin, convince it to fly him to Foxmouth, he'd definitely beat Torsten there. It was a foolish thought, really. Olvalthar had only helped him because of Nestol, so there was no guarantee the griffin would help him again.

Damn it all. He had to try.

'Olvalthar? Can you hear me? Olvalthar!'

Nothing replied. Not even birds sang in the trees.

His tunic had been ripped, and a tattered wedge of fabric dangled at his waist. Apollo tore it off and wound it around his arm as tightly as he could. Leaving a trail of blood would only invite danger, whether it was an Inquisitor tracking him or some animal looking for an easy meal.

Grasping his injured arm, Apollo shuffled forwards as quickly as he could, careful not to leave more damaged foliage in his wake. After the long horse ride, the torture, and the chaotic escape, he was about ready to drop from exhaustion.

Trees surrounded him on all sides, and what little light filtered through the canopy didn't reveal much about his location. As he walked, he considered just how far the griffin had flown them. There was a small patch of woodland between Eastbrook and Foxmouth—likely where he was right now. If that was the case, he only needed to head north to get home. It was a stroke of luck that griffin had taken him halfway there without realising.

He tripped over a dead log, cursed, and kept moving. More than once, he checked over his shoulder to make sure nothing crept up behind him. As a boy, he'd lost his best friend to a forest cat that had snuck up on them, and he didn't want a repeat of that experience.

Apollo focused on the rhythm of his breathing as he stumbled onwards, looking for the griffin but mostly trying to get away from the site of the crash. After the initial shock had faded, he was left with his own thoughts. The Myr on the horizon, attacking Eastbrook. There had been so many of them, a mass of shadows moving towards the coast. They'd even shot him down from the sky—although he didn't know if it had been a lucky strike or if he and the griffin had been targeted.

It was the beginning of another war.

One *he* was responsible for.

He could head east, make for the coast. It would be much easier to follow it up to Foxmouth, but it would be easier for Inquisitors to spot him, too. He *had* to use the trees as cover for as long as he could, even if the going was tougher.

After hobbling along for several minutes, Apollo realised the darkness above wasn't a raincloud or a growing storm. The air wasn't humid enough. It took him another moment to understand it was *smoke*, the acrid stench of it only just reaching him under the canopy. Had the fires at Eastbrook raged so much that the smoke had carried this far?

That didn't bode well.

The thought of the Myr so close urged him on. He didn't want to think about those magical monstrosities anywhere near Malora or Renys.

There were no insects chirping or birds singing, and it made him more wary than usual. He forced himself onwards, focussing on the positives instead of worrying. It was the queen's job to worry about the Porsenthian Empire, not his, regardless of the part he'd played in causing said problems. One foot in front of him, that was all he needed to think about. Getting home before it was too late. 'I'm coming, Mal.'

With the thick smoke in the air above the canopy, there was no sun to navigate by, so he simply headed where the ground sloped upwards. It was the best chance of going in the right direction, given Foxmouth's proximity to the Nethal Mountains, and he soon settled into a rhythm.

Apollo pushed past a particularly thorny bush, when the forest darkened as if a thick cloud had passed in front of the sun. Apollo halted, senses on high alert, as pitch-black blanketed the trees.

A low groan sounded just ahead, not quite a hiss, not quite a rumble. He couldn't think of any animal that made a noise like that. Mouth dry, he shuffled towards it as quietly as he could, ears straining for whatever was there.

The groan shifted into...chewing? A wet, sucking noise sent creeping dread through his gut. Despite goosebumps raising on his arms, he pushed on, every step measured, until he spotted movement in the darkness perhaps twenty feet away.

Something domed and black crouched between two trees. The colour in the ground around it faded as the creature shivered.

Apollo gasped.

A face from within the dome-shaped blackness spun around to stare at him, amber eyes glinting.

Freezing, piercing cold covered every inch of Apollo's skin when his eyes locked with the creature's. He staggered, dropping to one knee, and the creature shifted again, sharp teeth grinning wide. Its purple-black skin sucked in all the light around it, and the air surrounding the creature was hazy.

One of the *Myr*.

A boar raced out in front of him, two tiny, striped piglets following, heedless of the danger. She gave him a disapproving snort, and hurried off into the undergrowth.

Immediately, the cold receded from Apollo's arms and legs, and he stood up again. He looked back to the Myr, only to find it gone. A patch of dead and wilted plants remained in a circle where the creature had been feeding, sucking energy from everything around it.

Draining the life from the forest.

Apollo shivered, wondering whether to try and follow it or get away, when a twig snapped somewhere behind him. His blood ran cold. Leaves rustled as if being shoved aside. This wasn't a city that he knew, where he could choose from a dozen hiding spots or back alleys and disappear in a flash.

He was injured, exhausted, and in the middle of a forest he'd never been in before. And after seeing the Myr, he was more afraid than he'd been in years.

'...broken trees this way!' Someone shouted behind him.

Shit.

Perhaps it was a curious traveller, or someone who lived in one of the smaller, unmapped hamlets who had seen the griffin crash and come to investigate. Someone who was a friend, not an enemy.

But it was just as likely to be an Inquisitor, and Apollo didn't fancy his chances if it was.

He backed up to a tree, careful not to trip over one of its exposed roots, and knelt down in the large ferns that grew around its trunk. If he ran somewhere else, the movement or noise would give him away. Best thing was to stay low and quiet. Patience was often the most effective asset when it came to avoiding capture, and Apollo had patience in abundance.

He was careful to keep his head down, underneath the vast green leaves, though he had enough visibility to peek through the ferns. Only a few seconds after he'd ducked away, three people appeared between the trees. They were each in grey armour, short swords at their hips, and one carried a pike.

Apollo held his breath and watched one of them crouch down, pointing at the ground and gesturing to the others. They were too far for him to make out their words, but it was clear from their body language that they were tracking something.

Apollo prayed they were hunting the Myr and not there for him.

One of them stretched their arms high above their head and leaned on a tree, apparently tired from whatever they were doing. Another made their way off, heading deeper into the trees. The third, the one with the pike, straightened up from where he'd been pointing at the ground and looked around.

For one heart-splitting moment, their eyes connected, then his gaze drifted off towards the rest of the foliage nearby.

Apollo couldn't be sure whether the man had seen him or not, and he couldn't risk sticking around to find out. Careful to keep hunched below the growing ferns, he shuffled away from the tree, backing away one cautious, quiet, step at a time.

The soldier resting against the tree didn't so much as open their eyes, and the pike-wielder followed his comrade, away from his hiding spot.

Once clear, Apollo spun around and sprinted—straight into an Inquisitor's uniform.

'Well, well, well. Where are you off to in such a hurry?'

Apollo didn't recognise the man's voice, though he sounded younger than him by some years, and he didn't stop to take a closer look, either. Darting around the Inquisitor, Apollo hurtled off into the undergrowth without a second thought. His tunic snagged on branches, and he continued on, uncaring if some of his clothing ripped further.

Shouts followed him, then footsteps muffled by the soft forest floor.

This was just his luck.

Escape Torsten's torture, get out of the palace on griffin-back and survive a crash landing, only to be scooped up by Inquisitors moments later.

Apollo held his arms up, protecting his face from branches and leaves as he raced past them. Many scratched his skin, and one ripped open the cotton around his arm, but he ignored them, hurrying as fast as he could—leaping over roots and vines, using every instinct he had to lose his pursuers in the undergrowth.

Fuelled by adrenaline, Apollo put a fair amount of distance between himself and the young Inquisitor, reaching a narrow stream that cut through the trees. Although this forest didn't have a spirit, there was always magic in water, as there was throughout Porsenthia—particularly close to East-brook. A faint hum of music sounded where it splashed against rocks, as if someone played a harp nearby.

The bank was steep on the opposite side, but the stream flowed directly across his path. Gritting his teeth, he ran towards it and jumped, leaping over the water in a single movement. The bank was muddy on both sides, and his boots slipped, but he didn't fall. Apollo scrambled up the muddy slope, hurrying to get up it as quickly as possible.

The moment he reached the top of the bank, he froze.

Horses thundered through the trees, ten of them, each ridden by an armed, armoured soldier.

Apollo shook his head in disbelief, and as adrenaline left his body, aching pain ripped through it. Perhaps he *should* have gone to the coast. Staying in the trees was too obvious. He wiped sweat from his forehead, grimacing when he realised he'd just smeared blood across his face—his wound had bled through the ripped cotton.

Perfect.

Just perfect.

The horses were already turning towards him, spurred on by their riders. Behind him, on the other side of the stream, the Inquisitor and the soldiers from earlier flanked him, cutting off his retreat.

Trees spread in either direction, but didn't offer much cover. He considered jumping into the stream and letting it carry him away, but it didn't look deep enough.

With a groan, he pulled out his chipped sword and held it up. There was nowhere left to run, but he wasn't going down without a fight.

'Put that stolen sword down, Apollo.' Torsten's cold voice cut through the cacophony of horse hooves.

Apollo kept it held up, unable to believe how badly the tables had turned for him. He'd had the perfect opportunity to escape, and he'd messed it up.

And why was Torsten *still* after him? 'Shouldn't you be on the front lines fighting the Myr? Or are you happy to abandon your queen in her time of need?'

The pale grey horse came to a stop only a few paces from him, nostrils snorting as Torsten reined it in. 'You've some nerve to say that, traitor. It was *you* who gave the Myr cause to rise again!'

Apollo spat a glob of bloodied saliva onto the ground by the horse's front leg. 'You're the one who's left your queen and city. Surely I'm not worth all this effort?' He gestured widely to the other horses and soldiers there, turning to include the young Inquisitor behind him in the movement. 'You're worse than a dog with a bone!'

Torsten's horse whickered as the others came to a halt, forming a semi-circle around Apollo. Smoke from overhead began to filter through the trees, further darkening the forest.

Torsten muttered under his breath, one hand clutching the hilt of his sword. He shook his head and blinked, seeming to come back to himself. 'I am a Master Inquisitor, Apollo. Not some common grunt out on the front lines. Queen Surayo has plenty of protection.'

Apollo narrowed his eyes, wondering whether something was wrong with the Inquisitor. It wasn't like Torsten to lose focus. 'Something else on your mind, Torsten? Another distraction?'

'Ignorant thief. I have been ordered by my queen to get answers. And it was a good thing I came after you, Apollo. Once a thief, always a thief, I see. On top of your other crimes, you stole a griffin. It belonged to one of our Olmese guests. That is another unforgivable act, you know. I wonder what they do to griffin thieves in Olmir? Beheading? Live burial? I wonder...'

Apollo couldn't believe it. 'A griffin isn't a horse or dog. You can't just steal one! It flew me of its own accord!'

'And yet, I'm disinclined to believe you.'

'Go ask it and find out for yourself, then.'

'Funny you should say that. We found the creature unconscious. It'll probably die soon. Now none of us will know the truth aside from you. Such a shame. Although, as you do have a habit of twisting the truth, it's probably for the best.'

Apollo's mouth dropped open. Torsten was one to talk about twisting the truth. But the Inquisitor's words unsettled him. 'Olvalthar?' How could something so huge, so built for battle, die after a small crash?

Torsten snorted. 'Don't try and pretend you care, now.'

'Well perhaps if you weren't using Myrish creatures to torture your prisoners, I wouldn't have been forced to flee that way!'

A murmur of unease rippled through the mounted soldiers at the mention of the Myr. Some stared curiously at the Master Inquisitor, and their horses nervously pawed the muddy ground.

Torsten's eyes glazed over. He drew his sword and pointed it down at Apollo. 'You could not *possibly* comprehend what I must do.'

Apollo stepped back, unsure. It wasn't like Torsten to be so direct. Usually the Master Inquisitor enjoyed building up suspense, or gloating when he had the advantage. He'd only seen him a few hours before in that damned chamber. Why had he changed so much?

He supposed it didn't matter. Not when he was surrounded. 'How many of your comrades know you use one of their ancient enemies as a simple torture device?'

Torsten let out a grunt that was more hiss than anything else.

Apollo continued, 'And I understand well enough what you do. Met plenty of cold-hearted bastards in my time, believe me, and you're just another one on the list. You're not anything special.'

'Why you impudent wretch!'

Apollo grinned. It was lopsided, pulled down by his fatigue, but he'd managed to get under Torsten's skin again, despite the Inquisitor's odd behaviour.

'Sir?' one of the soldiers ventured, nudging his horse closer. 'Your orders?'

Apollo wanted to tell them about the Myr he'd seen in the forest, that they would do better to go after that instead of him. But it didn't matter what he said, now. Torsten had that look in his eyes. He'd made up his mind, and there was no way Apollo could talk himself out of the Master Inquisitor arresting him. Or worse.

He might as well go down fighting.

Apollo darted forward, waving one arm high and

thrusting his sword towards Torsten's horse. It was a feint, but, startled, the horse reared up.

Torsten grabbed hold of the reins and held on without being thrown, but he was off guard—and Apollo arced the blade up to slash across the Master Inquisitor's cheek. Satisfied at the blood drawn, he rolled forward between horses's legs and caused more chaos.

A few blades darted down towards him—one caught him on the back of his neck—but Apollo managed to stir up the horses more than get struck by the soldiers' swords. Horses brayed as they stumbled into each other, and men struggled to control their mounts.

Apollo couldn't help but grin at his handiwork.

He turned to flee—he could definitely hide until things quietened down—when Torsten was suddenly in front of them. Whether he'd been thrown from his horse or had jumped, Apollo couldn't tell, and the Master Inquisitor had his sword in hand, complete with rust spot.

Though Torsten glared at him, his eyes were unfocused. 'This ends now.' With a grunt, Torsten lifted the tip of his sword towards Apollo and muttered something under his breath.

Apollo stepped back, out of Torsten's reach, his fingers tense around the hilt of his own sword. Maybe he could chop off a finger or two before it was over.

Flames shot from Torsten's sword, enveloping Apollo in burning fire. He sank to the ground with a scream—it licked his arms and legs, peeling flesh as easily as a knife through butter. He smelled his own hair burning, and rolled away blindly, hoping to find the slope down to the water.

'No more of this stupidity, Apollo Tamlin.'

But Apollo wasn't listening. The cold, wet mud slopped up his arms, dousing some of the flames. He opened his eyes to check where he was, and on seeing the lip of the bank, pushed himself down it.

Water sang around him as he plunged into the shallow stream. The voices whispered incoherent words, soothing him as they washed away the heat of the fire.

Apollo gritted his teeth, willing more strength into his body so he could stand and fight, when a sudden weight pressed his head down, forcing his face into the silty river bed. Bubbles streamed from his nose as the air was forced from his lungs. As his vision dimmed, he scrambled for purchase, to push away from the water, to get rid of whoever was holding him down.

But his fingers flailed and he couldn't get free.

Apollo jerked as the last of his breath left him, when someone grabbed the back of his tunic and fiercely pulled him from the water. He was thrown onto his back, the wind knocked out of him, and he coughed violently, blood and water dribbling down his chin. He tried to breathe through his bruised chest.

Torsten scowled down at him, his cheek bleeding from where he'd been cut. 'Any last words?' He held his sword out, the tip of the blade hovering above Apollo's throat.

Apollo's vision was a blur of shadows, but one thought was stronger even than the realisation he was about to pass out. 'Mal...'

The last thing Apollo wanted to see before he died was Torsten's face, and he was about to close his eyes and accept his fate when something swooped down towards him, and dark feathers filled his vision.

APOLLO SLOWLY BECAME aware of muffled voices talking around him. They spoke softly, as if trying not to disturb his sleep.

Gingerly, he opened his eyes, confused when he didn't see the green leaves and forest canopy—instead, he was in a

495

warm, low-ceilinged room, beds on either side filled with injured people. A large fire burned merrily on the opposite wall. Looking down at himself, he realised the arm he'd cut in the forest had been bandaged up, the foul scent of glinoc paste strong under the linen.

Several people moved carefully between beds, offering soothing words of comfort or water skins to those resting, and he even smelled creamy herb-filled potato soup.

A sick room?

Where was this place? How did he get here?

He didn't recognise the building, and the few windows were too small and too high up for him to see out of and figure out where he was. He took a few deep breaths through his nose. There was no scent of the sea, but the door was closed and none of the windows were open. It had to be Foxmouth, didn't it?

But there were no Inquisitors or soldiers in the room.

Had Olvalthar carried him here?

Wincing, he tried to sit up in bed, but he had no strength in his legs, and slipped back down into the pillows with a grunt of pain.

'Careful, lad. You were covered in blood and bruises when you were brought in. Doubt they've healed yet.'

Apollo glanced to his right, where an elderly man in the bed beside him grinned. He had a bandage on his head, covering one eye, and was missing several teeth. 'Took a beating too, eh? We're all the same in here.' He gestured to the other beds with a wrinkled arm. 'Damned Myr. Can't believe it.'

'Where...?' Apollo asked, his voice barely more than a creak. He clutched his throat, wondering why it was so raw.

'Westbook. This used to be part of the village hall, but Dalio and his husband turned it into a makeshift hospital. Had no choice, really.'

So he wasn't in Foxmouth. That was frustrating. 'Dalio?'

Apollo recognised the name. 'Isn't he a winemaker?' He'd ordered hundreds of bottles of wine over the years for *The Grumpy Fisherman*, most from Westbrook Orchard.

The old man nodded. 'Well, we're all doctors now, I suppose. Gotta help each other how we can.'

Apollo's stomach turned as he remembered what had happened. 'The attack on the palace?'

'Terrible thing it was. Could see the smoke for days.'

'Days?' Apollo's heart pounded. 'How long was I asleep?'

'Must've been three days now. Of course, you were unconscious when that Olmese lad brought you in, so might've been longer than that?'

Olmese? Apollo didn't know anyone from Olmir, did he? His mind whirled, confusion muddying everything. He could worry about his apparent rescuer later, once he was fit enough to think straight and walk.

Wait. Three days?

Torsten would have made it to Foxmouth by now. 'Oh, shit. Are there pigeons here?'

'Sure. Plenty of pigeons, thank Toriaken.' He held up a small bundle from under his pillow. 'I'm sending this to some family of mine down in Horush. I can send something for you, too?'

Apollo shook his head. 'I need to get a message to Foxmouth. My wife and daughter are there.'

The man's smile fell, his mouth widening in surprise. 'Oh...oh! I'm so sorry, lad. Didn't think there was anyone from there anymore. Foxmouth is gone.'

'What...?' Apollo was sure he was delirious.

The old man gave him a kind, sad smile. 'It was attacked by the Myr, too. Neros rose to fight back, but...the town was destroyed. It's completely gone.'

497

30

THE DRAGONS

FENN

Fenn grabbed the priestess before she hit the icy floor. Her skin was burning up, as if she'd been standing beside a hot fire for hours. 'Selys? Selys, talk to me! Are you okay?'

She didn't respond.

Fenn held Selys carefully, crouched on the floor. His breathing shook as he suddenly realised he was alone and responsible for looking after her. There was no Calidra to take charge, no Jisyel with her light-hearted humour, no Varlot to offer his gruff advice.

'Selys?' Fenn called again, shaking her gently.

Nothing.

He could feel her breath and heartbeat, which was some relief, but he didn't know what to do. The injury on her shoulder was bleeding, and whatever Neros had done to her body had obviously taken its toll. He needed to get her help, and soon.

He shrugged out of his cloak and bundled it up on the floor, resting her head on it like a pillow. Then, he paced the chamber, thinking. They were in the middle of the mountains, and the outpost was the closest place he could go to for help. It was also where the Inquisitors were based, and Varlot could still be there, too.

But after what she'd done to the Inquisitors? She was likely to be arrested on sight.

He couldn't risk going there.

Somewhere south-east was Nethal, he recalled. Again, a large town that would likely have supplies. Doctors. But also Inquisitors.

Fenn turned to Vermecio. 'Can you heal her?'

'*I cannot.*'

He rolled his eyes. Then again, the reason it had been able to help him was because his pain and weakness had been due to the Myrish curse. It made sense the Myrish construct could help him but not Selys.

But that thought sparked an idea. Perhaps he should get her to the Lasseen Ocean? It was Neros's domain, after all. And the dragon who apparently never blessed her priests and priestesses had just broken that rule. He didn't understand why, and doubted Selys did either, but getting her to Neros was probably his best bet.

He squeezed his eyes shut, tried to think. A shrine would probably be able to help, too, but he had no idea if there was one anywhere near. The ocean was easy to find, though. He'd seen it in the distance when they'd climbed up the mountain. He just hoped that Neros actually cared for her priestess.

Fenn sat down and rooted through their meagre supplies. There was dried fruit, smoked fish, and a couple of small, sour apples. It wasn't much, but he wolfed it down, one eye on Selys in case she stirred. It had been almost a whole day since he'd last slept, but thanks to Vermecio's help, Fenn knew he could make it back down the mountain—even carrying Selys—without too much trouble. And given her condition, he ought to get going sooner rather than later.

Her desire—or rather Neros's desire—to destroy the bastion was a concern. Right now, it was his only chance at getting his memories back, and he had no intention of letting that chance be taken from him.

Food eaten, he stood up and wiped his hands. 'Vermecio. I *will* be back with the thing you asked for, and you will restore my memories.'

'*I look forward to your return, Fenn.*' Vermecio grinned again, teeth glinting in the dawn light that spilled into the cavern.

The gesture was unnerving, and Fenn quickly looked away. 'Come on Selys, we need to get you some help.' He carefully pulled her up and over his shoulder, then picked up her glaive, which was surprisingly light. Once he adjusted their bags, weapon, and Selys herself, Fenn took a deep breath and made his way back down the tunnel to the mouth of the cave.

It was strange, retracing his steps but without the ability to see any of the dark mist that he had before. He smiled. It was the next piece of evidence that the curse—in part—had been lifted. He just hoped there weren't any Myrish spirits around that he wouldn't be able to see, now.

Fenn was greeted by a cold, brisk wind blowing across the face of the mountain. There hadn't been any more snow-fall, for which he was grateful, and the rising sun gave him plenty of light to navigate by. With another deep breath, he headed east, towards the Lasseen Ocean and help for the priestess of Neros.

It took until well past midday before Fenn reached the tree-line near the base of the mountain. A river flowed between the peaks, and he followed the sound of that for most of the afternoon, breathing a sigh of relief when he saw the distant trees.

His feet were numb with cold, yet sweat rolled down his

back from the effort of hiking downhill while carrying Selys. She hadn't stirred at all during the trek, and Fenn was beginning to worry something was seriously wrong.

How did the spirits' magic work, exactly?

Trying not to think too much, he continued on doggedly through the snow towards the shelter of the trees. It had been so long since he'd had any energy at all that it was difficult to work out when he was becoming tired.

Periodically, he checked on Selys. He stopped to rest, checked the wound on her shoulder, made sure she was breathing easily. The wound hadn't healed at all. It was an angry red and swollen. He rinsed it with the cold river water, half-expecting the shock to wake Selys, but she didn't so much as twitch.

Lumps of ice drifted down the river, sinking every so often only to pop back up to the surface with a splash. Fenn wished he could sit on them and be swept downriver—it would certainly let them cover ground more quickly.

The quiet was disconcerting. He'd become so used to the voices in his head, or the chatter of his companions, that being left alone with his own thoughts and footsteps crunching through the snow was almost too much for him to cope with. He tried not to speak aloud, but by the time he reached the treeline, Fenn was having full conversations with Selys—even if she couldn't answer him.

He narrated his movements and thoughts, reassuring her every so often that she would be okay, and that Neros would know what to do when they eventually made it to the sea. He also joked several times that the going would definitely be faster if she was awake and walking.

Thankfully, the trees provided some shelter from the wind—although it was less bitter lower on the mountain than it had been closer to the peak—and Fenn carefully cleared away snow before gently setting Selys down, resting her up against the trunk of a tree.

'Let me just get this place tidied up a bit,' he muttered, aware how foolish he sounded but taking comfort in the illusion of conversation. He kicked away rocks and broken twigs, clearing a wider space under the branches of the fir tree he'd picked to rest underneath. There were a number of pinecones, too, and he was sure to move those out of the way.

They were still relatively high up, and Fenn was afforded a clear view of northern Porsenthia. The trees grew into a small patch of forest directly to the south, fed by the river he was currently camped beside. The river meandered downhill, cutting through the snowy fields until it became grassland, where a small town sat just before the horizon. Further down the mountain, a herd of deer made their way through the snow, nosing away slush to get to the grass underneath, their thick, russet coats blowing in the wind.

Fenn returned his attention to the town, squinting as he tried to make out more details and see if it jogged any memories. But no matter how hard he tried, he couldn't so much as recall the name of the place.

Far to the east, beyond a larger forest than the one he rested by, lay the coast and the Lasseen Ocean. Something dark lingered across the treetops, and Fenn blinked, frowning as he questioned what he'd seen.

The shadow disappeared.

Had it been a trick of the light? Or his mind?

Columns of black smoke rose on the horizon, adding to his uncertainty. He wished he knew where he was, wished he could remember the towns and cities of Porsenthia. Damn the Myr for taking something so small, but so essential.

After spending a couple of minutes watching, Fenn turned back to the small camp. Selys hadn't moved, and he was beginning to wonder if she'd wake up at all. He threw his cloak over her and got a fire going, enjoying the warmth and light from the gently crackling flames.

'How are you holding up, Selys? Having too good a dream you don't wanna wake?' Fenn wrapped his arms around his knees. 'Can't say I blame you. It's not great out here. Must be a fire or something further ahead. Can't tell where, though. But there's a lot of smoke.' He rested his chin on his knees. 'I don't suppose you've had any more ideas about the thing Vermecio wants?'

The priestess said nothing, letting out a quiet snore as her eyelids fluttered.

Fenn sighed. 'Yeah, me either. Gold. Blade. Bow. Gold. Blade. Bow…' He closed his eyes, letting his mind wander, trying to piece together a puzzle he hardly understood.

If Calidra and Jisyel were with them, they'd probably have some useful ideas. Those two would probably be in Foxmouth by now. Had Calidra found her sister? He hoped she wasn't anything like Furyn. That woman had bigger anger issues than Varlot.

At the thought of his old friend, Fenn's stomach turned.

Varlot.

Betrayer.

He shook his head, annoyed with himself for being such an idiot. For not listening to Calidra. For hoping that people weren't as selfish as she'd warned him they were.

As his mind whirled, Fenn slipped into a doze. The rustling of birds roosting in the tree above him, or falling twigs, disturbed him slightly, but it wasn't long before his tired body gave in and he fell into the sleep he'd been putting off for a day.

Instantly, Fenn was in darkness. With certainty, he knew he was back on the edge of the spirit world again.

'You are no longer weak. Vermecio helped you, as I said it would.'

Fenn felt the cold around him before he heard the Myr talk, although the fire in his chest kept much of it at bay. Now he wasn't at death's door, now he knew what he faced, a

503

slow fear trickled in. 'Vermecio removed the curse. Well, part of it. It didn't restore my memories.'

'It is good that you live. Almost all the other echoes have crossed into the spirit world.'

The hairs on the back of his neck stood up, but some invisible force kept him from turning to face the creature that addressed him. 'It said it could help me with my memories, if I helped it.'

'Interesting.'

'It wanted me to find something. Some sort of riddle.' Fenn thought back to the details—in this place, everything was a blur, from his vision to his mind, and it was difficult to tell what was real and what was imagined. 'A sliver of...gold? A blade that you can't fight with. And a bow—'

'From which an arrow cannot fire,' the Myr finished for him.

'You know what it is?'

'What you seek lies far to the east. Beyond the dragon of the sea.'

There was a flare of cold, as if the Myr had allowed some emotion to be released for a split second, then it regained control of itself.

'Why don't you tell me what it is?' Fenn whirled around, his desperation to lay eyes on the creature that taunted him overwhelming his fear.

He gasped at the sight, and the fire in his chest burned fiercely.

The Myr stood about half a foot shorter than him; skin blue-purple, with snake-like yellow eyes that watched him intently. It appeared humanoid, despite a domed back, with smooth black hair and a slightly oval-shaped head. It had two pairs of arms—each ending in three clawed fingers, which looked vicious. The strangest part of the Myr's appearance was the small, pitted nose above a mouth filled with dagger-like teeth. *'We are dying. We need your help.'*

Fenn swallowed. Everyone he'd met had told him how

terrible the Myr were. The atrocities and deaths they'd caused. They had even cursed him, not that he could remember how or why. The creature in front of him was terrifying, yes, in a deeply primal way that he couldn't explain. But it wasn't as terrifying as the dragons.

Discovering whatever Vermecio wanted would certainly help the Myr. And helping these creatures went against the Iron Crown.

But without them, he wouldn't be able to restore his life. Find friends and loved ones.

The Inquisitors wanted him locked up, anyway.

Would helping them truly be so terrible?

His chest tightened with a flare of heat, and it was suddenly difficult to breathe. 'What will you do once Vermecio has this…this…object?'

'The bastion will restore your memories. As promised.'

He frowned.

'We honour our promises. Will you?'

Fenn's eyes snapped open. It was getting dark. Beside him, Selys was sitting up, poking the fire, his cloak wrapped around her shoulders.

'You were talking in your sleep.'

He swallowed, relieved that she was awake, and afraid at what he might have been saying. 'Oh. Um. Good to see you're awake, Selys! How are you feeling? Do you remember what happened in the cave?'

'Neros.' The single word sent a shiver through him. 'You carried me down the mountain, I suppose?'

Fenn nodded. 'You're injured. You need help.' He pulled his bag over and offered her some of the apples they had left.

Selys shifted, reaching to grab one, and winced. She clutched her shoulder and shook her head at it. 'I shouldn't have let myself be caught by that Inquisitor.'

Guilt stabbed Fenn through the gut. 'It was my fault. They were after me. If—'

'No. Don't blame yourself, don't you *dare* blame yourself!' Selys spat, a viciousness lacing her voice that he'd never heard before. 'Varlot is the one who caused it.'

She wasn't wrong, but it didn't make him feel any better about the situation. Trying to change the subject, Fenn said, 'I thought Neros never blessed anyone? You were glowing pretty brightly back in that cave.'

Selys lowered her gaze, her hand dropping from her shoulder to her chest. 'I feel her fire. It's here, within me.'

Fenn's eyes widened at her words. He had a fire in his chest too. 'Wait...what?'

She smiled. 'All those blessed by a spirit carry their fire. They're part of you, and you them.'

His breathing quickened. Was *he* blessed, too? The thought flooded him with fear. 'You...does it hurt? The fire? Inside you?'

Selys shrugged. 'It can. Depends on you and the spirit. If you're not used to it, I imagine it's uncomfortable. It'll certainly take me a while.' She leaned back, the hint of a smile on her lips, the apples forgotten. 'I can't believe Neros chose me. Of all people, of all places! Fenn, Neros has never done this before. Do you understand what that *means*? How important this is?'

Fenn tried to share in her jubilation, but was too stunned by what she had said about fire. His chest had burned with heat since...well, since he could remember. Voice trembling, he asked, 'What was it like?'

Selys giggled, sounding more like Jisyel than herself. 'It was wonderful. I was the sea, Fenn. The *sea*! There was nothing else but the water.'

He frowned. 'You don't remember what you said?'

'I spoke?'

He chewed his lip, debating whether or not to tell her. 'Said something about destroying the Myr.'

'Well, that's not surprising.' She raised her trembling

hands and studied them. 'I've been chosen, Fenn. By a *goddess.*'

IT TOOK them two days to hike along the river, making their way towards Westbrook. When Selys had named the town, Fenn nodded, as if he'd always known what it had been called.

Selys's strength grew every hour, and it wasn't long before she didn't need to lean on him. It was a relief. Fenn hadn't been sure the priestess was even going to wake up, let alone be able to walk unaided.

Her shoulder wound had darkened, and although she'd rinsed it several times in the freezing river, it wasn't improving. Yellow pus had started to leak from it, along with blood.

'We need to get to Westbrook quickly. They'll have medicine,' Selys said. It was easy enough—they simply had to follow the river.

So far north, there was no path, no people. Just leagues and leagues of icy hills, deer racing from them and eagles circling high above. It was a far cry from his journey with Selys and Jisyel through Bragalia, where they saw dozens of people every day and the intense heat was a constant companion.

Up here, it was expansive and lonely.

When they saw a small group of horses and riders heading their way, Fenn's first emotion was hope. Perhaps these people would have medicine if they were used to travelling these frigid hills.

When he saw the dark uniforms and grey dragon insignia, his stomach dropped.

'Inquisitors, all the way out here?' Selys drew her glaive. 'Not when we're so close to safety!'

'But they aren't coming from Nethal or further west.

507

Maybe they won't know about...what happened?' Fenn asked, standing his ground. He didn't want to draw his sword and appear as a threat.

'Perhaps.' Selys acknowledged, though she didn't sound convinced.

There was no point in running. The group had spotted them, and mounted as they were, could easily catch up. Better to appear cooperative.

Fenn chewed his lip nervously. Although his curse had been removed, they'd still consider him a lost soul without his memory. He prayed to Neros that the Inquisitors would listen to Selys.

'Good day, Inquisitors.' Selys bowed her head as they approached, the horses' hooves a roar after so long in the empty tundra.

'*You!*'

Fenn backed up as one Inquisitor pushed his way past the front of the group. There was no mistaking his arrogant sneer. 'Master Inquisitor Torsten.'

'Out causing trouble again, I see?' Torsten got down from his horse and strode towards him, a dark look in his eyes. A deep cut grazed his left cheek, and his uniform looked like it had been punctured by a dozen needles. Through the holes in his cloak, Fenn saw blood lined his right arm. The sight was a far cry from impeccable intimidation he had been in Ballowtown.

Selys glared at him. 'Fenn is my apprentice. We're on our way to Toriaken's Shrine. I have papers—'

'Oh, he is, is he? First an apprentice to Varlot, and now an apprentice to a priestess? Fenn, you must be an expert in combat after your training. And with a spirit on your side, too? What another convenient lie.' Torsten spat, ignoring Selys, his gaze locked on Fenn. 'I should have dealt with you much sooner. Now, what have you done?'

'I...I haven't done anything.' Fenn was genuinely confused

by the accusation. Torsten might have had an instinct for those flouting the rules, but he had no idea what the Inquisitor thought he'd done. Nor did he understand why Torsten was so full of rage. It wasn't the cold, calmness he remembered from before.

'Priestess. You're injured?' Another Inquisitor got off his horse. He was younger than Torsten by at least a decade, with sandy-coloured hair and a stocky frame.

The third Inquisitor, a woman with dark, braided hair stared at Torsten with narrowed eyes. She kept quiet, observing proceedings atop her piebald horse.

Fenn watched them carefulley, certain he'd seen both somewhere before, but unable to quite place where.

'You have medicine?' Selys asked the sandy-haired Inquisitor,.

'Sarron, stay out of this. I will deal with Fenn, first,' Torsten snapped.

'I thought we were looking for that thief Apollo, sir?' Sarron asked, frowning. 'And this priestess has a wound on her shoulder. We must offer her aid.'

'The Myrish traitors take precedence.'

'How can you be so sure he's a traitor?'

'I'm sure.' Torsten's voice allowed no argument. The sword in his hand flashed and he squeezed the hilt until his knuckles whitened.

Sarron frowned, backing up to where his colleague watched. 'Is it just me, Nadja, or is he behaving more strangely than usual?' Though his voice was low, Fenn caught the words, which mirrored his own thoughts. Clearly they and the other soldiers weren't sure about Torsten's orders, but didn't have the courage to question them.

Torsten glowered at Fenn, unaware or uncaring of his comrades' uncertainty. 'And you, Fenn? You escaped my grasp once before. Looks like Varlot isn't here to protect you this time!'

The same rust spot he'd seen before was on Torsten's sword. Fenn was about to comment on its strangeness when the fire in his chest roiled, sending spikes of pain along his limbs. He clutched his chest with a grimace, trying not to sink to the ground. Appearing weak in front of the Master Inquisitor was the last thing he wanted to do.

Torsten lunged before Fenn knew what was happening. Through sheer luck, he sidestepped the strike, stumbling backwards in the slushy snow.

'Torsten! Is this necessary?' the third Inquisitor asked, getting off her piebald horse. She and Sarron stood together on the edge of the battle.

Fenn couldn't pay her any attention. His own sword held up defensively across his chest, he blocked Torsten's barrage of blows one after the other—backing away from him after each strike. After the fifth or sixth blow, his arms went numb, and his grip on his sword faltered.

Torsten grinned with grim satisfaction and pressed the attack, striking at Fenn's legs.

With a yelp, Fenn tripped over, dropping his sword as the edge of Torsten's blade slashed into the meat of his thigh.

'That's enough. The lad is disarmed,' said Nadja.

Torsten ignored her. He stood over Fenn, the tip of his rusty sword ready to strike.

Fenn stared up at Torsten, breathing hard. The Inquisitor's gaze flickered, pupils widening, but his eyes were unfocused. 'I know what you are. I know you have the Myrish magic inside you,' Torsten hissed, his voice low. 'After what happened to the palace, I'm not taking any chances. Every one of you traitors will be killed on sight.'

'No! He's with me!' Selys screamed.

Torsten didn't bother to turn and face her, more intent in savouring his victory. 'The Myr dared to attack our coastline. I shall make it my personal goal to ensure not a single Myr-touched person is allowed to live.'

Fenn grimaced as pain laced up his leg, his own hot blood staining the snow underneath him. He turned his head, eyes widening when he saw Selys.

'Torsten!'

Fenn didn't know who shouted, but the warning held enough urgency to grab the Master Inquisitor's attention. Torsten whirled around in time to be struck by a wave of fire shot from Selys's body. The flames burst in all directions, scorching the ground and melting snow—leaving the grass underneath blackened.

Selys's action gave Fenn time to scramble to his feet. Gritting his teeth, he hobbled towards the priestess.

'You are *not* getting away from me again!' Torsten fumed. 'Miroth!' He raised his sword, which lit up like the sun. A plume of fire shot forth, charging towards Fenn and incinerating anything that hadn't already been burned.

Fenn dropped to his knees as the crackle of flame exploded around him, burning the hairs on his arms.

Selys strolled forward, snow melting under her feet with every step. 'Torsten. By order of Neros, you will leave Fenn alone or suffer the consequences.'

Torsten spat. 'You stand in the shadow of the Iron Crown! You are under the control of the Porsenthian Empire! You belong to Queen Surayo, and you will obey our rule. This boy is Myr-touched. Only death awaits him!'

Fenn swallowed, getting to his feet with difficulty. What had happened to Torsten? He was acting like a man possessed. He'd been cold and cruel, yes, but this was something else. 'I've done nothing! I'm trying to *help* the Iron Crown!'

'Sure you are.' Torsten dismissed him with a wave. 'My only goal is to rid the world of the Myr. Your magic poisons everything. Steals life. It cannot be allowed to remain.'

Before Selys could get any closer, Torsten sent another plume of smoke careening into her.

She halted in place, as if caught between bracing for the attack and diving out of the way. Fire slammed into her, the force of it knocking her off her feet.

'Selys!' Fenn cried in panic, and the fire in his own chest surged.

'Do not repress me. Fight back. Miroth is weak and I am stronger.'

'Who...who are you?' Fenn gasped, as the voice in his head spoke louder than ever before. It was the same voice he'd heard in the deadlands, who'd urged him not to give up. To stay strong. It was warmer than the Myr's voice had been in his visions. Stronger and more righteous. 'You're...the *fire*?'

'I will be your armour.'

Fenn had no idea what was going on. Knees weak, he faced Torsten. 'But...but Torsten is an Inquisitor!'

'I said I would watch over you, tainted one. Raise your sword. Let me defeat this weakling.'

Fenn did as commanded, although he wasn't sure how much of the action was his own. Sword pointed at Torsten, he exhaled once. Heat and energy built in his chest, so powerful it was as if he was lifted off his feet.

Power raced through every vein, every muscle, and even the wound in his thigh faded to nothing, as fire exploded from him. He thought it would hurt. Thought there would be the smell of burning, the choke of soot, but the fire was pure and clean and *alive*.

It flew through him, through his fingertips, through the sword, and straight into Torsten's side.

The Master Inquisitor screamed, throwing up his shield at the last minute and blocking the rest of Fenn's fire.

'He *does* have a spirit!' one soldier gasped.

'Torsten! He was telling the truth!' Sarron yelled.

'How could he be Myr-touched if he has a dragon spirit?'

Torsten lowered his shield. 'He is in league with the Myr!

512

Can't you see? Are you blind? Stupid? I'd recognise that filthy stench anywhere!'

Fenn responded with another plume of fire. He wasn't conscious of his movement, as if something deep within controlled every action, every breath. But the fire was greater than Torsten's and broke through the Inquisitor's defences. Flames caught Torsten's arm, burning through the uniform and singing flesh underneath.

'Torsten! I've seen enough. We need to report back to the palace! What if you've angered Neros through your misguided actions?' It was Nadja. She raced across the battle, heedless of the flames, and grabbed hold of Torsten. She tore away his burning sleeve and dragged him backwards through what was left of the snow, dousing the fire.

'Nadja. Don't be fooled by Fenn's lies! It's some Myrish trickery!' Torsten's gaze was distant, his voice, desperate.

'I know what I see, Torsten. Fenn is certainly blessed. And you've hurt a Priestess of Neros. We need to get back to East-brook. Leave Apollo wherever he is, and aid the queen against the *real* threat.'

'No!'

'Sir. It is my opinion that you need these injuries seen to if nothing else.'

'Apollo started everything. We must find him! That boy is part of it. You mark my words!'

Nadja shook her head. 'Sarron. Help Torsten back to the palace.'

The sandy-haired Inquisitor bowed at her order, and hurried over to Torsten. The Master Inquisitor continued to shriek incoherently.

Nadja frowned at Selys and Fenn, who were crouched beside one another, panting. 'I apologise for our conduct here. Tensions are high with the Myr, as I'm sure you can appreciate. I hope your spirits are able to see we are only human, ruled by our emotions and fears, and forgive us for our transgression.'

Fenn didn't know what to say, too stunned by the power flowing in his veins.

Selys nodded. 'Thank you, Inquisitor. I will ask Neros to be merciful.'

Nadja bowed, then got back onto her horse. With Sarron aiding Torsten, and the scent of burning flesh filling the air, the group headed off, down the rolling hills and into the distance.

Selys spun to face him. 'Fenn, what in Neros's name was *that*? You've been blessed this whole time and never said anything? How in all of Tassar did I not *see*?'

Fenn gasped as the surge of energy left him. He sank to his knees. 'I think...I think the Myrish curse had something to do with it?' His breaths were ragged. Now the fire had died down, the pain in his thigh flared. 'Covered it up somehow. I didn't realise...until very recently...'

Darkness overtook his vision as Fenn collapsed onto the blackened ground. In his mind, the dragon spirit laughed.

THE AFTERMATH
CALIDRA

C alidra was drowning.

Cold, dark, seawater was the only thing she'd known for...how long? Hours? Days? She was lost in a shapeless, murky void of green and black. It was all-encompassing. The cold sucked the strength from her body, stiffening her limbs, making it harder to move or think, let alone swim.

She stared up at the surface, startled at how the light played through the water, giving the world above a strangely dream-like quality. Light drifted across the surface; orange and red fire from burning ships, pink and yellow sunlight, white-hot flames from Neros. It all blurred together in a haze of delirium.

Bubbles gushed up from her mouth and nose. From her frustrated, weak flailing.

The surface edged away from her.

No.

She was sinking.

Thoughts of Jisyel, Malora, and places from her childhood floated into her mind's eye. Places she'd never go again. People she'd never see again.

The panic that had been suffocating up until that point melted away, and aside from the cramp building in her arms and legs, she was…peaceful. She couldn't hear anything other than the low thrum of the water swelling around her, and Calidra wondered why she'd ever feared it before.

Something exploded above the surface, the sound muted. A shockwave rippled through the water, its pressure jarring. Distantly, she knew she needed to keep swimming, to get back to the surface before she ran out of breath. But she simply couldn't anymore. The stress, shock, and sheer, unrelenting terror had left her numb.

She no longer felt the cold.

No longer felt much of anything…

Suddenly, she was flying up—shooting headlong towards the surface. Lights grew brighter, forcing the darkness and cold away, lost behind her. Water splashed, white foam spraying over her face, and Calidra could breathe again.

Her focus sharpened, and with it returned the cold, the biting pain, the searing heat of her lungs desperate for air. And the realisation Jisyel wasn't with her. She *had* to find her.

'Mama! You got another one! Big fish!'

Calidra coughed, her eyes stinging in the salt water. A small boat floated above her, big enough for perhaps five or six people, if they all squeezed up together. It had a small mast and a wide sail, neither of which were on fire.

Two figures peered down at her, obscured by the dazzling sunlight above.

Calidra struggled to keep her head above the water, and when she slipped under, something yanked on her collar to keep her where she was. She tried to take a deep breath, but only managed to cough.

'Ren, mind yourself. I'm trying to get her into the boat!' A woman said, her accent distinctly Bragalian.

Calidra was confused. She'd been in the Lasseen Ocean beside Foxmouth. Had she floated so far south she'd reached the gulf between Bragalia and Olmir? Her memories were fuzzy after the ship had collapsed on top of her, with significant stretches of time completely blank.

Before she could give it any more thought, something sharp tugged on her collar again, hauling her towards the boat the woman and the little girl watched her from. Calidra yelped as she was pulled, then her fingers were scrabbling against the side of the boat.

'No, not there! You come up *here*!' The girl pointed to a short ladder as if it were the most obvious thing in the world.

Calidra shuffled along the boat's side, water slapping into her face, then she heaved herself up. Every movement was agony, weighted down by her sopping wet clothes, and when she finally collapsed into the boat, she retched.

The girl crouched beside Calidra and peered down at her for a few seconds. 'You shouldn't swim so deep.' She pushed some of Calidra's hair out of her face. 'Pretty lady.'

'Ren, get back. Give her some space.'

At—presumably her mother's—orders, the girl backed away from Calidra. 'She been swimming too long, mama.'

'I'm sure she has. Come and sit down, help me get the next line ready.'

Calidra heard Ren sit down as instructed, gleefully opening boxes and reaching in for supplies.

'I'm sorry about Renys. She's so inquisitive. Are you hurt? Other than the water you took in, I mean. I'm surprised you're still conscious!'

Calidra didn't even have the strength to lift her head. She tried to look up at the woman, but retched again, spewing up seawater and bile. Suddenly embarrassed, she shuffled forward and vomited over the side of the boat, emptying whatever was left in her stomach into the Lasseen Ocean. 'Where...?'

'We're on the edge of the Polar Sea, just north of

517

Foxmouth,' the woman said. 'I'd head further south for more supplies, but who knows if the Myr are still there. It's been two days since the attack, but I'm not taking any chances.'

The Myr.

So it *had* been real.

Calidra had hoped her mind had cracked, that she'd imagined the enemy or it had been part of some terrible nightmare.

'You're the fifth person we've picked up today, and you won't be the last.'

Calidra remained leaning over the boat, not trusting her stomach under the swell of the waves. Over her shoulder, she said, 'Have you found a woman called Jisyel? Jisyel Herbst? A Porsenthian?'

'Possibly? All of the people we've found so far have been Porsenthians, aside from you. Most of them sailors. No-one's been awake, though.'

Calidra's head thumped and she vomited again—this time there was more substance. Shaking, she didn't fight it, just let the sickness wash over her, as awful as it was to experience. The woman's voice was comforting. It wasn't often she was able to hear the accent of her homeland, especially not so far north in Porsenthia. 'You...you're a long...way from home,' Calidra muttered in between bouts of retching and coughing.

'Married a Porsenthian who hates the heat.'

Calidra laughed, then grimaced when her stomach twinged. 'I understand that...My partner is Porsenthian, too.'

'Oh? Where from?'

'Isle of Salt.'

'Yeesh.' The woman laughed goodnaturedly. 'I guess you don't care for curses?'

Calidra shrugged as much as she could while leaning over the side of the boat. Her view was limited to a mash of green-blue water churning up underneath the hull, broken up by the occasional splash of white foam. Neros was no longer in view, thank goodness, but the sea was rough and choppy—no doubt a reflection of the spirit's mood at being attacked. Debris littered the water—boxes, barrels, and sacks were scattered among bits of burnt ship. Wood, sails, and anything else that could float drifted past.

'Have the Myr…really gone?' Calidra asked, once the latest bout of vomiting had passed, still not trusting herself to turn around.

'For now, thank Neros. But they'll be back. They *always* come back,' she said, bitter.

Calidra wiped her face and delicately leaned back, keeping her gaze low. She didn't care that she was kneeling on the floor—she couldn't stand staring out at the sea any longer. 'Are you making for land soon? I…I'm not good on the water.'

'Mama! Another one!' Renys leapt to the side of the boat and pointed eagerly over the edge.

'Good girl. Let me see if we can help. Ren, can you get a towel for this lady, please?'

'Okay!'

The woman walked over to where her daughter gestured, though Calidra could only see her legs from her low position. She still didn't have the strength to look up, nor did she want the woman to see her with vomit streaked down her chin and her clothing in such a sorry state.

When Renys approached her with a towel and a blanket, Calidra gratefully took them. It was thick, made of a soft blend and in an ogee pattern, common in Bragalia. It reminded her of the blankets in her bedroom back in Fellwood. She frowned at it, feeling the warm material between her thumbs.

'Where…in Bragalia are you from?' Calidra towelled her face and hair, trying to get clean and dry as quickly as possible. She'd already started shivering.

The woman didn't answer, too busy getting her line ready to fish out another survivor from the Myr attacks.

Renys squatted down beside Calidra and poked at her face. 'I like fishing in boat with my da. We always get *big* fishes that are silver and blue and...and...' She screwed up her face, trying to think of what she wanted to say. 'And they're tasty!'

Calidra peered down at the child. She couldn't have been more than four or five years old and had an utterly fearless nature. 'Well, I hope you don't eat me!'

Renys burst into fits of laughter. 'No, silly! *You're* not fish!'

Calidra smiled, despite herself.

'*Renys*! Get back to the middle of the boat.' The woman charged past, pulling a rope to adjust the sail on the mast.

'Mama?' Renys's bottom lip poked out at her mother's brusque voice. 'But...we help the people swimming!'

'We can't help this one.'

Calidra looked over the side of the small boat and instantly regretted it. A bloated corpse floated on the water's surface. He wore a tattered sailor's uniform, which had discoloured after so long in the sea. There was a gaping wound where his right arm should have been, and already flies and maggots had festered in what was left of the bloody pulp, squirming together in the sunlight.

Renys shouldered her way past Calidra, heedless, to get a better look. Calidra grabbed her by the waist and pulled her away gently. 'Go and sit down, like your mother says.'

'I wanna see! Is it a big fish? I'm not scared!'

'No. Do as you're told.'

Renys poked out her bottom lip again, eyebrows furrowing deeply, but she didn't argue—just huffed and went to sit down on the bench in the middle of the boat.

By the time the corpse had floated out of view, they were heading towards land. It wasn't much more than a large, rocky outcropping, where tough, hardy grass grew, but it

520

wasn't on the sea and Calidra was happy about that more than anything else. Dozens of brown and grey goats chewed nonchalantly on the grass, watching the boat approach without reaction. They were obviously used to people coming and going.

A tall tower had been built of stone—its exterior weather-beaten and slightly disfigured—with open windows near the top where oil lanterns had been lit. A lighthouse. A large stone dragon had been carved beside the entrance. It was too badly misshapen for Calidra to tell which spirit it was supposed to represent, but she assumed it was Neros.

'You brought the survivors here?' Calidra asked.

'Yes. Several of us did. It was far enough away not to be caught up in the battle, and frequented enough that there were already supplies here. There weren't a lot of options.'

Calidra got to her feet, the towel wrapped around her shoulders. Once certain she wasn't going to topple over, she turned to finally face the woman who had saved her life. 'I didn't thank you for helping me out of the water. I'm Cali—'

She gaped. It couldn't be. 'M...*Malora?*'

Malora hardly looked a year older than when she'd last seen her, despite having had a child and living in this awful climate. Her hair had grown, and her eyes had a few crow's feet around them, but there was no other significant change.

It made the realisation all the more shocking.

How could she have been on the same boat as her sister and not realised?

'*Calidra?*' Malora was equally incredulous. 'What...what are you *doing* here? How did you get here? What...?'

As the boat nudged land, coming to a stop on the pebble beach at the rocky island's base, the two women hugged each other tightly. Calidra no longer cared about her appearance, about the vomiting. This was her sister. Who she'd thought had died *years* prior. Whose death she'd blamed herself for.

Calidra's whole body trembled, and for one terrible

521

moment she was afraid she was about to vomit all over Malora. Then, tears fell down her cheeks. They stung her raw skin but she didn't care.

She had *found* her sister.

'Mal, it's…it's such a long story.' Calidra wiped her face, embarrassed, and stepped back. 'I need to see if Jisyel is here. I can't…I'm shaking so much. I don't know what I'll do if she isn't here!'

'If she isn't, we're still looking for people.' Malora bent to scoop up Renys. 'Come on. I'll take you inside and you can look.'

THE LIGHTHOUSE WAS MUCH BIGGER INSIDE than Calidra had expected.

There was a long, stone building built into the bottom of the tower—no doubt to provide accommodation for those working there—and it was being used as a base for the survivors found amongst the wreckage.

Calidra was impressed at Malora's ingenuity. It was a cosy maze of rooms, with low ceilings, crooked beams, and uneven walls that had probably been shaped more by years of wind and sea than the original stonesmiths who'd crafted them.

An enormous cookfire burned in the kitchen, used so often for so long that the flagstone floor around it had been charred black. It heated the building, and Malora had arranged beds in the rooms directly beside the kitchen to keep them warm.

In the first room, nine sailors rested. They each sported injuries, but none were life-threatening.

The second room held a woman who had been burned badly down one side of her body.

More people were in the third room. At least a dozen.

None were sailors, and from their shell-shocked expressions, Calidra assumed they were all citizens of Foxmouth, caught off-guard in the attack. There weren't enough beds to go around, so the people in this room had to make do with floor mats and bundled up clothing for comfort.

Calidra was about to leave for the next room when she spotted auburn hair poking out from under a patchwork blanket. Heart in her throat, she darted over. 'Jisyel?'

She held her breath and knelt down beside the blanket. Gently, she shook the woman's shoulders.

'Too...early...'

Calidra cried again as relief flooded her. She'd been through too much recently to bottle up her emotions anymore, and she didn't even try to stop her tears. 'Oh thank Neros. Jisyel, are you okay?'

Jisyel rolled over, her hair sticking out at all angles, one eye shut with sleep. 'Is the boat...in Foxmouth yet?'

Calidra threw her arms around the woman. 'I had to find you, Jisyel. I had to get back, and know you were safe.'

'Back...? I haven't gone...anywhere. I've been...asleep.' Jisyel slurred.

Calidra wiped away her tears. There was no need to explain the atrocities to her just yet. She could enjoy her rest —she needed it. 'It's okay. You can sleep. I'm here.'

'Mmmm.' Jisyel's other eye closed.

Calidra gently laid her back on the mat and pulled the blanket over her shoulders, content to let her sleep.

Malora found Calidra in the same position some hours later. 'It's not the best, but it'll help.' She handed her sister a steaming mug of coffee. 'No cinnamon I'm afraid.'

At the smell of hot coffee, Calidra smiled. 'Mal, I lo—' She cut herself off. She *did* love her sister, but they'd parted on such poor terms, the thought of saying it aloud made it awkward. She hadn't even had the time to apologise yet. 'I've really missed you.'

Malora grinned. 'I know your favourites.'

Calidra gasped, suddenly remembering. 'I...I actually brought you some pickles from Fellwood. But they...but the ship...'

'It's okay,' Malora said, 'why don't you get up from the floor. I know it's warm and toasty in here, but you need to stretch your legs.'

Calidra's gaze drifted back to Jisyel.

'She'll be fine. A few of us from Foxmouth are running shifts here, keeping an eye on the people we've brought in, cooking food, getting supplies. She won't be alone.'

After considering it for a moment, Calidra nodded. She followed Malora out of the warm room, through a few narrow hallways, and outside. It was some time past midday, judging by the sun's position, and surprisingly warm.

The grass here was kept short by the numerous goats that roamed freely, although it was thick and full of hardy wild-flowers. A stone wall surrounded the lighthouse grounds, providing a secure area for them and Renys—who raced up and down the grass without a care in the world.

Several people were also in the garden—the people from Foxmouth her sister had mentioned, Calidra assumed—many were digging an area for vegetables, others were sorting supplies and hauling in barrels. A few small boats the same size as her sister's bobbed in the sea beside the light-house, where more survivors were brought in to have their injuries checked.

Another two boats were already heading towards the island, gently cutting through the churning sea.

'The Myr attacked Eastbrook first,' Malora said, without preamble. She took a sip of her own coffee and sat on the stone wall. 'Toriaken fought them, of course. Drove them up the coast, away from the palace.'

'Straight to Foxmouth?' Calidra raised an eyebrow.

'I don't know if it was intentional.'

Even though the small island was some distance from Foxmouth, Calidra had a clear view of the smoking ruin. Swathes of fire were yet to be extinguished, and most of the buildings were rubble. It was hard to believe.

A town had stood there one minute. Now, it was gone. 'I'm so sorry, Mal. I'm glad you and Ren were able to get out. It's...it's lovely to meet her.' She watched her niece as she picked flowers and showed them off to anyone who would pay her attention. 'She's bold, isn't she?'

'Yes.' Malora beamed.

Far above, against the white-grey clouds that covered the sky, griffins flew. Their high-pitched cries could be heard for leagues, and Calidra had never lost that child-like sense of awe when she stared up at them.

She wondered whether Amsel and Hailathlyl were there, soaring alongside their warrior brethren, or whether they were still in Fellwood at Furyn's disposal. She wondered whether anyone in Fellwood had heard of the attacks, yet. Briefly, she considered mentioning their childhood home, talking about her mother, about the funeral. But Calidra wanted to savour her reunion, and talking about home would sully it.

Eastbrook and Foxmouth, both attacked, but only one had survived. Toriaken was the only real defence against the Myr, that much was clear. Although Neros had been powerful enough to drive them off, Foxmouth had been lost.

'I...I want to ask Chryam for his blessing again.' Malora said after a time.

Calidra was stunned. 'What? After everything that spirit put you through?'

Malora shook her head. 'I know. Of course I know! But if I'd had the spirit's power, fewer people would have died. Foxmouth might still exist.'

'Mal, if Neros couldn't save Foxmouth, *you* couldn't have.'

'How do you know that? Perhaps I would have made a difference.'

Calidra sighed. She couldn't believe what her sister was saying. 'You must've swallowed too much seawater because you aren't making any sense.'

Malora pursed her lips and looked away, her gaze drawn to her daughter as she played with the goats and their kids, chasing them up and down the rocks while they brayed in protest.

Two boats nestled in beside the others already docked, and Calidra glanced over as several people disembarked. They brought more injured with them—one, a man who had lost his left foot, who hopped along while leaning on the people on either side of him. Another was a woman who clutched a broken arm.

Calidra was in shock at the devastation the Myr had caused in a single attack. It wouldn't be long before they ran out of survivors and started finding bodies instead.

One tall man approached them from the second boat. He wore a breastplate and helm of iron, but his face was young, with a thin moustache. 'Malora Tamlin?'

'Yes?' Malora straightened up.

'A letter for you. From the palace.' He held out a rolled up parchment, which had been burned at the edge.

Malora glanced at Calidra. 'From the palace?'

'Yes. It was tied to one of those red pigeons the Inquisitors use. Found the poor thing half-dead in the dovecote. I don't suppose anyone had thought to check it after...everything.'

'Thank you.' Malora took the parchment from him, offering Calidra a confused frown as she did so. It was torn and weather-beaten, blackened at the edge. If the message had turned up in this condition, it was a wonder the pigeon had survived the flight.

Malora unrolled it and read, quickly. 'Oh no.'

'What?' Calidra was by her side a moment later. 'What does it say?'

Malora offered no resistance as Calidra took the message from her.

MALORA TAMLIN,

I write to inform you of your husband's situation.

The queen's Master Inquisitor is currently interviewing him. I expect the process will take some time, and a guilty verdict is likely. Should this be the case, he will be executed without delay for crimes against Tassar, and high treason to the Iron Crown.

I suggest getting your affairs in order at your earliest convenience.

Inquisitor Nadja

CALIDRA PURSED HER LIPS. Her own journey had started with news of her father's death. She wondered whether Malora's would start with news of her husband's imminent one. She didn't remember much about Apollo Tamlin, other than the man was a thief who'd managed to steal from their mother.

He'd had a charming way about him, she could admit that, but he was a crook.

Calidra had shared in her mother's distaste for Apollo, and she'd assumed he'd led Malora into a life of crime and, ultimately, a terrible end.

'He's alive. I know it.'

Malora's whisper was so low that Calidra almost missed it. 'Mal...He's in the *palace*. No-one escapes from there. And what crimes against Tassar has he committed? What have you got yourself involved with this time?'

'It doesn't matter.'

'Of course it matters! Why else would Torsten have him?

I'm sorry, Mal. He's a dead man.' Calidra shook her head. 'Think of Ren. You have to—'

'He's *alive!*' Malora whirled around to face her, tears in her eyes. 'I don't *care* about Torsten! I don't care about the queen! I don't care if it was Toriaken himself!'

Calidra understood her sister's fury, her fear. 'Getting upset isn't going to help—'

'And what would *you* know about getting upset? You were always the one who never laughed, never cried. Had to get a barrel of ale down you before you'd even *talk* to me like a real person!'

Malora's words stung. Calidra bit back the argument that was already on the tip of her tongue, considering her words before she spoke them. She missed their closeness from childhood. It had been shattered once they'd reached their teens, once Malora had been blessed by the Spirit of Gold and whisked away by some Porsenthian thief.

She *needed* to move on from the past. So, she shook her head and raised her hands. 'I know. And that was just how I coped with mother. Like *you* coped by running away.'

Malora pursed her lips.

'Neither of us were right, but what's done is done. We're here, now. Together. Let's not drive each other away again. Especially not after all this.'

Malora's lip trembled. 'Apollo is my husband, Cal. I can't...I can't...'

'It's okay.' Calidra embraced her sister, wrapping her arms around Malora's shoulder. 'It'll be okay.'

Calidra had to be strong. Had to be the older sister, who looked after Malora. She didn't care for Apollo, even less if what he was being charged for was true, but she loved her sister, and that was all that mattered. S

he wouldn't let her down.

Not ever again.

THE CURSE

FENN

S
purred on by their dragon spirits, Fenn and Selys reached Westbrook shortly after dawn the day after their encounter with Torsten. Selys's shoulder wound had worsened through the night, which had slowed her down somewhat. Thankfully after several hours of sleep, Fenn had awoken stronger than ever. He'd quickened their pace as much as possible, especially when a fine sheen of sweat broke out across her face. His own leg stung from the wound on his thigh, which thankfully wasn't deep.

Seeing the Master Inquisitor behaving so erratically had been terrifying. Fenn couldn't help but worry if Miroth really was the cause of strange Torsten's behaviour, what was to stop it happening to himself or Selys as well?

It also begged the question of how much of his own actions were a direct result of the Myrish curse. He couldn't remember *who* he was. How was he supposed to know which thoughts were his own and which were driven by the Myr?

Not being in control of one's own desires was a kind of madness that frightened him beyond words.

Selys, as usual, was a voice of reason even through her injury. She had dedicated years of her life to Neros, working in the shrine and helping those who needed aid or sought the dragon's wisdom. Neros behaved very differently towards her followers than Alnothen, or Toriaken, or any other dragon spirit to their followers.

As people's personalities differed, so too did the dragons'.

It was one reason Selys gave for Torsten's behaviour being so different to another person blessed by a spirit. Miroth's desires were different.

Fenn wondered what Neros desired, how she would influence Selys, and whether the priestess would be receptive to it. Torsten had appeared to be fighting something within. What if it was Miroth's influence. Or actual control?

Fenn shuddered at the thought of losing control of his body. If it were possible, then he was opening himself up to be a pawn, used as if he were an unwitting piece in a game of *Rehkaro*.

Had Torsten been at Miroth's mercy, too? Had Miroth been acting *through* him? Perhaps Torsten could be forgiven for trying to kill him.

Fenn could imagine Calidra scowling at him for being so naive and forgiving.

He almost felt sorry for the Inquisitor. So many people were chosen at random by dragons, and blessed or cursed without their consent—sometimes without their knowledge. Even *he'd* been unaware of a spirit's presence within him until the Myrish curse had been lifted. He shook his head at his foolishness. Alnothen herself had asked why her brother had touched him, and Fenn hadn't understood it at the time. He'd been too busy coming to terms with her accusation of Varlot.

Now, it made sense.

Now the fire in his chest wasn't being repressed by the Myrish curse, Fenn had more knowledge than before— chief among which was the spirit's name: Hassen. It shouldn't have been surprising. The dragon spirit had flown *through* him during their first encounter on the Isle of Salt, and everything had turned to flame. He'd had the knowledge of the forest for a split second, as if the world had suddenly opened up and magic had spilled into him like a fountain.

Even if Fenn hated the idea of being under the control of something else, Hassen *had* kept him alive when the Myrish magic should have killed him. Without Hassen, he would have ended up lost in the spirit world, just like all the other echoes. He frowned, unsure about the power imbalance between himself and Hassen, and the guilt it caused.

Selys had no such trepidation. Not that she showed outwardly, at any rate. She was as excited and joyful as he'd ever seen her before. And why shouldn't she be? Selys was the first to be truly acknowledged by Neros. The first to be blessed by the sea.

One thing drove him now—figuring out the answer to Vermecio's riddle, finding the item, and returning it to the bastion. It was by far the most important thing.

If he was honest with himself, it was the *only* important thing.

Fenn found himself thinking about Calidra, Jisyel, and Varlot. What would they make of him now he had Hassen with him?

He wanted to forgive Varlot, wanted to take that rage and burn it away with his spirit's fire. The man had been his *friend*. 'Why shouldn't I forgive Varlot?' He hadn't meant to blurt it out, but his emotions were high after everything that had happened since getting off that ship.

Selys didn't ask for clarification. 'Varlot, again?' She let out a sigh, but didn't slow her pace. 'A better question is why should you?'

Fenn rolled it around his mind, wondering whether Hassen would jump up to throw in an opinion, but the dragon spirit remained quiet, his fire burning low but steady.

He hadn't reached a decision, even by the time they reached the edge of Westbrook.

'Everything's in chaos,' Selys said.

Unlike most of the towns Fenn had passed through since leaving the Isle of Salt, the market town of Westbrook had no gates or wall surrounding it. It was built in between two rivers, just north of where they joined into one. Vineyards fanned out from the town to the south.

The cobblestone streets of Westbrook were wide, built for plenty of carriages and people. Neat buildings with low, thatched roofs lined the streets, each happily sitting in its own plot. Most of the doors and windows were barricaded shut, weeds poked up through the stone cracks, and no smoke rose from chimneys. It was as if half the town's buildings had been abandoned.

People hurriedly made their way along the streets, many of whom were carrying bags of supplies, and none paid Fenn and Selys any attention. One man, perhaps in his fifties, held up a parchment, showing it to the people who were going about their business. 'Please. My son! Have you seen him?' He drifted from person to person, holding up the parchment and begging for news.

'What's going on? Why isn't anyone helping him?' Fenn frowned. None of the people the man spoke to gave him more than a curious glance, evidently too busy going about their own tasks.

'Can you smell the smoke on the wind?' Selys asked, halting in place, her chin upturned. She clutched her chest. 'The Myr.'

'What? Here?' Fenn whirled around, half-expecting the shadowy creatures to be strolling down the street behind him. 'Are you sure?'

'Neros is.'

Fenn took a good look at his surroundings, but there was no shadowy haze or amber eyes watching. Finding the town to be Myr-free, he said, 'I think we're safe for now. We need to find a doctor for your shoulder, or you won't be able to lift that glaive anymore.'

Selys grimaced, gently peeling back the linen bandage wrapped around her shoulder. She wrinkled her nose at the sight, and quickly returned the bandage. 'Definitely.'

'Excuse me. Where is the town's doctor?' Fenn asked the man looking for his son.

'My son? Have you seen him?' the man replied, ignoring Fenn's question and shoving the parchment in his face. It was a crude drawing in charcoal of a man's face. 'He's twenty-six. Will be twenty-seven this summer. Dark hair. Brown eyes. Skin paler than mine. Please? He's been missing three weeks now!'

Fenn shook his head. 'I…I'm sorry. I haven't seen him.'

'Please help! My boy…' The man abandoned Fenn and approached Selys, sinking to his knees when he reached her.

Selys gave him a sad smile. 'I'm afraid I don't know either…'

'Why not? You're a *priestess*, aren't you? What's the point if you can't help people in need? My son has been missing for weeks! His wife is pregnant! What are we supposed to do?'

Fenn was taken aback by the man's sudden anger, even if it was understandable. He didn't see how it was Selys's responsibility—she wasn't at her shrine, where people came for aid, and she had her own problems to deal with.

Before Selys could reply, the man continued, 'Eastbrook was attacked! Foxmouth was attacked! What use is the bloody Iron Crown if it can't even keep us safe from the damned Myr?'

'Foxmouth?' Fenn repeated, staring down at the man. 'Foxmouth was attacked…by the Myr?'

'Open your bloody eyes boy and look around! Peace is over! Damned fool queen lied to us about the armistice! And my boy *isn't here*!'

'Sir. I won't lie to you. I don't know where your son is. He might very well have crossed into the spirit world if he's been gone for so long,' Selsys said, grabbing the man's attention.

'You...you can't mean that!'

'It's a possibility. What have you done to search for him? Have you spoken to the Inquisitors? Sent messages to other towns where he might have friends or relatives?'

The man gulped. 'No! He doesn't have that! He lives here in Westbrook with me!'

Selys looked at Fenn.

He knew what she was thinking. Perhaps this man's son was another lost soul. Although he and the others had been cursed by the Myr, there was no explanation as to why, how, or where it had happened. There was every chance this man's son had been as unfortunate as Fenn.

If that was the case, there was a good chance he was now dead. 'I'm sorry. About your son.'

'No! No, he isn't dead! He must've got lost somewhere on the road. Or sidetracked, you know how young lads are! Time passes them by when they blink!' The man clutched Selys's boots. 'Please!'

'I hope so. But if not, you'll need to take steps to help your...daughter-in-law? Visit Toriaken's Shrine, ask the priests there for aid.' Selys gestured to her wounded shoulder. 'I need a doctor. Is there one in town?'

The man covered his face, shaking his head. 'We don't have a doctor. Town hall is a hospital, now.'

'Thank you. May Neros bless you and your family, and Toriaken, too.' Selys left the man kneeling in the middle of the street and headed deeper into Westbrook.

Fenn watched the man for a long moment, wondering if there was anything he should do or say, before he hurried after Selys. 'Did you hear what he said? The Myr attacking Foxmouth?'

'I heard.'

'But...Calidra? Her sister? What if...' Fenn didn't want to give words to that dark thought. Even if it had already happened, voicing his fear would make it more real.

'This must be why Neros reacted,' Selys said, her gaze on the path in front of her. 'Something's happened that has allowed the Myr to rise again. A chink in Queen Surayo's armour, perhaps? Or something more insidious? Neros must need help to face them. It must be why I was chosen.'

'Why you, though?' Fenn asked, thinking back to Neros's Shrine. 'There are lots of priests and priestesses at your shrine?'

'Perhaps I was the closest when the Myr attacked.' It was a simple answer, one that Selys said with no emotion. 'If that's true...was it just a coincidence that our paths crossed, Fenn? That you were Myr-touched? Or something more? It all had to happen for me to be where I was, for Neros to bless me.'

Fenn didn't like where she was going with that thought. 'You're saying I had to suffer so you could be blessed?' If it were up to him, none of this would have happened in the first place. He'd still be living his life, happily unaware of what the dragon spirits or the Myr were planning.

'Fenn, I didn't mean it like that.'

He scowled but didn't argue further. After Varlot had tried to sell him to Inquisitors for gold, and Selys now saying his suffering had been required so she could gain a blessing, he was sick of people using him for their own gain. Of being caught in the middle of who knew how many different factions. Was it so bad that he just wanted to look after himself for once? Do what he wanted? He tried to keep his mood from darkening. His leg was twinging again after their forced pace, which didn't help.

From the way Selys spoke of spirits, he should be grateful that one had decided to aid him. But when he concentrated on the ball of fire in his chest, he felt frustration more than anything else.

The village green in the centre of Westbrook was large, dominating a wide area. Trees had been planted in its centre, and neat rows of flowers lined the edges of the lush grass, although like the streets, many weeds had started to grow. It seemed the people of Westbrook no longer had the time to tend to their plants.

Under the shade of one of the trees, an enormous war griffin lay curled up, asleep. It had rich, black feathers that shifted into dark fur, its head resting atop massive talons.

'Isn't that...Hail...Hail...uh,' Fenn struggled to remember the griffin's name.

'Hailathlyl,' Selys finished for him. 'What's the griffin doing up here? I thought she was part of Fellwood's defences?'

'If she's here, then Amsel would be, too?'

'Maybe we should find him? He might know more about the Myr?'

'Let's get your wound looked at first. Then we can figure out more.'

They approached the largest building on the eastern side of the green—the town hall. Its steepled roof was made of layers of blue and grey slate tiles, and the spire's peak held a brass bell. Supply crates of food were lined up against the wall, and one man stood beside the stack, portioning out fruit, vegetables, meat, and cheese into smaller boxes. He looked up as they approached and frowned at their appearance. 'Need medicine and food?'

'Just medicine.' Selys gestured to her shoulder and pulled the bandage down.

He inspected it, then leaned back sharply. 'Oooh, that looks bad. You're a priestess, aren't you? How did that happen?'

Selys covered up the wound. 'Sometimes my work is dangerous.'

'Are you in charge of the injured?' Fenn asked, looking past them through the open doorway, where movement had caught his attention.

'Yes, I'm Motzha, and I'm running this place with my husband. He should be back any minute now with more supplies, actually. Can't believe we cleared through our stock of glinoc paste in six hours! Took another day for the shrine to send us more materials. We're used to making wine, not medicine.'

'I don't suppose you have a bottle going spare?' Selys asked, a small smile on her lips.

He laughed. 'Always have a bottle or two somewhere. Didn't know you priestesses drank?'

'I worship Neros, but I *am* human. There's nothing wrong with a drop of good wine every so often. Considering our situation, I'd say it was more than appropriate right now!'

'Aye. It's a dark time.' Motzha shook his head. 'Can't believe we're seeing the day the Myr are back.'

Fenn pushed away the guilt that immediately appeared at the mention of the Myr, and even the fire in his chest sputtered briefly, as if showing its distaste.

Motzha pulled a small sack of herbs from behind the crates of food and handed it to Selys. 'Sorry, we don't have the manpower to make it for you. But there's plenty of supplies inside. Find somewhere you can sit down and help yourself.'

'Is there anything we can do?' Fenn asked.

'Sure. I'm portioning food for the people inside. You can give them out. Glad to see a couple of friendly faces! You start handing out food, and I'll see if I can find you some wine to thank you for your help.'

Fenn took the armload of boxes and followed Selys inside. Two rooms led off on either side of the corridor.

People in the first room were already eating, so Fenn made his way into the second. There were twelve beds inside, and all but one were occupied. Thankfully, no-one here was too badly wounded, and probably needed rest to get over the shock of what had happened more than anything else.

As Motzha had said, there were plenty of tools and equipment laid out on a long table against the wall. Selys grabbed a pestle and mortar and crossed to the room's far side. She perched on top of a barrel in the corner and began to create the paste. Despite the awkward position, she didn't appear the least bit uncomfortable.

Leaving her to it, Fenn moved from bed to bed, handing each occupant their small box of food. They were all grateful, and it made him wonder about the work the shrines did during times of war. As Selys had warned, there would need to be a lot more of it in the coming weeks.

The man in the final bed was sitting up and staring at the wall, his gaze distant and unfocused. Cuts and bruises adorned his face and upper body, though most of them were hidden under layers of bandages, and his nose looked broken. He ignored the offered box of food.

Fenn placed it down on the bed beside him. 'Hey, you okay?' Was this man one of the lost souls?

The man didn't reply.

'Excuse me? There's food here for you.'

'Give it to someone else.' His voice was flat.

'Why? You need to eat.'

The man turned to look at Fenn. His eyes were bloodshot, as if he'd been crying recently and was on the verge of starting again.

'What happened?'

'It doesn't matter anymore. They're gone. They're gone and I wasn't there to help.'

Fenn had heard similar stories from so many people that he was getting numbed by their intense sadness. It was a time of war. People were going to die or go missing. There was so much hurt and loss and death that you couldn't be upset for everyone. 'I'm so sorry.'

The man leaned back, resting his head against the wall. 'Maybe it's my punishment.'

'Punishment?' Fenn echoed.

The man raised his arms, gesturing to the room. 'All this. My fault.'

'What do you mean?'

'You'll hear about it soon enough.' He was despondent.

Fenn sat at the end of his bed, which creaked under his weight. 'I don't know what you've done, but it can't be that bad, can it?' They were going to be here a while, and he considered how he could cheer him up. 'I'm Fenn.'

'Apollo,' the man replied, after a pause.

Fenn clutched Apollo's hand in greeting—and the room disappeared around him. He was on a mountainside in deep snow, while a blizzard raged overhead. He watched three figures trudging along, huddled in thick cloaks of fur, and snow up to their knees. The wind battered them, impeding their progress.

'*Another Myrish vision.*' It was the fire's voice again. Hassen's voice.

The scene flashed, changing to another time. Apollo sat beside a large fire, no doubt having made camp, and stared at a smoking box by its base. The wind had ceased, and a gentle snow fell all around him. Apollo reached for the box with gloved hands, upturning it. Beside him, a dark-skinned woman leaned forward, her mouth open as she stared at the box, enraptured.

Fenn couldn't help but think of Calidra when he looked at the woman.

Something fell from the box into Apollo's hands. A sliver of gold flashed in the firelight.

A key.

The fire in his chest thrashed around, as it had always done in the presence of anything Myrish, and Fenn gasped. The surety of it couldn't be denied. It was the answer he had been searching for, and it seemed so obvious now he saw it. 'The blade and bow...of a *key*! This is what Vermecio wants?'

The vision blurred, and Fenn jumped back, releasing Apollo's hand. His palm was clammy and sweat dripped down his nose, but no amount of time appeared to have passed. Fenn breathed heavily as he recovered from the sudden, intense vision.

'Lad, you okay?' Apollo asked. 'You need to sit down?'

Fenn couldn't believe it. This man had touched the Myrish object. This key. Wherever it was.

He gasped for breath. The visions in the deadlands had been from a battle against the Myr from years ago. Who knew how long ago this vision had been from? Breathless, Fenn asked, 'Apollo? What was that key you had?' The question was direct, but there was no need to dance around the issue anymore. This man *would* lead him to his answers.

Apollo stiffened. 'What are you talking about?'

'The key. I saw it. You were on a mountain. There was snow, a blizzard and—'

'Sshh! You can't talk about that so bloody openly!' Apollo was more animated than before, his movements taking on a wild, chaotic nature.

'Of course I can!' Fenn replied, confused.

'No. You *can't*. This is Porsenthia. You can't talk about the Myr!' Apollo glanced around, as if expecting people to be eavesdropping on their conversation.

'What are you talking about? The Myr attacked Eastbrook and Foxmouth. I expect everyone in this makeshift hospital was injured in that. Weren't you? Now is the *best* time to talk about it!'

Apollo buried his face in his hands. 'It's all wrong. It's all gone bloody wrong!'

'Tell me. What *was* that key? Where was it? What did you do with it? I have to know!'

'Why do you want to know?'

'It's extremely important.' Fenn didn't want to tell a veritable stranger the details of his situation, but he needed to gain Apollo's trust. It was the only way he was going to make any progress. And the man appeared on the brink of a breakdown. 'Apollo. I'm cursed by the Myr.'

Apollo slowly turned to look at him. 'You are?'

'Yes. Lost souls, the Inquisitors are calling people like me. The Myr took my memories, took my knowledge and history. Stole it from me. And this key is the *only* way I can get it back.'

'That key is a problem.' Apollo exhaled slowly, his breath trembling. 'I knew a man once who'd been Myr-touched. Same as you, I guess. Had something to do with this bloody key, too. It didn't end well for him.'

'It's a risk I'll take,' Fenn said, pleased he was finally getting somewhere. 'Without it, I'm lost. I don't have anything, anyone.'

'Maybe you should walk away. Trust me, anything to do with the Myr isn't going to be good for you.'

Hassen's fire roared in agreement. Fenn ignored it. 'What, you mean, just *give up* on finding answers?'

Apollo shrugged. 'Would that really be so bad? Starting over? You already have friends.' He gestured to Selys, who was in the process of applying the freshly made paste to her shoulder. 'People who care for you. Why not start a new life? Believe me, it's easier than you'd think.'

'And what about the friends and family I already have? The people who are probably convinced I'm dead? You're saying I should just leave them to their fate, too?' Fenn knew he was raising his voice in frustration, but he couldn't do anything about it.

Apollo shrugged again.

'Tell me where it is, please. I *have* to get it.' He thought quickly, trying to come up with ways to convince Apollo. 'It's more than just my chance of finding myself again and getting back home. It could stop the war with the Myr!'

Apollo shook his head and massaged his temples. 'Lad. I appreciate you think this thing can help. I do. But it's not worth it. I'm a dead man. My wife and daughter are probably dead. Nothing matters anymore.'

'You know where the key is?' Fenn asked.

'Of course I know where it is.'

'Okay. This might sound strange, but...let me just hold your hand again. It'll only take a second.' Fenn wasn't sure he was ready to deal with more visions, but if Apollo wasn't going to tell him, then perhaps he could *show* him.

Apollo wrapped his arms around his torso, tucking his hands under his armpits. 'Fenn, I don't want any more to do with the damned Myr and their bloody magic!'

'Fenn? What's going on?' Selys approached, a wad of glinoc paste on her shoulder, covered with a fresh bandage. 'You're causing a scene.'

Guiltily, Fenn turned around to find several curious faces peering over at himself and Apollo. He cleared his throat. 'Selys, this man, Apollo, he knows where the key is!'

'Key?'

'The thing Vermecio wants! A sliver of gold? Blade and bow that aren't weapons? It's describing parts of a *key*!'

'How can you be so sure?'

'When I shook his hand, I had another vision. I saw him with the key. It's a Myrish item. I'm Myr-touched. There must've been the same magic for the connection. Like with Varlot in the deadlands.'

Apollo raised his hands. 'Look, look, I don't know what you two are talking about—'

'You *have* to help!' Fenn cut him off.

Selys looked Apollo up and down. 'I'm Selys, priestess of

Neros. This is Fenn, who has Hassen's blessing. The knowledge you hold is imperative to my spirit. I can see you're injured. Maybe a few days' rest here will be everything you need and then you can take us—'

'Stop it! Both of you! I've just learned my home was destroyed! My wife and daughter might well be dead, buried under rubble. Can the pair of you shut up and give me some room to breathe? If you're priests, maybe you should show some damned sympathy!'

Fenn jumped at Apollo's shout, suddenly feeling awful about being so pushy. 'Apollo, I'm sorry. I just…that key means *everything*.' He knew he was being rude and selfish, but he was so tantalisingly close to getting his life back that he didn't care.

Apollo raised his head from his hands, a deep frown on his face. He looked at them both for a second, then his mouth dropped open. 'Wait…Selys? Selys Ioran?'

Selys pulled up sharply and scrutinised him. 'Neros, I don't believe it. Apollo Tamlin? I didn't recognise you under all that blood and those bandages.'

Fenn frowned. 'You know each other?'

Apollo shook his head in disbelief. 'I knew her from years back. The Ioran warband down in Segandis. I heard you'd left for Neros's Shine.' He gestured at the tattoo up her arm. 'Guess you made it as a priestess. Spirits take me, you look different. You cut all your hair.'

Selys shifted her weight. 'That was a long time ago, Apollo. I was another person.'

'Still got your brother's glaive? That helped us out of a pickle or two, didn't it?'

'I'd rather not remember.' Selys folded her arms, not relishing their reunion. 'Apollo, you've clearly been through a lot. Fenn and I were insensitive, and we apologise for that. We'll be in town if you change your mind. Fenn, let's see if we can find Amsel. See if there's an update on the Myr in

543

Bragalia. We need to do what we can to ready ourselves for more fighting. Our spirits will need us.'

Fenn nodded, though he kept his gaze on Apollo, and allowed Selys to steer them out of the makeshift hospital and back out onto the green. He knew the man was suffering, that he'd experienced unimaginable loss, and asking him to do anything other than grieve was selfish. Everyone in that town had probably lost someone.

Overhead, smoke from distant fires continued to darken the sky.

Fenn wondered whether he'd ever be able to access the answers that Myrish key would unlock.

And even if he was able to, whether he would be too late.

THE KEY

APOLLO

As Fenn and Selys left the room, Apollo sank back into the thin, scratchy pillow of his hospital bed, the springs creaking noisily under him. His body ached in a way it never had before. Muscles he didn't know he had screamed in pain, and every joint was fiery agony.

Worst of all were the pieces of his heart. He'd never cared about anyone before. Not until Malora. Not until Renys. He knew there was a chance they were okay. There were people in Eastbrook who'd survived the Myr attack, after all. Why shouldn't there also be those from Foxmouth who'd been lucky?

But he couldn't dare hope.

If he did, if he convinced himself they were safe, then returned home to find everything a smouldering ruin, he would lose his mind.

So he accepted the worst. Assumed they were gone, like the town was. Like he might as well be.

He was angry at that pair of blessed bastards trying to dig up the past. Where in all of Tassar had they come from? Selys, he could hardly believe was there. She'd swapped fighting in Segandis and sailing on her family's ship for spouting Neros's word and a set of priestess robes.

And how could Fenn *possibly* have known about the key? The lad had said something about visions, and that worried him. Was he like Nestol in some way? He said he'd been Myr-touched. There could be a connection.

Could Fenn somehow pluck information and memories from his body, too?

If that damned key had been *so* important, why hadn't the queen told him? He wasn't a moron. Perhaps if she'd been more forthcoming, the whole damned world wouldn't be on the brink of war again.

In one, aggressive motion, he upended the box of food Fenn had brought for him, sending vegetables rolling on the stone floor. Apollo raged, glaring holes into the ceiling of the hospital. He wished it would fall and crush him. It would make everything so much easier.

He was angry at the queen for not telling him. Angry at Torsten for gloating. Angry at Nadja for making him realise what he'd done, and all the guilt that went with it.

And he was angry at himself—what he'd done would affect Renys.

He *knew* he needed to go to Foxmouth and see for himself. Determine once and for all whether he still had a life worth living.

But after everything Torsten had done to him, and his subsequent griffin crash, he wasn't sure he'd be able to walk any time soon, let alone travel. Why had everything fallen apart so quickly?

A hush suddenly fell upon the hospital room, tension rising, silencing conversations.

Apollo twisted in bed to peer over the other people, trying to get a better view of the doorway. Dario the wine-maker was speaking with a woman in polished armour, her back to him. After a moment of talk, he escorted her inside.

It was Inquisitor Nadja.

Fuck.

She wasn't in uniform, but he'd recognise her anywhere.

Judging by Dario's reactions, and those of everyone in the room, they all knew exactly who she was, too.

His heart thudded. There was nowhere for him to escape. Nadja had come through the only door to the room, and none of the windows were big enough—or accessible enough —for him to get out.

He shuffled over on his bed, pulling the sheet up over his shoulder to obscure his face.

What in Neros's name was he going to do?

'I bring official reports from the Iron Crown.' Nadja's voice projected across the room, and everyone stilled to listen to the Inquisitor. 'I apologise this information was not as prompt as is our usual way, however Eastbrook has suffered after a direct attack...by the Myr. We are scrambling to bolster our defences and send aid where it is most urgently required first. Toriaken's Shrine will, of course, provide shelter to those without homes.'

Chatter immediately sprang up between those in sick beds and those tending to them.

'Foxmouth, also, has fallen to our ancient enemy. Though the great spirit Toriaken drove off their attack, I am sure the Myr will try again. Perhaps tomorrow. Perhaps a month from now. Whenever they come, I assure you, we will be ready.'

'How is this possible?' one man called.

'Queen Surayo promised us a lifetime of peace!' a woman added. 'Five years is hardly a lifetime!'

Nadja said, 'We believe there was a traitor among us. A Porsenthian who may be responsible for allowing the Myr's resurgence.'

Apollo stopped breathing.

Nadja continued, 'This man is to be dealt with by the Iron

Crown, and the Iron Crown *alone*. Queen Surayo, in her wisdom, will know how best to proceed. Her priority remains the safety of the Porsenthian Empire, and I am sure you will all contribute to that.'

The chatter quietened.

Nadja strolled down the room in between the beds. Even though he didn't dare look up, Apollo heard every booted step grow closer.

'This man, this traitor, may be among you now. A casualty of the battle in Eastbrook, yes. But he has played his role in what has happened.'

More gasps.

'Apollo Tamlin. Show yourself and I swear on my honour as Inquisitor, you will be treated fairly until justice can be delivered.'

Apollo was certain his pounding heart would give him away. He couldn't remember which people he'd spoken to, whom he'd told his name. *Someone* was going to give him up.

Nadja had all but named him the cause of the destruction they'd endured. The losses they'd suffered.

Muttered voices to his right made him sweat. They were going to tell her.

Deciding there was nowhere to run, no way out of his situation, and unwilling to be called out by anyone in the room, Apollo lifted the cover off himself and sat upright. 'I'm here, Nadja.'

A cacophony of noise broke out as the other people hurled accusations at him. Shouts crossed each other, and Apollo flinched at the din.

Nadja approached the foot of his bed. Even without her Inquisitor's uniform, she was imposing. 'We must talk. Alone.'

Apollo groaned. If things weren't bad enough with Fenn and Selys, now he had an Inquisitor to deal with. And it had to be *Nadja* of all people.

He coughed weakly. 'Inquisitor. I'm afraid you might be too late...I'm so worn out...Not sure I'm up for talking...'

'Good. This will be over faster if you are quiet and listen.'

Apollo scowled, then broke into coughing laughter. 'Fine. Fine! There's a supply area at the back. Has extra linen and bed sheets. We can talk there.'

'*I* will talk to you there. *You* can listen.' Nadja gestured for him to rise, and she followed him across the room, ignoring the angry stares from the other people.

He hobbled most of the way, his legs screaming in protest at being used again. He expected more jeers, more displays of aggression, but he had to remember these people were ill and injured. As far as they could see, Nadja was about to handle his justice.

Once inside the cramped room, Apollo sat down heavily on a large crate and looked up expectantly at the Inquisitor. If she wanted him to hold his tongue, he could provide a reasonable effort.

'Before you ask. Yes. I did send a pigeon to Foxmouth. However, as you have escaped, I see it wasn't necessary.'

Apollo bit hard on his lower lip. It was the only way to stop tears building. He hadn't expected Nadja to send a letter. Hadn't expected her to open their conversation with that. If Malora had received that message in time, she might've decided to bring Renys to the palace. It would be just like her to try and put things to rights. She would have left Foxmouth. Would be *safe*.

But if the letter hadn't made it in time...? If she was still in *The Grumpy Fisherman* when everything happened...'Foxmouth's gone.'

'I know.' Her voice belied no emotion other than cold comprehension of fact.

Apollo held his sobs back, staring hard at a spot on the wall until he was sure he had his rage, sadness, and fear under control. 'You finally found me, then. Better than what Torsten could do.'

At the mention of the Master Inquisitor, it was Nadja's turn to look uncomfortable. She shifted her weight and readjusted the longsword at her hip.

'Oh. You noticed him slipping up too, did you?' Apollo pressed, taking pleasure in degrading the Master Inquisitor while he had the chance. Anything was better than thinking of Foxmouth. 'Or are you here to march me back and have me beheaded? That was quite a speech you just gave.'

'I reserve judgement on you, Apollo. What I do know is Torsten is...afflicted by something. He is not himself, as I'm sure you saw.'

Apollo kept his mouth shut, unsure whether agreeing or arguing with her would be the best course of action. Second-guessing Inquisitors was never fun.

Nadja didn't seem bothered by his silence. 'I don't know what he did to you, and it isn't my place to ask or question my queen. But I want answers. I want the *truth*. And I don't think I will get that in Eastbrook.'

Apollo frowned, trying to understand what she was doing. She hadn't executed him on the spot. She wasn't in uniform. She'd come alone. And he wasn't in irons. 'Wait. You're *defecting*?'

'I'm taking an extended leave.'

Apollo laughed. 'Bet that went down well, what with the Myr back?'

'That is not your concern.'

He couldn't believe it. 'If you aren't an Inquisitor anymore, what are you doing here? What do you want with me?'

'I am still an Inquisitor. Do not confuse the issue. I am simply acting alone for a brief period of time. A time I hope to use to find answers that will help my queen and the Porsenthian Empire. Perhaps all of Tassar.'

Apollo swallowed. His head throbbed and his body ached just from the brief walk across the room. 'So what *exactly* do you want?'

Nadja straightened up, considering her words. 'It isn't easy to circumvent Queen Surayo's magic. And you *have* used her pardon graciously—by giving up your life of crime and owning a reputable establishment, even starting a family. As far as I could see in the records of that tavern, everything is above board and imported legally. You even pay your taxes on time.'

'Malora won't let me do otherwise,' Apollo muttered.

'So I do not believe you acted in spite. Selfishly, perhaps, but that's hardly a crime. And you did complete your task in essence, if not to the letter. As you weren't given all the facts at the time, and have lived peacefully and within the law of the Iron Crown for the past five years, I cannot blame you for that.'

Apollo couldn't believe it. An Inquisitor with a mind of their own. With *common sense*. 'You aren't here to drag me back to the palace, then?'

Nadja shook her head. 'If you are responsible for this, executing you will not help.'

Apollo dropped his gaze, not trusting himself to say anything that wouldn't ruin the chance that was clearly being laid out in front of him.

'But I *will* make sure you fix it.'

'What?'

Nadja flicked her hair out of her eyes. 'Torsten wants you dead. If I'm honest, it feels more like a personal grudge than any sense of honour or duty. Yes, the queen commands those guilty of high treason are to be executed, and Torsten will always carry out her orders.' She paused and studied him. 'But I see no benefit in that when you can fix things.'

'Inquisitor?'

'You know where the Citrine Key is. You know what must

551

happen to it. You will complete the task given to you five years ago by feeding it to Paragos, and you *will* undo what you have caused. Malicious or not, people are dying, and I won't stand for it when it can be solved.'

'Do you have any idea what you're asking?'

Nadja's expression remained impassive.

Apollo could see she wasn't giving him any way out of this. Honestly, the chance was more than he deserved. He dragged his hands down his face. 'Fine.'

'I'm not giving you a choice, Apollo. Whether you agree or not, this is what will happen. I'm going to make sure of it.'

He snorted. Nadja was definitely still an Inquisitor. 'I'm a bit out of sorts, if you couldn't tell.' Apollo held up his bandaged arms. 'Gonna be slow going.'

'Slow going is better than no going. I'm happy to carry your belongings if needed.'

He shrugged. 'What you see is what I have.' He thought about Fenn and Selys, and their desire for the key, too. 'As long as you get your answers, I don't suppose you care if anyone comes with us?'

Nadja furrowed her eyebrows. 'This is a matter that concerns the Iron Crown only. Who else would come?'

'A couple of priests.'

'Well...I can't really stop them if it concerns their spirits.'

'Good. They're already outside, and I guess they'll be as keen to leave as you are.'

APOLLO HAD BEEN happy to die in bed less than an hour ago.

Now, he would go to Foxmouth to find his own truth.

Nadja needed him for the key. So did Fenn and Selys. That gave him the advantage, and he wasn't going anywhere without returning to Foxmouth first. At least if Mal and Ren were gone, he would be able to join them by throwing himself into the sea. And if that was where everything was going to end, he'd have priests there ready to perform burial rites.

He held onto the morbid thought tightly as he limped across the green in the centre of Westbrook. The grass underfoot was soft, with a few wild flowers dotted here and there. Fenn and Selys were already under the trees talking to an enormous griffin with glossy black feathers. It was easily as large as the brown and red-feathered one outside Eastbrook, and far larger than Olvalthar.

There was something familiar about it, but he wasn't sure what. It could well be a result of encountering the creatures so recently, and the stress his body had been put under. Events and days were starting to blur together.

'Apollo! I thought you'd be bed-ridden for a lot longer,' Fenn said, his voice light. 'Changed your mind about that key?'

Apollo had to hand it to Fenn, the lad was determined. 'I couldn't lay there and mope any longer.' Every step was painful, but he'd endured worse.

'Amsel and Hailathlyl have been waiting for you.'

The names meant nothing to him. 'Who?'

Fenn bowed low, gesturing to the griffin. 'I think you owe Hailathlyl some gratitude.'

The griffin pawed at the grass with one taloned foot. 'You are husband to the daughter of the woman we are protecting. She sent us north when word reached us of the Myr's strike.'

Apollo gaped at the griffin's words, mind whirling to connect the dots. 'The daughter of the woman...You work for Mal's *mother*?'

The griffin fluttered her wings. 'For now. We brought warnings of the Myr to Bragalia. Our brethren carried them to Porsenthia, too, although it does not look like our words were heeded.' She turned her beady orange eyes to the sky, where black smoke lingered. 'Perhaps if the Iron Crown took the Myr more seriously, fewer would have died. The scent of death lingers in the air here.'

Apollo winced at the griffin's words. He glanced over his shoulder, where Inquisitor Nadja watched and waited, her arms folded across her chest. 'You know about the attack on Foxmouth? Mal might...she was there when...and they...' Apollo trailed off.

The griffin snapped her beak. 'Yes. This is why we must fly there. But Amsel said to wait here and make sure you lived. We have been waiting days. We need to fly!'

'Why wait? If Mal survived? If she's injured, she'll need your help! And sooner rather than later!'

'Because Amsel wanted to give Malora the news you live.'

Apollo shook his head. Hailathlyl was giving him hope when he didn't deserve it. And yet the griffin spoke with a certainty that rivalled any Inquisitor. 'Will you fly me to Foxmouth?'

'Of course.' Hailathlyl stood up and opened her wings with a high-pitched cry. 'Once Amsel returns, we can fly at once.'

'Hold on a second,' Fenn said, raising one hand. 'Hailathlyl? You and Amsel are protecting Furyn and the rest of Fellwood?'

The griffin tilted her head. 'You know this.'

'And you're going to help Furyn's daughter? You mean... Calidra? But...But Apollo isn't her husband?'

Apollo gulped. 'Uhhh...I'm married to Malora. Calidra's her sister.'

Fenn paled. 'Oh no. Foxmouth. Foxmouth!'

'You know Calidra?' Apollo asked, stunned.

'Yeah.' Fenn turned to Selys. 'Calidra. Jisyel! In Foxmouth!'

Selys tapped her chest and took several deep breaths. She didn't look at Apollo. 'I don't know, Fenn. Neros fought the Myr outside Foxmouth. They might be okay...'

554

'What about getting the key?' Fenn asked.

'I'm not going anywhere until I've seen Foxmouth. Until I've found...Mal and Ren.' Apollo wasn't budging on that. There was no chance. '*If* my wife and daughter are safe, we'll talk about the key.'

'But—'

'Stop quarrelling. We have our orders. We will fly to Foxmouth,' Hailathlyl cried, her voice sharp and painfully loud. She flapped her wings, sending gusts blasting in all directions.

At the griffin's cry, an Olmese man approached them from the other side of the green. He was young, barely in his twenties, with a bright smile, and carried a heavy-looking sack over one shoulder. His smile faltered when he reached them. 'Fenn? Selys? What are you two doing here?'

'Amsel!' Fenn bowed low like he had done to the griffin. 'It's been quite a journey since we left Fellwood.'

'I can imagine.' Amsel bowed back, then appraised Apollo as he rested the sack on the ground. Its contents jingled. 'Apollo Tamlin? An honour to meet you, at last. I'm glad to see we reached you in time.'

'What?'

Amsel patted Hailathlyl's neck affectionately. 'Rescued might be a better term for it. That Inquisitor was moments away from slitting your throat.'

Everything clicked into place. '*You're* the one who swooped down! I thought...it was another.'

'Do you know many griffins?' Amsel laughed.

'One. Olvalthar. Helped me esca—helped me earlier.' Apollo swallowed down the word in case he accidentally offended Amsel and Hailathlyl. A brief flash of guilt stabbed through him. If Torsten hadn't been lying, Olvalthar might well be dead somewhere in that patch of woodland.

Just another crime to add to his apparently regrowing list.

'Looks like I'm heading to Foxmouth with an Inquisitor escort.' He pointed over his shoulder. 'She's not someone you really want to argue with, so I'd hold your tongues if I were you.'

Amsel nodded, picked up the heavy sack and clambered up Hailathlyl's harness, where he secured it into place behind the saddles. There was a raised wooden rail that looked like it would offer some security in flight, a far cry from his hasty journey with Olvalthar.

'An Inquisitor with us will be a bonus.' Amsel raised his hand to Nadja, waving her over. 'If you're ready? The Myr have moved quickly and we can't afford to waste anymore time. Come. Climb up.'

Apollo laughed at the irony. The key had been the start of his freedom, and now it seemed to be locking him back into a prison.

Nadja reached them and paused beside Hailathlyl, staring at Fenn. 'Wait…do I know you?'

Fenn stood his ground, chin raised defiantly. 'Selys and I saw you on the mountain yesterday.'

'No. Before that.' Nadja shook her head.

Fenn scratched his nose, then his eyes widened in sudden realisation. 'You were with Torsten at the tavern in Ballowtown.'

Apollo raised his eyebrows. 'Fenn, you know this Inquisitor?' Somehow that was stranger than he and Selys being reunited.

'Ah yes. You were one of the lost souls. Didn't Varlot stop Torsten from arresting you?' Nadja narrowed her eyes. 'Wait. You fell into the river!'

'I did. With Jisyel. Are you going to try and arrest me again?'

Nadja pursed her lips. 'I should have recognised you on the mountain, but I was too distracted…'

'She's off duty!' Apollo gave her a broad smile. 'Come on, I need a hand up. We can talk on the way.'

Amsel and Nadja helped Apollo up the heavy leather harness around the griffin, who was easily large enough to carry another couple of people if she needed to. It was no wonder the Olmese used griffins instead of horses for war. A fleet of those might be enough to keep the Myr at bay.

Hailathlyl lowered her head to make it easier for the group of five to get on board, snapping her beak in irritation only once, when Fenn accidentally pulled on her feathers instead of the handrail.

Nadja sat behind Apollo. Though she wore her armour, she'd eschewn her Inquisitors uniform, and the iron dagger that went with it. Nadja was, if nothing else, a woman of her word—which was more than could be said of Torsten.

Credit to her, she didn't fight when told they were flying to Foxmouth first. She'd probably taken one look at Hailathlyl's beak and talons, and decided it wasn't worth the argument.

Apollo knew she was worried about Torsten. He wasn't sure if he preferred the regularly flavoured bastard or the new, chaotic one. Either way, there was no chance the Master Inquisitor could do anything to him while he flew with a griffin.

He grabbed hold of the handrail, grateful Hailathlyl was far larger than Olvalthar, and took a deep breath. If this flight was anything like his previous one, it was going to get bumpy.

Fenn, blessed by a dragon spirit, was more of an enigma. He was desperate to find the Citrine Key, desperate to rid himself of the Myr's touch. Selys was keen to travel with him, no doubt for her own spirit's reasons. Nadja wanted the key to be destroyed.

They all had different reasons for chasing it, and he didn't need to be a fortune teller to know it was going to end in chaos. Perhaps in blood.

Nadja was an adept fighter and negotiator, but up against two priests? He didn't think she stood a chance. He pushed the thought from his mind. Their battles were not his concern.

Foxmouth was gone. But he prayed to whichever spirit would listen that Malora and Renys were not.

As Amsel guided Hailathlyl into the smoky air, apprehension settled in his gut. Streaks of black and grey whipped past his face as the griffin flew higher, and Westbrook faded to a dark smudge against a backdrop of stained green fields.

To the west, the Nethal Mountains rose from the ground —an eternal landmark that lined northern Porsenthia. To the east, the Lasseen Ocean swelled—a churning mass of water that rarely promised safe travel.

And beyond the ocean, he would face whichever vengeful spirits awaited him.

END

EPILOGUE

TORSTEN

Blood dribbled down Torsten's arm in slow rivulets. His uniform was in tatters, just as bad a mess as it had been in the Battle of Marlrush. To be less than impeccable grated on him even more than events of the previous few days.

Nadja had left, and he was angrier about that than he'd realised.

'You don't need her. You don't need anyone. You have me, brother.'

Torsten exhaled slowly through his nose, trying to calm himself.

Nestol was gone. The whole box had been stolen like a loaf of bread left unattended.

Apollo.

Torsten was furious with himself for allowing the thief to escape—twice. Sloppiness wasn't something he tolerated from his Inquisitors, which made the entire sorry situation all the more infuriating. 'He has a wife. He has a daughter. They will pay for him.'

By the time he'd managed to get back to the palace,

Miroth had ceded control, chased away by Selys and Fenn's wrathful spirits. That had been a shock.

Fenn had no tattoo, but his blessing couldn't be denied. How the magic of the dragons and the magic of the Myr coincided, he had no idea. It all pointed to Fenn being a traitor not just to the Iron Crown, but to all of Tassar. Some abomination that couldn't be allowed to live any longer.

And perhaps Fenn was just as responsible as Apollo for allowing the Myr to return.

He returned his attention to his spirit. 'I know I have you. But Nadja and the others are helpful when you are...' Torsten stopped himself before he said the word.

Miroth seethed. '*Go on. Say it.*'

'When you are *weak*.'

Torsten knew what happened to Miroth wasn't the spirit's fault. Lakes and forests came and went over time, as did the spirits that were brought forth from the abundance of life energy in those places. Miroth hadn't been a strong spirit to begin with, made worse by the salt poisoning the lake at Tonmouth and people moving away to live and work in Eastbrook. As life diminished in the area, so did Miroth's strength. And it had always been difficult to get people to visit the shrine and offer the lake dragon their worship.

He felt Miroth's shame and fury as much as he'd felt his own as a boy, when he'd been at the mercy of everyone else bigger and stronger than him.

The palace doctors saw to Torsten's injuries with minimal fuss—cleaning his wounds and bandaging his arm. They warned him he was going to have a scar across his cheek from Apollo's sword.

Once seen to, Torsten prowled the palace, making his way up to his own quarters in the east tower, which afforded a view of the roiling Lasseen Ocean. Letters had been left on his desk, updating him on the situation in Eastbrook while he'd been chasing down Apollo and the Myr-touched Fenn.

He hadn't meant to allow Miroth control for so long, but the spirit had been incensed once the Myr had begun their attack, and Torsten hadn't the strength to fight the dragon.

He'd only ever needed to call upon Miroth's aid in emergencies before. This was the first time Miroth had forced his control upon Torsten outside of the shrine. It was as if sensing the Myr in Fenn had made the dragon spirit more volatile.

News from the Olmese who'd flown along the coast confirmed that Foxmouth was in ruins, utterly destroyed. Good. Perhaps Apollo's family had been crushed under it.

Eastbrook had fared much better, and aside from a few chunks of stone missing, the palace itself hadn't been damaged in the surprise Myrish attack. But the response had been twofold—Queen Surayo had declared the Myr were indeed a threat again after five years of peace. But she had her scapegoat, naming Apollo as the cause.

Secondly, she'd drafted in mages from across her empire to aid in thwarting the Myr once and for all.

There were to be no more peace talks. No more truce.

Queen Surayo was going to wipe them from the face of Tassar.

A hesitant knock on his door grabbed Torsten's attention. He took off his tattered cloak and threw it over the back of his chair. 'Yes?'

The door opened, admitting a short, balding herald in cream robes, a dragon insignia across his chest. 'Master Inquisitor. I apologise for disturbing you so soon after your return. I'm sure you would prefer the time to recover and—'

'Get on with it.'

The herald bowed low. 'A man arrived just before dawn to see you. I thought the queen should know, but...I was reminded you wanted to see him if ever he returned.'

Torsten frowned. He hadn't the faintest idea who the herald was talking about. 'Where is he?'

In response, the herald bowed low and stepped aside.

The man who walked into the room took up the entire doorway. Tall, with broad shoulders and a thick, bearskin cloak, Varlot looked every bit the wild, ferocious fighter his reputation suggested. Even outside the heat of battle, the man was imposing.

'Thank you. You may leave us.' Torsten dismissed the herald. He stared at Varlot, emotions flying through him. Hate was near the top of the list. Surprise was a close second. Indignation, too. A pinch of fear.

'We will burn him!'

Torsten ignored the dragon. 'Why have you come back, Varlot?' He kept his voice neutral.

'You've done some terrible things, Torsten. So have I. I'm done grinding this axe. I want to come back and serve my queen.'

Torsten laughed at the absurdity of the comment. 'Serve the queen? Varlot, when have you *ever* served anyone other than yourself?'

'Could say the same for you.'

'They won't let you back. You murdered your own wife and child in a drunken rage. Surayo will never allow you back in her ranks.'

Varlot's lip curled at Torsten's words. 'And what will Surayo do when she finds out *you* paralysed her cousin? You torture prisoners to death and claim they were ill. How do you think she'll react once she learns you've gone too far with the small amount of power you've been given?'

It was Torsten's turn to bristle.

Varlot continued, 'Remember the lad in the tavern from Ballowtown? He's the linchpin in everything that's happening with the Myr, I'm sure of it.'

'Yes, I met Fenn recently.' Torsten held up his right hand, the flesh burned from Fenn's fire.

'If we work together and stop him, we could claim victory over the Myr. Think of the glory! The gold!'

'And what do you want for that?'

'Let me come back, that's all I ask. Not as a soldier. I'm done being on the front lines.'

'What, then?'

'An Inquisitor.'

Miroth's fire flared. *'You don't need him, brother! We can kill the Myr-touched one!'*

Torsten couldn't ignore the fact he wanted Fenn dead as much as he wanted Apollo dead. If Varlot had knowledge on how to get to Fenn, it would be a start.

Ignoring his spirit's objections, Torsten raised his unburnt hand to shake Varlot's. 'Fine. Lead me to Fenn and I'll consider your request.'

Continued in Book Two:
The Shadow Gate